P9-CAD-783

CRITICAL SPACE

Also by Greg Rucka

Keeper
Finder
Smoker
Shooting at Midnight

CRITICAL SPACE

GREG RUCKA

BANTAM BOOKS

NEW YORK · TORONTO · LONDON · SYDNEY · AUCKLAND

Critical Space

A Bantam Book / October 2001

Book design by Heather Saunders.

Library of Congress Cataloging-in-Publication Data
Rucka, Greg.
Critical space / Greg Rucka.
p. cm.
ISBN 0-553-80132-5
I. Title
PS3568.U2968C75 2001
813'.54—DC21 00-066694

Published simultaneously in the United States and Canada

Bantam Books are published by Bantam Books, a division of Random House, Inc. Its trademark, consisting of the words "Bantam Books" and the portrayal of a rooster, is Registered in U.S. Patent and Trademark Office and in other countries. Marca Registrada. Bantam Books, 1540 Broadway, New York, New York 10036.

PRINTED IN THE UNITED STATES OF AMERICA

BVG 10 9 8 7 6 5 4 3 2 1

This is for Nunzio Andrew,
who was there when Alena was born.

Thank you for all the stories already told,
and for all the ones to come.

ACKNOWLEDGMENTS

Gratitude and thanks to the following people for helping with the creation of this work:

First and foremost, The Triad—Alexander Gombach, Gerard V. Hennelly, and Scott Nybakken. From samples of *dit da jow* to weapons selection and expertise to holding the stopwatch while riding the Staten Island Ferry, you truly are the best men I could have had for the job. The Three Stooges had nothing on you guys, and yes, that was a *huge* rat.

Special thanks to my agent, David Hale Smith, who encouraged the risks and never flinched at the results, and who spurred me forward when I wanted desperately to go back. I couldn't ask for a greater advocate or friend.

Particular attention to the following people: Daria Carissa Penta, who once again stepped in at the right time with the right words and a critical gaze, and who showed me what a *pas de deux* is all about; Matthew Brady and Steve Woodcock for their chemical and pharmaceutical knowledge, and for taking the time to not simply assist in research, but to guide it, as well; Sara Bellamy for assistance with the peerage and The Season; Rick Burchett, for enduring rants, raves, curses, and for listening almost as well as he draws.

Quick nods to: Dr. Jessica Parrish, Dr. Han Sin Shi, Max Kelleher, Nick Barrabas, Yuri, and Lev.

This work could never have been possible without the enthusiastic and unflagging support of several individuals who have asked to remain anonymous. A special thanks to all of you.

Finally, to Jennifer and to Elliot, who kept me grounded while allowing me to fly.

Now my name it is Mulvaney
And I'm known quite famously
People speak my name in whispers
What higher praise can there be?

—Richard Thompson,
Cooksferry Queen

CRITICAL SPACE

PROLOGUE

It was, she realized later, an audition of sorts.

Then, however, it was simply a murder. The calculated death of a target named Oksana Zurkowska.

The way she described it, I could imagine the details she omitted from her story. I filled it all in, the texture and the color, the sound and the smell. I could see the institutional washroom, feel the fog of steam from the showers, hear the drip of water onto the gray tiles of the floor. The clouded mirrors, sheets of polished metal rather than silver-backed glass. The porcelain sinks along the wall stained with rust brought up from the pipes. The smells of bleach and mildew and soap clung to the walls and ceiling, and the condensation rolled in beads to the floor, trickling to the drain in the center of the room.

She told me it was bright and sunny that day, but for some reason all I see is a shade that falls listlessly to the floor from high transom windows never opened to the outside. I see it in winter, oppressive and bitterly cold, but, as best as she could remember, it was spring.

The stalls had no doors, so she hid in the one farthest from the entrance, standing on the bowl, her feet on either side of the seat. It didn't matter that the concealment wasn't total. Oksana always used the sink nearest the entrance, she knew. Even if it was being used, Oksana would wait. Oksana liked that sink; it had the best water pressure of any in the building.

She waited for Oksana to close the door and start the water, hearing the pipes rattle and knock in the old walls. She listened, and when she heard the sound of the brush scrubbing teeth, she moved.

It was, she told me, like sitting in the back of an empty and dark theater and seeing oneself on the screen. She understood her motion and intent, and yet there was no attachment to the action. She was moving, she was acting, and she felt nothing at all.

She remembered that she found that curious.

Oksana Zurkowska, brushing her teeth, was taken entirely by surprise. The first blow drove her against the edge of the sink, crushing the air out of her. The second hammered her forehead against the tile at the base of the metal mirror. So did the third, and fourth, and fifth, until blood was coming off the wall, mixing with the foam of the tooth powder and water floating in the sink. Oksana hardly made a sound.

When she felt Oksana's head alter, felt the skull stop resisting the blows and finally yield to the pressure, she stopped and let the girl fall.

It was like shattering an unusually tough pumpkin, she told me.

On the floor, Oksana's left arm was still moving, jerking from side to side, as if pulled by a puppeteer's string. Then that stopped.

The sound of the water filling the sink came back to her. She reached out and shut off the tap, and the water stopped, and she saw herself reflected in the mirror. Blood had streaked the pitted surface, and then she realized that it had streaked her as well. It was on her hands, on her shirt, on her face.

She stripped and set her clothes by the radiator, so they would stay warm. Then she got into the shower, standing motionless beneath the water as it took its time changing from ice cold to scalding hot.

She wasn't feeling much of anything, she told me. Mostly, she just wanted to get the blood off herself. She remembered trying to decide what she would do about the shirt, that she had resolved to throw it in the furnace and to take a replacement from Oksana's own closet. They all wore identical clothes in the orphanage and she doubted anyone would notice anything except that the new shirt would be too large on her.

Oksana, after all, had been a big girl, ten years old.

She, on the other hand, was only eight, and small for her age.

PART ONE

CHAPTER ONE

The ashtray didn't surprise me as much as the quality of the throw behind it.

Perhaps when Skye Van Brandt was still in high school, before she was "discovered" and turned into one of *People*'s Fifty Most Beautiful Faces for two years running, before she'd netted two Oscar nominations and one Golden Globe award, maybe she'd pitched softball or even hardball at some point in her youth. Not that her youth was over: the woman on the other side of the hotel room was only twenty-two.

At least according to her publicist.

Skye was beautiful. Her hair was long and blond, just a shade too dark to be strawberry, and her large eyes were deep and soulful and tailored for close-ups during love scenes. Her lower lip was just a little pudgy and lopsided, and it gave her a perpetual almost-pout that reviewers described with words like "irresistible" and "wanton." Her dental work was perfect. She was one of those people who remain stunningly beautiful no matter what they're doing, be it smiling or screaming.

She was screaming at me right now.

"God dammit, Atticus! Take my bags!"

For the third time, I said, "I can't do that, Miss Van Brandt."

Skye dropped the suitcase in question and stormed my way, to where I stood just inside the front door. We were in the sitting room of the

Presidential Suite at the El Presidente Hotel in El Paso, Texas, which meant that Skye had a lot of ground to cover, and that I had plenty of time to get out of her way. I didn't bother. To my mind I was doing the job I'd been paid for, doing more than it, in fact. It was now mid-morning of Day Eight on what was supposed to have been a six-day location shoot. I'd been hired to provide Skye's personal protection while on location, two thousand dollars a day, plus a stipend from the studio. I was, for the time being, Skye Van Brandt's bodyguard.

Not her valet.

The job, like so many other things in my professional life, was bullshit, for show and nothing more. But it was still a job, and I took it seriously, and there was no way I was going to pick up Skye Van Brandt's overpriced Tūmi luggage and carry it to the lobby at her command.

She stopped three feet from where I was standing, hands on her hips, that wanton lower lip jutting a little more in her fury. For all her grace and beauty and presence on the screen, she was a tiny woman, nearly a full foot shorter than my six feet.

"I'm *paying* you! You do what *I* tell you!"

She jabbed in the direction of her bags with an index finger as if gouging at someone's eye. There were three bags—one garment, one small duffel, and one larger duffel with a shoulder strap. All were black leather, all bulging with clothes, scripts, cosmetics, and the witch's brew of new-age elixirs and homeopathic medicines Skye used to keep herself fueled.

"Take them downstairs to the car," she ordered.

"You know I can't do that," I said. "I have to keep my hands free. Wait until the bellman—"

"God dammit! What fucking word don't you fucking understand? Pick up my fucking bags!"

I waited until she was done and catching her breath. Then I said: "No."

Skye Van Brandt raised her right hand and I figured she was going to slap me, but then she spun off and stomped away, swearing louder. The way she swore reminded me of my Army days, and I wondered how *People* might've altered their rankings if they heard Skye Van Brandt shrieking things like "shit-eating goatfucker" and "fart-breathed ass-miner."

When she passed the executive desk with its fax machine and multi-line telephone and leather-bound hotel directory, she grabbed the ashtray on its corner and flung it at me without pause or warning. The ashtray was small, cut glass, and surprisingly aerodynamic. I had just enough time to turn my head, and then it hit and bumped me out of the world for a moment. For an instant I felt like I had been knocked down a well, and I was surrendering to gravity when somehow I managed to arrest myself, leaning back against the wall until I was sure I wouldn't collapse.

Blood was coming off my forehead as I straightened, blinding my left eye. I felt thick and sluggish, and it took a while to get my hand up and my glasses off to clear my vision. Each time I swiped, more blood came to replace it. I put my glasses back on and tried to focus on my principal.

Skye Van Brandt stood behind the couch, her hands at her sides. There was no repentance or apology in her expression.

"Now," she said sweetly, "pick up my bags, motherfucker."

"I quit," I said.

The doorman hailed me a cab to the airport, and I spent the entire ride with my handkerchief to my forehead. Facial cuts, as any guy can tell you, bleed a lot. I caught a glance of myself in the rearview mirror during the drive and, over the reflection of the hack's curious gaze, saw the gash above my left eyebrow. It wasn't deep, but the skin had split and I was probably going to need stitches.

When I hit the terminal I gave the cabbie an extra twenty for a tip—expense money—and then made straight for the monitors inside, trying to find the next departure to any of the New York area airports. There was a flight to Newark that was boarding, another to Kennedy that was leaving in thirty minutes. I got into line and weathered a storm of stares. I couldn't tell if the stares were because of the wound or because I'd been recognized, and frankly didn't care.

"You ought to do something about that cut," the customer rep said in a gentle Texas drawl. He looked sincerely concerned.

"I am doing something about it," I said. "I'm going home."

I checked my bag with my weapon inside, and as he was swiping my credit card, my cell phone started ringing. I shut it off, took my boarding pass, and then stopped at the first gift shop I could find on the concourse, where I paid too much for a package of Band-Aids. Then I found a men's room and examined myself in the mirror. The appraisal didn't help my mood. Blood had speckled my cheek and the collar of my shirt, though the wound was now content only to ooze. I looked tired and sallow and generally unpleasant, though maybe that was the lighting.

I ran some warm water, cleaned myself off carefully, then used my pocket knife to slice the bandages into makeshift butterfly sutures. It hurt when I applied them, but the wound appeared closed and I guessed I'd earned myself a companion scar to the one on my cheek from when I'd been pistol-whipped a couple years back. I tried to remember a time when I hadn't had any scars on my face, realized I really was thirty years old, and then ran some more water and cleaned my glasses. I pushed a couple fingers through my hair, straightened the two hoops in my left ear, and made it to the gate as they were closing the door.

My seatmate was white and in his mid-thirties, wearing a blue suit with a green-and-gray-striped tie. A leather laptop case lay by his penny loafers, stowed under the seat in front of him. He had all the marks of a business traveler, and I prayed that meant he'd leave me alone. With some squeezing I made it past him and then folded myself into the window seat, and with additional contorting, managed to assume a position that was merely uncomfortably cramped rather than genuinely painful. We were another forty-three minutes on the tarmac before actually lifting into the air, during which time the headache from the tête-à-ashtray invited a few friends over to throw a really big party.

Then we were rising and I stared out the window, watching as Texas faded away beneath me and wondering how I'd become someone who was expected to carry the bags of the likes of Skye Van Brandt.

The call had come in February, five months earlier. It had been a bleak winter, filled with rain and slushy snow, and a wind with teeth that never seemed to let up, day or night. I'd been cold and often irrationally lonely. My "don't call me girlfriend" Bridgett Logan had entered rehab just a few weeks prior, and Erika Wyatt, my almost-baby-sister, had started NYU, and moved out of the apartment we'd shared and into student housing. My home, which had never seemed spacious to me before, felt cavernous.

I was stretched out on the sofa in Dale Matsui's living room, squabbling with Natalie Trent about whether or not we were so desperate we needed to take out ads in some of the less-reputable trade journals. I was on Dale's couch because we'd been using Dale's house in Queens as our offices, and I was arguing with Natalie because our company was in serious danger of going belly-up.

"Can you think of another way to get clients?" Natalie asked. "Because without clients, we don't have a business."

"Security firms that advertise in the publications you're considering do not, in my opinion, engender confidence," I said. "And if we're protecting someone's life, I think confidence is kind of important."

"Don't be snide. We build confidence by protecting clients. To get clients, I'm suggesting we advertise."

"No," I said.

"Sentinel advertises."

"Well, by all means, then," I said.

She scowled at me, and I kept my tongue still, knowing that I'd cut too close to the bone. Natalie and I have a confused history that includes things like her dating my best friend, that friend dying, her blaming me for his death, and, eventually, the two of us making up to such an extent we ended up sleeping with one another off and on for almost a year. That the friendship has survived such things is a testament to its quality and our stubbornness.

Even knowing that, though, the crack about Sentinel was probably a cheap shot. Sentinel Guards was the biggest security firm in Manhattan, run by Natalie's father, Elliot Trent. Our firm—KTMH Security—was founded, in part, due to a falling-out between Natalie and Dear Old Dad, and she and I liked to think of ourselves as an alternative to the old-school protection firms that Sentinel personified. That was still, in my opinion, a worthy goal, and one that I knew Natalie shared.

The problem was that personal protection is an intimate community. Most work comes from referrals, either via former, satisfied, clients or from other agencies. Since we were a new firm we didn't have any former clients, and the rumor was that Elliot Trent had pretty much blacklisted us from the start, so no firms, from Sentinel on down, were giving us referrals.

I used my elbow to prop myself up and looked at Natalie, who had now turned her scowl to the window that looked out onto Dale's backyard. Outside, a light sprinkling of snow was twirling down onto the lawn. Dale, in the other chair, was looking at me like a disapproving parent. I've actually known Dale longer than I've known Natalie—he and I were in the Army together on a couple of the same details. He is, without a doubt, the nicest person I know, genuinely kind.

As a result, his disapproving look is pretty darn devastating.

"You know what I mean," I said to Natalie.

"I don't appreciate being compared to my father."

"That's not what I was doing, Nat."

She looked back at me, and her green eyes lost their focus briefly in their contemplation. Natalie is just shy of my age, tall and fine-boned, with red hair that she'd recently had cut into a bob. The new haircut showed off her facial features, the line of her neck and jaw. While the four of us in KTMH—Natalie Trent, Dale Matsui, Corry Herrera, and I—are equals, there is a hierarchy when we're at work, and Natalie is my strong second-in-command. She's as good as I am at the job, if not better.

"We're living on credit right now, you are aware of that, aren't you?" she asked.

"Painfully aware," I said.

"And you understand that our credit is almost gone?"

"Yes," I said.

"So you tell me, Atticus, what are our options? Keep waiting, hoping that the phone is going to ring? Or do we do something proactive, do we take out some ads and see where that gets us?"

"The question may be moot," Dale said. "We may not have enough money to advertise, at least, to advertise anywhere that'll do us some good. We need a corporate account."

"I am not going to just wait for business to come to us," Natalie said. "We need to *do* something."

"I agree," I said.

"What, then?"

"I have no idea."

She was ratcheting up her glare when the phone rang. Dale moved to answer it, and Natalie let the glare go, went back to frowning at the backyard.

"It's for you," Dale said, holding out the phone.

"Who is it?" I asked.

"Sergeant Robert Moore. Of the Two-Two SAS. You remember him?"

I nearly tripped over the coffee table going for the phone. "Robert?"

"Atticus, how've you been, mate?" The connection was good, and I couldn't tell if Moore was calling from England or across the street. "World treating you just?"

"I've got complaints, but you don't want to hear them," I said. "What's up?"

"This a bad time? I can ring you later, you like."

"No, now's fine."

"Called your apartment first, got this number off the machine. I've left the Regiment, didn't know if you'd heard."

"News to me."

Moore laughed in my ear. "Figured I was getting too old to be running through marshes with full kit. Day comes you know the Beacons are going to beat you rather than the other way around, a man thinks about retiring. I'm in your line of work now, matter of fact."

"No kidding?" I said. Natalie and Dale were both watching me, curious, and I made a half-wave with my free hand, trying to indicate that I knew as little as they did.

"Dead serious," Moore said. "And it so happens that I've got a principal coming across the water in a couple weeks, has some speaking engagements. Pseudopolitical, lots of photo opportunities, things like that. Wondering if you'd be interested in handling some of the crowd for me."

"What are the dates?" I was motioning frantically for someone to give me something to write with and to write upon. Natalie tossed me the *GG&G Industries* catalogue sitting on the coffee table, and Dale handed over a ballpoint.

"End of the month, twenty-fifth through the third of March," Moore said. "You free?"

"Absolutely."

Moore laughed. "Didn't have to check the schedule, then?"

"No, I've got it memorized," I said, scribbling the word "JOB" on the catalogue and holding it up for all to see. "Can you tell me anything more?"

"I've got a packet I can fax you, if you give me the number. Dates, itinerary, so on. You can review it then give me a ring back, we can discuss terms."

"Hold on," I said, and covered the mouthpiece. "Do we have a fax number?"

"We have a fax number," Dale said.

I removed my hand and repeated the number Dale gave me to Moore. "When do you need an answer?"

"Can you ring me tomorrow?"

"Done."

"Talk to you then. Cheers."

I hung up the phone and turned back to share the news, only to discover that the room had suddenly emptied, and that Dale and Natalie were now in the office at the end of the hall. Dale was making certain the paper tray was loaded, and Natalie was staring at the fax machine as if it would start reciting Homer at any second. As I entered, though, she pulled her look from the machine and put it on me.

"Well?"

"Robert Moore has left the SAS and is now in the personal protection business. He's got a job in New York and he wants us to assist. Details to follow."

"Who's the principal?"

"Didn't say."

"But presumably it's someone who can pay?"

"I'd expect."

Natalie gnawed her lower lip for a moment. The fax machine bleated, once, then began humming, and within seconds pages were spewing forth. Dale grabbed them as they hit the out tray, handing them over, and Natalie snatched the first sheet before I read it.

"Lady Antonia Ainsley-Hunter," she said. "Moore is protecting Lady Antonia Ainsley-Hunter."

"I'd say she can pay," I said.

Natalie socked me in the shoulder.

Lady Ainsley-Hunter was, at twenty-three years old, one of the most visible advocates of children's rights in the world, and the founder of Together Now, a grass-roots group that had started in the U.K., similar to Rock the Vote. Hunger, disease, abuse, exploitation, ignorance—all of it was on Together Now's hit list, and the organization worked closely with UNICEF and the ILO to reach its goals, with Lady Ainsley-Hunter spearheading the assault. She was blond and attractive and surprisingly innocent-looking despite all she had undoubtedly seen, and her mission occupied most, but not all, of her waking moments. In interviews she could talk as easily about her favorite bands and foods and films as about mortality rates among infants in the Third World and incidences of child and spousal abuse in emerging nations.

The media absolutely adored her, both in Britain and the U.S. It was that visibility as much as anything else that made her a force to be reckoned with: She got the message out.

It was that visibility that also made her a target, because every wacko in the woodwork knew who she was.

For the next three weeks, we buried ourselves in advance work, covering everything we could think of, just to be safe. All four of us knew that Moore had thrown KTMH a life preserver, and we weren't planning on letting it go. This was our big break, our chance to show all watching that we knew our stuff, that we were on the stick.

And there would be people watching, none of us doubted that at all.

We just didn't know who.

Natalie and I started with close surveys of all the locations Lady Ainsley-

Hunter would be visiting, from the hotels to the restaurants to the apartments, right up to the front entrance of the United Nations. We took photographs, made maps, racked our brains trying to imagine the worst that could possibly happen, and what our actions would be if it came to that. We practiced entry moves, debus moves, went so far as to put in extra range time. The last week of February alone, just prior to Lady Ainsley-Hunter's arrival, Natalie and I put a combined two thousand rounds through our weapons.

While we were busy on the ground, Dale and Corry were working on the road, planning primary, secondary, even tertiary routes, driving them over and over. Wherever they were in the city, they knew the nearest hospital, the nearest precinct house, and the quickest routes to get there. They did the drives in daylight and darkness, at dawn and at dusk, learning the traffic patterns, learning where to expect delays and planning how to react should any occur. Corry repaired, overhauled, and polished all of our equipment, making certain it was in good order; he even paid for new radio batteries out of his own pocket.

It was some of the best advance work any of us had ever done, and when Lady Ainsley-Hunter landed at Kennedy and we met her and Moore and the rest of her entourage, we were as ready as we could be. We were confident but cautious. We knew what we were doing.

Unfortunately, when it finally came down, none of that mattered. Not the prep. Not the gear. Not the two thousand rounds, or the hours spent driving the routes and poring over maps, or the brand-new batteries in the radios.

When it finally came down, what mattered was luck.

Pure dumb luck.

Even before she arrived in New York, the invitations had begun pouring in, various celebrated people all trying to contact Lady Ainsley-Hunter, inviting her out to dinners, concerts, and clubs. For the most part, she turned them all down, sending regrets and thanks, but preferring to stay at her hotel and work.

Until Carson Fleet invited her to attend the premiere of his new blockbuster, *Long Way Down,* starring—amongst others—Skye Van Brandt.

"She'll want to go," Moore told me, after he'd read the invitation. One of his duties was to screen any incoming mail, and he'd opened and read the letter as a matter of course. "She loves Fleet's movies."

"You think it'll be a problem?" I asked.

"Nah," he said. "Invitation is for the movie and then a bash at Pastis on

Ninth afterwards. She'll do both, we'll have her back by two in the morning, no later. She's not much of a party girl."

"For which we are all extremely grateful."

"You and Nat want to run the route, I'll let her know we've got security in place."

"We'll do it this evening, after she's buttoned up for the night."

"Right, then," Moore said. "Should be a no-brainer, really."

Ingress was flawless.

Egress was another matter entirely.

We were using two cars, one driven by Dale to ferry Lady Ainsley-Hunter, Moore, and myself from location to location, and then a second car to follow, driven by Natalie, and loaded with Corry and Lady Ainsley-Hunter's personal secretary, a young woman named Fiona Chester. The vehicles were kept lined up around the block, and as each celebrity departed, the event staff would radio to tell each driver that they were free to move. Because we didn't trust the event staff to know their jobs, Dale and I were waiting on word from Moore.

"Sleepy coming out in thirty seconds," Moore said over the radio.

"Confirmed," Dale answered, and as he started to roll us into position, I got on my radio and echoed the order to Corry. Natalie confirmed before we'd come to a stop, and I was out, holding the door open at the end of the red carpet, scanning both sides of the line. Natalie and Corry fell into position on either side, where photographers and autograph seekers were lined up three and four deep beyond the velvet ropes. The flashbulbs started exploding.

Moore's voice came over my earpiece. *"Sleepy coming out."*

"Confirmed."

They appeared at the end of the carpet, making their way toward us. Lady Ainsley-Hunter was smiling, waving to each side, and Moore was sticking close to her, and there was another barrage of flashes, followed immediately by a yell, and without warning a fight erupted amongst the paparazzi that spilled onto the red carpet. Moore's left hand shot to Lady Ainsley-Hunter's shoulder, pulling her back toward him and tucking her in, and he tried to power through to the car using his body as cover. I stayed on post, watching as Nat and Corry did their damnedest to keep the route clear.

Cops started swarming in, the gawkers got involved, and suddenly there was a furball of people pushing and pulling. The brawl was escalating, punches starting to fly wildly, and Moore abruptly went down like a dropped brick, a flailing photographer's elbow connecting with the former soldier's face, taking him utterly by surprise. For one horribly long moment Lady Ainsley-Hunter was motionless, alone, standing on the red carpet with the melee around her.

I went off the car, diving in after her, using my hands to knock people out of the way. Over my earpiece, I heard Moore shouting for an evac.

Lady Ainsley-Hunter gripped my arm as I reached for her, and I pulled her into me, looking for a path out. "Got you," I told her. "Got you, you're fine."

"Bloody hell," she muttered.

"Hold on," I said, already turning to fight a path back to the car.

Then Corry was shouting, "Gun! Gun! Gun!"

His name was Samuel Jeppeson, and we learned later that he was forty-three years old and recently released from Bellevue, where he'd been undergoing treatment for paranoid schizophrenia. When the cops finally managed to get a semicoherent statement from him, they learned that he'd stopped taking his medication four days before Lady Ainsley-Hunter arrived in New York. Jeppeson then explained that he had merely been trying to keep the British Crown from reclaiming the Colonies. What we didn't understand, he said, was that Lady Ainsley-Hunter was actually a member of the One World Government's Covert Action Staff, on a mission to New York City to seduce the mayor and recruit the NYPD to her cause.

He never explained where he got the gun, which was a Llama Model IX, a semiautomatic pistol manufactured in Spain, with a magazine capacity of seven nine-millimeter rounds. The gun hadn't been well cared for, and specks of rust were visible around the barrel and along the slide, though they certainly wouldn't keep the weapon from firing.

Any other weapon, and things could have turned out very differently. But Jeppeson brought the Llama, and from that single decision everything else sprang forth.

By the time Corry was shouting "gun" a second time, I had my hand on Lady Ainsley-Hunter's shoulder and was pushing her down into the crouch, hoping that Moore had drilled her on this, hoping she wouldn't go flat. If she went to the deck, down on the carpet, it would be impossible to move her quickly. She stopped on her haunches, and it's to Her Ladyship's credit that she remembered what she'd been taught, and she was in her crouch when I spotted Jeppeson.

He was in full lone-gunman mode, making straight for us, right into the critical space, the pistol out in his right hand, shouting some condemnation that I never actually heard. My stomach had shrunk to the size of a marble, I didn't have time to index my own weapon, in fact I didn't really have time to do anything at all. I remember thinking, quite clearly, that if Jeppeson shot Lady Ainsley-Hunter I'd end up getting blood all over my only suit, which was from Brooks Brothers and which I was rather fond of, and which I didn't think I could afford to send to the dry cleaner because certainly if our principal died I'd never get work again.

He broke through the line with people moving to get away, and I stepped in front of him and grabbed the pistol with my left, trying to force the slide back and out of battery, trying to keep the hammer from falling on the bullet in the chamber. It wasn't a conscious attempt to do anything clever; it was a move of panic more than anything else, an act to do something—anything—to keep the Llama from firing.

The force of my grip on the gun drove Jeppeson's arm back against his body, and I started to reach up between us, to grab his elbow and pin him back. There was the vibration of something metal snapping in my hand, and then my grip on the gun was gone, so I reached for him again, catching his right shoulder with my left hand, catching his elbow once more, and then I pivoted and pitched him headfirst into the carpet. The flip dislocated his shoulder, and Jeppeson hit the deck howling.

As soon as my hands were clear I indexed my weapon with my right, scanning for another attack, and shouting at Lady Ainsley-Hunter, "Get in the car! Get in the car!"

She sprang up from the crouch, and I fell in behind her, looking at the mass of people, wincing at the onslaught of more flashbulbs. Lady Ainsley-Hunter slid into the backseat, and I pitched in after her, slamming the door shut and then literally covering her body with my own. The engine had been running, and we were out into the street in roughly a second, Dale accelerating, speaking quickly into his radio.

"We're clear, we're good," Dale told me, after a minute. "Moore and the others are en route, they'll meet us at the hotel."

I rolled off Lady Ainsley-Hunter and helped her sit up, then began running my eyes and hands over her body, making certain she hadn't taken a wound I might've missed. Given enough adrenaline, a person can take a bullet and keep moving for quite a while, and I didn't want us to arrive at the hotel only to discover that we should have been headed for the hospital instead.

"Fresh," Lady Ainsley-Hunter said.

"You'll forgive me," I said. "You're all right? You feel okay?"

"I'm fine, Mr. Kodiak."

I took my hands off her and slid back. She was flushed, still breathless, but as best as I could see she was telling the truth. "We're taking you back to the hotel."

"I heard. Somehow I didn't think Mr. Matsui was racing us to the party. It would be anticlimactic after all of that, I think," Lady Ainsley-Hunter said lightly. She smiled.

Then she put her hands on her thighs, doubled over, and vomited.

I pulled her hair out of the way, realized I was holding something in my left hand, and tried to imagine what it could be.

When the heaves became dry, Lady Ainsley-Hunter pushed my hands away, then sat up once more. Tears were streaking her face now, shimmering in her eyes, and her mascara had run. She wiped her nose with her fingers, and I found my handkerchief and handed it over.

She took it and blew her nose energetically, dabbed at her eyes, tried the smile on me again. "I'm sorry."

"Not to worry. It's a natural reaction."

"I'm afraid I've made a mess."

"Dale'll clean it up."

She laughed, just barely, but I took it as a good sign. Then she focused on my left hand. "What's that?"

"I'm not sure," I said, and opened my hand to see a chunk of metal about four inches long. "I think it's the slide."

"The slide?"

"From the gun."

From the front seat, Dale said, "From the *what*?"

"The slide-stop must've snapped when I was trying to force it back," I said. "Came off in my hand, and I was too amped up on adrenaline to drop it."

Lady Ainsley-Hunter leaned back and used the handkerchief again. "Nicely done," she said. "Taking the man's gun apart like that."

"Oh, hell yeah," Dale said. "He so meant to do that."

"How do you know I didn't?" I asked.

"I know you."

The plane was descending into Kennedy, and I was watching the sunset light slide away from Rockaway below us, thinking it was a beautiful thing, that it would be a beautiful image to keep and preserve. Much more worthwhile than yards of videotape and mountains of photographs that almost, but didn't quite, tell the truth.

It was the cameras that did it, that lofted me and the rest of KTMH into the same orbits as Skye Van Brandt and Carson Fleet and even Lady Antonia Ainsley-Hunter. The still photos and the endlessly looped videotape that showed, again and again, what appeared to be my magic trick, the effortless one-handed dismantling of Jeppeson's gun. The full-color photo that, for one week, was on the cover of *Time,* taken the moment after Jeppeson hit the deck, showing me with the slide in one hand, my weapon in the other, and Lady Ainsley-Hunter dashing past, sprinting for the car.

Within days of the attempt on Lady Ainsley-Hunter, we were swamped with requests for our services, everything from legitimate protection work to puff show jobs to one query asking if we'd be willing to fly out to Idaho for a week and train a militia unit in the finer points of personal protection. We took a pass on that one; we said yes to just about everything else. We were invited on talk shows, including a couple of national ones. We appeared on *Charlie Rose* and *Larry King Live. New York* magazine did a cover story, entitled "The New Security." Natalie, certainly the best looking of us, got singled out for particular attention, with one photograph of her running with the caption, "Cover me!"

We weren't working out of Dale's house in Queens anymore. We had an office in Manhattan, below the West Village by the entrance to the Holland Tunnel, in what was once the Printing District. We were almost rich, and certainly comfortable. We had more work than we could handle, and of late Natalie and Dale had been agitating for hiring on another couple of hands, just to help with the load.

We were, by all reckoning, successful.

My dumb luck.

CHAPTER TWO

It was six past nine when the cab let me off in front of my apartment building in Murray Hill, and I unlocked the foyer door and checked the mail, discovered the box empty. I took the stairs two at a time to the top and let myself into the apartment. Elvis Costello was playing on the stereo, and beneath his voice I heard others, though those stopped when I shut the door. I locked up after me and tossed my bag into the bedroom, which is inconveniently right off the front hall, then turned around and saw Bridgett Logan as she came around the corner from the living room.

She smiled when she saw me, and that made me feel better. I'm a sucker for her smile, for the way her mouth opens and the way the lower left corner of her lip kind of tugs off to a side a little bit. Then again, I'm a sucker for just about everything about her, and in more ways than one, from the hoop through her left nostril to the tattoo on the back of her right calf. She's an inch taller than me, long and lean and with pale white skin that makes her black hair and blue eyes all the starker, and I think she's a total knock-out, but I freely admit to a bias. We've known each other just over three years, and in that time we've gotten together, pissed each other off, made separate, concerted efforts to sabotage our relationship, and finally returned to one another in a shaky comfort. A year ago, we were barely speaking.

Things change. When she got out of rehab, we began spending more and more time together. Now, often as not, Bridgett was at my place as much as her own apartment in Chelsea. She had a shelf in the bathroom for her toiletries, two drawers in the bureau for clothes, and slowly books and music from her collection had been migrating across town.

In May, I'd asked why she didn't just move in already and get it over with, and she'd told me that this was enough, then cut off further discussion by saying that she didn't want to be pressured. She asked me not to ruin it.

So I tried not to ruin it.

That didn't keep me from saying, "Hi, honey, I'm home," though.

Her smile broadened and she came down the hall toward me, so I moved to meet her. We caught up with each other at the kitchen and necked briefly, and then she pulled off the kiss and I put my face into her shoulder, and we held one another like that for a bit longer. She was wearing a black tank top, and her skin was warm and smelled of the oatmeal soap she now kept in my shower.

"Never, *ever,* say that to me again," Bridgett said.

"Let's go to bed," I told her shoulder.

"Hmm." She moved her mouth closer to my ear, and I heard her teeth clink against my earrings. "Tempting, but you've got company."

I let her go, straightening my glasses to see Natalie waiting at the end of the hall, watching us. She was in slacks and her blazer, and she didn't look very happy, and I guessed that she'd come from work.

"Hey, Nat."

"Atticus."

I opened the refrigerator and got myself a bottle of Anchor Steam, then offered one to each of the two ladies. They said no. I had a swallow, then dropped into one of the chairs at the table and began removing my necktie.

"That Skye Van Brandt's autograph?" Natalie asked.

"She's got a hell of an arm." I smoothed the tie down on the table, trying to get the creases out.

"Her manager called this afternoon, screaming his head off," Natalie said. "Says you walked out on her. Then Skye called, asking where you were, if you were coming back, sounding pretty distraught—"

"She's an actress," I said. "She gets distraught if her makeup isn't right."

"She's a movie star, actually," Natalie corrected. "Then her agent called, and he got shrill with me, saying that Skye couldn't work like this, whatever that means. Then Skye called back, but this time she had a bitch on, and when I told her I hadn't been able to reach you—"

"I shut off my phone."

"So I'd gathered. When I told her I hadn't been able to reach you, she called me several four-letter words, in a variety of combinations, then hung up. Then her manager called back and said you were fired. So, essentially, as a result of whatever happened in El Paso, I was verbally abused by the Skye Van Brandt organization this afternoon. Would you like to tell me what happened in El Paso, Atticus? Because I'm really curious."

"You know I wouldn't just walk out for no reason," I said.

"I do," Natalie said. "I also know that Skye Van Brandt's a spoiled brat, and that you should have been done with the job two days ago. Did she do that?" She indicated my forehead with a manicured nail.

"With an ashtray."

"Why?" Bridgett asked.

"I wouldn't carry her luggage."

They looked at each other. Bridgett began to giggle.

"That's nice," I said. "I'm glad you're amused, because I sure as hell wasn't. Aside from the pain that comes from being beaned with a glass ashtray, I nearly lost consciousness, I had blood in my eyes, and I couldn't see."

"You poor thing," Bridgett said.

I ignored her, speaking to Natalie. "She made it impossible for me to protect her."

"By walking out on her you left her exposed," Natalie said.

"To what? Back strain? Skye Van Brandt didn't need a PSA, Nat, she needed a babysitter. I was for show, that's all. And, for the record, I wasn't fired—I quit."

"It could make it hard for us to get more work."

"You mean more of that kind of work, and no it won't. We bill them as normal, and if they make a stink, we'll let them know our attorney will be in touch."

"You'd sue over this?" Bridgett asked.

"Of course not," I said. "But they won't dare trash our reputation, and if they get even the least bit snarky I've got no qualms about threatening them with a civil suit for assault."

"Ooh, he *is* pissed off," Bridgett told Natalie.

"Damn right I am."

"You might want to get that under control," Natalie said. "We've got clients coming into the office tomorrow at one, they're going to want to meet with you."

"Is it a real job?" I asked.

Natalie looked at me skeptically.

"One where we actually do what we're trained to do," I explained. "Not another dog-and-jackass show."

"Is that what you think we've been doing?"

"Don't you?"

"No, but this clearly isn't the time to discuss it. I'll see you tomorrow."

"I'll walk you out," Bridgett told her.

They left me alone in the kitchen, and I could hear them talking softly at the front door. Natalie and Bridgett have a friendship that predates my knowing either of them, and while it'd been stormy in the past, they seemed to have worked most of their difficulties through. I finished the beer and heard the door close, and Bridgett came back as I was rinsing the bottle out in the sink.

"Okay, sport," she said. "What are we going to do about your mood?"

"My mood's fine."

"True, you do sullen so well."

"Don't start."

"And feeling sorry for yourself even better."

"I asked you not to start."

"You did not, you *told* me not to start, and you know how I respond to that." She leaned back against the wall, arms folded across her chest. "I'm going to ask again, what do you want to do?"

"I want to shower. I want to have something to eat. I want to go to bed."

"That it?"

"Well, I'd prefer not to do these things alone."

"Then we have a problem, because I already ate."

"I can go without dinner."

"Problem solved."

A little after midnight I discovered that going without dinner had been a bad idea, and we got out of bed and pulled some clothes on, then went back into the kitchen. I boiled some water for Bridgett's herbal tea, fixed a glass of juice for myself, and we sat at the table and munched on sliced apple and cheese and bread. Bridgett had pulled on her tank top and a pair of my shorts, and I could see the track marks on her arms, puffy scars that were hard to the touch. She caught me looking at them.

"I'm fine," she said.

"I know," I said. "They just make me sad."

"Scars can do that. You've got a couple that make me feel the same way."

"And now a new one."

"Skye Van Brandt hasn't earned the right to scar you. It'll heal clean." She put some cheddar on an apple slice, munched, and chased it with a sip of tea. "She's not what's bugging you, though."

"How about the ennui of the working class?"

"Try again."

I swirled the cranberry juice around in my glass. "I shouldn't have walked out on Skye. That bugs me, but I'm not sure if it bugs me more than the fact that I took the job in the first place. I knew it was bogus going into it, but I did it anyway."

"The money was good," Bridgett said.

"I didn't do it for the money."

"Star-fucking, then?"

"I beg your pardon?"

"Not literally, you dope. Just wanting to be close to the *glitterati*. There's a glamour in it, admit it."

"The glamour has long since worn thin. I've seen how the other half lives, Bridgett, and I'm not interested. It's not that."

"Why then?"

I finished my juice, looked at the empty glass in my hand. "Something to do, I suppose."

"There are better ways to combat boredom."

"Don't I know it."

She finished her tea and we cleared the table, then shut off the lights and got back into bed. Bridgett curls up when she sleeps, and she pressed her back into me, settling, and was asleep in minutes. It took me much longer to relax, and nearly another hour before I managed to doze.

Then Bridgett was nudging me awake, and I was wincing in the sunlight, listening to her tell me that I was wanted by the FBI.

CHAPTER THREE

"How many times are we going to do this?" I asked Special Agent Scott Fowler.

"Hell if I know," he answered. "Until they don't have any more questions, I expect. Get in."

I took the passenger seat and Scott waited until I had buckled up before starting the engine and pulling out into the traffic on Lexington Avenue. It was an unseasonably cool summer morning, and pedestrians who had opted for shorts and tank tops were walking with the brisk purpose of people desperate to get warm again.

Scott himself seemed comfortable, though I knew to him anything below sixty-five degrees was, by his own definition, "freezing." We were both Californians by birth, but Scott was from SoCal, and grew up spending his after-school hours and weekends catching waves along the lower Pacific Coast. He's got four years on me, wears glasses, has two earrings, and looks perpetually ready to hit the beach at the drop of a hat. But for his suits, which are uniformly blue or gray, you'd be hard-pressed to tell just by looking at him that he works for the FBI.

"You were out of town," Scott said. "The lovely Skye. Nicely done."

"What the hell are you talking about?"

"It's in the paper. 'Seen canoodling at The Grey Moss Inn outside El Paso,

Texas, smoldering starlet Skye Van Brandt and celebrity protection specialist Atticus Kodiak.' "

"Whoa," I said. "Back up. What?"

"Page Six. The *Post*. There's a copy on the backseat." Scott was grinning like he'd snuck a mouthful of some very tasty and forbidden treat. "Bridgett know?"

I was twisting around for the paper, finding it already folded open to the celebrity gossip pages. There was a small file photograph of Skye, and the copy was pretty much as Scott had quoted with the addition that, "Van Brandt's publicist denies any involvement between the two."

"This is utter crap," I said.

Fowler laughed, negotiating the merge onto the FDR. "They make all that shit up anyway. You'd never be caught dead canoodling anyone at The Grey Moss Inn."

"Wait until tomorrow," I said. "They'll run a story saying that she and I had a fight and that we're 'headed for Splitsville.' "

"Oh, I'm sorry to hear that. You and Skye were so good together."

"Shut up and drive." I tossed the paper back behind the seat. "Did something happen?"

"No idea. The SAIC just told me that the Backroom Boys wanted to see you again, and could I get you into the office this morning. I told him I'd try."

"That's it?"

"If I knew anything else, I'd tell you, Atticus," Scott said. "Probably more of the same. Somebody somewhere found something someplace and they're hoping you can shed light on it."

"Here we go again," I muttered.

"Here we go again," Scott agreed.

We parked in the garage, and then Scott led me up into the Federal Building, where I got my visitor's pass and was escorted past the metal detectors, then into the elevator and up to the Bureau offices. What had once seemed a maze of corridors and turns had now become familiar, and we went past the pictures of the President, the Attorney General, and the Director, walking along floors carpeted in gray and blue, passing agents and secretaries until we reached the same conference room as every time before.

They were waiting for us inside, already seated, six of them this time, which was the most who had been present for quite a while. There were five men, three of them at the table, two seated with their backs against the far wall, and one woman, also at the table. The man at the head of the table was Hispanic and in his fifties, with a stack of file folders to one elbow, and I pegged him for American before he spoke, either CIA or NSA or State, though the odds were he wouldn't identify himself as such. To his right sat two more men, both Asian. The woman was to his left, black, perhaps shy of fifty, and when she spoke, her accent was South African. The men seated at the back were both white, but the lights were dimmed for the presentation, and I didn't get a good look at their features.

These were the Backroom Boys, and so far they had never been the same group twice. This was the sixth time I'd been summoned to appear before them in the last eleven months, and I was resenting it like hell right now. The first couple of times hadn't been so bad; there'd been a novelty value, and I'd been eager to help the cause of international law enforcement, to offer what small insight and experience I could. Now, even if the cast kept changing, the parts didn't, and I knew all the lines by heart.

The man at the head of the table rose and said, "Thank you for coming, Mr. Kodiak. My name is Marietta. I work at the State Department."

"Sure," I said.

Everyone except Scott put their eyes on me for a moment, taking stock. I was wearing old jeans and a T-shirt and my Army jacket. The butterfly sutures I'd put on my forehead the previous night had come off, and I hadn't had time to shave. I imagined that I looked pretty sordid, less a professional security specialist than some thug who had wandered into the wrong line of work.

Fine by me. If everyone was going to play a part, I'd play one, too.

Marietta indicated the woman, introducing her as a representative from Interpol's headquarters in The Hague. The two men on Marietta's right worked for the South Korean Intelligence Agency. He ignored the men behind him, and from his manner I assumed that all of us present were to do the same. Which meant they were probably spooks.

When the introductions had been completed, Marietta started the presentation, using a sleek black laptop linked to the LCD projector on the table. He directed his speech to the three at his end of the table. The rest of us might as well not have been there.

"Mr. Kodiak is a personal protection specialist based here in New York. Almost a year ago he headed the protection detail surrounding a man named Jeremiah Pugh. Pugh had been targeted by a member of The Ten, by the assassin now referred to as Drama. What is so remarkable about this, aside from the fact that Mr. Kodiak kept himself and his principal alive, is that he had personal contact with Drama on multiple occasions, mostly by telephone, but including three physical contacts, one of which was a conversation that occurred in his own home."

Everyone at Marietta's end of the table looked at me again. I raised my right hand and gave them a small wave. What Marietta wasn't telling them is that before Drama and I had chatted in my apartment, she'd stripped me to my underwear and that she'd held a gun on me the whole time. There was still a bullet hole in the couch from where she had fired a warning shot.

"As of this date," Marietta continued, "Mr. Kodiak is the only individual known to international law enforcement and intelligence to have had contact with Drama and survive. He is considered to have unique insight into the workings of The Ten. . . ."

I tuned him out, mostly to keep from registering my disgust. I am an expert on The Ten the way Scott Fowler is a member of the Beach Boys. Drama had been hired to kill the man I'd been hired to protect, and the fact was, I didn't like talking about her, and neither did any of my partners. We'd miraculously survived the experience without harm, without losing life or limb. Mentioning her name at times seemed a little too much like tempting fate, as if she might be summoned from the depths where she slept to wreak havoc on all of our lives once more.

The Ten were stone-cold killers, ghosts of the modern world who murdered without pause or flaw, without politics or emotion to cloud their judgment. They did what they did for money, and they were good enough that they commanded millions for their services. Nearly nothing was known about them but for a handful of code names, a cloud of rumors, and a few very anemic and dubious facts. Even the name "The Ten" was misleading, since it referred to a theoretical ten best, and nobody in their line of work was particularly interested in providing an accurate census. There could be three or five or fifty of them, for all anybody knew.

People don't like to admit it, but death and killing have long been part of how power travels, how governments do business. The Ten were the logical and inevitable result of that; each had undoubtedly been trained by governmental or military programs, had learned his craft in service to a country or agency before going rogue. Which meant that, in some cases, the organizations hunting members of The Ten would be counting on the same people who had *created* the members of The Ten; and if the data those people provided wasn't accurate, or forthcoming, or useful, that was hardly a surprise. It made The Ten all that more dangerous, because in the face of total lack of knowledge, the few facts that might be discovered would almost always be viewed as suspect.

Worst of all, most of the time you never knew one of The Ten was coming until he or she had already gone, until the body was cold, and even then, maybe not. Got a witness you need to keep from testifying? Oh, look . . . he had an AMI in his sleep, how convenient. Member of parliament making things difficult for your business? Wouldn't be that same Right Honorable Gentleman who was found dead in his apartment, naked, with the body of his young lover, would it? Car crashes, fatal falls, mysterious illnesses, unexplained disappearances, tragic fires . . . The Ten could create them, it seemed, on demand.

Drama was one of them, and she scared the shit out of me. The only reason that Dale and Corry and Natalie and I hadn't blown town and taken to living in shacks in Antarctica after our encounter with her was that we knew it wouldn't do us a damn bit of good.

If Drama wanted us dead, we were dead.

Just the same, in the first weeks after protecting Pugh, all of us lived in perpetual paranoia. Natalie went to France for a month, saying she'd been meaning to get back to Paris ever since she'd lived there her junior year of college. Corry took his wife and son to visit family in Ecuador; Dale and his lover, Ethan, spent four weeks driving cross-country "in search of America." I stayed in the city, trying to pretend that everything was normal.

Nothing happened, and we all relaxed, though when Christian Havel came around to all of us, working on her book, asking for interviews, we'd gotten nervous again. Havel was a crime reporter for the New York *Daily News,* and had bullied her way into Pugh's protection, then spun that involvement into a feature story, and most recently, a soon-to-be-released book. Last I'd heard, she was calling it *Drama: A Window into the World of Protection and Assassination,* and from what I and my colleagues knew about it, Havel pretty much laid out everything that had happened. She hadn't bothered to change our names, as far as I knew, and I wasn't looking forward to the new wave of public scrutiny that would come with the book's release.

Somehow, I didn't think Drama was, either.

That I and my friends were still breathing I took to mean that we were beneath Drama's notice, and that was just fine by me.

That was just how I wanted it.

After Marietta's presentation they went to the slide show, the LCD projector shining grainy surveillance photos acquired from God-knows-where on the wall at the end of the room. The first set were of Drama, though in a couple of them it was impossible to tell if it was her or just a light gray smudge with breasts. Most of the slides were black-and-white blowups from security tapes or long-range lenses, but there were a couple of color shots, too.

She was a tall woman, my height, and fit, maybe around one hundred and forty pounds. Her hair had been blond the last time I'd seen her, shoulder length, though in the various photographs now projected on the wall that was constantly changing along with the rest of her appearance. Her eyes, as I remembered them, had been blue. She was deft with the little changes that make recognition difficult, though apparently didn't bother with advanced disguise techniques like latex and heavy makeup. In four of the photographs she wore eyeglasses or sunglasses, never the same pair twice, and the frames helped to hide and alter the shape of her face.

Marietta ran through the slides, finishing with the most recent picture of her, taken just minutes after I'd seen her last. The shot was focused on a fire engine that had parked outside of a building on Broadway, and had been snapped by a tourist who was passing by at the time and merely interested in capturing the FDNY in action. Drama was barely in the frame, walking north up Broadway, and it was clear she didn't know the camera was there, because she wasn't hiding her face.

There was a click, and the slide was replaced with an enlargement of the same, now cropped around Drama. This was the only truly good picture of the batch. The FBI had managed to obtain the negative from the previous shot, and working from that had finessed the current image. She was mostly in profile, looking straight ahead, her right hand coming up with a set of sunglasses ready. She was wearing tan slacks and a black unstructured blazer, and her hair was dirty blond, straight, and to the base of her neck. Her mouth was just a tad open, as if she was speaking, and the corner of her upper lip was tugging back, as if in the first or last moments of a smile.

I'd seen it before, and every time I saw the shot I wondered what her expression meant. She had just tried to kill me and Dale and Pugh with a bomb, and there was a chance that, as she was walking up Broadway, she believed she had succeeded, that we were dead. Maybe it was satisfaction, that she'd done what she'd set out to do. Maybe it was pride in her work.

The laptop chirped and the wall where Drama had been was bathed in white light. There was a pause while Marietta concluded his narration, and then he opened the floor to questions. The woman from Interpol seemed fascinated that I'd spoken with her face-to-face.

"How did that come to pass?" she asked.

"She ambushed me in my apartment."

"Why would she do this? Why did she not merely kill you?"

"She had bugged the apartment, and that was where we'd been planning most of our operation. I was more useful alive."

"And she spoke with you? For how long?"

"About ten minutes."

"Why?"

"My theory is that I'd come home just after she'd placed the bugs and she wanted to distract me, to keep me from noticing that anything was out of place in the apartment. And she wanted to psyche me out. Most of her phone calls were for the same purpose, to gain a psychological edge."

The two Koreans spoke to each other quietly. One of them asked, "Could you determine her national origin?"

"No. Her English was colloquial and fluent. She spoke with a slight mid-Atlantic accent, so it's possible English is her native language."

"Anything about her training?" the other Korean asked.

"She implied she might have been a bodyguard, once. She didn't say where."

"How old would you say she was?"

"I'd put her around my own age, say early thirties. That's a guess."

"Which hand did she favor?"

"The right."

"Would you say she's technology-dependent?" Interpol asked.

"No, I think she uses the best tool at her disposal. If a pointed stick will do the job she wants done, she'll use it. But she's adept with technology, on the cutting edge. The mains transmitters she used to bug my apartment were maybe two millimeters long, half that wide. She also built her own explosives."

Interpol liked that answer and made some notes on her pad. "You spoke with her for ten minutes. Could you comment on her personality?"

"She made a couple of jokes, morbid ones, and she seemed to enjoy engaging in wordplay. At the time we—meaning my associates and I—were operating on the premise that she might have a partner, though that turned out to be mistaken. She had fun with that. She was almost flirtatious."

They all stared at me and I waited it out. It was the word "flirtatious" that did it. Whenever I used it, the people asking the questions would look at me like I was holding out on them, as if something more had happened, though nothing had. The conversation with Drama had ended not with a roll in the hay, but rather with me getting 120,000 volts from a stun gun, which pretty much put me out of the amorous mood until well after her departure.

Marietta cleared his throat, and the questions resumed. This took most of the next hour, and covered everything from the equipment Drama had used and the ways in which she'd used it, to what techniques we'd found effective in combating her and which ones had been failures. The Koreans were very interested in our countersurveillance procedures, and wanted to know all the specifications on the devices that Drama had planted in my apartment.

When that was finished, the lady from Interpol handed Marietta a CD-ROM, and he loaded the new images, then ran them through the projector.

"We have some people we would like you to look at," Marietta told me. "Let us know if you recognize any of them."

"I won't," I said. "I never have before."

"Yes, we know," Interpol said. "Please, humor us."

There were forty-seven pictures, mostly surveillance shots, presumably all of men and women suspected of being members of The Ten. The ethnicities were broadly mixed, though whites seemed to predominate.

As predicted, I didn't recognize a single face.

Interpol took a piece of paper from her briefcase and set it in front of her on the table. "I'm going to read you a series of names we've compiled. Tell me if you've heard of any of them, if, perhaps, Drama mentioned any of them."

"You got it."

"Pontchardier, Claude? Also known as Dupuis, Jean-Claude and Breda, Marlon? Sometimes called The Fireman."

"No."

"Holcomb, Benjamin? He might be referred to as Dancer."

"No."

"Ebbertine, Jennifer or Garza, Teri—it's with one 'r' and one 'i.' Sometimes referred to as Lilith?"

"Nope."

"Rai, Ravi. Also Munez, Roberto? Called Gomez—"

"You mean from *The Addams Family*?"

She looked up from the sheet at me. "What?"

"Nothing, sorry," I said. "That's a nope."

"Pallios, Andreas, or Ben Havar, Simon? Known sometimes as Lawrence."

"No."

She frowned at Marietta, then replaced the sheet tidily in her attaché case. I thought about asking Interpol where they came up with these code names, and if she really thought that The Ten used them amongst themselves.

Somehow I couldn't see Drama picking up a phone and, say, giving Lilith a ring to swap tips about neck-snapping and checking the going rate for a car bombing. The code names are used by law enforcement and intelligence, just a way to label people who had lost their true names long ago and now went through aliases the way water passes through coffee grounds.

Everyone at the far end of the table now had their heads together, and were speaking intently. I looked over at where Scott was seated, and he shrugged, so I cleared my throat. The conversation continued, so I did it again, louder. Marietta raised his head.

"Yes?"

"It's been fun," I said. "But I have somewhere to be."

"Of course," he said, getting to his feet. "Thank you for coming in and taking the time to speak with us."

"My pleasure," I fibbed.

Scott rose, and we headed for the door. Just before we exited, I heard Interpol asking Marietta if it was true that I was dating Skye Van Brandt.

CHAPTER FOUR

Scott was kind enough to drive me back uptown, to the office. The clear morning sky had vanished, replaced with a low-hanging gray that seemed to drip water.

"That wasn't so bad," he said, as he turned the car onto Canal Street.

"Not for you," I said. "But you got to catch up on some sleep."

"I was never actually asleep. I just didn't want to strain my eyes."

"Who were the two in the back?"

Scott shrugged. "Pick three letters of the alphabet, mix them together, there's your answer."

We turned off Canal before we hit the traffic battling to get through the Holland Tunnel, and Scott circled the block until we were on Hudson, parking opposite the building where KTMH had its offices. The building took up the entirety of the small block, and once had been the home of some serious printing, with the presses right on the premises. Now the printing industry in Manhattan was dead, and as a result the building was in the process of major renovation. Seventeen stories tall, the property was owned by Trinity Church, and they were doing their best to turn the location upscale. Construction had begun on an additional two floors at the top, and scaffolding surrounded the building on three sides.

Scott let me out and told me he'd try to call in the next few days, and I crossed the street and got pelted by drops from the air conditioners working in the windows above me. A new coat of paint had been put down on the walls in the lobby since I'd left for El Paso, and the smell of it was still rich. I waited at the elevator with a small cluster of people, mostly students from the New York Restaurant School, which was located on the sixteenth floor. There seemed to be a lot of people about for midday, and then I looked at my watch and saw that it was six past one, and realized that this was the lunch crowd returning from their meal.

The car came and I rode up in a mass of students, mostly black and Latino, listening as they talked to one another about their "mad skills with the béarnaise." I left them at fifteen and made my way to the solid wooden door at the end of the hall. There was a plaque mounted on it, brass, that read, "KTMH Executive Protection." The door was unlocked, and no one was in the reception area, not even a receptionist, but that didn't surprise me. We'd been having bad luck finding someone who could master the intricacies of answering the phone, taking messages, handling light typing, and greeting visitors to our offices. More often than not the receptionist's desk was vacant.

For a moment I stood still, listening for voices from down the hall, and then I heard the front door click behind me. Corry Herrera came in, carrying a box of doughnuts from Krispy Kreme, one in his mouth.

"Why aren't you in L.A.?" I asked him.

His response was lost in the doughnut, and he gestured with his head to indicate that I should follow him as he went down the hall, so I did. We've got a lot of space, enough so that each of us has our own office with windows and nobody had to fight for a good one. We also have a coffee room, a file room, a conference room, an equipment and storage room, two bathrooms—one with a shower—and three more rooms that are empty until we decide what to do with them. The walls are off-white and most of the floor is a fake wood laminate from Sweden that looks like the real thing but doesn't get scratched. It's a pretty nice space, and I like to think that when you enter it for the first time, it's comfortable rather than officious.

Corry made for the coffee room, and after he'd set down the box and finished his doughnut, said, "We got back this morning."

"Obviously. But you were supposed to be in L.A. until next week." Both Corry and Dale had gone out on a consulting job shortly before I'd left for El Paso, contracted by one of the major studios to act as technical advisors on some sort of production. As they'd explained it to me, this meant teaching young actors how to hold fake guns in a realistic manner. "Did something happen?"

"No, they just finished with us early, said we could leave." Corry opened the cupboard and got down a plate and three mugs. The coffeemaker on the counter had a full pot, and it smelled freshly brewed. "Dale couldn't get out of there fast enough. He's at home now, but I thought I'd come in, just check things out around the office."

"And bring doughnuts and make coffee," I said.

"These aren't for me. Will you grab the pot? My hands are full."

I took the pot and followed him out of the coffee room and back down the hallway, which I thought meant we were heading for Natalie's office.

"What happened to your forehead?" he asked, over his shoulder.

"Nonsmoking incentive program."

"Natalie said you and Skye Van Brandt had a falling out."

"Skye Van Brandt and I never had a falling *in*. Where's Nat?"

"Your office. We're entertaining, in case you hadn't guessed."

"I guessed. Who is it this time? Some spoiled rock star who wants someone to help him trash a hotel room? Or maybe another movie celebrity who needs an extra pair of hands for stroking his ego?"

My door was on the opposite side of the hall from Natalie's, and Corry stopped in front of it, adjusting the balance of the plate on his hand. He's five inches shorter than I am, with a wrestler's body and black hair, and one of those smiles that makes you think he doesn't have an enemy in the world. He didn't show me the smile, though; he showed me his frown, looking up at me with his eyes rather than by moving his head.

"Get the door," Corry said.

I opened it, still looking at him. "Just tell me the principal isn't another totally insufferable brat."

"Not unless vomiting in the backseat of automobiles counts," Lady Antonia Ainsley-Hunter said.

"So how long are you in town?" I asked.

"Just the day," Moore said. "We're flying back tonight."

"Quick trip."

"Her Ladyship had an appointment at the U.N."

Natalie, Corry, and I all looked at Lady Ainsley-Hunter, who was sitting in the chair beside Moore, and who had just put a rather large piece of an old-fashioned chocolate in her mouth. We caught her with her cheeks puffed out, and she raised one hand to hide her face while she hastily chewed and swallowed, and with the other gestured generally that we should find something else to look at for the time being.

"Clearly they didn't offer her any doughnuts," I said.

"No, just tea," Moore said.

"It's not anything to fuss over," Lady Ainsley-Hunter said. "It was just a *meeting*, that's all."

"Right, only a meeting at the U.N.," Corry said. "I mean, I had an appointment there just last week."

"So did I, come to think of it," Natalie said. "The Secretary-General is in my book club. I had to drop off the reading list."

"They're mocking me, Robert," Lady Ainsley-Hunter said. "Make them stop."

"Listen, you lot, stop mocking Her Ladyship," Moore said.

"Hey, our ancestors fought a revolution for just that right," I pointed out. "She doesn't want to be mocked, she shouldn't take such greedy bites."

"Bloody colonials," Lady Ainsley-Hunter said. "Don't they know they're speaking to a member of the Royal Family, a hereditary peer of the United Kingdom?"

"They know," Moore said. "Problem is, they don't give a damn."

"Perhaps they might be more appropriately respectful if they knew I was soon to be named an Honorary Goodwill Ambassador of the United Nations."

"That might do it. Would that do it?"

I looked at Corry, who looked at Natalie, who looked at me, and we all nodded in agreement.

"Yes, that would do it," Natalie said.

Lady Ainsley-Hunter smiled her approval, and we offered our congratulations. It seemed she was a little embarrassed by the honor, and it took some coaxing before she explained that Together Now had been working with the U.N. Special Commission on the Rights of Children, and the appointment had come as a result of her involvement. Nothing had been released to the media yet, and the actual appointment wouldn't be made for another three weeks.

"Which is what brings us here," Moore told us. "I've tried talking her out of it, but Her Ladyship is insisting that you motley bunch give me a hand with the protection. Pretty much the same as last time."

"Though preferably without the paranoid schizophrenic," Lady Ainsley-Hunter added.

"What's our schedule like?" I asked Natalie.

"We can clear it for this."

"Then you've got us," I told Moore.

"Brilliant," Lady Ainsley-Hunter said. "I'll leave you and Robert to discuss the details, and the rest of us can head out for a late lunch."

We all rose when Lady Ainsley-Hunter did, and Natalie and Corry headed to the equipment room to draw radios and other gear. They came back with their jackets on, guns in place, and we all headed to the front door. Moore made arrangements to rendezvous with the three of them later that afternoon, and then Lady Ainsley-Hunter said goodbye to me with a peck on the cheek.

"I'm so glad you can do the job. I was worried you might be too busy."

"We're never going to be too busy for you," I answered.

Moore and I waited until they were in the elevator and heading down before we went back inside, returning to my office. We each poured ourselves a cup of coffee, and I got out the laptop and settled back on the couch, rather than at my desk. Moore took the same chair again and lit a cigarette, and we began going over what would be required. He's one of the most disciplined men I've ever met, partially as a result of serving in the Special Air Service, which is considered by many who know to be the best special forces unit in the world, and perhaps also because he's black and has had to deal with prejudice all his life. He's in his mid-forties, and his face shows the lines of over twenty-five years of hard soldiering. Even working in the public sector, he still kept his hair in a military crop.

"Going to be a five-day stay in Manhattan," Moore said. "We're arranging for the usual press and speaking engagements, though once the U.N. announces the appointment we'll be getting more requests, so I'm trying to keep some of her schedule free. We'll let you know as more dates get filled."

"Where will she be staying?"

"The Edmonton. You know it?"

"Off Central Park, yeah."

"We'll be taking a suite on the eighteenth floor."

"Can you get a room closer to the ground?"

Moore shook his head. "You know she likes the suites at the Edmonton, and there aren't any below twelve."

"How many people will you be bringing over?"

"It'll be her, her personal secretary—young lass named Fiona Chester, you remember her—and myself. That's it."

I looked at him over the laptop. "No one else?"

"Her Ladyship thinks that's ostentatious," Moore said.

I laughed. "You have no idea how refreshing that is to hear."

"No, I do. I saw the *Post* today."

"Are we going to need extra guards?"

Moore dragged on his cigarette, then jetted smoke from his nose with a slight grimace. "I don't know, honestly. My professional paranoia keeps getting in my way."

That got a nod, because I understood exactly what he meant. If money and time and appearance were no object, both Moore and I would have preferred that Lady Ainsley-Hunter travel wrapped in Kevlar, and with a rotating detail of twelve guards that included emergency medical personnel.

He tapped ash into his now-empty coffee cup. "Threat level against her has been very low of late, especially since the burgeoning peace in Northern Ireland. Used to be that the IRA was the major worry, but not any longer. She gets the occasional letter, that's about it."

"What are the letters like?"

"Oh, standard nutter, mostly sexual. Fantasies, scenarios, and even those are rarely violent. I forward them to Scotland Yard as a matter of course."

"I'll want to see all of them, and the list of names, if any of the authors have been identified."

"Not a problem."

I typed up some more notes, then showed Moore what I had. He read it over and made a couple of changes, and by four we had a solid plan. I told him we'd get started on the advance work the next morning, and he promised to keep us informed as things developed on his end, especially as more appearances were confirmed. Then we spent another five minutes going over the price, and he got pissy with me when I tried to give him a break on the rate.

"You're a bloody awful businessman, Atticus. You should charge us what you're worth."

"You get a discount for being the people who made us famous."

"Shouldn't make a damn bit of difference, you berk. Now give me the *real* rate and I'll wire you the retainer tomorrow."

"Six thousand for the week, plus expenses."

"What's the bloody matter with you? You should be asking at least ten, and you know it."

"I can't believe we're arguing about this. Eight thousand, and that's my final offer, take it or leave it."

He took it and I got out a blank of our standard contract, filled in the appropriate information, and we each signed it. I made a photocopy and handed it over, saving the original for our files, by which time Moore said he had to be going. I escorted him to the door, we shook hands, and then he left.

I went back to my desk and filed the contract, then cleaned up the empty plate and mugs, dumping Moore's cigarette butt down the toilet. I washed the dishes and put them away, wiped down the counter in the coffee room, and rinsed out the dregs in the pot. Then I went back to my desk and sat down behind it. The lights were off and the shadows were growing long. To my left, opposite the couch, hung the framed covers from *Time* and *New York* magazine, and a couple of the front-page photographs from different papers. In the dimness, the newspaper shots reminded me of the slides I'd seen earlier in the day, the way the details blurred and the grays ran together.

When the light grew too faint for me to see what was inside my office I spun my chair and looked out the window. Traffic down below was backing up as more and more cars tried to squeeze their way into the tunnel, their headlights and taillights reflecting white and red off glass and painted metal. Once in a while the sound of a horn or a siren seeped in from the city around me, but other than that it was quiet.

I thought about Antonia Ainsley-Hunter, about how much I genuinely liked her, about how impressed I was with the way she used her life. I was proud to have protected her.

I was proud that she trusted me to do it again.

CHAPTER FIVE

Ten days later, Dale and I were working in the conference room when the temp at the front desk buzzed us on the intercom. We'd spent the morning on a risk analysis for the area around De Witt Clinton High School in the Bronx, where Lady Ainsley-Hunter would speak in the morning on the second day of her visit. She was going to address the students in the school auditorium, then do the meet-and-greet with members of the local Together Now chapter. Dale and I had driven the area, checking the approaches, then done a walk-through. We'd snapped three-dozen photographs and drawn maps, then dropped the film off at a one-hour place and grabbed lunch.

Now we were back in the office, trying to determine what the safest route to and from the school was, rather than the quickest. Dale was tacking the relevant pictures to the corkboard at the far end of the room and I was going through the Hagstrom atlas of the five boroughs, tracing out our route and transcribing it longhand onto a legal pad. Natalie and Corry were at the Edmonton, performing yet another walk-through of rooms.

When the intercom on the phone beeped, I poked the button with the pen. "Yeah?"

"Mr. Kodiak?" the temp said. "A Ms. Chris Havel is in reception. She doesn't have an appointment. She says she has something to give you."

"I'll just bet she does," Dale muttered, thumbtacking another photograph to the corkboard.

"Tell her I'll be right out," I told the intercom, then came off the button, capped my pen, and got up.

"If she only brought a copy for you, I'll be insulted," Dale said.

"If she only brought a copy for me, you'll have every right to be," I said.

She was waiting at the end of the hallway, smiling as I approached. It'd been almost seven months since I'd seen Chris Havel last, and she didn't look different, but there was a new air about her. Her short hair was artistically disheveled, and her skin had the luster that people get from either healthy living or expensive salons. What I knew about her led me to believe it was the latter. She had a book-bag hanging from one shoulder, black leather, Italian, and that was new; her old book-bag had been canvas, olive drab, Kmart. In her left hand she had a paper shopping bag.

"Thanks for seeing me," Chris said. "I probably should have made an appointment, huh?"

"I can give you ten minutes without the world ending," I assured her, then gestured to my office. When we got inside, she moved straight to the gallery wall, studying each frame. I settled behind the desk and waited for her to finish. When she had, she flopped on the couch like an exhausted teenager, letting her book-bag drop to the floor and putting the shopping bag on the coffee table. From inside she removed a stack of gift-wrapped packages, gold foil paper with a blue ribbon tied neatly around each.

"That it?" I asked.

"Oh, yeah." She took the top package from the stack, then flipped it my way as if throwing a Frisbee.

It was a hardcover copy of her book. The dust jacket was in matte black, with two traditional theatre masks on the cover, both in an embossed, glossy silver. One of the masks was Tragedy, the other Comedy. In Tragedy's left eye glistened a tear of blood. On the back of the dust jacket were quotes from a whole bunch of people I'd never heard of before, saying things like "Terrifying!" and "A revelation!" and "Possibly the most definitive work on the subject ever!"

Her signature was on the title page, with an inscription. The inscription read, *To Atticus—Thanks for almost blowing me up.*

"You're welcome," I told her. "Next time I'll try harder."

"That was murder to come up with. I never realized how damn hard it is to inscribe a book." She patted the stack. "You were the easy one, too. I had no idea what to say to Corry and Dale. Are they here?"

"Dale's working in the conference room. Natalie and Corry are out right now. If you want to leave the books with me, I'll make sure they get theirs."

"You're busy."

"We are," I agreed.

"I'll leave these with you, then." She settled back on the couch and put her feet on the coffee table, giving me no sign that she was ready to leave. "I tried to do well by you guys. Tried to be honest. You'll have to let me know what you think."

"I will," I said, closing the book and putting it to one side of the desk, by the phone. "Any word on how it's doing?"

"The book's not officially out until Monday, and we've already sold through the first print run just on the advance orders. My publisher is going back to press, this time fifty thousand copies in hardcover, can you believe it? They're talking about the *Times* list like it's a sure thing."

"I'm impressed."

She shook her head and made a vague gesture with her hands, telling me to wait, that there was more to come. "Gets even wilder. I mean, I've got a literary agent, he's just sold my second book, the publisher wants it ASAP, and the advance is an *embarrassing* amount of money, believe me. I've got another agent, the Hollyweird one, and he called this morning with an offer for the movie rights, and *that* makes the advance for book two look like the change you'd find in a gutter."

I realized that what I'd thought was delight in her was actually shock.

"I go on tour next Monday, I'm supposed to do radio and television and Internet chat rooms and PBS and the whole shebang. People are calling my agent, badgering him to get interviews scheduled and crap like that. I'm waiting to wake up, Atticus, waiting for someone to call and say there's been a terrible mistake, they don't mean *my* book, they mean someone else's book, some other Chris Havel."

"I'm happy for you," I said, and I was, but my voice didn't carry the sincerity, and she caught it. Hurt crossed her face for a second, then vanished.

"No, no, I didn't use your names," she said. "All the names were changed."

The relief was like a car rolling off my chest.

"Was that it? What was bugging you?"

"That was it," I said. "Thank you, Chris."

"Maybe you shouldn't thank me, yet. You're in the acknowledgments, you and the rest, and I mention the firm, too. Anyone paying close attention, they'll figure it out, but . . ."

"We can survive that."

Havel straightened on the couch, letting her feet drop back to the floor. "That scared you?"

"The thought of more publicity actually makes my blood run cold," I confessed.

"Is that it? Not that you're afraid she'll, uh . . ." Havel made a gesture with her right hand, as if shooting a gun.

"Not anymore."

She came forward on the couch, perching on the end, actively curious. "Really?"

"It would be pointless. It's too late to keep the book from being released, so the only other reason to come after us would be revenge, and I don't believe that factors into her world."

Havel considered, then sighed, leaning back once more. "There were a couple of times when I was writing, I got really scared. Working on a passage, and it would hit me that this was *real,* that I was writing about this secret, that she was out there, she and others . . . and I was afraid to go outside, I was afraid to stay indoors, I was afraid to be with people, I was afraid to be alone. . . ."

"Been there," I said.

"Yeah, I'm sure you have."

For a couple of seconds we shared a silent appreciation of fear.

"I'm supposed to be working on the next one," Havel said. "My new book. They want it yesterday, kind of a sequel to the first one, something along the same lines. Another book about The Ten."

"Good luck with the research," I said.

"I was kind of hoping you could help me with that."

I said nothing.

Havel looked over at the wall of photographs. "I want to talk to her."

I choked on a laugh.

"Yeah, I know how it sounds," she said. "But she talked to you, a couple times, so it's not that outlandish an idea, is it?"

"No, it is," I assured her. "Chris, you don't want to interview this woman, trust me on this. And come to think of it, I don't imagine she'll be all that willing to grant an interview."

"Have you heard from her? Since the Pugh thing?"

She said it like Drama was my ex-girlfriend, as if we'd parted amicably. "Are you nuts?" I asked curiously.

"I was thinking that if you had, you know, then you could arrange it." She rose, looking at the wall, crossing back for a closer look at the photographs. "I'd be willing to pay her for her time."

"You're not listening to me," I said. "I haven't talked to her. I don't *want* to talk to her. And honestly, neither do you."

"No," Havel said. "Don't tell me what I want, Atticus. It would be an amazing interview, it would be an amazing book."

"I can't help you."

"Meaning you won't?"

"Meaning I haven't heard from her, Chris. Leave it at that."

She turned away from the wall, studying me at my desk. "She hasn't been in touch with you?"

"You sound like the Feds. No."

Her frown was brief, gone again when she asked, "Can you tell me how to contact her?"

"I already said—"

"That's not what I mean, I'm talking about like, if I wanted to hire her, you know? How would I do that?"

I gave her a stare that was hopefully more eloquent than everything she'd been ignoring out of my mouth. She met it with a stare of her own, then shrugged and moved back to the couch, gathering up her book-bag.

"I can figure it out, you know," she said. "Asking you was just the quick way."

"Chris," I said. "You really don't want to do this. You start trolling for one of The Ten, they'll investigate before they even begin to make contact, and they'll find out who you are. This time, they'll know about the first book, and they'll see you coming a mile away. You'll be lucky if they simply ignore you."

With her right hand, she adjusted the leather strap on her shoulder, giving me a smile. "Fear is not a reason to not do something."

"Maybe you ought to examine the source of the fear. Self-preservation is a valid motive."

"You don't get it, Atticus," Chris Havel said, heading for my door.

"Chris—" I tried once more.

"The name of the game is publish or perish," she said as she went out.

"The nut file," I said, dropping the folder on Bridgett Logan's desk.

"What does that look like to you?" she asked.

"I beg your pardon?"

Bridgett sighed and pointed up. We were in her office at Agra & Donnovan Investigations, and she was slumped in her chair behind her desk, ignoring me and focused on the light fixture that hung above. I followed the direction of her index finger, saw the bowl of frosted glass attached to the ceiling. A tarnished brass bolt secured the fixture in place.

"A light fixture," I said.

"Yeah, but what does it look like?"

"Is this a trick question? It looks like a light fixture."

"You have no imagination," she said.

I pushed the file forward across her desk until it was even with her keyboard. It wasn't the thickest nut file I'd ever handled, but it had meat on its bones, and when I pushed it, pages slid out the way playing cards slide from a newly opened deck. "Courtesy New Scotland Yard," I said. "By way of Robert Moore."

"And how is that SAS bastard?"

"Ex-SAS."

"And how is that *ex*-SAS bastard?"

"Counting on us to make certain his principal doesn't take harm in our fair city. I need you to start on this right away."

"We're on the clock?"

"Lady, I'm here as the man who is subcontracting your services to assist our protective effort, not as the man who is pleasuring you nightly."

"You think mighty highly of yourself, don't you?" She sat up in her chair, flipping the folder open and beginning to scan the pages. "These have been vetted?"

I nodded and took the seat across from her. "Moore or one of his detail screens the mail. They don't like what they read, they forward it to the police and the cops take it from there. That's a copy of the official file, with Moore's notations."

Bridgett kept scanning the pages. "Notes are remarkably free of anti-Irish sentiment so far. You've reviewed this already, I assume."

"I have."

"Any in particular you want me to pay attention to?"

"I flagged the letters that got me twitchy."

She found the pages I'd marked, removing them from the folder and spreading them out to view side by side, then resting her elbows on the desktop and her chin in her hands. She read carefully. There were four that I'd noted as worthy of a closer examination. Three were sexual, two of them signed and from the same author. Both letters were couched in romantic phrasing until degrading into more disturbing fantasy when the author described what he wanted to do with Lady Ainsley-Hunter. While his descriptions weren't explicitly violent, the tone as each progressed became more aggressive and bitter. The third was written anonymously, a graphically detailed rape-murder fantasy. Scotland Yard didn't think the author of the first two and the author of the third were the same.

The fourth letter was a vitriolic death threat, in which the writer stated that he had been "close enough to do it" on more than one occasion. That letter also referenced the Jeppeson attempt, saying that, "you can't be protected all the time."

Bridgett's mouth tightened to a line.

"Just read the bit about the meat cleaver and the drill, huh?" I asked.

She nodded and kept reading, moving one hand to open her desk drawer. I thought she might be going for a Hi-Liter or a pen, but she produced a tin of cinnamon Altoids and popped three in her mouth. The tin stayed open on her desk.

When she had finished reading she separated the two that had been signed. "These worry me the most."

"Those are the ones postmarked out of Connecticut?"

"Hartford, yes. Signed, 'Love always, Joseph Keith.' Not Joe, Joseph. We know who the hell Joseph Keith is? Anything on him in here?"

"No. That's why I'm hiring you."

She crunched the Altoids in her mouth. "When does Lady Ainsley-Hunter get in?"

"Monday."

"Five days."

"Yeah."

"Okay, I'll get on this immediately. Have you talked to Special Agent Dude?"

"Fowler said he'd be happy to take a ride to Hartford with you."

"I'll call him now," she said, reaching for the phone. "If I head to Hartford, I'll be out of town for a couple days. I'll need you to go by my place and bring in the mail, water the plants. You guys backed up?"

"It's always like this the closer we get to a deadline. The details begin unraveling."

She stopped dialing long enough to let me come around the side of her desk and kiss her on the cheek.

"I should have started on this Keith guy a couple weeks ago," she scolded me.

"We didn't get the file until this morning. Moore had some trouble getting the copy released to us."

"It's not enough time, Atticus."

"It's all we've got."

"I'm sure that'll be a consolation to Her Ladyship when the shit hits the fan," Bridgett said.

CHAPTER SIX

"So where is he, then?" Moore asked.

"That's the problem," I said. "We don't know."

There was a slight crackle from the speakerphone as Moore, across the Atlantic, considered what Natalie and I had been telling him. It was the middle of a Sunday afternoon, the day before Lady Ainsley-Hunter would arrive, and Natalie and I were spending it in the office making certain our end of things was in order. In Queens, Dale and Corry were giving the vehicles their final once-overs, and checking that the rest of our gear was ready for action.

"I thought the FBI was assisting with this," Moore said. "Can't they find him?"

"They're looking."

"And?"

"And they're looking, Robert," I said. "Bridgett Logan and Scott Fowler went to Hartford. They found his apartment, but he wasn't there, and so far the word is that he hasn't been back."

"Christ."

There was another silence. I reached for my coffee cup and found the contents ice cold. I drank it anyway.

"All right," Moore said. "I have to ask, are we just being paranoid?"

"Hard to say," Natalie said. "Logan did some interviews with the neighbors. Keith was at his residence until sometime early last week. Bridgett went to his place of employment—he worked for a temp agency, white-collar, secretarial—and they told her Keith picked up his last check the Friday before last, at which point he told the service he'd be out of town for a couple of weeks."

"Christ," Moore said again. "Next you'll tell me he owns a rifle."

"If he does, it's an illegally acquired weapon," I said. "According to the FBI, Keith doesn't own a firearm."

"Good news, I suppose. There more?"

"Yeah, but you're not going to like it. Bridgett got a look at his apartment—"

"Legally?"

"I'm sketchy on the details. He had a lot of literature on Together Now and Her Ladyship. Not a shrine, Bridgett was very clear on that, but a substantial collection."

"Like what?"

Natalie consulted her notepad. "Pictures, magazine articles, clippings. Copies of articles written by Lady Ainsley-Hunter. Some of it was recent, including the press release about her appointment from the United Nations."

The groan that floated from the speakerphone made Moore sound like a disgruntled ghost. "How is that not a shrine?"

"No incense," I said.

Natalie gave me a proxy of what Moore's glare must have looked like.

"Bridgett got a picture of Joseph Keith," I said. "Confirmed it with the neighbors. We've had copies made and the FBI is handling distribution to the local authorities."

"Is that all?"

"There's not much more that can be done. Keith hasn't committed a crime, and until he does we can't get a full law enforcement press. Bridgett's been chasing down background on him, but she hasn't found anything in her interviews that sheds more light on what he's up to. We have to work with what we have."

"You trust Logan?"

"If there's something to find, I trust her to find it, Robert."

There was another pause, this one so long that I wondered if we hadn't been cut off.

"Right, then," Moore said softly. "Professional opinions, if you please. Do we cancel?"

Natalie's look was pained, and I nodded slightly in agreement. We didn't need to talk about it; each of us knew the other's mind on the subject.

"Will Her Ladyship accept a recommendation to cancel?" Natalie asked Moore.

"Not unless we're absolutely certain. Unless we tell her we have definite fears for her safety, she'll insist it's still on. I can pass on our concerns, but all that will serve to do is make her nervous, if not outright frightened. It won't keep her from making the trip."

"So this is going to be our decision?" I asked.

"No, for this one, I'm being a bastard," Moore replied. "It's your decision, the two of you. I'm asking you: What's your gut saying?"

What my gut was saying was that I shouldn't have finished the cold coffee, and I felt myself getting cranky. Whoever the hell Joseph Keith was, he suddenly had the power to dictate not only the lives of me and my colleagues, but of the people who had hired us. I'd wanted this job, wanted to do it and to do it well, and now we were looking at leaving it half-finished all because a possibly crazy man had a crush on a young woman he'd never met, and that maybe that possibly crazy man now wanted to do that same woman harm for reasons known only to him and whatever demons had taken up residence in his brain. We had a handful of circumstantial evidence hinting that Keith was up to something, nothing more than that.

Natalie was waiting for my answer.

"We'll see Her Ladyship tomorrow," I said.

From the phone came the sound of Moore's low chuckle. "She'll be happy to hear it."

"Are you going to tell her?" I asked.

"It would be an unnecessary burden at this point," Moore said. "Wish us a safe trip, mate."

Moore cut the connection on his end and I reached over and switched the speaker off. Natalie finished jotting her last notes on her pad, then set both pen and pad down and stretched in her chair, twisting her torso once to each side with her arms extended high over her head, and finally settling back with a sigh.

"For a moment, I thought you were going to tell him to bag it," she said.

"For a moment, I was."

"And then?"

"And then I remembered that this is what we're paid to do. If Lady Antonia Ainsley-Hunter wants to come to the Big Apple and see the sights and do good works, our job is to allow her to do that with the least risk possible."

"It'd be so much easier if the principal would just pay us to lock them in a room and guard them twenty-four hours a day."

"I favor encasing them in Lucite."

"Then the principal would suffocate," Natalie pointed out as the phone on my desk started ringing.

"Yes, but they'd be perfectly preserved." I picked up the phone. "Who is this and why are you calling my office on a Sunday afternoon?"

Scott Fowler said, "I'm at your door. It is locked. Please unlock it and step outside."

"And why should I do such a thing?"

"Your presence has been requested downtown."

Natalie arched an eyebrow. I told Fowler, "I'm kind of busy."

"I appreciate that. This is urgent."

"Urgent how?"

"Urgent enough that I'm not going to say anything more to you while I talk on a cellular phone, Atticus," Scott said, and his tone had altered, and I heard the change, and suddenly I was really regretting having finished the cold coffee.

"I'll be right there," I said.

The lights in the conference room had already been dimmed, and at the head of the table, in the acid glow of a laptop's screen, I could see the shapes of two men. The laptop rested beside a small LCD projector, and as we entered, the image of a blue sky with white cumulus clouds appeared on the wall to my side.

The man working the laptop and projector said, "Mr. Kodiak, please take a seat." His voice was soft but rushed, nearly breathless.

"What's going on?"

"You'll figure it out," the other one said. His voice was louder and deeper. "Take a seat."

I looked at Scott, saw the reflection of the clouds flaring from the lenses of his glasses. He motioned me forward with an almost apologetic look, and I could see from his expression he hadn't expected this treatment, and that he didn't much care for it either. We made for the chairs midway down the conference table and I was pulling out mine when the first voice piped up again.

"Thank you, Agent Fowler. Please wait outside."

Scott stopped, wincing into the light, and the shadow from his frown made it appear even deeper. "I'm under orders to baby-sit Kodiak whenever he's in these offices," he said.

"Please wait outside, Agent Fowler," the second voice said. When he said

Scott's last name I caught the edge of a Boston accent. "You're not cleared for this briefing."

For a second longer Scott seemed willing to argue, then he shook his head slightly and patted my shoulder once. "I'll be outside."

I stayed standing until he had left and the door was shut.

"Take a seat, Mr. Kodiak," the second voice said.

"This is very Tom Clancy," I said. "I'm impressed. Why don't you turn on the lights?"

"Not yet," the first voice said. "Sit."

I contemplated staging a minor protest, a stand-in, then realized that would accomplish nothing other than to eventually hurt my feet, and so I finished pulling out the chair and did as ordered. As soon as I was down, there was a soft chirp from the laptop and the clouds and sky disappeared, replaced with a crisp color image of what appeared to be the exterior of some sort of storage facility. The containers were large, painted dark orange, in some sort of compound. The center container had its doors open, and a lot of bright light was shining on the entrance. In the background, above the line of tops of the containers, the sky was the color of an overripe plum.

"This was taken last night in Dallas," the first voice said. "A rental company called Total Storage. The photograph was taken by the Dallas Police Department."

There was another chirp; the exterior photograph was replaced by an interior of the container. The colors were vivid but dark, in the way that all crime scene photographs seem under- and overexposed at the same time. The container was large, filled to perhaps half capacity with boxes and crates of varying size. On some of the boxes were brand names I recognized—Toshiba, Sony, Zenith—but most were unlabeled. It didn't matter. The boxes weren't the focus of the photograph.

The bodies were.

There were three of them, men. They looked to be roughly in the same age group, between late twenties and mid-thirties, and all were similarly dressed in the Texas casual I'd seen so much of when I'd been in El Paso. Cowboy boots, jeans, T-shirts. One of them wore a denim jacket. All had been shot.

The floor was raked slightly on all sides surrounding a small drain set at the center of the container, designed to keep any water that might leak in from pooling near stored objects. The lights shining on the scene made the blood that had flowed to the drain look like tar.

From behind the projector one of the two coughed, and the laptop chirped again, and the projector put up a new picture, a close-up of a Hispanic man. He had been shot in the head, from the side, and most of the top of his scalp was missing. It looked like he'd taken the bullet at close range, perhaps even point-blank.

"Joaquin Esteban Alesandro," the second voice said.

Another chirp, and the Caucasian man was now painted on the wall. Best as I could tell, he'd been shot four times, a tracking line that ran from the sternum up to the center of the face. The grayish white of bone was visible where a couple of rounds had stripped flesh and gore away. A discarded revolver was on the ground near his right hand.

"Richard Montrose," the second voice said. "And no, he didn't get a shot off."

The image changed; the last victim appeared on the wall. Unlike the other two, he lay facedown. The exposure was a little dark, but it appeared he had taken a bullet to the base of his skull. Probably while he had been on his knees.

"Michael Ortez," the second voice said.

The laptop chirped; the image dissolved into the Hallmark blue sky and white clouds once again.

"Never heard of any of them," I said.

"We doubted you had," the first voice said. Each time he spoke it sounded like he'd just run up a flight of stairs. "The murder weapon was recovered at the scene. A Smith and Wesson Model ninety-nine, nine millimeter. No prints."

"All three men were suspected by the Dallas PD in a string of burglaries over the last couple of years," the second voice said. "Electronics, vehicles, jewelry, guns—anything they could sell, but no narcotics, no drugs. Nonviolent offenders, as far as that goes. You following?"

"I'm following," I said. Funny how the mind works. They show me three photographs, two of explicit violence, and the one that's going to stay with me is the one where I couldn't really see the victim lying in his own brain.

"In doing the inventory, DPD has recovered a number of items that have been reported stolen." The first voice, again. "There are significant gaps in the collection, however. Presumably those items that had been sold off prior to the murders last night."

"No guns," I said. "No ammo."

"Correct. No weapons were found in the facility. There are several possible explanations for this. They could have been stored elsewhere. They could have been sold. Or they could have been removed by the killer after the crime. Each of these, or a combination of any of them, is entirely plausible."

"Didn't this place have security of some sort?" I asked.

"The gate requires a key code, but that's hardly a deterrent," the second voice replied. "Static cameras are placed at the office in the front, at the gate, and along each row of containers. Unfortunately, the cameras outside this particular container had been disabled."

"But," I said.

"But," the first voice answered, "DPD recovered the following image from the camera at the gate."

The laptop made its bird call, and a black-and-white picture, presumably pulled from the surveillance tape, appeared. It showed a large GMC truck moving out of shot, followed by a sedan, what looked like a Ford Taurus. The time stamp on the tape read the previous night, 23:49 hours. The camera had been placed on the right-hand side of the gate as one entered, and none of the drivers were visible.

"Entry," the first voice said. "We tried to augment the image, but we couldn't pull anything usable."

"But," I repeated, this time more to myself. I knew what was coming; I had known the moment Scott had picked me up at my office on a Sunday afternoon.

"But we were able to do something with the exit shot."

Chirp, and the Taurus was leaving alone. The time stamp read 00:08 this morning. The driver's window was down and a figure was partially visible, but only a portion, as if the driver was trying to stay out of the camera's line of sight.

Then the picture was replaced with an enlargement, pixilated and fuzzy at the edges.

"Is that her?" the second voice asked.

She was wearing spectacles, thin wire-frames not unlike my own, and she had once again altered her hairstyle, now wearing it very short so that the shape of her head was clear. But it was a token disguise, and there was no doubt that the woman on the wall in front of me was the same woman who had killed three men just minutes before; there was no doubt it was the same woman who had tried to kill me and Dale and Pugh the previous summer; there was no doubt at all.

I waved my fingers at the picture, cutting the light of the projector with the shadow of my hand.

"Hi, Drama," I said.

She didn't wave back. She couldn't. It was only a picture.

The knowledge didn't make me feel any safer at all.

The one with the Boston accent introduced himself as Ellis Gracey. Gracey was pushing into his fifties, with black hair that had lost its battle against encroaching gray, worn short and neat. He used a Montblanc fountain pen to take notes, and he smiled whenever he asked a question. The smile was blatantly insincere, and never reached his eyes. His companion was introduced as Matthew Bowles; I figured him to be twenty years Gracey's junior. Both men wore suits, but Bowles appeared the more fastidious of the two, keeping his tie tightly knotted at his throat.

Both claimed to be from the CIA, and considering what I'd just seen, I had no reason to doubt them.

"Has she contacted you?" Bowles asked.

"Twice this week I've been asked that," I said. "If she had contacted me, you would have heard about it, believe me. I'd have screamed so loud the whole damn city would be on notice."

"Twice this week?"

"A journalist I know asked."

Bowles fussed with his necktie, making the knot, if anything, tighter. "Chris Havel?"

"Read it, have you?"

"Book's gonna be a bestseller," Gracey said with a grin. "We've all read it. Hot stuff."

"Why did Havel want to know if you'd been in touch with Drama?" Everything Bowles said came out in the same rapid hush.

"She wanted to know if I could arrange an interview for her. I couldn't. Are you two saying that Drama's on her way to Manhattan?"

"We don't know, you believe that?" Gracey's smile grew momentarily brighter. "She could be in the city already, we haven't got a fucking clue. Only thing we know for a fact is that she ain't in this room at this moment, and that's it."

"Is she on the job?"

"You saw the crime scene shots, what do you think?"

"I think she's hunting, but I'd really like it if you told me I was wrong."

"You're protecting Antonia Ainsley-Hunter starting tomorrow, Drama was in Dallas as of fifteen hours or so, give or take a few minutes. Those are facts. Infer what you like from them."

"What I'm inferring is not something I like," I said.

"We have no confirmation Drama's hunting, and no evidence indicating that, if she *is* hunting, she's hunting your principal. Does that help?"

"Not much," I said.

Bowles had disconnected his laptop from the LCD projector and was setting the computer inside the briefcase. Finished, he opened the top folder in front of him. The folder was stamped in red ink with some impressive but dull-looking warnings about security violations and national secrets. He removed an eight-by-ten black-and-white and set it out, facing me. I was still seated too far from them to get a good look, and so I got up and moved closer, taking the chair at Bowles's elbow.

"Have you ever seen this man?" he asked.

The picture was of a pseudo-military unit of some sort, a group of eight men in a mixture of fatigues and what might have been hunting garb. The men were all white, and ranged in age from early twenties to late fifties, from the looks of them. The figure Bowles was interested in had been circled with red ink. He looked to be six feet tall, perhaps two hundred pounds, with balding hair and a narrow mustache clipped tightly over his lip. In the photograph, all of the men were holding weapons—long guns, either rifles or shotguns—though the man in question appeared unarmed.

"Who is he?"

"Have you ever seen him before?" he repeated, with no change in inflection.

"Not to my knowledge."

Bowles took back the photograph. I looked at Gracey, who shrugged, as if he didn't know who the picture had been of, either.

"Who is he?" I asked again.

"He may be a colleague of hers," Bowles said.

"You mean another one of The Ten?"

Bowles finished replacing his things in his briefcase, and Gracey gave his Montblanc a final twirl before nesting it in his breast pocket. It was clear neither was going to give me anything more.

"Tell me you're on top of this situation," I said. "That you're doing your best to locate her."

"We're on top of the situation, and we're doing our best to locate Drama." Gracey's smile dropped away and the expression he was offering now was veering dangerously close to sympathy. "You do what you do for Ainsley-

Hunter, and you let us know if you hear from our lady friend or anything like that, all right?"

"That's it?"

"We're finished, at least for now. Nothing more we can tell you, and apparently you've got nothing you can tell us. If Drama appears on your radar, tell Special Agent Fowler—he'll let us know. Otherwise just keep your head down and your back to a wall."

Gracey got to his feet. Bowles hesitated a moment longer, then reached across the table, offering me his hand. I looked at it, then at him, wondering if he thought this had really been worth a handshake.

After another second, Bowles retracted his hand, gathered his things, and followed Gracey out the door. Before he stepped out he looked back to where I was still seated.

"Sorry," he said.

It sounded to me like an honest condolence for my failings.

CHAPTER SEVEN

Natalie was in her office, flipping through the stack of location photographs we'd taken over the last few weeks, checking them against our maps. I entered without knocking.

"Call Dale and Corry, get them here now," I told her.

My look as much as my tone kept her from asking the obvious question, and I went back to my office without another word, making straight for my phone. I tried calling Moore at home and got his machine, left a message for him to contact me. Then I tried his cell phone and got his voice mail, so I left the same message again. I was hanging up as Natalie came in.

"What happened?"

"I'd rather wait until everyone's here."

"Is this about Lady Ainsley-Hunter?"

"Wait until they're here, Nat."

She looked around the office, then said, "I'll order dinner."

"That'd be good."

"By the way, Bridgett called."

"What'd she say?"

"I'll wait until they're here, I think."

We glared at each other, and I realized I was being a prick. I also realized that my stomachache had sent colonists up to my head to see if they could get some action of their own started.

"As of eight minutes past midnight this morning, central standard time, Drama was in Dallas, Texas," I said. "She killed three men at a storage facility, and in all likelihood armed herself with the weapons they kept there."

Natalie lost her voice for a second, her mouth opening slightly but no sound following.

I knew what she was trying to ask. I said, "I saw the photographs. There's no confirmation that she's coming here."

"But she could be."

"It's possible. I think it's unlikely."

She kept staring at me. After a second I saw that her look wasn't actually fixed on me, but had slipped to a side, and was focused past my shoulder.

"What?" I asked.

"The blinds are open."

I turned around and looked out the window behind my desk, realized just how exposed my back had been to the world. From my view, there were easily dozens of perches where a sniper could roost and take a shot into the office. I felt the edges of panic returning, the same feeling that had clung to me in the first days after Drama had vanished. The urge to hide under my desk was suddenly powerful.

"She's not after us," I told Natalie.

"There's this book, you may have heard of it. It's on display in store windows and people are talking about it on the radio and it's all about this professional assassin and these protection specialists who stopped her from killing a man."

"It doesn't make sense that she would be after us."

"Shut the blinds, Atticus."

"She's being sloppy, she let herself be photographed in Dallas, and she's better than that. She knew the camera was there, she had to have known."

"Everything she does, she does for a reason, and she's got a reason to come after us now. We have to call Havel."

"Why would Drama let us know she was on the move? She had to have known we'd find out. She can't be after us or Chris. She can't be after our principal."

"She loves games, Atticus." I heard Natalie shift on the carpet, and her voice stayed soft, but her words started accelerating. "Shut the blinds. My paranoia, I know that. Yours is cars, mine is snipers, and I'm asking you please, Atticus, shut the goddamn blinds now."

I stared out the window, using one hand to shield my eyes from the sunset. Nothing that looked like someone who wanted to kill me leaped out from in or on the surrounding buildings. Below, the Holland Tunnel traffic was writhing its way to and from Jersey.

"For God's sake . . ."

I closed the blinds and turned back. Setting sunlight ran through the slats that covered the window, cutting the shadows in the room with narrow strips of orange and gold. Natalie had moved out of the doorway, and her expression surprised me. I'd known her a long time, and I'd seen most of her emotions—the ones she was willing to wear on her face, at least—and I had seen her nervous, I'd seen her worried, I'd even seen her afraid. But I'd never seen her terrified.

"It's all right, Nat."

"No, it isn't. We can't do it again."

"She's had a year. Why now? If it's the book, then why now, when she can't do anything to stop it?"

"We should have canceled. We have to call Moore."

"I tried reaching him, I left messages. We'll be fine."

She regarded me with the fondness one normally reserves for an exceptionally naïve child. "You're crazy, Kodiak."

"Yeah, but it's that good, devil-may-care, rides-his-motorcycle-in-the-rain crazy," I said. "This is no different than what we were dealing with earlier today, it's the same situation as with Keith. It's circumstantial evidence, nothing more, and it can't keep us from doing our job."

She shook her head. "You can't compare the two, it's not the same at all, Atticus. Keith is a *potential* stalker. And we don't even know if he's prone to violence. But a professional killer—we know what she's capable of, we've seen her work."

"An assassin is just a stalker who is better at his job, Nat. And at least with Keith there's evidence proving an obsession with Lady Ainsley-Hunter, if not an intent to do violence. With Drama we don't even have that. I don't believe that Drama is after us, and I don't believe that Drama is after Lady Ainsley-Hunter."

Her jaw flexed. "Then why did the CIA feel it necessary to inform you she was in the country?"

It was a question I'd already asked myself, and since I didn't know the answer, I brushed past it, saying, "It doesn't matter. We muddle through, we stick with what we're good at, we protect our principal. If worse comes to worst, we'll shoot a lot of people."

"Or get shot a lot ourselves." She closed her eyes, willing herself to relax, and when she opened them again the last hints of her fear had vanished. "You *are* crazy, you realize that, don't you?"

"I have never argued that point," I replied. "What did Bridgett say when she called?"

"She's on her way to Philadelphia to interview Keith's brother. She said she'd call later if she found out anything of use."

"Okay, good. See? We're on top of this."

"Oh, yeah, we're all over it." She moved back to the door, then stopped. "Sorry about that."

"Ain't no thing. She scares the crap out of me, too."

She frowned and went into her office. I headed for the conference room. It was dark in there, and I closed the blinds before switching on the lights.

Dale and Corry arrived at six-twenty, apologizing.

"Weekend traffic," Dale told me. "You'd swear they put these drivers on the road just to annoy me."

"Or worse," Corry said. "I thought he was going to run one guy off the road."

"I could have done it, too." Dale puffed out his chest boastfully. "I know how."

"Yes, we're very proud of you, Speed Racer," I told him. "Conference room, if you please. We've ordered dinner."

I waited until they had gone down the hall, then doubled back to the front and locked the door and switched on the alarm. My belief that Drama wouldn't be coming after us was sincere, but the precaution seemed wise all the same, although if she were coming here, our security system wouldn't do much more than annoy her.

Natalie caught my eye when I joined them, and I nodded. Dale and Corry were already seated, digging into Thai food that had been delivered just before they arrived. Natalie was putting the finishing touches on the diagram she was drawing on the dry-erase board, a map of the route we'd take from the street into the Edmonton Hotel, through the kitchen and to the elevator banks. Other maps were spread out on the table, held down with the paper containers of *tomyum gai* and *nue gra pao*. Photographs and notes were tacked to the corkboard and taped to the walls.

Corry slid me a soda, saying, "Okay, so why the rush?"

I popped the top, watching the whiff of carbon dioxide that escaped when the seal was broken. "Fowler took me to see the Backroom Boys again this afternoon."

"You learn any cool code names?" Dale asked.

"No new ones."

The sounds of eating stopped.

"Oh fuck me," Corry said.

They took it better than either Natalie or I had done, I thought. Maybe they just did a better job of hiding the fear. Neither of them interrupted me as I repeated what Bowles and Gracey had said.

When I was finished, the debate began as to what we were going to do with this new information, and how we should best proceed. Once more, the question of aborting the op came up, this time voiced by Corry.

"It may be too late," I said. "I tried reaching Moore when I got back here, and all I managed was to leave him messages that haven't been returned. They're already in transit, either on the way to Heathrow or already in the air."

"So we boomerang them when they land," Dale said. "Head to the airfield as planned, just don't let them off the plane."

Natalie said, "Which would be a sound thing to do *if* Drama is after Lady Ainsley-Hunter."

"You don't think she is?" Corry asked.

I said, "I think the primary threat against her is still Keith. All we know about Drama is that she was in Dallas this morning, that she murdered three men. Extrapolating that she's after our principal—or us—is alarmist."

"We *are* talking about one of The Ten," Dale said. "And Drama has reason to be pissed off. Havel's book is everywhere."

"She doesn't care about the book."

"You can't know that."

"You think we're overreacting?" Corry asked me.

"I'm not saying we shouldn't worry. But I think we have to put this in perspective, we have to go back to what we know."

"And we know Keith has a thing for Lady Ainsley-Hunter," Corry said.

Dale made a face. "Anything new on that end?"

"Waiting to hear from Bridgett. But we're going to proceed as before on that. No change."

I cleared the remaining food from the table, moving it to the fridge in the coffee room, where I prepared another fresh pot of coffee. Back in the conference room we chased theories about Drama and Keith for a while longer and then, from a little after seven until almost eleven, we went over the plans we'd already drawn up, honing the final details. I set the stand-by call for six the next morning, when we would all gather at the office before heading out to the airport in New Jersey for Ainsley-Hunter's arrival. The four of us together took down all of the paper we had up in the conference room, and while Dale went to store it in the safe and I cleaned the dry-erase board, Corry and Natalie went off to the storeroom. They returned with four vests.

"Kevlar," Corry said, handing one to me. "The gift that keeps on giving."

I did a walk-through of the apartment when I got home just after midnight, switching on lights and checking rooms, trying to remember if the mess I was seeing now was the same mess I'd left behind that morning. Bridgett, I had discovered, was a surprisingly sloppy person, constantly leaving out books and papers and CDs, though the clothes that she kept in my bedroom were always neatly folded and stowed. Between the near-constant work I'd been doing preparing for Lady Ainsley-Hunter's visit and Bridgett's natural entropy, there was a lot of picking-up that needed doing.

Even so, everything looked to be in its place. I got out of my jacket and then the vest, hanging both from the hook in the hallway before entering the bedroom and stowing my weapon in its lockbox. I rummaged through the drawers in the kitchen until I found the set of tiny screwdrivers that I kept for repairing my glasses. Armed with the largest of the flatheads, I worked my way from room to room, dismantling every light switch cover and electrical outlet, checking them all for bugs. When we'd protected Pugh, Drama had bugged the apartment with a mains-powered transmitter hidden in an outlet in the kitchen, the one I used to run the coffeemaker. I doubted the same technique would be used twice, but I wanted to be sure.

I didn't find anything but some mouse droppings and one desiccated spider husk.

After I'd finished with the outlets, I sat down at the kitchen table to start with the phones, then stopped when I caught a glimpse of my hands. My fingernails were chewed and chipped from wrestling with the outlets, and I'd scraped the knuckle of my right middle finger groping around inside the wall. These days, there are hundreds of ways to monitor and intercept phone calls, be they cellular or landline, and almost none of them requires that the device be planted on scene. There wasn't really a point to taking apart the phones: If there was a bug and I removed it, that wouldn't guarantee my calls would be secure; if there wasn't a bug, it didn't mean that the line wasn't being intercepted somewhere farther down the pipe.

The answering machine finally caught my attention while I was debating with myself, and I saw that there was a message waiting. I was about to play it, when the phone rang.

"You're still awake," Moore said when I answered. "What's with all these messages?"

"You on an open line?" I asked.

"Yes. If we need to be secure this'll have to wait."

"No point."

"I'm assuming there have been developments in our situation?"

"Yeah. Your girlfriend with you?"

"She's nearby, out of earshot, but she's moving about. What's happened? You find more about Keith?"

"Not about Keith, no," I said, and then laid out the situation with Drama as succinctly as I could. If she truly was listening in, she'd at least be amused.

"Where's this coming from?" Moore asked when I finished. He didn't sound all that concerned, more annoyed.

"Company men."

"Odd."

"In a word."

"No, I mean that doesn't match with what I've got. I checked with Interpol and the people I know at Six before leaving, and they gave me a pointer, but it wasn't about our lass Drama. They say there's another one on the move, a bloke they've named Oxford, they think he's in the States, somewhere on the East Coast. Don't know if he's hunting, just that he's been moving about."

"Are you saying there are two of them on the prowl?"

"There are at least ten of them, you forget. And they're usually hunting."

I felt very tired, suddenly. "Jesus, Robert."

"Was going to wait until we were with your lot and on the ground before sharing the news, but you sounded insistent in your messages."

"Insistent was then. Verging on panic-stricken is now. What's the deal with Oxford?"

Moore made a hissing noise into the phone, then said, "It'll have to wait 'til I'm there."

"She's back in earshot?"

"You could say that, and you'd be correct."

"You trust your source on this?"

"Hold on," he said, and for almost a minute I heard nothing but the slight hiss from the line. It occurred to me that he was calling from the plane, that he and our principal were already over the Atlantic. When he came back on the line, he resumed as if there hadn't been a break. "I've known my people for years. No mention of your lady friend. Far as that goes, word is she went on hiatus after your last dance. You trust your information?"

I gave it about two seconds of consideration. "I saw pictures," I said.

"Easy enough to fake those," Moore said, and he was getting testy. "Awfully convenient that the Company shares this tidbit with you a mere twenty hours before we're to arrive, don't you think?"

"I do think. But given the nature of the intelligence, I felt it was kind of important that I pass it on. I don't see how it's going to change the operation as it's been defined so far. Unless you decide it's cause to abort."

"I do not. Way I'm reading it, situation is the same, Keith is still Threat One."

"I agree."

"I'll call my people again, see if anything's developed."

"But you doubt it."

"I do, I truly do. Action as before, Atticus."

"Are you going to tell her?"

"Are you daft?"

"Everyone keeps asking me that. See you soon."

"G'night," Moore said.

I set down the phone, then rose and replaced the screwdriver in its case and put the case back in the drawer by the sink. I filled a glass with water from the tap and drank it, wondering if we weren't teetering on the brink of a disaster. Of the intelligence available to me, I was more inclined to trust Moore's than that of two men I'd never met until today. And Moore was Ainsley-Hunter's PSA; even more than myself or my colleagues, he was responsible for her welfare. If he felt that we were safe in proceeding, then he was making that determination with her best interest at heart. Whoever Oxford was, whatever threat he posed, it hadn't been enough to keep Moore from putting Her Ladyship on a plane to cross the ocean.

Except that Moore was also ex–Special Air Service, and the SAS didn't strictly train bodyguards, even though they had an Executive Protection program. They trained men to be soldiers, "complete soldiers," as Moore himself called it. Soldiering and protecting are two different beasts, and while elements of the work exchange, the jobs are nowhere near identical. And Moore wasn't one to back down, I knew that from past experience. It wasn't that he didn't take threats seriously; it was that he had absolute certainty in his ability to ultimately control and conquer any situation he might face.

I finished my water and started for the bedroom, and again saw the light blinking at me from the answering machine, so I stopped and finally played back the message. It was from Bridgett. She left a number and told me to call when I got in, "no matter how late."

The clock on the coffeemaker said it was eighteen minutes past two, but I took the directive seriously, and dialed the number she'd left. When the call was answered, a receptionist told me that the Embassy Suites Hotel in Philadelphia would be pleased to assist me. I asked for Bridgett Logan's room, and after a slight pause for the switchboard to route the request, the phone began ringing. She got it between the third and fourth rings.

"Hummf?" Bridgett said.

"Hey, it's me."

"Dark," she said, and then mumbled something that I took to mean she wanted me to wait. I heard the phone get bumped down and the sound of her moving, then silence. Then there was what might have been water running. Then the phone got picked up again.

"It's two-thirty, you know that?" Bridgett asked.

"It's two-twenty, and you said to call no matter how late."

"I did say that. Yes, I did indeed say that. I'm trying to remember why I said that."

"Because you missed me."

"No, that wasn't it. Hold on." I heard her yawn. "Okay, I remember now. Joseph Keith has a brother named Louis. I talked to him this evening. He's worried about his brother."

"Worried how?"

"Louis Keith says that Joseph has had, and I'm quoting, a thing for Lady Antonia Ainsley-Hunter since he was in college."

"Where'd he go to school?"

"Philadelphia Community College. He was a member of the Together Now chapter there. Brother Louis tells me that Joseph ran for chapter president not once, not twice, but four times. Lost each time."

"Does that qualify him as a disgruntled worker?"

"Not as such, no, but the last time he was defeated, his membership was revoked. Shortly afterwards, he was expelled."

"More details, please."

Bridgett yawned again. "Don't have them yet. It was Sunday, the school offices were closed. I'll go by first thing tomorrow morning, see what I can see. There is something else, though. Not certain what to make of it, but it could shed some light."

"Go ahead."

"Louis Keith told me that his brother believes in past lives. And that, about a year ago—this was Thanksgiving—Joseph told Louis that he and Ainsley-Hunter were married."

"Married," I said.

"Right. This would have been, oh, roughly five or six thousand years ago, in ancient Sumer."

"Sumer," I said.

"*Ancient* Sumer. Apparently, and Louis was a little embarrassed to relay this last bit—"

"He wasn't embarrassed to relay the first bit?"

She ignored that. "Apparently Joseph was not only her husband, but they were royalty. And Louis reports that his brother said that—I quote once more from my notes—'the sex was amazing.' "

I stared at the front of my refrigerator. Erika had given me a Magnetic Poetry set a couple of months back, and houseguests were forever messing with it. Bridgett herself could spend upwards of an hour mixing and matching words. The phrase "beautiful but without rice" caught my eye.

"Wow," I said.

"Yeah. The sex must have been really something if Joseph can still conjure it after six thousand years."

"Okay, so he's sprung."

"Potentially sprung. Belief in reincarnation is not a mental defect."

"Fair enough," I said. "Find out why he got expelled."

"First thing in the morning. And how was your day, snookums?"

"I could tell you. But it would take most of an hour, at least. You might want to sleep."

"Nah. I'm lying here with the phone in my ear. If you bore me, I'll just nod off."

"You're in bed?"

"Yup," she said. "Naked, even. Tell me a story."

I told her about my day. She didn't nod off.

When I finished, she said, "I'm coming home."

"Why? You're doing more good following up on Keith than you can do here."

"I'm afraid for you, that's why."

"Don't be. There's nothing that can be done tonight. Moore thinks the Drama stuff is bullshit, anyway."

"Moore doesn't impress me the way he does you," Bridgett said, and I could hear her moving, imagined her rolling up onto an elbow. "Drama's already visited you once when you were alone in that apartment. I don't want that happening again. If I'm there, you've got a little more protection."

"I'll tell you what I told the others, Bridie. Even if she is on the move, she's not coming here."

"And I'll tell you what they should have said in response, Atticus, which is that you cannot possibly know what she will or will not do. From what you've told me about her, she made a point of singling you out. She's targeted you before."

"She singled me out because I was running the operation. If she's truly after Lady Ainsley-Hunter, she won't come here, because that'll tip her hand. Which means that the only other reason to come here would be a personal one, and since she didn't bother to hunt us all down after everything with Pugh had been resolved, I'm inclined to believe she's not interested in taking things personally. Havel's book hasn't changed that."

"Oh, fuck you," she said softly. "I hate it, I absolutely hate it, when you start using logic."

"Well, I do it so rarely," I pointed out.

"You got that right. Just be careful."

"I will be," I said. "You, too. Get some sleep, I'll talk to you tomorrow."

"Don't worry about me."

"It works two ways, you get to tell me to be careful, I get to worry about you."

Her silence seemed suddenly sullen. Then she said, "Is that how it works?"

"Did I say something wrong?"

"It's late, Kodiak. I'm tired. Drama's maybe gunning for you. You'll forgive me if my tone isn't everything it should be." She wished me safe rest, and hung up.

I went to bed, thinking that the phone never had been my friend, and never would be.

CHAPTER EIGHT

We met at six on the nose the next morning, all of us in our work clothes and Kevlar vests, and before we did anything else, I shared Moore's news about Oxford. At first, they all thought it was a bad joke.

"My sense of humor, while damaged, is not quite that morbid," I told them. "Moore has reliable intelligence that another of The Ten is on the prowl in our neck of the woods."

"Jesus Christ," Natalie said. "Two of them?"

I nodded. "This one's called Oxford. There is a positive, however."

"Her Ladyship has canceled her trip?" Corry asked hopefully. "She has taken vows and entered a convent in Upper Volta?"

"Not that positive," I said. "Moore's intelligence mentions nothing of Drama, and in fact, indicates that she has been inactive for much of the last year."

They considered that. Then Dale said, "So Moore's intelligence on Drama is basically that he has no intelligence on Drama."

"It's better than him confirming what Gracey and Bowles told me yesterday," I pointed out.

"Becomes a question of who we believe."

"Yes."

"Which leads us again to the question of why did the CIA bother to tell you she was on the move in the first place," Natalie said.

"Yes."

They all looked at me as if I had something more to add. I did, but it wasn't very insightful.

I said, "Let's get to work."

While Natalie and I handled the final weapons and radio checks, Dale and Corry went to the garage up the block from the office to retrieve the vehicles. It took them a little over thirty minutes to make certain that the cars were secure, and by a quarter of seven we were on our way to Jersey. Natalie and Dale took the Benz, leaving Corry and me with the Lexus. Both cars had been purchased for the firm, and both vehicles were hardened top to bottom, though the Benz was the more heavily armored of the two, sporting gun ports, Run-Flat tires, and a fire-suppression system in addition to the standard reinforced frame and bulletproof glass.

Corry drove, following Dale's lead in the Benz. The traffic out of the city was as heavy as the traffic on its way in, but worse. A lot of the delivery trucks making runs from the outer boroughs liked to cut across the island and use the Holland Tunnel, trying to cut down on tolls. When you're boxed in by three four-ton trucks, it doesn't matter if the car you're in is reinforced or not.

I kept my eyes moving the whole time, looking for tails front or back, until we were past Newark and turned onto 280. We had an almost two-hour drive ahead of us, though Dale was moving quickly, punching through traffic as efficiently as possible to keep us on schedule. If we arrived at the airport early, that would be fine; it was arriving late that we couldn't allow, and though I knew that Moore wouldn't let Lady Ainsley-Hunter off the plane unless we were present and in position, I didn't want to keep them waiting.

Natalie's voice came clear over the radio in the car. *"Dale says we're good, looks like we're free and clear."*

"Wonderful," I said.

"Hey, Corry?" Dale asked. *"Is Atticus white-knuckling it?"*

"I'd check, but then I'd have to look away from the road, and then he'd freak out," Corry answered.

"Drive, damn you," I said.

Over the radio speaker, I heard Natalie and Dale chuckling.

"ETA roughly one hundred minutes," Dale reported. *"Out."*

Corry grinned, adjusting his grip on the wheel. Past West Orange the views changed, the industrial heart of Jersey fading to a more pastoral countryside. Our route had been chosen to take us past a number of airports, both large and small fields, just to keep any potential tails guessing. Past Parsippany, we turned north onto 287, the Boontown Reservoir to our east. The traffic here was lighter, and we accelerated to almost eighty for a short burst. No tails revealed themselves.

"How'd you sleep?" Corry asked after a while.

"Well, just not for long. Ended up staying on the phone with Bridgett for almost two hours after I got home. You?"

"Not badly, all things considered. It took me an hour just to make certain the house was secure, you know?"

I laughed, and Corry nodded.

"You, too?"

"Me, too," I said. "What'd Esme say?"

"Well, I woke the baby up when I was checking the nursery, and Esme didn't much care for that. Asked me what the hell I thought I was doing. I told her I was just making certain the place was safe."

"You didn't tell her about Drama?"

He grimaced, shook his head. "It would've just kept her up all night. She needs her sleep. Did you tell Bridgett?"

"Yeah, but it's a different situation. She's working for us on this, so I figure she needs to know all the facts."

After a moment, Corry said, "I don't like keeping things from my wife."

I thought about how to answer, and then my cell phone rang. It was Bridgett.

"Hey, you," she said. "You'll never guess where I am."

"Philadelphia Community College."

"Oh, you are good." If she thought our last call had left a tension, there was nothing in her voice to acknowledge it. "In fact, I am in the Office of Campus Security at Philadelphia Community College, where I have just finished speaking with Chief of Campus Security George Abrega, who runs the show here. And the Chief has very generously shared with me some details about Mr. Joseph Keith, class of year before last."

"Such as?"

"Such as Mr. Keith was expelled."

"We knew that."

"Yes, but we did not know why."

"And why was he expelled?"

"He brought a weapon to school."

"What kind of weapon?"

"A knife."

"Knife how?" I asked, ignoring the look that Corry was shooting my way and wishing he would get back to watching the road. "Knife pocket? Knife switchblade? Knife machete?"

"Knife as in it was confiscated and I'm looking at it right now," Bridgett said. "It's one of those big movie things, long blade, serrated edge. It's got a handle that you can unscrew and store things in."

"And what was he doing with the knife?"

"Brandishing it at a Together Now meeting. He did not actually threaten anyone with it, but it was enough to get him booted. The college has a very firm no-weapons policy."

"Sensible. I'm assuming no charges were filed?"

"That is correct. Mr. Keith did not appeal his expulsion, either, which to me indicates that he knew he shouldn't have been waving the knife around to begin with."

"Anything else?"

"Well, it was only two years ago, so I'm thinking that maybe a couple of the students who were present at the incident and who knew him might still be attending classes. I'm going to take a look around, see if I can find where the Together Now crowd hangs out, and ask some more questions."

"Good," I said.

"You're at work?"

"We're in transit."

"I'll call if I find out anything more."

She hung up and I slipped my phone back into my jacket pocket. Corry said, "Well?"

"Keith waved a knife around school once two years ago," I said. "He was expelled for it."

"Predisposed toward violence."

"Maybe. Maybe he was just showing it off to friends."

Corry made a face. "Like you for a second believe that."

We were in Passaic County now, and there was no other traffic on the road but for our two cars, and I almost relaxed. The Benz took a turn off the main road, and we followed, passing a sign with a picture of an airplane on it. We were working our way uphill, through scattered forest, pretty much approaching as middle-of-nowhere as one could get in New Jersey. After another twelve minutes, the Greenwood Lake Airport came into view.

It had been Moore's idea to keep Lady Ainsley-Hunter from arriving at any of the major area airports, and he'd been pleased with how Natalie and Corry had handled the advance. The two of them had scouted out the smaller fields in the New York/New Jersey area and rejected almost all of them for one reason or another—usually because most of the airfields couldn't handle small jets. They'd settled on Greenwood Lake because of its ability to handle a small jet landing and because of its seclusion. We'd taken the roundabout way to reach it; our return trip would be more direct. Corry and Natalie had made all the arrangements for our presence on the field themselves.

Lady Ainsley-Hunter had arrived in the United States almost three hours earlier, her flight from Heathrow landing at Logan Airport in Boston rather than New York in order to keep her final destination secure. After clearing customs, Moore, Her Ladyship, and Chester—the PA—had waited to board a chartered Lear for the final leg. At the time Moore had requested the plan, the security had seemed a tad excessive.

Now I wasn't so sure.

The airport was one or two bad days from being dilapidated, a small terminal building with a closed coffee shop that, in part, occupied a garishly painted and presumably gutted DC-9. A handful of single- and dual-prop planes were parked on the tarmac, and farther along the main runway was another long, low hangar. We skirted the building, turning onto the tarmac, and Dale came to a stop ahead of us. I watched Natalie get out of the Benz and run to the hangar at the side. She came back out in under a minute followed by two men, each looking to be in their late teens to early twenties, and each wearing jumpsuits with a faded eagle painted on the back over the words "Eagle Charters."

Over my earpiece, I heard Natalie say, *"Tower says they're inbound on final, three minutes."*

"Confirmed," I said.

Natalie climbed back into the Benz as the two in jumpsuits pulled back the gate. One of them waved at us as we drove past. From his expression I could tell he knew who we were.

"What'd you tell them?" I asked Corry.

"Who?"

"Those two. When you and Natalie arranged all this, what'd you tell them?"

"Nothing. Just that we were a security team and that we'd be picking up a VIP."

"He recognized you."

"Not me, man. Natalie."

"She ought to dye her hair or something," I said.

"That wouldn't solve the problem. Gaining fifty pounds and wearing baggy clothes, *that* would solve the problem."

"I'll tell her you said that."

"You do and I'll be forced to harm you."

We were out on the tarmac now. Corry parked beside the Benz, nose facing the field, keeping the engine running. In the rearview, I could see the two men in their jumpsuits taking their time to join us.

"They're for the luggage," Corry told me.

"I knew that." I unfastened my belt and got out, moving to meet Natalie as she exited the Benz. Like Corry, Dale was staying behind the wheel. Over the sound of the cars I could hear the plane, distant but coming closer.

"Ready for this?" Natalie asked.

I nodded, thinking that in fact, I was. Even with everything that had happened, everything that could possibly happen, I felt good, and fairly confident. One of the pleasures of working with such a small group of colleagues is that I had no doubts about our individual abilities or commitment to the job. There comes a point in every protective effort when all the planning and all the preparations must give way to the event itself, and to the randomness that comes from simply living in an ever-expanding universe. Those things that we could control were actually very small, and we had already exerted as much power over them as we could. From here on out we were game on, and would have to take each complication, each situation, as it arose.

The plane touched down at the end of the runway with a puff of smoke from the tires and a rising whine from the engines as the pilot played with the throttle, slowing down. Natalie and I watched as the Learjet passed, burning off the rest of its speed. For a moment I thought the plane wouldn't stop in time, that it would sail off the end of the runway and into the trees rimming the hilltop, but it was fine, and the jet turned at the opposite end of the field, taxiing back our way.

Natalie thumped on the roof of the Benz, and Dale started forward, moving to greet the plane as it came to a halt. He brought the Benz around so the trunk was presented to where the plane had finally come to rest, and then Corry moved the Lexus up and around, taking the lead position for the egress. When the car was in place, Natalie turned and waved the two men forward, pointing them to the fuselage. We watched as they opened the baggage compartment and began moving the luggage from the plane to the Benz. It took them four trips to fill the Benz, and there were still bags left over.

I pressed the button in my palm, spoke to the mike on my lapel. "Corry, we're going to need the Lexus's trunk, too."

"Gotcha," he said.

Natalie directed the two to load the remaining bags in the other car. When they were finished they headed back to the gate without a word, leaving the trunks open. I shut the Lexus first, then the Benz, then moved around the passenger side and did another check of the perimeter. Aside from the two still heading back to the gate, there was no one visible in my line of sight.

My earpiece crackled slightly, and then Moore came on the net, saying, *"Check, Check, this is Hook, how do you read, over?"*

On the radio, I heard Natalie respond, *"Smee reads you five-by, Hook."*

"Understand. Wendy and Peter are standby."

Natalie turned to make eye contact with me, and I gave her a thumbs-up. She nodded, and I heard her over the net again. *"Tink gives all clear."*

The door on the plane opened, and the stairs unfolded. I waited until Natalie had moved into position at the bottom, then opened the front and rear passenger doors on the Benz.

"Coming out, coming out," Moore radioed.

Natalie mounted the steps, stopping just outside the door as Fiona Chester emerged. She was in her late twenties, small, with short and curly brown hair, wearing a long black wool skirt that must have been very uncomfortable for July. She carried a computer bag over one shoulder, with a smaller duffel bag in her left hand. Chester hesitated just long enough to be sure of the angle on the stairs, then began her descent with Natalie at her side. When they hit the tarmac, Natalie escorted her over to the Benz. Chester climbed into the backseat, sliding over to the window, and Natalie turned and went back to the plane, this time stopping at the bottom of the stairs.

Antonia Ainsley-Hunter appeared in the doorway. She was in blue jeans and a green shirt, pulling on a tan windbreaker. She kept her head down and didn't pause, and Moore emerged right behind her, close behind. As Her Ladyship reached the bottom step, Natalie started forward.

I kept watching the perimeter, noting that the two who had helped with the luggage were now watching from the mouth of the hangar. Other than them, however, there was no motion, nothing.

When Natalie reached the car she peeled off, stepping around me and making for the Lexus. I moved back, away from the door, still scanning, as Lady Ainsley-Hunter climbed in, Moore after her. He closed the door after him and I took a last look, then slid into the front passenger seat. I had barely shut my own before Corry pulled out, and Dale put us into gear, and then we were accelerating off the runway. We were already doing forty by the time we reached the intersection at the end of the access road.

"Looking good," Dale told me. "We're clear."

"Pick your route," I said.

"Bravo."

I used the handset for the car radio, relayed the choice to Corry in the Lexus. He radioed back a confirmation, and when I acknowledged, I felt as much as saw Moore relaxing in the seat behind me.

"Everything's good?" Lady Ainsley-Hunter asked me.

"Everything's fine," I said.

"All right, then," she said, and leaned forward from the backseat, reaching around and giving me a rather awkward hug. "Nice to see you, Tinkerbell."

"Nice to see you, too, Wendy."

"Anything new?" Moore asked. All I could see of him was a bit of his shoulder and the side of his head as he kept watch out the rear window.

"Minor things. I'll brief you after Wendy's been buttoned up at the Edmonton," I said.

He turned in the seat long enough to meet my eyes in the mirror, curious, but he knew better than to ask and, after a second, went back to watching the traffic from his window. Lady Ainsley-Hunter asked Chester a question about the evening's schedule, and Chester opened her computer bag, producing a sheaf of papers. They continued to talk quietly as we followed 287, the Lexus always in our lead. Natalie's voice came over the radio, giving us regular updates on changes in the traffic and potential delays.

It took another ninety minutes before we reached the city, coming in across the George Washington Bridge, then down the West Side Highway, and then an additional half an hour to make it the three miles through the crosstown traffic to the Edmonton. We followed the Lexus around the hotel, past the roundabout at the entrance to the service side, opposite Central Park. Natalie was out of the car before it had come to a complete stop, and I waited until she had secured the door to the building before climbing out myself. Moore, Natalie, and I debussed Lady Ainsley-Hunter quickly, bringing her through the kitchen as planned, as Dale, Corry, and Chester went around the front to check in and deal with the bags. A couple of waiters and chefs gave us stares as we came through, but most ignored us, having seen this sort of thing before; the Edmonton was used regularly by visiting dignitaries, and the hotel staff was experienced with the procedures and peculiarities of security work.

"I feel very important," Lady Ainsley-Hunter confided as we were riding up to the eighteenth floor in the service elevator. "And extremely embarrassed."

"There's a Holiday Inn off Times Square we can put you in, if you'd prefer," I told her.

The elevator stopped and Natalie stepped out to check the hall, reporting back that Corry had already gotten the room opened up. Together, the four of us made our way to eighteen twenty-two, a suite of four rooms that included a central sitting area complete with a fireplace. Moore got Lady Ainsley-Hunter seated on the sofa there, and Corry headed back down to the lobby to supervise the transfer of the luggage. Natalie and I gave each room another look over, decided that if there was anyone or anything lurking with intent to do harm, it was hidden beyond our ability to spot it, and rejoined Moore and Her Ladyship just before the rest of the group arrived, now in the company of a bellman and his heavily laden cart.

Chester tipped him, and when he left, Moore shut the door and then turned the dead bolt and threw the locking bar. We spent another ten minutes moving the bags, and then Lady Ainsley-Hunter announced that she wanted to take a nap, and that she thought Fiona ought to do the same. They each retired to their respective rooms.

Moore and I exchanged looks, and he gave me a little nod of the head, so I got on the phone and ordered up sandwiches and sodas from room service, watching while the rest of us got settled. Moore had his equipment bag out and was loading spare clips for his Browning. When I hung up, he reached into his bag again and removed a folder, dropping it on the coffee table in front of him. He waited until I had taken my seat, along with Natalie, Corry, and Dale, and then unfastened the string holding the folder closed. Inside was a stack of photocopies, what looked like copies of reports and photographs.

Moore fished a single photograph from the stack, and held it out to me.

"Meet Oxford," he said.

It was the same picture that Gracey and Bowles had shown me the previous afternoon, the one of the mock military unit. The man who had been picked out with red ink before was this time highlighted in fluorescent yellow.

"Son of a bitch," I said.

"Real name unknown," Moore said. "Been identified as one of The Ten for coming on fourteen years, now."

I handed the picture to Natalie, who looked at it carefully for several seconds before letting it continue around the circle.

Moore went on, now laying out a sequence of new shots, mostly color copies, and all of crime scenes. "The I.D. picture is at least four years old, though Interpol only began distributing it last September. Taken in Croatia. He's called Oxford because the first hit put to him was the murder of a Cambridge don in '87, an old wheeze named Kepper. That's him."

He tapped a black-and-white copy of a picture with his index finger. The shot showed a man in his late fifties or perhaps older, in his bedroom and on his side. The noose was around his neck, tied at the other end to the headboard. A television and VCR were visible near the edge of the photo.

"Staged as autoerotic asphyxiation," Moore continued. "The video player had a tape in it of some very dodgy behavior between human beings and other members of the animal kingdom. Extraordinarily humiliating, since Professor Kepper taught, amongst other classes, Christian Ethics."

"You said a Cambridge don?" Natalie asked.

Moore managed a grin. "The gag—if you'll pardon the pun—is that one of the detectives who figured it for murder made the comment that the assailant must have been 'an Oxford man.' "

None of us laughed.

Moore slid the other photographs around. They depicted acts of exceptional violence, rarely with a single victim, and universally related to sex in one fashion or another. Bodies were bound in rope or chain, cut and stabbed, as if the pictures were all production stills from a series of snuff films.

"You can see his M.O.," Moore said. "He's considered a specialist, the fellow you hire when murder just won't do the trick, and you need to assassinate character as well. He consistently plays a sexual angle, either because that's his pathology and it gets his horn up, or because sex is almost always sensational and scandalous. Maybe both. In most cases he capitalizes on already existing relationships—affairs and the like—but he's willing to fabricate from whole cloth if need be. Most of the time the stagings don't hold up, but by the time the facts are known, the media's already finished Oxford's work for him. The victim's reputation is destroyed."

There was a silence while we all studied the photographs, then Moore began gathering them up again, casting a glance at Lady Ainsley-Hunter's closed door. We'd been keeping our voices low, conspiratorial, and Moore's glance made me feel suddenly guilty, even though I knew better. We were keeping things from our principal, but all of us knew that was for the best. Better that she remain ignorant for now than terrified for no reason.

"Why do your people think he's here?" Dale asked Moore.

"Couple days ago a listening post intercepted a call that should've gone through Rome, ended up being routed through London instead. I don't have the details of the conversation, but whatever they heard was enough for them to tell me Oxford was headed to the States."

"So nothing's to say if he's actually after her or not," Corry said.

"No, but she's a viable target," Moore answered. "She's pissed off people who make their living off trading flesh, in particular the flesh of children. Those are people with money, and they might well want her not only silenced but discredited."

We were all silent for a few seconds, thinking. Moore replaced the closed folder in his bag, and as he did so room service arrived. Dale signed for the food and Natalie brought the cart in, and everyone but me descended on the meal, cracking open cans of soda and taking halves of sandwiches.

When everyone had taken their seats once more, I said, "The CIA showed me a picture of Oxford yesterday, but they didn't identify him as such. Why would they do that?"

"Intelligence gathering?" Corry ventured. "They wanted to know if you'd seen him before."

"But they had to have access to the same sources Robert has," Natalie insisted. "Which means they had reason to believe Oxford is on the move, and potentially moving against Lady Ainsley-Hunter."

Dale shook his head. "They know something that they aren't sharing. Something about Oxford or Drama. A connection between the two, maybe."

"Like?"

"Like maybe they're working together," Corry said.

"Okay," Dale said. "But I have to ask, is that likely? We know for a fact that Drama works alone, and that's not unusual for someone in her line of work."

Moore said, "If Oxford's hunting Her Ladyship, he's hunting alone. There's been nary a whisper about Drama."

"It doesn't hold, anyway," I said. "Drama doesn't have a partner."

"Doesn't have to be a partner," Corry countered. "Just someone she's working with on this one job."

"That's a lot of money to spend to take Her Ladyship," Natalie pointed out. "Just guessing, but if it costs a million dollars to hire one of The Ten, it's got to be at least twice that for two."

"Some people might think it was a bargain," Corry said.

Natalie frowned and turned in her seat, tossing her empty soda can into the trash by the desk. "I agree with Atticus on this. Drama and Oxford are not working together. Doesn't fit the M.O."

"But it would explain why both are coming to New York, if in fact both are," Dale said.

"We don't know if either of them are coming to New York," Moore said. "All we know is that Oxford is on the move in the U.S., but not where. And if we believe what Atticus was told, we have the same problem. It's the same problem as ever with this lot, children—we know just enough to be justly dribbling down our legs, and not enough to do anything more."

"We also know that The Ten work constantly to preserve their anonymity," Natalie said. "If two work together, all of that gets blown to hell. The difficulty doesn't double, it explodes exponentially. Alone, Drama and Oxford can keep their own counsel, modify their plans as they see fit. If they partner up, they've got to worry about all sorts of new problems—including communication. And the more they communicate the greater the chance of being discovered or compromised. It'd be too risky. Even if we assume both of them are on the move, that both of them are coming to New York, that both are after the same mark, we still can't assume they're in it together."

Corry grunted, ceding the argument.

"There's one more strike against Oxford, now that I think of it," Dale said. "If he's after Lady Antonia, he'll have to get her alone to stage the hit. He needs to assassinate character along with life, right? So he's got to make her look really bad, and we know that he'll try to make that bad be some sort of sex thing. He'd need to get her alone to make that work."

"And he'd need prep," Corry added. "A lot of prep. We're talking not only props, but another person, potentially."

"Not necessarily," Natalie said. "He could use one of us."

We all looked at her.

"He could," she said. "Bodyguard in Tryst with British Peer would make great copy. Any of us would do."

"Wouldn't work," I said. "Oxford would want it to look like Lady Ainsley-Hunter was the perpetrator, not the victim. The nature of the relationship between us and her is such that no one would buy her taking advantage of us. If Oxford sets it up to look like any of us jumped her, it'd make Her Ladyship into a martyr."

Dale coughed. "Make us look pretty bad, though."

"Oh, that's a lovely thought," Natalie said. "Oxford's not after *her,* he's after us? Why?"

"Maybe Drama hired him," I said. It was a joke. No one laughed.

Moore cleared his throat, then asked if we had any new information on Keith.

"Logan called from Philadelphia," I said. "Joseph Keith is turning into a very interesting guy. He is on record as saying that he and Her Ladyship were, once upon a time in ancient Sumer, husband and wife. And he was expelled from Philadelphia Community College for possession of a knife."

"He cut anyone?"

"No, but that may be for lack of trying. Details of the actual event are sketchy."

"The photograph is being distributed?"

Natalie reached into her blazer pocket, produced one of the flyers we'd run off, offering it to Moore. "We've run off a hundred and fifty copies to hand out at every location. They'll go to local security and the like, mostly."

Moore stared hard at Keith's portrait before flipping the paper over and reading the back. We'd done the original on a color inkjet printer and the reproduction had worked very well. On the back of the sheet we'd printed out the protocol we wanted followed in case Keith was spotted. It wasn't terribly elaborate, the instructions straightforward—if Keith was seen, the protection team was to be notified in person immediately. We didn't want Keith engaged, simply monitored. We would take it from there.

The corner of Moore's mouth curled in a slight smile. "Very dolly, very nice."

"Glad you like it," Natalie said. "It'll be included in the bill."

Moore dropped the sheet into his equipment bag. "I gave Her Ladyship and Ms. Chester the standard briefing on the plane. Both of them had heard it before, but it never hurts to emphasize the particular bits. I made certain they understood that when we were mobile they were to take direction from us without argument or hesitation."

"Chester was good coming off the plane," Corry said. "She done this before?"

"Not like this, actually. But she's a quick study."

"How long she been on Lady Ainsley-Hunter's staff?" Dale asked.

Moore grinned. "She's safe. I vetted her myself. She's been Lady Antonia's PA for almost a year, now. If she's working for one of The Ten, she's been waiting a long time for her opportunity."

Dale brought his hands up with a shrug, and then we moved on to the other topics at hand, beginning with Her Ladyship's plans for the evening. Lady Ainsley-Hunter had a dinner at eight-thirty with some of the U.N. folk that would be held at one of the consular residences. After that, the plan was to return her to the hotel and button her up for the night. The next day would be the big one, with the formal announcement and ensuing press brouhaha.

Everyone had finished eating, and I pushed the cart back into the hall, returning to find that Moore had already retired to his room for a quick nap. Dale and Corry left to check the cars, which left Nat and me alone in the sitting room.

It grew very quiet, the way silence spreads in a space where more people are asleep than awake, and it was infectious, and neither of us spoke. Natalie read the complimentary copy of *New York* magazine that had been put out with the phone book and the hotel directory, and I dug out my copy of the flyer and spent some time memorizing Keith's face.

He looked utterly normal. Black hair and brown eyes, and perhaps his nose was a tad sharp, but not so sharp that it was a distinguishing feature. His expression in the photograph was mild, as if he'd been about to laugh, and the photographer had jumped the smile by a fraction of a second.

I set the paper back down and sighed heavily, despite myself, and Natalie looked at me over the top of the magazine.

"Relax," she said.

"Two members of The Ten and one lone nut, and you tell me to relax? You *are* bossy."

"We're just getting started."

I nodded slightly, thinking that it wasn't the start that had me tense.

It was wondering how it was all going to end.

CHAPTER NINE

We were rotating the live-in duties at the hotel, and the night after the U.N. appointment my turn came up and I slept at the Edmonton, on the sofa bed in the suite's main room. The previous day had been exhausting, and the sofa bed comfortable enough, and I slept deep and well, but woke early all the same to hear Fiona Chester cursing softly.

She was working at the desk in the main room, dividing her attention between the laptop open in front of her, the fax machine positioned at her left elbow, and the telephone to her right. My understanding was that she always started work early, but all the same I was surprised to see her up. The light seeping through the windows was just beginning to hint dawn, and from the look of Chester, she'd been up for a while. She'd switched the desk lamp on, and the illumination was enough to see that she was already dressed for the day, skirt and blouse and makeup all perfect. I got my glasses on while she continued with the phone, and I could tell she'd been trying to keep her voice low, but her frustration was getting the better of her.

"She had their word," Chester was saying. "No, that's unacceptable. . . . Her Ladyship—I beg your pardon?"

I sat up and swung my legs out of the bed, and Chester noticed me moving. She shot me a quick and apologetic smile before turning her chair to avoid my near-nakedness. I'd slept in my undershorts, and while she continued her conversation I pulled on my pants from the previous night and got my shirt on and half buttoned. The conversation had turned, was growing heated, and now, with me awake, Chester no longer felt a need to maintain restraint.

"They bloody well *did* promise," she snapped into the phone. "Now . . . no, listen to me, please. I am *not* threatening you. But you would be well advised to tell Orin and his brother that I'm not the woman they have to worry about."

She slammed down the phone as if squashing a very large, very ugly bug.

"Who are Orin and his brother?" I asked.

"Musicians. Rock stars. Imbeciles."

"Is this something I should worry about?"

"I don't think so." Chester rose and smoothed her skirt, which was navy blue, then headed for Lady Ainsley-Hunter's room. As she passed me, she said, "Very sorry I disturbed you."

"I had to get up in another hour or two," I said.

She might've smirked, but I didn't see it, because by then she was tapping on Ainsley-Hunter's door. She waited a moment, then slipped inside, so I set about stowing the bed back into the sofa and replacing the cushions, then searched around for the room-service menu. I ordered up two pots of coffee, two of hot water for tea, and some orange juice. Then I took my overnight bag into the bathroom and got myself sorted for the day.

When I emerged again, Chester was back at the desk, working at the laptop, and Lady Ainsley-Hunter was standing beside her, speaking on the telephone. Unlike her personal assistant, Her Ladyship apparently hadn't been awake for very long; her hair was still mussed from her sleep, and she was wearing one of the terrycloth hotel robes. The emblem of the Edmonton was stitched in gold thread over her heart. She glanced over at me as I dropped my bag by the sofa, and her expression was different from any of the others I'd seen her wear.

She was pissed.

There was a knock at the door, and I answered it and wheeled in the room-service cart, then threw all the locks once more and fixed myself a cup of coffee. Lady Ainsley-Hunter got off the phone. Chester and I both looked at her, me for an explanation of what had them in a dither, Chester most likely awaiting orders.

Her Ladyship ignored both of us for most of a minute, staring at the edge of the desk, apparently deep in thought.

"What was scheduled for this evening?" she finally asked Chester. She sounded only mildly curious.

"You're lecturing at Sarah Lawrence," I said. Both of the women looked at me with mild surprise. "It's Natalie's *alma mater,* that's why I remember."

"Cancel," Lady Ainsley-Hunter told Chester. "Then find out where the party is and make damn sure we're invited."

Chester nodded and picked up the phone. Her Ladyship started back to her room.

"Wait a second," I said. "What's going on? Why the change in plans?"

She stopped and gave me a look that was as surprising as her earlier anger had been. For a moment I thought she was going to demand who I thought I was, asking her such questions. Then she seemed to remember that was what I'd been hired to do.

"You know Rorschach Test?" she asked. "The band, not the psychological exam."

"I've heard of them," I said. Erika had played me one of their albums, a synthesis of acoustic rock with electronic music, before moving out for school. She'd thought it was good. I'd thought it sounded confused and self-important.

"We're going to the launch party for their new album."

"You're canceling a lecture at a liberal arts college to attend a launch party?"

"They're one of Robert's favorite bands. He'll enjoy it."

I frowned and started to ask the logical next question, but she cut me off.

"You'll excuse me, I'm going to get dressed."

She returned to her room.

At the desk, Chester shot me a look that I couldn't begin to interpret.

The party was held at a club called Lot 61, in the meatpacking district, and not more than a stone's throw from the bondage club I'd bounced at a couple years back. Lot 61 is the kind of club I make a point of avoiding, and usually that's not a problem, because it's also the kind of club that never lets people like me inside. Whatever fame I and my colleagues have, it doesn't even begin to register on the management's radar.

Lady Ainsley-Hunter was another matter entirely.

The party started at eight, but we didn't arrive until almost eleven, because Her Ladyship said she wanted to wait until the press was all present. It made me wonder why she'd canceled the Sarah Lawrence expedition, but I didn't ask her, and the only explanation I could come up with was that she had, indeed, been pissed, and consequently not thinking very clearly. But whatever that anger was, it had passed early in the day; there'd been no sign of it since I'd caught her on the phone that morning.

Dale dropped us off in front of the club where a gaggle of poseurs and poseurs-in-training stood waiting behind the velvet ropes. Because he was driving the Benz, which wasn't a limo, nobody paid us much attention, at least not when Moore got out of the car, taking the lead. When Lady Ainsley-Hunter emerged a buzz started, and it continued as I followed her and Moore to the front door. The bouncer—who was probably more of a male model than a security guard—didn't even bother to check his clipboard before ushering us inside, and I barely had time to tell him that there were four more in our party before we got swamped by the wave of music that sprayed from the open doors.

Moore led us through the crush to a bar area, decorated with seventies furniture and an enormous fireplace. People were writhing against one another on the dance floor, and the noise was tremendous, and I spotted security—both plainclothes and uniformed—scattered around the main room.

Lady Ainsley-Hunter got herself a flute of champagne from a passing tray and turned on a radiant smile, scanning the crowd. I glanced at Moore and he just shrugged; if he had a better idea why we were there than I, he'd been doing a fine job hiding it. Certainly, he didn't seem displeased at the chance to meet the members of Rorschach Test.

It took less than a minute for the first reporter to find us, a young black man with dreadlocks who wrote for *Spin*. Her Ladyship greeted him like an old friend, made introductions, and then the two of them bent their heads together and shared a shouted conversation at the bar. While they were talking, I saw Natalie enter with Chester, Corry, and Dale following.

"Where the hell are you?" she radioed.

I tabbed the button resting in my palm. "At the bar."

She and Chester were stopped twice before they reached us, each time by men wearing the latest styles, and though I couldn't hear a thing, it was clear they were being invited to dance. Nobody paid Corry and Dale any mind, except to sneer at their fashion sense as they went past.

Her Ladyship and the reporter from *Spin* talked for several minutes longer, and when they were finished she gave him a kiss on the cheek. He shot a couple grins back her way as he returned to his table closer to the fireplace.

"Lovely man." She was shouting in my ear, and it was still difficult to hear her. "James Rich, he did a piece on Together Now last year. The week after it came out, our membership in the U.S. bumped almost eight percent."

"Seems nice enough."

"What?"

"I said, he seems nice enough."

She nodded, waved at someone across the room who was standing under a Damien Hirsch painting of multicolored spots. The person waved back, began making his way over to us. With the crowd the way it was, I guessed he'd reach us sometime after we'd all gone home and gone to bed.

With Natalie, Corry, Dale, and Moore all present, I felt safe in putting my full attention on Lady Ainsley-Hunter for a moment, so I shouted, "I'm going to ask this again—why are we here?"

She sipped her champagne for the first time, gave the glass a look of mild surprise, then set it on the bar and leaned over to where Moore was standing.

"Robert, would you like to meet the band?"

He grinned, shook his head. "That's a bit unprofessional, my lady."

"Not at all." She smiled at him. "I need to speak with Orin anyway, Robert."

"If Your Ladyship insists."

"She does," she said, and with that, we went to meet the band.

Rorschach Test was really only three members, the two McLaughlin brothers—Orin and Judd—and a drummer who went by the name Digger. If it was a first name, a last name, or a nickname, I never found out. Orin and Judd clearly had come from the same tree, though Orin, the elder, was also taller and heavier than his brother. All hailed from Sheffield, England. All three were dressed unpretentiously, and I wondered if they'd had any trouble getting into the club that night.

We found them in one of the VIP rooms at the back of the warehouse, seated on more of that seventies furniture, lit by lamps designed by Jorge Pardo. The room was awash in a haze of smoke, both tobacco and pot. A sideboard was laden with caviar, smoked salmon, fruit, bottles of champagne, and, frighteningly, Coors. Groupies or roadies or other support staff clung to the corners of the room.

Moore and I accompanied Her Ladyship inside, leaving the others out on the dance floor, and no sooner had we entered than Orin sprang from where he'd been lounging on a sofa and gave Lady Ainsley-Hunter a hug. It seemed genuinely warm, and she returned it enthusiastically. Judd grinned. Digger ignored us and took a hit off the bong in his lap.

"Lady Antonia," Orin said. "Didn't know you'd be here."

"I could hardly miss the opportunity. This is Robert Moore, he handles my security. He's a fan."

Orin was perhaps a year or two older than Lady Ainsley-Hunter, and when he grinned, he looked even younger than she did. "Truth?"

"Truth," Moore said.

Orin stuck out a hand, shook Robert's warmly. "Always glad to meet a fan. You pick up the new album yet? We've got copies lying around here, hold on." He turned and shouted at a middle-aged woman who was pouring drinks at the sideboard. "Libby, we got a copy of the new one lying about? Could you bring it here?"

"It's not necessary," Moore said.

"It's no bother, mate. Here it is. Enjoy it, it's the best one yet. We really hit our stride on this one."

Behind him, on the sofa, Digger nodded, then let out the smoke he'd been holding. He didn't cough.

"My PA spoke with your manager this morning," Lady Ainsley-Hunter said. "He told her that Rorschach Test won't be on our album."

"Yeah, we're really sorry about that, Lady Antonia," Orin said. "Just that if you want to have the album out for Christmas, we've got to lay down the track in the next month or so, and we're on tour. We don't have time. You know how it is."

Lady Ainsley-Hunter nodded, sympathetic. "Yes, you're extremely busy. Headed straight for the top of the charts with this new one, I understand."

"That's the hope, eh?"

"You gave me your word, Orin. You said Rorschach Test would provide the lead track. You promised me an original song that would really—and I'm using your words now—make a difference."

Orin McLaughlin made a pained face, glanced back at where his brother was seated. Judd was watching the conversation. Digger looked like he was about to nod off.

"I did do that, yeah," Orin said. "Things change. We can't."

"You will."

It was how she said it; it frosted the air between them, and Orin snapped his head up as if she'd slapped him.

"This November, Together Now will release an album to raise funds for child rescue in Southeast Asia and Africa," Lady Ainsley-Hunter said. "Our fund-raising target is fifty million dollars, and I have every intention of not only reaching that mark, but surpassing it. To that end I have assembled, very carefully, bands that appeal to a certain buying demographic, a youth market.

Rorschach Test is about to become enormously popular to those buyers. Despite my bodyguard's enjoyment of your music, you and I both know he's not the demographic I want.

"You gave me your word. You will keep it."

"Lady Antonia, it's not that we don't *want* to, it's that—"

"I didn't come here to listen to your excuses, Orin, and I didn't come here for a contact high. I'm explaining to you the way it will be. You will write me my song, it will be bloody brilliant, and you will have the track recorded and ready for the album before the end of August."

Orin shook his head, angry and hurt. "I don't care if you are a sodding *peer.* You don't talk to your friends like that, eh? You don't push me around like that."

"This isn't about friendship." She was furious, and her voice dropped, and she took a step forward, and for a moment I wondered if I was going to have to restrain her. Moore, standing at her other arm, still holding the CD, was motionless. "It's about *work.*"

"You can't force us—"

"I can." She took another step closer to him, and there was no friendliness in the approach. "Now, you'll give me my song. Or else you had better start asking for proof of age from every groupie who offers you a blowjob, Orin. Because I promise you, if just one of them is underage, I'll find out about it, and I'll make sure everyone who has ever even heard of Together Now knows how much you *love* children."

The threat turned Orin pale. Judd had gotten to his feet, looking as shocked as his brother. Digger was snoring.

"My PA will expect a call from your manager in the morning." Lady Ainsley-Hunter turned on her heel and headed for the door so briskly I had to scurry to catch up.

Moore followed a second later, mumbling an apology and a thank you. When I caught his expression out of the corner of my eye, I knew that Lady Ainsley-Hunter had humiliated him as much as she had Orin.

"It's always about the children," he muttered as we made our way back to the dance floor.

CHAPTER TEN

Three days later, everything went to hell in a handbasket.

It actually started the night before, with me getting in late, cranky and hungry and with a headache. I'd made a bowl of oatmeal and finished the orange juice in the pitcher, and that had taken the edge off by the time I fell asleep.

All the same, when my alarm went off at a quarter of five my head felt thick, my muscles ached, and I knew I was moving slowly. A look at myself in the mirror when I'd finished shaving confirmed the worst. The bags under my eyes looked packed for a long trip, and my tongue was coated. I was coming down with something.

In the kitchen, I popped a handful of the assorted vitamins that Bridgett kept in the cabinet with the canned goods, made a fresh quart of juice from concentrate, then used most of it to chase the pills down. I dressed in one of my nicer suits, hooked my radio and gun to my belt, and stumbled downstairs. It was still dark outside, and I nearly tripped over Midge, my downstairs neighbor, who was stretching against the doorframe in preparation for her morning run.

"You should be in bed." Midge said it in the same perky way she said everything, no matter how sad or depressing or tedious the observation might be. Everything about her was perky, from the sweats to her permed blond hair.

"Gotta work," I told her.

"You look like you have a fever."

I nodded and made my way down the block to the corner of Third Avenue. Midge followed me, bouncing on the balls of her feet.

"Haven't seen much of Bridgett for the last week. You're still friends?"

"She's been working out of town," I said. When Midge had first moved into the building, Erika had been living with me, and she had assumed Erika was my sister. Erika, in turn, had implied that our relationship was far more intimate than that, and it had taken several months before Midge realized the joke. As a result, Midge was careful in how she referred to Bridgett, always as my "friend," although given the lack of insulation between floors there was not a doubt in my mind that she knew what the relationship was.

Midge helped me hail a cab on the corner, and as I climbed in she wished me a good day and headed off in the direction of the East River. I told the cabbie that I wanted to go to the Edmonton. The traffic was still light, and the cabbie sped enthusiastically. He had to wake me up when we reached the hotel, and I paid him and headed through the lobby, and maybe it was the extra ten minutes of sleep, but I felt significantly better.

Moore let me into the suite after making the appropriate checks through the spyhole, and as I passed him, he echoed Midge.

"Christ, you look like warm shite."

"Fuck you very much. Is there coffee?"

"Cart just came up."

He followed me into the sitting room, where Chester was working at the desk. I could hear a shower running in Lady Ainsley-Hunter's bedroom, and I used my head to indicate the door, which was a mistake, because the headache—that had been just waiting for an excuse—took that as its cue to make a grand entrance.

"Natalie in there?"

"Of course." Moore grabbed the cup out of my hand. "Tea for you, mate."

"Coffee's fine."

"Tea is better for you." He took a fresh cup and used the second pot on the cart to fill it, then squeezed the juice from a lemon wedge into the tea.

"You're so British," I grumbled, taking the cup and a seat. " 'Morning, Peter."

" 'Morning, Tinkerbell," Chester said. "You do look a sight."

"I look worse than I feel."

Moore had been having eggs and hash browns and sausage, and a bowl of oatmeal, and the sight of it made my stomach look for a place to hide somewhere behind my liver. I averted my eyes as he wolfed down a couple of forkfuls.

"We should move me off the perimeter today," I told Moore. "Give it to Natalie."

"It takes a wise man to admit it when he can go no farther," he said. "Though I'm inclined to tell you to just head the hell home and get some sleep."

"My head's clear and I'm moving fine. We'll just swap me with Natalie today, and I'll back you up on the close support."

Moore appraised me like I was a recruit on his parade ground. Then he grunted. "We'll run with it. But if you start to head south, you notify, understood?"

"Yes, Sergeant." I finished the tea and stood to refill the cup. "Shall we get to business?"

Moore wiped his mouth with the napkin, nodding, then pushed his plate away. "Fiona, you want to come over here?"

Chester moved from the desk to the couch, bringing one of the typed sheets with her. "Her Ladyship's schedule for the day, gentlemen. She begins with an appearance on *Talk New York!* at ten, but the show's producer has asked we have her at the studio no later than nine to give him time to go over the questions she'll be asked. She's been invited to stay for the whole hour, after which Her Ladyship is free until one this afternoon, when she will lunch with the lieutenant governor and members of his staff at the Four Seasons. At two-thirty she has promised to attend a benefit auction for the International Red Cross in Scarsdale. The rest of her afternoon is free until six-thirty, when she will speak at NYU on grassroots political action as a means of fighting child exploitation. The lecture is supposed to end at eight, but in all likelihood, Her Ladyship will want to entertain questions as long as she can. When she is finished, however, she has promised to join some of the students for drinks at a local pub—excuse me, local bar."

While she spoke, Moore and I consulted our notes, checking off each item as it was listed.

"Scarsdale is new," I said.

"It was added last night, after dinner," Chester said, nodding. "The invitation was presented to her in person, just before we left."

"Checked it already," Moore said. "It's up-and-up."

"Well, it's a problem," I said. "It'll take an hour, probably longer, to get from that lunch midtown to Scarsdale. That's without serious traffic."

"But it's possible?"

"She won't have much of a meal," I said. "It'll be a rush."

"She can be a few minutes late," Chester said.

"I'll let Dale know. If he can find a route he likes, it'll fly."

"Agreed," Moore said. "The NYU lecture and drinks to follow, you know the location?"

"There's a bar in the neighborhood that I like. The Stoned Crow, it's small, entrance is on Fourth Street. Gets a regular crowd most weeknights, but there's a space in the back that's easy enough to secure. There's a pool table back there, some booths, a dart board. It'll be fine. We scouted it week before last."

"How do you want to handle the guests for that?"

"Well, we could search them."

"Her Ladyship would rather if you didn't," Chester said. "These are the people who make Together Now work. She doesn't wish to do anything that might alienate them."

I looked at Moore, shrugged. "Eyeballing works, too."

"All right," he agreed. "Anything else?"

"Not for now."

Moore checked the Rolex on his wrist. "I've got oh-six-twenty-three."

I checked my own watch. "I agree."

"How long is it going to take us to get to the studio?"

"Maybe thirty minutes. It's pretty much a straight shot over to the West Side."

"Then we'll egress at oh-eight-thirty."

We all seemed happy with that, so Chester headed for Lady Ainsley-Hunter's bedroom to inform her of the itinerary and I got up to use the phone on the desk, dialing Dale's cellular. He answered immediately, and I told him the news about Scarsdale, and he was surprisingly obliging about the whole thing.

"I'll pull the maps now," he said. "Anything else?"

"There'll be a change in the rotation. Natalie's going to take the perimeter today, I'll be backing up Moore with Lady Ainsley-Hunter."

"I'll pass it along to Corry when I see him. When do you want us there?"

"Quarter past eight. Radio when you're in position."

"See ya then."

I hung up the phone, drained the last of the tea in the cup, and refilled for a third time from the cart. "You were right," I told Moore. "The tea's helping."

"That's the restorative power of a cuppa." He glanced over at Lady Ainsley-Hunter's door, making certain it was still shut. "Any news on the Keith front?"

I tore open a packet of honey with my teeth, then said, "Bridgett and Special Agent Fowler are in New Jersey. Joseph Keith—or someone using his Visa card—bought a suit at a mall off Route Seventeen yesterday morning."

"A suit?"

"A three-piece suit, navy blue, and two dress shirts, three ties, a package of cotton handkerchiefs, and a pair of burgundy leather dress shoes. And some cuff links."

Moore rolled his eyes. "Well-dressed stalker."

"Well, you know, they were married," I said.

"Who was married?" Lady Ainsley-Hunter asked.

She had just emerged from her bedroom, Natalie and Chester following. She was wearing a white shell with a mock turtleneck collar that left her arms bare, and light silk pants the color of an avocado's flesh. She'd touched her cheeks, lips, and eyes lightly with makeup, and had spent some time on her hair, as well. In each earlobe was a small pearl on a stud, and its companion necklace was visible at her neck. Her feet were bare.

Lady Ainsley-Hunter looked expectantly from me to Moore, giving each of us time to come up with an answer. When neither of us did, she smiled.

"Right," she said. "Which of you is going to tell me about my stalker, then?"

"I've spent the last twelve years becoming very adept at listening to what people are saying behind my back," Lady Ainsley-Hunter said. "It's the world I was born and bred to. It's a required survival skill in a class-based society."

She was seated on the edge of her bed, pulling on a pair of white cotton socks that looked stunningly inappropriate. I'd taken the seat by the dressing table, and we were alone for the time being, the others waiting in the sitting room for the second round of breakfast—this for Her Ladyship and Natalie—to arrive.

"Neither you nor Robert want me to fret over something I cannot control. I suppose I could be offended or outraged or otherwise angry, and I am, a bit."

"You're concealing it well."

"Another trait I had to learn early." She finished tugging up her socks, then grabbed a foot in each hand and pulled them in against her thighs, rocking slightly on the mattress. "Is this man dangerous?"

"Possibly."

She pursed her lips and blew out a breath. Then she shrugged. "Very well."

"That's the most understated response I've ever heard from a principal."

"You don't know very much about the peerage, do you?"

"Not really."

"The women I grew up with, went to school with, the ones who are my age, they think I'm pitiful. As in, deserving of their pity."

The look I gave her made her laugh. It sounded bitter.

"Ninety percent of those women are anorexic or suffering from some other eating disorder," Lady Ainsley-Hunter said. "Everything is about appearance, about station, about finding a good husband. These are women who spend their whole year preparing for the Season, choosing what they will wear, who they will invite, who they will deign to speak to."

"It's that shallow?" I asked.

"It's not shallow at all, if you're a part of it. It's the culture." She let her feet go and reached down for the pair of black boots at the foot of the bed. "When I was nine years old, I went with my father to Thailand. He was with the Foreign Office then, going on a fact-finding tour, and I begged and begged to go with him. On that trip, I met a little Thai girl, my age, perhaps a year or two older. She was quite sweet, quite kind to me. She and I played by the pool at the hotel. She wore a black bathing suit, and I thought it was quite adult, because it didn't have frills or ruffles.

"One afternoon, while we were playing, two men came over, one of them Thai, the other I'm not certain about, but he was Caucasian. I thought the Thai man was my friend's father. And my friend left with them, and I stayed in the pool."

She paused, yanking the right boot on and then smoothing her pants leg down over it. "You know how when you're little you can occupy yourself with a pleasure for hours and hours? You can play with the same toy, you can read the same book again and again?"

I nodded.

"Growing up in the north of England, not really weather for taking a dip," she reached for her other boot, "one does not swim for fun. Only if one has fallen into the lake. I was in and out of that pool for hours. So I was there when she returned. She was happy to see me, she jumped into the water, wanting to play.

"As soon as she was in the water, though, blood began clouding around her middle. She'd been bleeding between her legs, you see, and the bathing suit, being black, had hidden it. But in the water, it sort of . . . billowed out. As soon as she saw it, she started to cry."

She looked at the remaining boot, still in her hand.

"The pool attendant came and pulled her from the water. I thought that he would call for a doctor, but he didn't, he began shouting at her. And the man that I thought was her father, he came running back, too. The two men started shouting at one another, my friend between them. The attendant was shaking her, and the water from her suit made the blood run down her legs. She kept crying the whole time.

"Then they left, or, more precisely, they were forced to leave. The man who I believed was her father—he was dragging her after him. He didn't seem like a very kind parent, I remember thinking.

"My own father arrived, and I told him what I'd seen. I wanted to know where my friend had gone, you see. I was going to be at the hotel, at the pool, for another three or four days, and I wanted to have someone to play with. My father went to talk to the pool attendant, and when he came back he looked as if he'd swallowed something both sour and sharp at once, as if it was in his stomach, making him ill."

Lady Ainsley-Hunter finished pulling on the remaining boot, then stood, stamping each foot to make sure she was set on her heels. With the back of her hand, she smoothed her hair.

"I badgered him, asking over and over what had happened, where she had gone. Asking if I could play with her again. I'm old enough now that I understand how hard it was for him, but then, I thought he was just being cruel, and I wouldn't relent. In the end, he sat me down and he said that I wasn't going to see her again. And I asked why, I asked if that meant she was sick, if she had died. After all, I'd seen her bleeding.

"My father was a reserved man, you understand. He could be quite passionate when it suited him, but he rarely revealed his emotions. But I saw tears in his eyes, and he held me close, and he told me that there were evil things, and that the worst evils were the evils done to children.

"And then he explained what evil I had just seen."

Outside, I heard the doorbell ring. Lady Ainsley-Hunter canted her head in the direction of the sound, listening. There was the rattle of a new cart being wheeled in, the old one being wheeled away. She sighed, checking herself in the mirror, finding me in the reflection. There was the hint of a self-mocking smile.

"I can't think of any work more important than what I do," she told my reflection. "I suppose some might think that arrogant, but I genuinely believe that there is nothing more important in the world than rescuing children. I have dedicated my life to a cause. I will never abandon it."

She finished checking herself in the mirror, then turned to face me.

"This man Keith, he worries you and he worries Robert. As far as I'm concerned, all that it means is that the money I'm spending on security is worth every pence. But Keith doesn't matter to me. He is, in all honesty, irrelevant. I have more important things to deal with. . . ." She trailed off, searching my face for some sign that I understood what she was saying and why she was saying it.

"All right," I said.

She nodded, taking her suit jacket from where it hung at the back of a chair. It was made from the same light silk as her trousers, the same green.

"And now I want my breakfast," she said.

The producer of *Talk New York!* was a man named Jordan Palmetto, and he met us in the dressing room when we arrived at the studio. He waited, patient and visibly amused, until Moore and I had finished our checks, then greeted Lady Ainsley-Hunter and tried to present her with a basket of fruit and cheese. Moore took it from him before Lady Ainsley-Hunter could, grinning and saying that he was starved. It was a more discreet—though ruder—way of indicating that he wanted to check the contents before handing it over.

Once she was seated at the makeup table, Palmetto began running through questions with Her Ladyship, Chester sitting with them. Her Ladyship was going to be the first guest. The other guests today were a stand-up comedian who had a new sitcom that had debuted this fall, and an author.

"But nobody's ever heard of him," Palmetto confided. "If it looks like we're going long, we'll bump him."

"What does he write?" Lady Ainsley-Hunter asked.

"Books," Palmetto said.

I took a post near the door to the dressing room while Moore headed back out to make a circuit of the stage area. Over my radio I listened as Natalie and he exchanged transmissions about the layout and the look of the audience. Dale was out back, keeping an eye on the two cars and the exit, and Corry was waiting in the lobby, in position to watch as people began filing inside. The studio had two hundred and twenty-eight seats, and all of them would be filled, though whether the seats were occupied by people who actually wanted to see the show or by people who were pulled in off the street was hard to tell.

"I'm going to talk to the square badges once more," Natalie radioed. *"Make certain they know how to use the copies of the handout."*

We all radioed back confirmations.

"Doors open in five minutes," Corry said.

Again, we radioed confirmations.

Palmetto finished with Her Ladyship, and it seemed to have gone well, because he left her laughing, then stopped to speak with me before leaving the room.

"Kodiak, right?" he asked, offering me his hand.

"Right," I said, trying to decide what to do with the potential shake. If I took it, one of my hands would be busy. If I didn't, I'd be rude. I decided it was safe enough in the room to be polite. "Nice to meet you."

"Hey, it's my pleasure." He smiled at me the same way he had at Lady Ainsley-Hunter. "Listen, you and your colleagues, you ought to do the show sometime, maybe next week, what do you think? We could do the whole hour with you guys, talk about your job, the work, Skye Van Brandt, stuff like that. We could even get that other writer, the journalist with the book. What do you think?"

"We're busy through the month," I said.

The soothe-the-celebrity smile didn't falter. "No problem. Tell you what, leave me a card or something, we'll get in touch, work it out."

"I'll do that," I lied.

He offered his hand again, and because I'd accepted the first time, I was obligated to once more. Then he went out into the hall, and I shut the door, turned back to see Lady Ainsley-Hunter saying something to Chester and the woman who was touching up her hair; both laughed. The hairdresser was gray-haired, very thin, and kept a long cigarette parked behind her ear.

"Tinkerbell," Dale said over the radio. *"Two of the Lost Boys are here to see you."*

"Stand by," I said. "Hook, check six."

"Check six, confirmed," Moore said. *"Be about a minute."*

Both Chester and Her Ladyship glanced my way.

"Nothing serious," I told them. "Moore's going to spell me here. I've got to step out for a second."

"Check six?" Chester asked.

"It's a sneaky way of saying 'I need to step outside,' " I said. "Keeps anyone listening from knowing what we're up to."

The hairdresser finished what she was doing and I let her out of the dressing room as Moore arrived. He took over my post, and I went down the long hallway to the back door, passing two security guards along the way. I stopped long enough to make certain both had the handout, asking them to each show me theirs, and they glared at me.

"We know who we're looking for," the younger of the two said. "We've been doing this for a while."

"Prove it to me," I said.

"Just because we're not famous doesn't mean we don't know how to do our jobs," the other one complained. He had the shoulders and upper arms of a person who has spent too much time lifting weights to the neglect of everything below the waist and, apparently, above the neck.

I smiled at the two of them, thanked them for their help, and continued out the back. Bridgett and Fowler were there, standing with Dale by the parked cars. Bridgett frowned when she saw me.

"You're ill," she said.

"And now cranky," I said. "Dale, get inside and have the two guards in the hall replaced with another set, please. They've got an attitude problem."

Dale rolled his shoulders and pretended to crack his knuckles, as if preparing to hand out a beating. "Me go be mean now," he said.

I turned back to Bridgett and Scott. "Keith's not in Newark?"

"We tracked him to a Best Western in Nyack," Fowler said. "He was there last night, checked out this morning. We missed him by maybe an hour. Got a positive visual I.D., but nothing on his transportation and no idea where he went next. He didn't make any calls and he didn't leave anything behind."

"But you two are here," I said.

Bridgett put the back of her right hand to my forehead, and I moved my head back, irritated. "You've got a fever."

"I feel fine. Why are you two here?"

"Because there's a chance Keith's coming here," Bridgett said, squinting at me, as if trying to see the virus clambering about in my bloodstream. "And we don't know where else to look."

"And we're both fans of the show," Scott said. "Where do you want us?"

"If you'd like to head around the front and meet up with Corry, two extra pairs of eyes couldn't hurt."

The door behind us opened and Dale emerged, grinning. "Taken care of," he reported. "I talked to Palmetto, he moved Heckle and Jeckle to the fire exits in the studio."

I nodded, then radioed Corry to tell him that the Lost Boys would be coming around to join him. All posts radioed back a confirmation, and Scott and Bridgett followed me back inside. A new guard was in the hall, and before we had even reached him, he had produced his copy of the handout and held it up for me to see.

"Thank you," I said.

The guard grunted.

When we reached the dressing room Scott and Bridgett kept going, but not before Bridgett stopped long enough to squeeze my hand and give me another kiss.

"Midge wanted to know if we're still friends," I told her.

"We're still friends."

"I'm asking for her sake more than my own."

"That perky bitch wants into your pants. If I sleep at your place tonight, I'll shoot her."

"How do you know she's after me? Maybe she's hoping you're available."

"The only thing that isn't straight about that woman is her perm," Bridgett said.

At oh-nine-hundred, Natalie came on the net to let us know that the house doors were being opened. I passed the news along to Her Ladyship, and we all settled in to wait. After fifteen minutes, the stage manager came back to check on us, saying that if Her Ladyship wished to move backstage, that would be fine.

I got on the radio again. "Wendy and Peter to station two."

The confirmations came back in their normal order, and we headed down the hall toward the stage. The set for the show was designed to look like the living room in some lavish penthouse apartment, with a fake Manhattan skyline painted on the backdrop. The audience noise was muted backstage, but it sounded like a lot of people. We stood to one side while stagehands scrambled back and forth with final preparations, and then Palmetto came by once more, just to check on everything, before heading to his position just off the stage.

"You'd think they'd introduce me to the hosts," Lady Ainsley-Hunter said.

"It's American television," I said. "The assumption is that you already know them."

"Is that really how it works?"

"I have no clue. I don't watch much television."

"Have you ever seen *Talk New York!*?"

I nodded.

"And?"

It took me a moment to find something to say. "You're going to reach a very large audience."

"Oh, my. That bad, is it?"

"Depends on what you think about papier-mâché centerpieces and fad diets."

The lights in the studio dimmed, and the stage lights came up. The audience began applauding, and from the opposite side of the stage the hosts came out, a man and a woman. Both were well dressed and heavily made up, and each carried a mug, presumably full of coffee, that had the show's logo on its front. Both hosts were very white, very friendly, and they began by addressing the audience, telling them that it would be a terrific show, that their "very special guest" today was an actual member of the Royal Family, Lady Antonia Ainsley-Hunter, and that she'd be with them for the full hour. There was a burst of applause, and from the corner of my eye I saw Her Ladyship shaking her head slightly, amused. The host and hostess went on to say who the other guests were, and they mentioned the author's name, so I figured his being bumped wasn't a foregone conclusion.

Then the stage manager announced that they were one minute from air, and everyone took positions, and the lights changed again. The theme came up over the speakers, then the announcer's voice, basically repeating what we'd already heard from the host and hostess. A sign by my shoulder lit up announcing we were on the air.

The crowd went wild.

Chester and I watched from the edge of the set. Across from us, I could see Moore in position, scanning the audience. The radio traffic was almost nonexistent, with Natalie or Corry or Moore occasionally noting some movement or action, but nothing major.

Lady Ainsley-Hunter went out on stage after the show returned from its first commercial break, and she got another thunderous round of applause, and she stopped when it began and faced the audience, giving them a good look and a modest bow. The host and hostess started with the obvious platitudes and questions, and she handled them gracefully and with self-effacing humor. After a couple of minutes they gave her the opening to talk about her work, and she explained why she was in New York, and she talked about Together Now, and the desperate plight of the world's children, and they put a tape up on the monitor, showing sweatshop conditions in Central America. The audience responded with the appropriate noises of sympathy, and when the clip was finished, the phone number, Web, and mail addresses of Together Now went on-screen. Then the show broke for another commercial, and when it resumed, the comedian came out and did a short routine, then joined the party around the table. He made a couple jokes about the English in general and got some laughs, and Lady Ainsley-Hunter was a good sport about it. After the next commercial break, the author came out and talked about his book—it was a cookbook—and everyone gathered in the faux kitchen to bake some low-calorie cookies and have a generally fine time.

Then it was ending, and the host and hostess were thanking everyone for coming and promising that tomorrow's show would be just as fabulous as today's, and the theme music came up again. The crowd was jubilant, perhaps because they loved what they'd seen. Maybe they were just glad the show was over.

Moore came around and got into position with me, and Lady Ainsley-Hunter came off the set. She was perspiring from the heat of the lights, and I took the lead as we made our way back down the hall to the green room, Chester following.

"I could do with some water," Ainsley-Hunter said as we reached the door. "They stick you into a sauna and the only thing they offer you to drink is coffee."

"We'll get you some water before we go," I said, and I opened the dressing room door to find Joseph Keith, the trousers of his new navy blue suit around his ankles, his penis erect and in his hand, masturbating furiously. The lights around the makeup mirror were on, and they lit him completely, and they spared no detail, and it was apparent he'd already climaxed once. His blue tie was flipped over his left shoulder, and around his neck hung a laminated card, and I realized it was a backstage pass at the same time that I realized he'd also brought with him a bouquet of flowers, a box of candy, and what looked like a short sword, all laid out on the table before him.

"Shit," I said, pressing the button in my left palm and grabbing Lady Ainsley-Hunter with my free hand. I had already started into the room, and I pulled her with me and then pushed her back against the wall, covering her with my body.

Chester swallowed a shriek, more of astonishment than of horror, and then Moore was past us. Keith had let go of himself and was now reaching with both hands for either the candy or the sword, but he never made it. Moore took him with a shoulder-check, knocking Keith back from the mirror and into the wall, and then grabbing his hair with one hand and his right wrist with the other. Keith howled in pain, then went quiet as Moore spun him about, and drove him headfirst into the wall.

That was the last I saw of it, because by then I'd turned back to Lady Ainsley-Hunter and started hustling her back down the hall, calling into my radio that we were evacuating, that Timmy should get the car going, that Tinkerbell and Wendy were coming out. Confirmations came back, tumbling over one another, and we were at the exit when Natalie came sprinting around the corner, making for the Benz. Dale had the engine going and Natalie yanked the rear passenger door open, scanning the sides. A cluster of autograph-seekers started to surge forward at the sight of us, then balked when they sensed they weren't watching a traditional, post-show departure. I climbed in first, guiding Her Ladyship after me, and then Natalie tumbled in, and we were moving into traffic when Moore came over the line.

"Hostile is down. Hostile is down and secure. Where's Wendy?"

"Tink and Smee have Wendy," I radioed. "Timmy's leading us back to the treehouse. Suggest you and Peter meet with Lost Boys to help with hostile."

"Confirmed. Advise John meet you at treehouse and unlock the door."

"Confirmed, out," I said, and then to Dale, added, "Take the long way."

"Way ahead of you," he replied.

Lady Ainsley-Hunter had both hands over her mouth and was bent in her seat, her head down, and Natalie had a hand on her back, her expression pure concern. My first thought was that, once again, Her Ladyship was vomiting, but then I saw Natalie start to smile, and she looked at me over our principal, and I realized that I wasn't hearing sobs but laughter.

"What the hell happened in there?" Natalie asked me.

Lady Ainsley-Hunter tried to explain, but couldn't stop laughing long enough to do it, so I did. "Keith was beating off in the dressing room."

Natalie's mouth opened in amazement. From the front, Dale coughed sharply.

"He was in a suit and tie and he'd brought *flowers*!" Lady Ainsley-Hunter managed to say. "I know it's not funny, I know, but . . . I barely had a chance to see him, the next thing I know Atticus has me against the wall and then Robert is flying through the doorway and there's this tremendous crash, and this poor man is against the wall, trousers at his ankles."

She covered her mouth again, unable to stop laughing.

"There was a weapon," I told Natalie.

That stopped Her Ladyship's giggles. "Was there?"

"A sword."

"Oh, dear. I suppose that makes a certain sense."

"How do you figure?"

"They had swords in ancient Sumer, didn't they?"

"Point," I said.

Her Ladyship sank back against the seat, and I took the opportunity to reach around her and get her seat belt fastened. She watched me, amused, and when I was finished she asked, "And what are we doing now?"

"Taking you back to the hotel."

"But it's over and done with, Atticus. Surely, Mr. Keith is not getting away from Robert, and I'm perfectly fine. I certainly don't need to go back to the hotel."

"It's SOP," Natalie explained. "We need to get you back to a secure location, to make certain that nothing else is brewing. We're giving Corry time to get back to the hotel first, to check that there aren't any surprises waiting for us in the suite. Keith could have been a decoy."

"A decoy?"

Natalie looked across Her Ladyship at me. "He may not be the only one interested in you."

Lady Ainsley-Hunter turned her attention to me. "What haven't you told me?"

"Keith isn't the only potential threat. We've no reason to believe there's anything else brewing, but it pays to be careful."

She started to ask again, then stopped and merely nodded. Then she started laughing again.

"All that work," Lady Ainsley-Hunter said. "Just to show me his little sword . . ."

Dale circled midtown until Corry radioed that he'd reached the suite and that all was secure. Natalie radioed back that we'd be there in five minutes, perhaps a little longer. When we reached the Edmonton, we debussed from the front, Natalie and I escorting Her Ladyship briskly through the lobby to the service elevator. When the car arrived, I keyed my transmitter.

"Wendy's on her way up," I said.

"Treehouse is cozy," Corry radioed back.

We got into the elevator, putting Her Ladyship at the back while Natalie pressed the button. I kept my eyes on the hall until the door was closed, and then the car started up.

"This is going to make me late for the luncheon, won't it?" Lady Ainsley-Hunter asked.

Natalie glanced at me, and I got as far as saying, "You shouldn't have to cancel but—" when the elevator stopped so abruptly Lady Ainsley-Hunter lost her footing, pitching into me.

"Motherfucker," Natalie said, and drew her weapon.

I followed suit, moving to put my back against Her Ladyship, to push her into the far corner with my body. I keyed my transmitter, opened my mouth to put up the alarm, and there was a screaming burst of static in my ear, feedback that threatened to open a crack from between my eyes to the base of my skull.

"We're being jammed," I told Natalie, and she started to curse again, but I never heard it, because the access hatch to the car was already opening, and just before the lights went out in the car I saw the grenade hit the ground between us, a flash-bang, and then another one. The darkness was complete, instant, and then it exploded into white, the light chasing after the concussion. The noise was incredible, disorienting, clogging my ears with echo and pain, and I felt Antonia's hands on my back, felt her fingers clinging to me as I went down. She had to be screaming, but I couldn't hear anything.

Then the burn started, finding my eyes and my lungs and my skin, the racing flame of pepper gas, and I had enough sense left to understand that was the second grenade. The car vibrated beneath me as something fell to the floor, and Lady Ainsley-Hunter's fingers were pulling at my jacket, she had wrapped her arms around me, and then her grip was gone.

Somehow, Natalie had managed to get her flashlight off her hip, the tiny Sure-Lite that we all wore, and the beam danced frantically for an instant, and I saw movement block the light. The car vibrated again and again, and the light fell to the floor, blinding me as it rolled free, and it caught Natalie's face as she hit the ground, the tears streaming from her closed eyes, the mucus and blood shining from her nose and mouth. Then the light rolled away again, and I saw a leg that wasn't Her Ladyship's, and I pushed off, bringing my gun up, and then my right arm went numb below the elbow and I lost the weapon.

I didn't take the hint, tried to keep going up, to find someone to attack, eyes to claw or flesh to bite, and then the club struck me again, and I was on the ground again, blood filling my mouth.

Natalie's Sure-Lite had rolled into the corner, and I saw the smoke and gas floating in the car, and then there was another pain as my hair was pulled, forcing my head around to look at the nightmare of bug eyes and deformed and shining black insect features. From beneath the Nightvision goggles and gas mask, I heard Drama say my name.

"Any alarm and she dies, Atticus," she said, her voice breathy and almost too soft to hear. "If you're not at home in thirty minutes, she dies."

I croaked at her.

"I've missed you, too," Drama said, letting go of my hair.

Then she kicked me in the face.

CHAPTER ELEVEN

My watch said I was a minute late as I came up through the apartment door, just in time to hear the phone's last ring echoing in the kitchen. I went for it anyway, diving across the table, but there was only the dial tone when I got the receiver to my ear. I hung up, trying to convince myself that I hadn't just killed Antonia Ainsley-Hunter, then broke into a fit of coughs that led to dry heaves and ended with me at the sink, running cold water over my head. I shut off the tap and straightened, felt the drops running down the back of my neck, beneath my collar, mixing with my sweat. Everything hurt, but the only thing I really felt was the drops falling from me to the counter and the floor.

I've killed her, I thought. I was as fast as I could be and I wasn't fast enough and I've killed her and—

The phone was ringing, and this time I answered it before it stopped.

"I told you thirty minutes," Drama said. "You're lucky I believe in redemption."

"I want to talk to her," I said.

"She's fine."

"Fuck you," I said. "Let me talk to her."

"Atticus," Drama said. "I could have killed you. I could have killed Natalie. That should tell you something."

"Put her on the line."

"Oh, all right," Drama said. "I'll have to go get her."

There was a thud as the phone was set down, then a silence. I heard the front door of the apartment open, and I pulled my gun and sighted at the corner, and Dale came into view and immediately threw up both hands. I lowered my gun, and each of us caught our breath. Over the phone I heard Drama telling someone to say hello.

Antonia's voice was thin, like a sheet that had been bleached one too many times. "Atticus?"

"Do what she says," I told her. "We'll get you back, just do what she says."

"I wi—"

Then she screamed, and the phone made another thud as it was dropped, and I started shouting for Drama to come back, to leave her alone. There was no answer, and I stopped shouting and started listening again, but there was nothing to hear. Dale was still standing at the edge of the kitchen, both fists balled.

The phone was picked up again. Drama said, "She screams like a girl."

"You hurt her—"

"Think it through, Atticus. Do you really want to be threatening me?"

I didn't say anything.

"Stay by the phone. I'll call when I'm ready. And I reiterate: Any word of her abduction, she dies. And I *will* know if you raise the alarm, Atticus."

Then I was listening to the dial tone, looking at Dale as he waited to hear the news.

The haze had started to lift by the time the elevator doors opened, and through the tears and the dissipating smoke and gas, I'd seen Corry running down the hall toward us, his gun out. All he needed was a glimpse, Natalie on her side and unmoving, me trying to find my feet, and it didn't matter that I was shaking my head, trying to tell him no, don't, he was on the radio immediately.

"Alarm alarm alarm," Corry said. "Repeat, alarm, Wendy is—"

"Dammit, shut up!" I shouted, and it felt like crushed glass was running in two directions inside my chest.

Corry gaped at me, but came off his transmitter. Over my earpiece, I could hear Dale and Moore each calling in for status.

"Help Nat," I wheezed. "See if she's okay."

Without another word, Corry holstered his pistol, took a deep breath, then stepped into the elevator.

The voices on my radio were getting frantic. I clamped down on my transmitter, said, "All units—this is Tink, stand by."

There was a pause, during which the elevator doors tried to close. Corry used his leg to block them, then slapped the emergency stop. Natalie was making a wet noise from the back of her throat, and as he took her by the armpits to drag her out of the car, she started coughing.

"Timmy standing by," Dale said.

"Hook standing by," Moore said. *"Request status."*

I pulled myself upright using the wall, fighting for breath. The only part of me that wasn't screaming from the pepper gas was my jaw, and that was because it had gone numb from the kick Drama had given it. My watch read eleven thirty-eight, and my best guess said I had to be at home, by the phone, by five past twelve. I tried to fill my lungs with good air, tried to sound as calm as I could before I transmitted again.

"All units, false alarm. Request Timmy to tree house at convenience, Hook landline in ten minutes. Confirm."

"Timmy confirms, en route."

"Hook?" I asked.

"Hook confirms."

"Tink out," I said, and came off the transmitter and the coughs I'd been fighting off struck back then, doubling me over. By the time the attack ended Corry had Natalie out of the hall and into the suite. I released the emergency stop on the elevator, started to follow, then realized my weapon was still in the car and managed to halt the doors just in time. I got my gun, then made my way after Corry.

They were in Lady Ainsley-Hunter's bathroom, Natalie already in the shower, Corry trying to sort her gear. He helped me get my radio off, taking the rest of my equipment as I stripped, then holding my glasses as I joined Natalie under the spray. He didn't ask any questions.

She was slumped against the tiled wall, her head down, diluted blood swirling at her feet. When she looked up at me I could see the source. Drama had broken her nose.

After taking a face full of icy water for thirty seconds, Natalie and I swapped places again. My watch was an Oris, water-resistant to one hundred meters, and I checked it again, saw that I had twenty-two minutes. The burning had stopped where the water was still hitting me, but everywhere else it still persisted, not as ferocious, but constant. There was nothing more I could do about it; pepper only relents in the face of three things—fresh air, cold water, and time—and time was the only sure cure.

Corry handed me a towel as I got out. Dale was now standing in the doorway.

The phlegm still bubbling in my throat made my voice thick. "Drama's got her," I told them.

It was on their faces that I was only confirming what they already knew.

"No word to the law, no alarms, nothing. The balloon goes up, she'll kill her." I dropped the towel, reached for my clothes. "I'm supposed to be at my place in twenty minutes for further instructions."

"I'll bring the car around," Dale said, and went.

"What do I tell Moore?" Corry asked.

"Have him and Chester come to my place as soon as they can, but tell them not to rush it. If the police catch a whiff, we're fucked."

"You think Drama's serious?"

From the shower, Natalie said, softly, "Absolutely."

I finished tying my shoes, grabbed my gun and radio. "There's another problem."

"Fowler's with Bridgett, and both were with Moore when the radios started," Corry said. "We're not going to be able to keep Fowler from coming here, or to your place, if that's where Bridgett is headed."

"Then don't try. Just make sure he doesn't find out why we've moved." I checked my watch, saw that I had just twenty minutes. "I'm gone. You and Nat follow as soon as you're able."

"What'd she say?" Dale asked.

"She wants me to stay by the phone. She says she'll call. She says again if we raise an alarm, Antonia's dead." I carefully replaced the receiver.

"What do we tell Scott?"

"Nothing."

Dale moved closer. "He'll know something's up, Atticus. He'll have to report this. He's legally and ethically obligated to report this."

"Then we'll lie."

"Atticus—"

"Dammit, Dale, Drama has her and the only reason Antonia's not dead is because she wants something else!"

He let go of my shoulder, scowling. "Don't shout at me."

I matched his expression with a scowl of my own, and then stepped past him. From the gun locker in my closet I took my Smith & Wesson, my extra clips for the HK, the ammunition I needed for both guns. Dale was where I'd left him, staring out the window. He turned his head enough to watch me dump everything on the kitchen table.

"We're going to need maps," I said.

"I have the Hagstrom in the car."

"Get it."

He went and as soon as I heard the door close I reached for the phone. Bridgett's cell phone rang twice before she answered, and before she could speak I started talking.

"Don't say my name. We've got a situation and it's bad and Fowler cannot be a part of it. Understand?"

"Uh-huh."

"Where are you?"

"Leaving Midtown North."

"Is he with you?"

"Uh-huh."

"I need you to come up with an excuse to separate from him."

"I can do that, but it might be a couple minutes. I'll have to go to the office first."

I was so worked up I didn't even appreciate the embellishment. "Moore told you where he was going?"

"Uh-huh."

"Dammit." That meant Scott already knew we'd moved from the Edmonton to the apartment, and that meant he'd be coming here anyway. "All right, don't worry about it. I'll call you back when it's safe."

"Well, safety is my middle name."

"Your middle name is Eileen."

She hung up, and so did I, and I stared at my spare gun and then set about loading the extra clips. I didn't have any immediate plan to use it; I didn't even have any immediate plan to wear it. But it kept my hands busy, it was something to do until the others arrived, until the phone rang again. Drama had as much as said we were now playing the waiting game, and I expected that she would make us wait long, to try and wear us down before she made further contact. The best thing to do would be to use the time well, and that meant getting ready for whatever might happen next. When the others arrived, we would discuss it, try to work out a strategy, a plan.

But just thinking that, I knew that there really wasn't anything we could do at all.

The pepper burn had finally relented, and now my insides felt raw. The illness I'd felt earlier seemed to have gone too, though if that was a result of the unending supply of adrenaline I seemed to have tapped or because I was actually healthier, I didn't know. I didn't much care. My face throbbed from where Drama kicked me, and when I touched my cheek, I could feel the swelling beneath the skin.

Dale came back with the maps, and a couple minutes later the intercom buzzed, and Natalie told me that she was downstairs with Corry, Moore, and Chester. I let them into the building, told Dale to cover the hall, then went out my apartment door to the top of the stairs. After a minute I heard them coming up, and when I saw Natalie leading the way, I waved Dale off. Wet hair clung limp around her head like sodden newspaper, and the swelling across the bridge of her nose had already begun turning purple and red. She swiped at a weak trickle of blood from her left nostril as she crossed the threshold.

Once everyone was inside, Dale shut and locked the door. Corry put Chester on the couch, sitting down beside her, and Natalie took the chair in the corner by the stereo. Moore remained standing. He waited until Dale joined us before asking if we'd received the call.

"She called," I said. "Her Ladyship's still alive, I heard her voice, not a recording."

"How'd she sound?" Chester was moving a glare over each of us, while the fingers of her right hand pulled at the upholstery on my couch, making a small hole larger.

"Scared." I looked at Moore. "They explained it to you?"

He nodded.

"We did everything we could."

He nodded again, and I knew he accepted what I'd said, but I also knew knowing it gave him about as much comfort as saying it was giving me. "Has she made demands?"

"She's primed the waiting game," I said. "Orders are to stay by the phone, wait for her call. If word gets out . . ."

"I heard," Moore said. "She hasn't said what she wants?"

"No."

"Doesn't make much fucking sense, then, does it?"

"Not so far."

Moore scratched at his eyebrow with his thumb, squinting as if trying to read small print. I waited for him to chase the thought, to see if he ended up at the same destination I had.

"How much time you figure?"

"It won't be until midnight at the earliest," I answered. "This is psych one-oh-one stuff; she's going to try to unbalance us. She can afford to make us wait, she knows that'll only make her position stronger, but she can only play that for so long—otherwise she risks the balloon going up whether any of us want it to or not. My feeling is we won't hear from her again until the long hours tonight. But we should start prep now."

"I agree. Natalie?"

She was already pushing out of the chair. "Dale and I'll go clean out the office. Anything in particular we should grab?"

"We don't know what we'll need," I said.

"So all of it?"

"Pretty much, yeah."

"We'll be back in an hour."

After they left, Chester asked, "Now what?"

"Now we wait," I told her. "We can't do anything until we hear from Drama."

"At which point what?" She was pulling pieces of stuffing from the hole in the sofa, apparently unaware she was doing it.

"She either tells us what she wants for Lady Antonia, or she'll tell us to keep waiting."

Her fingers stopped moving and she got shrill again. "We *can't* keep waiting, someone is bound to notice she's gone missing! I should be making calls as it is, I should be making excuses for her absence—"

"Soon as we get this sorted you'll be on the phone, lying through your teeth," Moore interrupted. "We have to wait until after the Fed is dispensed with."

She straightened, indignant. "I wasn't planning on saying that Her Ladyship had been kidnapped, Mr. Moore."

"She's got a point," Corry said.

"Of course not." Moore sounded annoyed. "The story should be that Her Ladyship has fallen ill, food poisoning will do fine. I'm not asking for any grand fabrication."

"That's not what I mean," Corry explained. "Drama's window is as limited as ours. She can't tease this out for too long, because as much as we try to keep the lid on, something's going to leak out. With all the media attention Her Ladyship gets, we can't have much more than twenty-four hours."

"Maybe a little longer," Chester said. "I can be very convincing."

"Good," I said. "Her life will depend on that."

Chester smiled ice at me. "At least she can rely on *me*."

The intercom went off again just before two, Scott Fowler asking me to please let him inside, and I responded by telling him instead that I'd be right down. I came off the button before he could ask why, told Moore I was going to be gone for a few minutes, and that if Drama called, to tell her I'd call her back.

Chester, still slowly destroying my couch, didn't think that was very funny at all.

Fowler was leaning against the side of the building as I stepped out, and the first thing he said was, "What the hell happened to your face?"

"Keith caught me with a wild arm," I said.

"Thought Moore bagged him."

"Hey, I helped."

One of his eyebrows rose slightly as he took another look at my jaw. "Why don't you want me coming upstairs?"

"I can't tell you."

"Why isn't Lady Ainsley-Hunter at the Edmonton?"

"I can't tell you."

"Why did you call Bridgett and try to pretend you were someone else?"

That threw me for a moment.

"Her cell phone identifies the incoming number." Scott tapped his forehead with an index finger. "Nothing escapes the ever-vigilant eye of the FBI."

"You're thinking of the Pinkertons."

"I'm thinking there's something going on and you're freezing me out. And I'm thinking there are a couple of reasons you might do that, none of them good, and one of them might have to do with the Backroom Boys." He shoved his hands into his pants pockets, frowning at me. "I'll ask again, and you can give me an answer."

"No, I'll give you a response, and it'll be the same one you just heard."

"What's going on, Atticus?"

I looked him in the eye and said, "I'm in a bad position, Scott. I know you're on the job, but so am I, and right now I've got a situation with my principal that requires my discretion."

"I'm listening."

"She's upstairs right now. She's well protected. She's also got company."

"Company how?"

I didn't say anything, hoping he'd do the math for me. He did.

"Male or female?"

"I can't say."

"You can tell me."

I shook my head. “I can’t, Scott. I’ve already said too much. She’s afraid you’ll report something back and that it’ll leak out of the Bureau office and to the media—”

“We don’t do that kind of shit, Atticus, you know that.”

“I know you, Scott,” I said. “She doesn’t. She’s used to dealing with the British tabloids, you understand? She’s gun-shy, she’s scared of being discovered, and my job is to protect not only her person, but her reputation. The thing with Keith this morning really rattled her, we got her back to the hotel, she told me that she wanted this arranged. She’s young and in love, what can I say?”

He searched my face a second longer, then looked up the side of the building, as if he might be able to see into my apartment windows. “And you’re using your place instead of the Edmonton because it’s easier to slip in and out unnoticed?”

“There’s a fear that some of the staff at the Edmonton could be bought. She’s worried about photographs.”

He accepted that with a nod, but I couldn’t tell if he was believing me. “So how long is this going to last?”

“No idea. She had Chester cancel her appointments for today and tomorrow. Food poisoning.”

“That’ll work for a while.”

“For a while. I’m hoping this won’t last more than the night.”

He smiled slowly. “What, you don’t like listening?”

“What kind of guy do you take me for?”

“The kind who likes listening.”

I laughed and he laughed, and then I said, “I need to head back up. I’ll call you as soon as she’s mobile again, all right?”

“Do that. And you can tell her that her secret’s safe with me.”

CHAPTER TWELVE

Bridgett arrived thirty-nine minutes after Scott left, just in time to help Natalie, Corry, and Dale unload the gear. Dale had driven over in the hardened Benz, but he came back driving his van, with Natalie following in her Audi. With the addition of Bridgett's Porsche, that gave us three cars in case we had to go mobile. Moore, Chester, and I sorted the equipment as it arrived, putting the weapons in the living room, the electronics in the office, and the radio gear in the kitchen.

Once everyone was in the apartment, Corry set immediately to work getting the electronics in order, beginning by taking all our radios and swapping their batteries with fresh ones. Natalie, Dale, and Bridgett went back downstairs, this time to put tracking gear in all of the cars. The Porsche, the Audi, and my motorcycle would all be outfitted with tracers. Dale's van would be excluded, because he'd have one of the receivers, and that meant that the other receiver would be hooked up in the apartment. The nature of tracking—unless one has access to, say, a spy satellite—is that two units have to be used, otherwise it's impossible to triangulate the signal. Assuming that we would, indeed, be mobile at some point, the tracers would be vital.

Nonetheless I was surprised when I found Corry in the bedroom, going through my underwear drawer.

"Having fun?"

"I didn't know you wore boxers. Well, not boxers, these are those mutant things, those boxer-briefs." He held up a pair and in all seriousness asked, "Are these comfortable?"

"They're one of my favorites."

"Good. I'm going to sew a tracker into the elastic."

"That will make them less comfortable."

"I want to be able to find you if you get lost." He pulled a spool of thread from his back pocket, and a small plastic box of sewing needles. "I'll let you know when I'm done, then you can model them."

"Sure. Fine."

He nodded and began threading the needle. "Like the silk ones, by the way."

"They were a gift."

"Sure they were."

The last person who had commented on my silk boxer shorts had been Drama, and maybe because of that, I decided to let the matter drop.

Dale, Bridgett, and I prepped the weapons, cleaning all of the guns, then loading them one by one, making certain the safeties were set and that everything was working properly. Chester watched from the sofa, her legs drawn up beneath her as if she was afraid to set her feet on the floor.

"Are you planning to go to war?"

"You don't know Drama," Dale said. "This won't be enough."

"God save us," she muttered, and then got up and headed into the kitchen.

Bridgett was loading the Benelli when she stopped suddenly and grabbed my arm. I was chambering rounds into the Mossberg pump when she did it, and I nearly dropped the damn thing. As it was, I lost the box of twelve-gauge cartridges, sending them rolling around the floor and under my misbegotten couch.

"Honey, could you please not do that when I'm loading a shotgun," I said.

She ignored me, putting her hand to the back of my forehead like she had earlier in the day. Then she scowled and told me to stick out my tongue. I did, and the scowl stayed put, so I put my tongue back in place.

"How are you feeling?" she demanded.

"You mean aside from having been kicked in the face and taken a lungful of pepper gas?"

"Yeah."

"A lot better," I said, and then I realized why she was asking.

Bridgett set the Benelli against the wall and got out of her chair, storming down the hall like she was intent on doing someone harm. I went after her, found that she was in the mess of our kitchen, standing in front of the open refrigerator, with both Chester and Corry looking on.

"Show me what you ate last night," Bridgett demanded.

"I made oatmeal," I said.

"Anything I should know about?" Corry asked.

"What did you drink?" Bridgett asked. "Did you make coffee? Tea? Did you have a beer? Any juice?"

My stomach suddenly felt as it had that morning. "Orange juice. I finished off the pitcher last night, made more this morning."

Without comment, Bridgett took the pitcher and dumped the remaining juice out in the sink. Then she took the open half-gallon of milk and dumped that out, too.

"I didn't have the milk," I pointed out, too late.

"Yeah, but there was no way she could know you wouldn't, was there?" Bridgett snapped the faucet on so hard I thought she might break the fixture from the wall, running the water until no drop of milk or juice remained.

"It's okay," I said.

"It is *not* okay, all right?" She swung around and looked at me, and for a moment there was naked hurt on her face. "For fuck's sake, Atticus, that bitch broke in here and poisoned your fucking food."

A quick survey confirmed that no one had taken food or drink in the apartment since their arrival, simply because that had been the last thing on their minds. Bridgett noisily cleaned out the refrigerator and then announced she was going to do some shopping. Chester, who had stayed in the kitchen, watching Corry work, volunteered to go with her.

"No way," Moore told her. "You're not leaving this apartment."

I thought she'd get shrill again; instead, she got quiet, and that made her frustration all the more evident. "I'm not in any danger, and I'm not doing any good here. I'm just being bloody useless and getting in the way."

"You're Lady Antonia's friend, and that makes you a target, Fi. You're staying put."

"You are not my employer, Mr. Moore."

"What Her Ladyship hired me to do extends to you. You're staying here."

"For how long?"

"For as long as it takes."

The two stared at one another for a couple seconds longer, and then Chester turned and slammed out of the kitchen.

"Maybe you should let her—" Corry started to say.

"I'm not going to lose both of them!" Moore snapped.

"You know what, I'll go alone," Bridgett decided. "I should be back in twenty minutes."

I locked the door after her, then stuck my head into the bedroom, where Dale and Natalie were working with the sweep equipment. "Almost done?"

"Almost," Dale said.

"Soon as you're finished, we need to talk about Chester."

On the monitor in Natalie's hand I could see the LCD readout cycling through frequencies in search of a signal that would indicate we were being bugged. She looked up from the screen to me, and her expression told me she knew not only what it was about Chester I wanted to say, but what conclusion I'd reached. Which meant she'd reached it, too, and therefore it wasn't just the bruising on her face making her appear so pissed off.

"When we're done," she said.

"Take your time," I said, and went back to the living room to load more guns.

"I know what you're thinking, Atticus," Natalie said. "Chester is a valid target, yes, she needs protection, yes, and that means she's got to be locked down until this is over. But I'm not the person for it."

"You're the only person for it," I said. "If we go mobile we'll need Dale behind the wheel of one of the vehicles, and Corry will have to man the gear."

Natalie pointed at Moore, who was leaning back in his chair with his hands folded across his chest. "Chester is his principal by proxy. He should do it."

"Like bloody hell," Moore said. "She's my secondary principal, if we're going to be picky, and if there's a prayer of retrieving my primary, then I'm on that action. It's got to be you or Atticus. Since Drama has already fingered Atticus as a player, it's you."

Natalie pivoted to face him, using both hands to indicate her bruised face. "I think this qualifies as a fingering, don't you?"

"Well, maybe as The Finger."

"Asshole!"

Moore nodded placidly. Natalie turned back to me, eyes blazing.

"You're the best one for the job," I said. "Even if it wasn't a question of vehicles and electronics, you'd still draw the straw, Nat."

"That's crap."

From the couch, Dale said softly, "Neither Corry nor I are as good at the close protection as you or Atticus."

That gave her pause. She ran a hand through her hair, then seemed to remember it had been cut, and scowled. Then she said, "Well, I'm not going to be the one to explain it to her."

We all looked at Moore, who said, "I'll do it, but after dinner. We've had one case of poisoning here already, no need to push our luck."

The meal helped ease the tension somewhat, and after that, Moore took Chester aside and spoke quietly to her, explaining she would be staying at the apartment with Natalie until we had a definite resolution to the situation. The two of them spoke for a long time.

I made up the bed in the office and told Corry he should take it. No one had even broached the subject of heading to their own home for the night; we all expected the call to come during the darkness, and no one wanted to be out of the loop. Additionally, there was safety in numbers.

"I called Esme," Corry said as he helped me make the bed. "She's taken Eddie to my mother's in the Bronx."

"Dale might want to call Ethan."

"He did at the office. Ethan said he wasn't going anywhere until Dale came home. They had a fight."

"I didn't know."

"Natalie told me about it while we were unloading the van." He plumped up the pillow, then dropped it on the bed. "This'll do me just fine."

"As long as you're comfortable."

"Speaking of, how's the briefs? The elastic loose?"

"Surprisingly snug, actually. Get some sleep."

"You, too."

I left him alone, shutting the door after me. Bridgett was already at the kitchen table with Moore, and she informed me that everyone else was down for their naps. We stayed in the kitchen, by the phone, and tried to keep from getting too much on one another's nerves, and it was a challenge because all of us were caught between a tension that wouldn't let us consider relaxing and the boredom that sets in when all you can do is wait. I made coffee and Bridgett made tea, and for a while Moore seemed unable to decide which he wanted more.

"Make up your fucking mind, dammit," Bridgett snapped at him.

He had one cup of each.

A few minutes after ten Bridgett stopped playing with the tin of Altoids she'd emptied hours earlier and said to Moore abruptly, "She's going to want Atticus to make the swap."

Moore, who was field-stripping his Browning for the fourth time, stopped his hands and considered, then went back to reassembling the gun. "Could do, yeah. Been thinking it's what she's got planned."

I put my back to the window, sitting on the sill. The closed blinds rustled against the glass when I bumped against them. "I don't," I said.

"Then you're being willfully naïve," Bridgett said.

"You're making it personal, between Drama and me. We don't have any evidence of that."

"She broke in here and poisoned you. She has history with you."

"And with Dale," I pointed out. "And all of us except you and Moore and Lady Ainsley-Hunter and Chester—"

"No, you were running the show when she last met you," Bridgett said, but it was less to me than it was thinking out loud, teasing out a train of thought. "She met you, she spoke with you, you're the one she made a connection with, however tenuous. Natalie's incidental, like she was in the elevator today. Using Keith as a decoy, that was to draw you out, not Her Ladyship."

"You want to explain that last bit?"

She looked at me curiously. "Again?"

"For the first time. That's new."

"I thought I had."

"No, it must have been lost in the rush."

"Keith had a backstage pass to the show this morning."

"Legit?"

"No, but a damn good forgery. Both Scott and I figured he'd made it himself, but the more I think about it, the more I think Drama picked him for the job. It would fit with what Keith told the cops when we took him to Midtown North." She began playing with the tin again, flipping the top up and down with her right index finger, snapping her fingernail against the metal. "His story was that he got a letter about three weeks ago saying that, as a member of Together Now in good standing, he'd been specially selected to meet Her Ladyship backstage at the show today. He swore up and down that he'd gotten the pass with the letter. We all thought he was lying."

"To do what you're describing, Drama would have had to access membership lists for clubs all along the East Coast," Moore said.

Bridgett shook her head. "The information is online. I've seen it myself, and we all know I'm not nearly as skilled as Drama is at these things. She could find it without breaking a sweat. Picks a chapter, starts searching through the names, sees if anything comes up. She found out that Joseph Keith had a thing for Lady Ainsley-Hunter, and was a little sprung in the head, to boot. So she wound him up and turned him loose."

"But there was no way she could control what Keith'd do backstage. Not unless he was in on it with her."

Bridgett snapped the tin shut again in annoyance. "Drama didn't *need* to know what he would do, she didn't *need* him to do anything other than be a warm body in the right place at the right time. If Keith had been backstage with nothing more than a smile and a bouquet of flowers—"

"He actually had both of those," I said. She ignored me.

"—you still would have gone lockdown, guns a-blazing. She counted on that, she knew his presence alone would force an evacuation, and she knew that you'd bring Ainsley-Hunter back to the Edmonton. Hell, she even knew when to expect you, since it wouldn't happen until after the show had ended. It's a lot of planning, but the way Atticus talks about her, I don't even think that would slow her down."

"It wouldn't," I agreed. "She got us doing exactly what she wanted at every stage without any of us ever thinking we were being played. Very precise, even elegant."

Bridgett snorted. "I wouldn't go that far."

I shrugged and let it go.

At eleven Bridgett went into my bedroom to rouse Natalie, and I went into the office and gave Corry a gentle jab in the ribs. He bolted upright the second I touched him, but either he was a little slow or I was a little fast, and he missed breaking my wrist. I told him there was fresh coffee, and that he should rouse Dale when he wanted company.

Bridgett was out of her pants and in my bed when I came back to my room. I took off my shoes and shirt, put my glasses on the nightstand at my side of the bed, and lay down on the covers beside her. She killed the light and for a while neither of us said anything, listening to the voices talking softly in the kitchen and the noises of the street beyond my window. Then she rolled onto her belly and put her chin on my chest, looking at me. My eyes are bad enough that even at eight inches she was blurry.

"This isn't about Lady Ainsley-Hunter at all," Bridgett said softly. "She's just bait. It's about you."

I put a hand on her head, ran my fingers through her hair.

"No comment?"

"If she wants to kill me, she could have done it in the elevator. She could have done it a year ago, she's had plenty of opportunity. Why would she wait until now?"

Bridgett adjusted slightly, keeping her chin on my chest, curling her legs up against mine. With an index finger, she began playing with the hoops in my ear. "Maybe she doesn't want to kill you. Maybe she wants to beat you. You beat her."

I thought about protesting that, about saying that I hadn't beaten her, and in fact had never had any interest in doing so. When I had protected Pugh, it had been Elliot Trent and Sentinel Guards who had gone after Drama, who had wanted that feather in their cap. They had wanted the capture, and Trent had gone to dangerous lengths in an attempt to accomplish his goal. But all it had ever been about for me was keeping the principal alive, and it seemed to me then, as it did now, that it was all it ever should have been about.

"You think she's trying to humiliate us?" I asked.

"I think she's trying to humiliate you, specifically, and KTMH, generally. Lady Ainsley-Hunter is the principal who made you guys famous. Add to that a bestselling book and lots of publicity. . . . If Drama takes Lady Ainsley-Hunter out on your watch, your career is finished."

The way she was flicking my earrings reminded me of her treatment of the Altoid tin, and it was annoying. I moved my head away from her hand. "Seems awfully petty."

"She murders people for a living, how come petty is so hard to accept? And don't tell me it's because 'she's a professional,' because that's a bullshit response. She's a professional killer, Atticus, and that means that something in her is broken, something in her head is wrong, and whatever that thing is, it allows her to do what she does." She squinted at the side of my head. "You should get another piercing."

"I'm almost thirty-one, Bridgett. The last thing I need is another piercing."

"Ageist."

"Suppose you're right, she still has to make it work for her, she still needs to call it a job. She needs that excuse."

"She does or you do?"

"What?"

"I'm wondering why you're justifying what she does," Bridgett said.

"I'm not. I'm trying to understand it."

She made a face and turned away from me, onto her back, so that we were lying side by side. The streetlight glinted off the hoop in her nostril, gave it an emerald shine like a star seen in a clear night sky. From the kitchen, I heard a chair scrape on the floor, a heavier foot moving away, down the hall. Dale.

"Okay," Bridgett said softly, and it sounded a little angry. "So what's that about?"

"What's what about?"

"This fascination with her. You talk about her like you actually like her, it's all admiration and shit."

I turned onto an elbow, but she wasn't looking at me. I gave it some thought, wanting to be honest, before I said, "She's very skilled. I respect her abilities. That doesn't mean that I approve of what she does."

"There's nothing about this woman that is deserving of your respect, Atticus."

"What she did to us today, it's not something many people could do even if they set their mind to it. The way she used Keith, if you're right about that—and I think you are—that was practically brilliance."

"No. It was sick."

I tried again. "I respect great white sharks for what they do, for how well they do it. This is like that."

It was the wrong thing to say, because she bolted upright and glared down at me. "It's their fucking nature, Atticus, they don't know anything else! We're talking about a woman who murders people for money! How you can even look at her and not be disgusted—"

"This from a woman who is pro-IRA."

"I've never been pro-IRA, I've been anti-occupation. I want the British out of Northern Ireland."

"You've justified, if not advocated, terrorist violence."

"There's a huge difference between trying to liberate an occupied nation and taking money to put a bullet in someone's head."

"Right, and bombing a high street and killing twenty innocent pedestrians, that's a blow for freedom? Terrorism is terrorism, Bridgett. At least what Drama does, she's honest about. She's not a monster, and it's a mistake to try and reduce her to that."

"What she does is monstrous," Bridgett argued. "By definition, she is a monster. And murder is murder, no matter if you're paid to do it or not."

"I'm not saying I approve of what she does. I simply respect her ability to do it."

"Well, I can't separate the two as easily as you can. It's sick. It's evil. It's seriously fucked-up."

"I think you're being a hypocrite. You'll allow for killing for a cause. Well, being paid to kill someone is a cause. May not be a good one, but it is a cause."

"I'm a hypocrite? You're the bodyguard who's defending the assassin, but *I'm* the hypocrite?" She got out of bed and began tugging on her jeans. "Fuck you."

"Bridgett—"

"No, seriously, fuck you." She finished buttoning her fly and pulled her belt tight, yanking it angrily. "You don't say that and then get to take it back. That you would even defend her behavior is reprehensible."

"I'm not defending her," I said softly.

"Liar."

I didn't say anything and she stuffed the tail of her T-shirt back into her pants, then went out the door. She didn't slam it. I heard Dale in the kitchen ask if there was a problem, and I didn't hear Bridgett's reply. I stared at the ceiling, tense and growing all the more angry.

It didn't bother me that she couldn't see what I saw. Few people could or would admit that they could. Moore, certainly, and Natalie, but even Corry and Dale would most likely balk at admitting to respect for Drama. But that wasn't the problem.

The problem was that Bridgett was so willing to equate that respect with approval. That she would so quickly take the moral high road and accuse me of taking the low.

That pissed me off, and when the anger finally ebbed, I was left with the feeling I'd had when I'd called her in Philadelphia six nights ago, the same sense of dull but rising disaster. I had tried everything I could, had tried for a long time now, and nonetheless I could see the new gap opening between us, as steep and dark and treacherous as the old.

Natalie woke me at a quarter of five.

The phone rang at three minutes past six.

CHAPTER THIRTEEN

"Starbucks on Third Avenue, two blocks from your apartment," Drama said. "Southernmost bathroom, seat-cover dispenser, instructions inside. It is now oh-six-oh-four hours. You have until oh-six-oh-nine."

She hung up.

"It's a run," I said, and started to relay the instructions. As I spoke, I removed my T-shirt, holding it while Corry began snapping one of the freshly charged radios onto my belt, running the leads to my ear and palm. Natalie was holding my Kevlar vest as if dressing me for a date, and Moore was rolling up my right pants leg, strapping the ankle holster with my Smith & Wesson in place.

"She's putting you on foot?" Bridgett asked.

"To start, yes. More instructions to follow."

"We'll get the vehicles. Three cars. You're wearing the tracer?"

"I've got a bug up my ass," I confirmed.

"He finally admits it," Natalie said, and helped me into the vest. While she fastened the Velcro on my left side, Corry pulled it tight on the right. When they were finished, I put my shirt back on and Bridgett handed me my coat. As soon as I had it on, Dale handed me my HK. I chambered the round, settled it in the holster on my waist, then checked my watch.

"Three minutes. I'll keep you posted."

Bridgett blocked my passage, fatigue and strain in her face.

"Sorry about last night," she said. "Stress."

"You and me both."

She moved her head, almost bobbing it, preparing to say more and then discarding the words for lack of time. Corry nudged me.

"Go," he urged. "We'll be with you the whole way."

"You better be," I said, and then I was out the door, taking the stairs as fast as I could.

The day quickly made it plain that I was wearing too much for the weather it had in mind. The humidity was rising, and I could feel the sweat on my skin as I ran east toward Third Avenue. The early August sky was thick with high clouds the color of cigarette ash, and several pedestrians were carrying umbrellas. Aside from my jeans, T-shirt, and jacket, I had my HK P7 at my waist, the Smith & Wesson 442 on my ankle, my switchblade, my radio, my wallet, and my cell phone. I felt like I was clanking with each step, though I knew everything on my body was secure.

At the corner of Third I checked my watch again, saw that I had ninety seconds, and crossed against the light, dodging traffic and nearly ending the run then and there when a taxi tried to run me down. There was no way to know if Drama was watching or not, either in person or through agents or surveillance of another means, and that meant I had to keep to her schedule. Risking death-by-cab seemed like nothing in the face of what the rest of the day might hold.

The façade of the Starbucks was being renovated, green-black scaffolding all along the front and around the southern corner of the building. Bills were posted on the wood all around, advertising either expensive jeans or an anorexic, party-all-night lifestyle, and upcoming concerts at the Garden and Meadowlands by bands I'd never heard of—yet another sign that I was getting old. There were two entrances to the coffee shop, and I went in the nearest, stopping just long enough to try to locate the bathrooms while noting the four patrons at various tables. I'd never actually been in the place before; much as I like coffee, I don't like Starbucks. They scare me.

There were two bathrooms located in an alcove on the northeast wall of the building, both marked unisex. A sign above each door said to get the key from the cashier, but I tried the knob on the southernmost one anyway. Locked. I turned and ran back to the cashier, a white kid who was rather obviously flaunting the fact that he had the latest issue of *Playboy* open in front of him.

"Bathroom key," I said.

"You going to get a drink?"

"I've got to pee, you think I need a diuretic? Can I have the key?"

I shouldn't have said "diuretic." It confused him.

"Give me a large of whatever is most like coffee and the key, please. Key first."

He nodded, checked the centerfold, who was not a natural blonde, and then retrieved the key. I took it and headed back to the bathroom, ignoring his shout for me to pay for the coffee first.

The bathroom was empty and the lights were on, and it was surprisingly spacious inside, almost ten by ten. The seat-cover dispenser was on the wall behind the toilet, and I reached through the opening and felt around until my fingertips hit the edge of something hard and cool. It took another two seconds to get a grip and pull it free, and I found that I was holding a box of Glory cigarettes.

Inside was a folded sheet of white paper. I glanced at my watch before reading it, saw that I had five seconds to spare.

The note, which looked like it had come from a laser printer somewhere, read:

> You can have her back.
>
> You must follow my instructions without deviation.
>
> You must keep to the schedule.
>
> You will proceed on foot north to 34th Street and turn west. At 7th Ave. you will turn north to West 35th. On the south side of the block between 7th and 8th you will find a 1999 model Lincoln Continental, navy blue, NY license H8X ND4, keyless entry code 443674. Further instructions are beneath the driver's seat.
>
> It is now oh-six-ten hours.
>
> You will be at the car at oh-six-thirty-six hours.
>
> Make me happy.

I folded the note and shoved it into my pocket, dumping the pack of cigarettes in the trash. I returned the key to the cashier, ignored the cup of coffee that was waiting for me, and headed out to the street.

Bridgett's Porsche was idling, double-parked, just outside. Farther down the block I could see Dale's van. Natalie's Audi was nowhere in sight. Wherever it was, Moore sat behind the wheel.

I turned north and started up the street, walking quickly. Drama had ordered me practically across the island, and she'd ordered it on foot. Thirty minutes was enough to make the location, but there wasn't going to be time to window-shop. I'd have to hurry.

Corry came over the radio. *"Where?"*

"She's sending me across town," I told my radio. "She's specified the route, and she's specified I do it on foot. Destination is West Thirty-fifth between Seventh and Eighth, there's a car there with further instructions. I'm supposed to cross on Thirty-fourth Street."

There was a pause, then Bridgett came on the line. *"That's Midtown South, she's sending you to MTS. Why in fuck's sake is she sending you to the busiest precinct in Manhattan?"*

"She's trying to draw you guys out, identify my cover. If you try to keep pace with me you'll back up traffic westbound. If you try to get ahead of me, you'll be loitering in front of a police station, and that'll draw attention."

"Which qualifies as alerting the authorities," Moore said. *"We can pull off, let you walk it alone, or we can put people on the ground to cover you."*

I was already at Thirty-third, crossing the street with the light and a cluster of pedestrians, a few of whom were trying to determine if I was talking to myself or to them. "Robert, I think getting out of the vehicles is an extraordinarily dangerous thing to do. At least in the cars you all have some protection. People start walking and she'll be able to pick them off at her leisure."

"You think she'll try to take us out?"

"It's a possibility."

"I do not like this," Bridgett said. *"She's trying to get you alone."*

"Turning onto Thirty-fourth now," I said. "I'm crossing to the north side of the street."

"I've got you," Dale said.

"I'm going to loop around," Bridgett said. *"Try to get ahead of you. I'll stay away from MTS until you're there."*

"Confirmed," I said, and fell silent. The foot traffic on Thirty-fourth was getting thicker, and I fell into a clump of pedestrians crossing Lexington. At the light I did another eyeball check, saw that Natalie's Audi was waiting at the light ahead of me, Moore at the wheel, and that Dale was still following behind him. There were a lot of people on the street, men and women moving with the strident purpose of people who have been forced by the need of a living wage to rise early and spend their day in toil.

When I reached Herald Square, Moore tried to slow down to keep me in view, which was a mistake and caused traffic to go apeshit. It wasn't bad enough that Thirty-fourth was a major east-west thoroughfare, at Herald

Square it was crossed on the north-south axis by not only the Avenue of the Americas, but also Broadway. Traffic there was always rotten, and by the time I reached Macy's, there was no doubt that, if Drama was watching, she'd made the Audi, which meant she'd pegged Moore. I got an earful of his curses before he gave it up and let Dale take over the tail.

By Seventh Avenue I was feeling the walk and beginning to perspire. The clouds had come together in a high and seamless cover. When I turned onto Thirty-fifth, my watch said it was six thirty-six in the morning.

The street was lousy with cops, either coming to work or leaving, or perhaps responding to some crisis. Cars were parked all along both sides, and the precinct itself was roughly in the middle of the block on the north side, a squat bunker on steroids. Sector cars were parked diagonally in front, and then, farther along in each direction, more vehicles in lines parallel to the curb. Just before the entrance, on the opposite side of the street, was the Lincoln Drama had specified.

"I'm at the car," I told my radio.

"Confirmed," Corry said, and immediately Moore and Bridgett echoed him.

The vehicle looked entirely in its element, complete with rust speckling its rear bumper and a dent in the front driver's side panel. Looking through the window as I approached I saw discarded bags of fast food, empty cans of beer crushed on the floor mats. The license plate matched, and the registration sticker was current. On the dashboard there was even a precinct parking permit, a laminated eight-by-ten sheet of paper, lime green, with the NYPD crest on it and the words "Restricted Parking Plate" and beneath it, "Midtown South Precinct." The permit would expire at the end of the year.

I unlocked the car, thinking that if she wanted to blow me up, this was a hell of a place to pick to do it. But the car accepted the code without anything more dramatic than the sound of the lock releasing, and the door opened just fine. Before climbing in I gave the street another look, both sides, back and forth, and there was nothing that caught my eye, and apparently I wasn't worth looking at either. In front of the precinct, six or seven uniformed officers were drinking from paper cups and talking, and not one of them gave me any attention.

Beneath the driver's seat was a folded Triple-A map of Manhattan, with a paper clip holding it shut. I opened the map, and a transit card fell out, along with a slip of paper.

One fare on the card.

Subway stop at the corner of 7th Ave.

Number 9 South to the Ferry Terminal——be in the second car.
It is now oh-six-thirty-eight hours.
You have 18 minutes.
Oh . . .
Open the glove compartment.

Like the last one, the note was typed.

I stared at it, then at the glove compartment, and the butterflies in my stomach went a little crazy for a second.

In the glove compartment was a cheap Motorola walkie-talkie, yellow, the kind marketed to suburban homeowners as a neat way to keep track of one another should someone get lost while working in the yard or walking their poodle. On a pink Post-it note stuck to its face was the command, TURN ME ON written in block capitals in black ink. There was a black knob at the top, by the antenna, and I twisted it, hearing the click, and then a short squelch of static. Then silence.

I kept it in my right hand as I got out of the car, making for Seventh Avenue. "She's sending me to the Ferry Terminal," I told my radio. "Subway."

"You go down there, we'll lose you," Corry said. *"Radios will be useless, so will the cell phone. I won't even be able to track you."*

"You're not telling me anything I don't know."

"We'll split it up. Dale, Moore, and I will go the long route. Bridgett, can you make the ferry?"

Dale broke in over Corry. *"Wait a minute. Did she tell you to get* on *the ferry?"*

"No."

"So she could be trying to split us up, send us out to Staten Island ahead of you, then make you double back."

"It's possible." I was at the head of the stairs down to the station, and from below I could hear the grinding of wheels on metal growing, the sound of a train coming. "Guys, I've got to move. You're going to have to work this out yourselves. I'll radio as soon as I can."

"You damn well better," Bridgett said.

Moore was on the line as I started down the stairs, asking Dale the best route to the terminal, and then I heard static. The radios we used for business, the one on my belt running leads to my palm and ear, were UHF, broadcasting on a repeater system that could be received throughout the boroughs. Powerful though they were, they couldn't penetrate the Manhattan streets. The Motorola in my hand was another story. It used VHF, and although it wasn't very powerful, it worked on a point-to-point system, basically direct line of sight. Which meant that if Drama was planning on talking to me, she'd have to have a relatively unobstructed view of my position.

The transit card had enough on it for my fare, and I made it through the turnstiles and to the doors of the car just as they were closing. The train started moving before I was able to get a handhold on anything, and I nearly slammed into a classic punk, decked out in black leather with a spiked dog collar and a torn Sex Pistols T-shirt, all topped off with a purple Mohawk. He brought his shoulders up in defense and turned a glare on me, but it changed to curiosity when he saw my face.

"Do I know you?"

"All men *are* brothers," I said, and wedged myself into the corner at the end of the car. There were no open seats, and at the next stop more passengers came aboard, dressed for work downtown. I tried to catch as many faces as I could, but it was pointless. If Drama was in the car, I couldn't see her.

I put the radio to my ear and heard static, the weak signal. A couple people gave me looks, wondering what the hell I was doing. Most couldn't have cared less.

Then her voice, far away, saying my name, over and over again, almost singing, like she was on a playground somewhere, eight years old and taunting me from the swing set.

"*—Atticus Atticus Atticus are you listening we've only got a few seconds you're taking the ferry* John F. Kennedy *it leaves at oh-seven-hundred go to the second foredeck by the ladder don't be late don't be late Atticus Atticus—*"

Then more static, and then silence.

I switched the Motorola off. The broadcast had been weak, too weak to be from the train. I'd caught the train she'd specified, so the only thing I could think was that she had been standing on a platform, maybe at Fourteenth Street, broadcasting as I went past. Which meant she wouldn't be on the ferry, which meant she could be anywhere by the time I reached Staten Island. There was no way Moore or Dale or Corry or Bridgett was going to find her in time.

It hit me that I already felt tired, and I'd been at this for less than an hour.

It hit me that I had been doing a very good job of hiding my fear up until this point, and that I didn't want to lose that now.

There was no longer any doubt in my mind that Drama was trying to strip me of my protection, of my support. The message about taking the ferry clinched it, proved beyond doubt that she wanted to get me alone. This was worse than a fool's errand, and there was only one way that made it make sense, only one reason to jump me through all these hoops to get me alone, to keep Antonia alive.

Drama wanted a trade. My life for Antonia's.

I dumped the Motorola in the first trash can I found, then sprinted up the stairs out of the station, already trying to get someone to respond to my radio call. Three lines of automobiles stretched around the corner of the terminal, cars waiting for their turn to cross New York Harbor, and I stood and scanned the line, looking for any vehicle I could recognize.

"Somebody come in," I said. "I'm aboveground, I'm getting on the ferry, somebody acknowledge."

"I'm with you, already aboard. Second row, middle. Where are you?" Bridgett's voice.

I was so relieved to hear her that for a moment I couldn't talk.

"Atticus?"

"I'm boarding. Supposed to go to the fore, second deck, and wait for instructions."

"Should I find you?"

I debated. Even if she could have reached the terminal before me, Drama wouldn't risk coming aboard, wouldn't risk trapping herself anyplace where there was no easy exit. But that didn't mean she couldn't have eyes present, someone or something to watch.

"No," I told Bridgett. "Keep your distance."

She hesitated before responding. *"Confirmed."*

The ferry sounded its horn, and I followed the remaining stragglers as they rushed aboard. I kept talking to Bridgett as I followed the walkway, passing an enormous anchor crammed into a corner, to the stairs and then up to the second deck. Most of the benches were occupied, and I could see a clump of early-bird tourists gathered on the aft observation deck to get a look at Manhattan as we pulled away.

"Why am I not hearing the others?"

"They cut out about three minutes ago. Could be signal loss, could be the batteries went dead."

"You have your cell phone?"

"I do."

"Call Natalie, see if they've checked in."

"Will do."

I turned to the fore, exited through the double doors onto the observation deck. We'd already left the terminal and I was surprised I hadn't even felt us go into motion. Continuing forward, I could look over the wall at the water beneath us, the short waves slamming into the ferry. The wind off the water was surprisingly cold, and the clouds had gone high again. Although the sky made the water look green and gray, visibility across to Staten Island was clear. On the starboard side, I could see the Statue of Liberty, stoic and stern and glorious, and she looked more to me like a guardian at the gate than an usher to the shore.

Behind me, under the awning and against the wall to the main cabin, I saw the ladder Drama had directed me to, marked with a sign warning that no one was admitted above. Attached to the awning, stowed above the beams that crisscrossed above my head, were old life jackets, faded safety orange, and nothing to trust your life to, from the looks of them. Faded paint noted that they were to be used in emergencies only.

I moved to the ladder and turned to face out again, waiting, listening to the wind and the gulls. The clump of tourists from the aft had moved forward, were emerging on my right, snapping photographs and talking in broken English and fluent German.

My radio crackled, and Corry came on, saying, *"Check, check, anyone read?"*

"Where the hell have you been?"

"A repeater went down somewhere, something, we lost communications when we left the Island. How are you reading?"

"Five-by," I said. "Where's Moore?"

"I'm here," Robert said.

"I'm on the ferry," I said.

"We heard," Corry said. *"Bridgett gave Natalie the update, we called in to let her know what was going on. You know your next stop?"*

"Other than Staten Island, no, not yet."

"We're just getting into Brooklyn, the bridge traffic nearly killed us. We're going to try and come across on the Verrazano. Keep us in the loop. Out."

"Out," I said. Off to the port side, I could see the bridge spanning the Verrazano Narrows, linking Brooklyn to Staten Island. It would take them at least another twenty minutes to reach it, by which time we'd be pulling into the St. George Ferry Terminal. Depending on what happened next, we'd either end up moving closer together or farther apart.

The tourists decided it was too cold and went back inside, and as they did, Bridgett came out, zipping up her biker jacket. She was wearing sunglasses, and she went to the railing and leaned over it, half of her six feet one dangling over the deck below, and with the wind blowing off the water making her hair fly, she looked impressive, and I knew she was posing. Then she pushed back off the railing and reached into a pocket. I guessed Altoids, but she came out with Cherry Life Savers and started chomping them down.

Something was beeping, and it took me a couple seconds before I realized that it wasn't coming over my radio, that it was a pager going off nearby, but there was nobody nearby with a pager as far as I could see. With my earpiece in, the sound was impossible to pinpoint, and I yanked it free, listening, then looked up.

One of the life jackets was paging me. I tried reaching for it and couldn't find anything, resorted to using the ladder, and on the second rung reached again. It was on top of the life jacket at the back, beside the opening onto the deck above, and I pulled it down, looking it over. It was black, new, with an LCD readout on the side for alpha-numeric messages.

I dropped off the ladder and turned it off, then used the buttons on the side to scroll through the message.

BLACKVWPASSAT . . . NJNADGAR . . . KEEPWATCHINGTHISSPACE. . . .

When I looked up again, Bridgett was at my shoulder and the St. George Ferry Terminal was looming large off the bow.

"Got all that?" I asked.

"Yup. Make sure I'm behind you when you leave the terminal."

"Keep your distance. She'll be watching, and if she thinks you're threatening her plans, she'll move against you."

She gave me a grin to humor me, then gestured that I should lead the way back down to the cars. As we worked our way back down I got on the radio and told Corry and Moore to stand by, that I'd have more information shortly. Bridgett stayed with me as I searched for the VW, even though I told her to back off, and we were about to hit the terminal before I found it. When she saw where it was parked, Bridgett swore, echoing curses off the walls around us.

"Bitch bitch bitch bitch bitch!" Bridgett said, and then she kicked the Passat for good measure.

It was the last car in the third row. Bridgett's Porsche was parked several cars ahead, and the way the vehicles were packed in, there was no way she'd be able to fall in behind me as we left the terminal. It meant she'd have to pull out as fast as she could and then circle back around, and hope that she'd be able to catch me before I got out of sight.

The ferry hit Staten Island with a gentle bump, and Bridgett shook her head once, then ran to her car. I tried the door on the Passat, and of course it was unlocked. It took me a few seconds to find the keys, checking the ignition, then the glove compartment, before I found them wedged between the roof and the passenger-side sun visor.

As I started the car, the pager began beeping.

DIRECTIONSUNDERFLOORMAT

I bent and lifted the mat, found a folded sheet of paper, typed in the same font as the others had been. Before I had a chance to read it, the pager went off again.

SHEKEEPSHERDISTANCEORSHEGETSHURT

Cars were beginning to move off the ferry. I dropped the pager in my lap, put the car in gear, and edged forward, then hit the transmit button in my left palm.

"Bridgett, you're going to have to back off."

"Like hell."

"I got another page. She just threatened you."

"Let her."

"Whoa," said Corry. *"She just what?"*

"Drama just warned Bridgett to back off," I said. "I'm getting messages by pager."

"Then Bridgett had bloody well better back off," Moore snapped. *"If Drama's twitchy, Wendy could end up dead."*

"You're assuming Wendy's still breathing," Bridgett retorted hotly. *"And Wendy isn't my fucking priority at this moment."*

I slammed the transmit button down again, breaking in before Moore could get a response off, snarling, "God dammit, that's enough! I want radio silence *now,* I don't want anybody saying anything until I come back on the line, is that understood?"

There was silence in my ear. The light at the intersection changed to green, and Bridgett's Porsche didn't move.

"Confirmed," Corry said.

"Confirmed," Moore said.

The cars behind the Porsche began honking their horns.

"Con-fucking-firmed," Bridgett said, and she must have popped the clutch,

because the Porsche ripped out of the intersection with a squeal and smoke. She took the left too hard, the 911 hugging the road, and then braked into the parking lot of a nearby BP station.

The Passat was an automatic, and I edged it forward until the light turned to red and the line stopped, then took the opportunity to review the sheet of instructions. Skimming them gave no hint of my next destination. Unlike the previous instructions, these were both incredibly vague and yet, at the same time, dictatorial.

There were twenty-nine separate steps I was to follow, given in distance and relative direction, no compass points. Number 29 itself was, "EXIT CAR. ANSWER PAGE." At the bottom of the page she'd typed, "DON'T WASTE TIME."

The signal turned to green, the cars in front of me began to move, and I turned left, activating the transmitter once more.

"I'm rolling. Turning onto Bay Street, coming out of the terminal. No way to tell where she wants me to go. I don't even have compass points to work with, just left and right turns."

"Damn," Corry muttered.

"That solves that," Bridgett said. *"I'm staying with him until we know where he's going. Anybody have a problem with that?"*

"No," Corry said.

Moore didn't transmit anything.

"Stay out of sight of the car," I said. "I'll radio you with the street names as I have them, follow at a distance. Corry?"

"Still here."

"You've got the map?"

"Hagstrom page 63, baby."

"All right, try to plot me on that, maybe you can figure out where I'm going."

"Confirmed. Have to say, we're way behind you. If something goes down, we may not be able to close the distance in time."

"How far out are you?"

"Maybe another fifteen minutes before we hit the Verrazano, even the way Dale's driving. Morning traffic."

"Don't worry about it," Bridgett said. *"I've got your back."*

The instructions led me from the ferry onto Victory Boulevard for almost three miles, past rows of dingy houses made dingier by the lack of color in the sky. Either the air conditioner in the Passat was broken or I didn't understand the controls, because the atmosphere in the car was thick and dead. I rolled down the window as I came up to Silver Lake Park, trading the security of a closed vehicle for the hope of air.

There was a grotesque monument to modern architecture opposite Silver Lake Park, a block of apartments that looked like it'd been built by the same firm that handled most of the U.S. Army's bunkers in foreign lands. My instructions had me continuing another 1.3 miles before a turn, and as I came over the crest of a small hill, with the Silver Mount Cemetery on my right, I caught a glimpse of the Porsche in my rearview mirror.

"You're still too close. Give me more room."

"There's plenty of room," Bridgett said.

"Give me at least half a mile, more if you can."

Her grunt was sullen in my ear.

I had another left coming up, and as the odometer confirmed the distance, I signaled the turn. "Left onto Clove. Heading roughly south now, maybe southeast."

Bridgett radioed a confirmation. Corry came back on the air, but there was a lot of interference, and I had to ask him to repeat.

"Said it looks like you're actually coming in our direction."

"Hope it stays that way," I said.

The traffic on Clove was busier than it had been on Victory, and I went another half a mile before hitting a light and checking the directions. I was on Step 11 now, and had another left coming up, in less than a tenth of a mile. Ahead of me, past the light, the intersection had been constructed around the Staten Island Expressway, and it looked like I had two choices: I could either make an almost immediate left or I could continue past the highway and make the left there. The odometer wasn't helping much.

The light changed, and I decided to err on the side of caution, making the left onto Narrows Road, then relaying the decision by radio to the others. Everyone acknowledged.

Step 12 said to continue .86 of a mile and then to make a right. Behind me, a black Camaro made its presence known by leaning on its horn. I ignored it, knowing that I was driving like a little old lady, and unwilling to take things any faster. The odometer ticked off eight-tenths of a mile, and I didn't see a right turn onto anything. The Camaro tried to get around me, found that it was blocked by a truck, and gave me more horn. The odometer was about to roll over another mile before I saw a right I could take, a busy intersection onto Richmond Road.

"Right onto Richmond," I radioed. If I had made a mistake, if I had taken the wrong turn when I'd gotten onto Narrows, there wasn't much of a point in sharing that.

Confirmations came back, and once again, Corry and Moore's transmissions were snarled with static.

Step 13 instructed me to continue 2.4 miles before making another turn, a left. The Camaro had gotten around me when I turned onto Richmond, and I drove, trying to monitor the odometer. If it was off, I was screwed, I'd have to double back to Narrows and try again. The road wasn't easy, either; Richmond was just as crowded as Narrows had been, and getting worse as more and more people left their homes to head to work. The Passat had a radio and CD player, and the digital clock informed me that it was now four minutes to eight in the morning.

I'd gone 2 of the 2.4 miles indicated when Richmond did a strange kind of left bank, merging with another road, and try as I might I couldn't get a glimpse of any sign telling me if the names had changed. On my right-hand side I could see a huge and well-tended golf course, but nothing said what I should call that, either.

"I think I'm off Richmond," I radioed. "I've got a golf course on my right, now, but I don't know what it's called."

There was a storm of static, and Corry's voice came through choppy, the words broken. I heard *"Richmond"* and *"club,"* but the rest of it was garbage.

"Corry, you're breaking up, I've got you at five by two, best. Can you hear me?"

More static, and this time I didn't understand anything he said.

She can't be doing this, I thought. She can't be jamming us like this, not unless she's very close.

"Bridgett?"

"Still here."

"Corry and Moore must have hit a dead zone."

"Could be on the bridge, it could be eating the signal. I'm still with you, don't fret."

"I've got another right coming up, Step 14, here . . ." I braked to a stop on the side of the road and stared at where Drama meant me to turn. I double-checked the paper and the odometer to be certain.

"Atticus?"

Once again, despite everything that was happening, I had to admire the skill of it. She'd picked the perfect place, just secluded enough to keep wandering eyes at bay, just public enough that our presence wouldn't raise suspicion.

Large open areas, and over the stone wall along the side of the road I could see the tops of trees, and that meant there'd be cover at the fringes, too.

"Atticus, please respond," Bridgett said, her voice harsher.

I put the car back into drive and moved forward, taking the right turn dictated on the paper.

"It's a cemetery," I said.

CHAPTER FOURTEEN

Steps 15 through 29 came quickly, one after another, miles in tenths, left and right turns along narrow roads that wound through the tended grounds. The entrance was past a set of wrought-iron gates into a wide gravel semi-circle, with smaller roads spanning off it like spokes jutting from a broken wheel. To the left I could see the administration buildings, the chapel, painted a depressing and smudged white. The cemetery was sprawling, and the plots spaced across sculpted hills and valleys, planted with grass and hundreds of trees of varying sizes. At one point a small bridge spanned a shallow pond with a fountain spewing a fan of water into the air. Picturesque. Most of the roads were unmarked, but a couple were named—Moldavia, Centennial, Restoration.

Cute.

Step 28 had me parking by a marble mausoleum on a slope, in the shade of several trees. I was at least half a mile from the entrance, and the buildings, the pond, all of it was hidden behind the foliage and monuments spread along the grounds. I killed the engine and set the emergency brake. A breeze had started up, making the leaves around me shiver. Through the open window, that was the only sound. There was no sign of anyone else, no mourners, no attendants, no one.

I got out of the car, and the pager started beeping.

BENCHBEHINDMAUSOLEUM . . . HAVEASEAT . . . HURRY . . .

"I'm out of the car," I radioed. "Moving around the back of a mausoleum marked Griffith."

"Wait!" Bridgett snapped. *"I'm not there yet, get back in the fucking car! Damn you, wait for me! I'm almost there!"*

"She knows I'm here," I said. "I don't have a choice."

"I'm coming up on the entrance, I'll be there in a minute, less, just wait for me, dammit!"

"Can't," I said.

A short stone bench, its back to the mausoleum, was positioned to look over a row of headstones running along the slope. As I was sitting down another page came through.

2NDONTHERIGHT

It took half a second before the letters carved in the granite made sense to me, and the fear burst so hard and intense it tried to steal my breath, tried to double me over. In my ear, Bridgett was snarling at me to stop, to wait, saying that she was past the gate, she was parking, she was getting out.

The name on the headstone was Logan.

I pressed my transmit button. "Get out of here."

"Fuck you, I'm coming to—" and then she shrieked, a noise I'd never heard her make, part fear and part surprise and so loud and so unexpected that I jerked my head instinctively to get away from the sound. She had kept her line open, and in my ear I heard the sound of breaking glass, a distant noise like the popping of a paper bag, and I was on my feet, turning to run, to try and reach her and in my hand the pager was shrieking, too.

"—shot at and took out the window. I don't know where it came from."

"Just stay in the car, stay down!"

"Like I have a fucking choice."

I silenced the pager, read the message. My hands were shaking as I pressed the button to scroll the LCD.

NEXT1INHERHEAD . . . MAKEHERGOAWAY . . . 60 SECONDS

"Bridgett."

"I can't see her, Atticus."

"You've got to go."

There was a pause, and then she asked, softly, *"What'd she say?"*

45SECONDS

"She's got a headshot. You've got under a minute."

"Oh." She said it as if I'd told her something of only minor interest.

"You've got to go," I repeated.

"Corry and Dale and Moore, they're not here yet, they're not responding to the radios, if I leave you alone . . ."

"She'll kill you."

"Atticus."

"Go. There's no time."

Seconds passed, marking her life.

I repeated myself, I shouted, I said, "Go!"

And she said, *"I'm going."*

Through the trees, I heard the growl of the Porsche starting again. I closed my eyes, listening for the gunshot.

Another page came.

LOSETHERADIO+PHONE . . . REACHUNDERBENCH . . .

I set the pager on the bench, pulled the radio off my belt and switched it off. I disconnected the leads, pulled the cords from inside my sleeve and under my shirt. I put them on the bench, added my cellular phone to the pile, switching it off first. On my hands and knees I looked under the bench, found a clear plastic bag stuck to the granite with duct tape. Inside the bag was a set of three keys and another printed note, cut into a small strip.

Up the slope. Ford Escort. Start the engine.
Leave the pager.

The car was last year's model, black, used, and parked just out of sight over the lip of the slope. One of the keys opened the door, and the same key started the engine. As soon as the power came on, there was a click from the cassette player, and her voice filled the car.

"Put it in drive. Accelerate to twenty. Follow the road, second right. Do it now."

The Escort was another automatic. She fell silent as I started moving, and I took the second right, and as soon as I did, she spoke again.

"The timing on this is absolute. No delays. I am *watching you. Accelerate to thirty."*

I was still in the cemetery, the roads still narrow, rising and falling, and thirty seemed about ten miles too fast for me. There was a bend at the foot of a long hill, and I moved my foot to the brake.

"Don't slow down," she warned.

It took an effort to get my foot back to the gas. The Escort sunk on its shocks as I made the bend, the wheels whining softly.

"First left, then straight. Accelerate to fifty until the gate."

The edge of the cemetery came into view, a service entrance. The gate was open. I slowed as I approached, and her voice told me to make a left and go with the flow of traffic. At the first light she told me to make a right again, and then, three blocks later, a left.

"Get on the Expressway, we're going to Brooklyn," she said. *"The traffic is going to be bad, so take your time with it. We've got all day, now, don't we? You should have a nice view of Far Rockaway as you cross."*

Her voice was soft and sure, very conversational. Her accent stayed mid-Atlantic, but when she said "Brooklyn" and "Rockaway," she rolled her "r"s almost imperceptibly.

"How about a little music?"

Her voice faded, and the Beatles filled the car, singing "Magical Mystery Tour."

"I like the classics," she said.

"Oh, shut up," I said, and after it was out of my mouth I realized that I was expecting her to answer.

She didn't.

Just as I hit the Verrazano, the music faded out.

"Traffic is going to be difficult once you get into Brooklyn, so don't worry about stopping or rewinding the tape if you get confused or fall behind. I want you to get where you're going, and I think you do, too. Now that I've got you alone, we have a little more time to get everything in order.

"I know you can't possibly bring yourself to believe me, but if you keep following my instructions, if you keep doing as I say, you will get her back intact. It should go without saying what will happen if you don't.

"You're wondering where I am right now. That will be answered soon enough. You're also wondering about her. That answer is coming, as well. You're certainly wondering how you can make contact with your friends, if,

perhaps, you can risk stopping at a pay phone to make a quick call. Believe me when I tell you that you can't. I'm monitoring you right now, Atticus, and if you stop anywhere other than the destination of my choosing . . ."

From the speakers there came the crack of a gunshot followed by a very stereotypical-sounding scream, both too clear to be anything but sound effects.

"Just so we understand each other. One last thing. Whatever it is you think is going on, you're wrong.

"Just something for you to think about.

"You're going to come off the Verrazano and exit onto Ninety-second Street. At the light, turn left. . . ."

It took until three minutes past ten for me to reach the destination, and she was right; the traffic was bad, and I had to stop the tape four times to keep from getting lost. Twice while driving through Brooklyn I saw NYPD cars, and each time I toyed briefly with trying to get their attention, but each time I thought better of it. How Drama was monitoring me I didn't know—there could be a tracer in the car, a microphone, even a camera sending her live video—but I absolutely believed that I was being watched. In its own bizarre way, we'd entered into a game of trust; Drama was trusting me not to do anything stupid, and I was trusting her to keep her word.

It seemed one-sided to me.

The directions took me through Bay Ridge, then north past Greenwood Cemetery and into the nicer homes of Park Slope. She kept me off the main thoroughfares, and several times had me making turns that reversed my direction or even took me in a complete circle. It was annoying; she'd already succeeded in cutting me from the rest of the herd, there was no longer any need to make certain that I wasn't being followed.

Finally the directions became more straightforward, and I went east through Prospect Heights, crossing Flatbush Avenue, and then south once more past Prospect Park, and it was then that I realized where she was taking me. The last time I'd been to this part of Brooklyn Natalie had driven, and at our journey's end we'd found the body of a man named Raymond Mosier. Mosier had worked for Natalie's father, part of the detail protecting Pugh before I'd been hired to take over, and he had been a glory-hound, the worst kind of guard. Drama had tricked him into accessing our security, and when she'd finished with him, she'd clipped the loose end by killing him.

Now, over a year later, I was pulling up outside Mosier's apartment once again. The building had received a face-lift since I'd last seen it, the brick exterior the color of an infected cut and the wood trim repainted. Flower boxes hung outside windows all along the first and second floors, tended and obviously loved. The tenants here had grown house-proud.

The cassette ended and flipped itself over automatically. Nothing came from the speakers but the hiss of magnetic tape. I stopped the engine and got out of the car, taking the keys with me. Aside from the key to the Escort, there were two others. The first fit the lock in the foyer, and the second opened the door to what had been Mosier's apartment on the third floor. I turned the key quietly, hearing the bolt snick back. The hallway was empty and quiet.

I turned the knob slowly, pushing the door just enough that the latch wouldn't fall back in its receiver. Then I replaced the keys in my pocket, took the revolver from my ankle and the HK from my waist, and filled my lungs with as much oxygen as I could draw. With my shoulder to the door, I shoved it open and then went in, low, crossing the threshold and looking for anything that needed a bullet put inside it.

Nothing.

I listened for several seconds and didn't hear anything but my own ridiculously labored breathing. I straightened, and used my foot to swing the door shut once more.

When Mosier had died here, the apartment had been spare, but furnished. There had been a Murphy bed and a big-screen television, a bookshelf, even a large erotic print hanging on one wall.

Now the place was bare. The only light came from the windows on the far wall. Even the Murphy bed was folded up, a note taped to the handle. I decided to ignore the note for the time being.

The bathroom was on the wall to my right, and farther along the same side stood the closet. Both doors were open. I hugged the wall, making my way to them, and peeked into each. Both were empty. The bathroom didn't even have a roll of toilet paper.

I holstered my guns and went to the bed, reading the note.

PULL GENTLY

The butterflies again got rowdy in my stomach.

Another potential booby trap. Or maybe another body, yeah, that would appeal to Drama's sense of irony.

With great loathing, I lowered the Murphy bed, and discovered it had been made, clean white sheets and an olive drab Army surplus blanket. Another note, tucked beneath the single pillow.

GET COMFORTABLE

I crumpled up the note and went to the window, which looked out onto the street below.

The Escort was gone.

I thought about what to do, and figured that if Drama wanted me to wait here, that was just fine by me. The tracker Corry had sewn into my shorts was hopefully still working, and that meant that the longer I stayed in one place, the sooner they'd be able to get to me. Even if Bridgett hadn't been able to raise Moore or Dale or Corry on the radio after she'd left the cemetery, she certainly would have called Natalie, and Natalie would have gotten in touch with them one way or another. Between Natalie at my apartment and Corry in the back of Dale's van, they could find me.

It was just going to take them time.

I sat down on the edge of the Murphy bed, rolled my head around, trying to loosen the tension resting in my shoulders. The Kevlar vest was tight around my middle, and now that I could spare a moment to think about it, pretty uncomfortable. My mouth was dry, and I realized I was thirsty, that I hadn't had anything to drink this morning but coffee, and with the humidity and the tension and the running about, I was in danger of dehydrating.

In the refrigerator I found a sports bottle of Gatorade, and another of fancy water with a label saying it came from a crystal-pure melting glacier in Greenland. There was also a box of baking soda in the far corner of the top shelf. I closed the refrigerator and turned on the tap in the sink instead, used my hands to drink my fill, then shut the water off.

While I was drying my hands on my T-shirt, there was a knock at the door. I went for the HK, backing against the wall, lining up a shot for what would ideally be the middle of the chest on an average-sized adult male.

There was another knock.

"Mr. Kodiak? I am coming inside. Please do not hurt me."

The voice was male, and had an accent. Russian. Or perhaps Ukrainian.

I didn't say anything, and the knob turned and the door swung open, and the man who stepped into the room was anything but average-sized. He was tall enough so that Bridgett would have had to look up to meet his eyes, two small, intense pebbles set deep and wide in a broad face. His nose was flat, with a ridge of scar tissue all along the bridge, and the shape of his mouth was defined and exaggerated by a sharp goatee, black hair. His head had been shaved sometime in the past few weeks, and the stubble along the dome of his skull made it seem like the top of his head had been smeared with charcoal dust. He looked in his mid-thirties, perhaps older, and he came through the door easily, his hands held casually at his waist, palms turned out to show me they were empty. He wore black jeans and work boots and a thin leather jacket that was unzipped and fell to below his hips. His T-shirt warned that it wasn't safe to mess with a big dog.

I adjusted my sights, raising to his head. He had big and strong down, but I didn't know about fast yet. Still, anyone wearing a leather jacket on a day like today was making a statement, declaring that either they didn't notice little things like heat and humidity, or that image was far more important than comfort.

My gut told me this guy didn't give a rat's ass about the weather.

He stepped inside, craning his head slightly, searching for me. When he finally spotted me against the wall, my gun on him, he smiled broadly and gave me a little nod.

"Hello."

"Close the door," I said.

"Sure, I was going to do that." He shut the door, showing me his back, then turned and motioned to the Murphy bed. "Should I sit down?"

"Not yet. Take off the jacket, slowly."

"Sure," he said again, softer, and he removed the jacket, dropping it to the floor.

"Hands on your head, lace your fingers and turn around."

He shrugged, did as I ordered. I couldn't see any weapons on him, no wires, nothing that looked like a radio.

"Now you can sit down," I said. He started for the bed and I let him get halfway there before adding, "There's fine."

"You want me to sit on the floor?"

"You got it."

Another shrug, and he got on the floor.

I stayed against the wall, keeping my eyes and the gun on him, until I reached the door.

"I already locked it for you." He watched me reach for the knob. "I'm not here to hurt you."

"Thanks," I said, and checked the door anyway. He was telling the truth about the lock. I moved away from it, farther down the wall, keeping ten feet between us, and readjusting my sights on him. "She sent you?"

" 'Tasha?"

"If that's what she calls herself."

" 'Tasha sent me, yes."

"And who are you?"

"She told me to come here and take you someplace."

"I've already figured that much out. Who are you?"

"Dan."

"You're Russian, Dan?"

"Ah, no, I am Georgian."

"Georgian, sorry. So Dan is short for, what, Danilov?"

He looked pleased. "That is right, yes."

"How do you know 'Tasha?"

"She is my friend."

I decided not to laugh.

Dan checked his watch, a big platinum thing around his left wrist, then started to get back to his feet. "We need to go."

"I didn't tell you to get up," I said.

The implied threat didn't stop him, which told me that either he wasn't afraid of taking a bullet, or that he knew Drama's leverage on me was such that my threat was a hollow one. He bent down and took his jacket, shaking it once to make certain that nothing from the floor was polluting it, then put it back on and made for the door. He stopped with his hand on the knob, smiled at me again.

"Please," Dan said. "We go now or else we are late. You can keep your guns."

And he went out the door, leaving me to follow.

CHAPTER FIFTEEN

Dan had a platinum-colored Mercedes-Benz Kompressor convertible that perfectly matched the color of his watch, and he drove it with the top down, oblivious to the threat of rain. The stereo was cranked just below painfully loud, rap music that Dan liked to share with everyone we passed. He drove with one hand, his left arm hanging over the door, thumping on the car in time with the beat.

"You want a drink, Mr. Kodiak?" he asked when we stopped at the first light.

"I'm fine," I said.

He twisted and reached into the space behind my seat, feeling around. The light changed and he glanced up, then let out the clutch and started us forward, using his thighs to control the wheel. It took him a couple more seconds to find what he was looking for, and he turned back around now holding two dripping cans of Bud Light in one hand. He dropped one of the cans into my lap, where the icy water instantly was absorbed by my pants, and then used his teeth to pop the tab on the other one. He still wasn't using his hands to steer the car.

I wondered what would happen if we got pulled over for having open containers, then took my can and set it again behind my seat.

Dan laughed and lit himself a cigarette, and when he caught me looking at him, asked, "What?"

"You're surprising."

He drained what must have been half of his beer before asking, "Why?"

"She's not this sloppy."

He grew instantly serious. "Oh, no, Mr. Kodiak. I am not sloppy. I know where there are police in Brooklyn and where there are not, and there are none in our way. 'Tasha, she trusts me to do what she asks."

"And what has she asked you to do with me?"

He smiled and didn't answer, and when the next song started, he sang along.

We ended up in Brighton Beach, which wasn't astonishing, since it's one of the major enclaves of the Russian mob in New York City, and Dan had *"mafiya"* stamped all over him. He stopped us outside of a bodega not too far from Coney Island Hospital, parking the car illegally right in front and then hopping out as soon as the engine died. He waited courteously for me to join him on the sidewalk, then held the glass door into the store wide for me, following close behind as I entered.

It wasn't a very nice bodega, dusty groceries stacked sloppily on the shelves, and the fruit and vegetables on display looked minutes from rotting. The cashier worked behind a smudged bullet-proof screen, and was a teen girl with bright red lipstick and eye shadow that made her whole face look tubercular.

Dan put a hand on my shoulder, gently, guiding me forward, and said something to the girl in Russian or Ukrainian or Georgian. Her response was surly, and he raised his voice at her, and she didn't say anything more, though she flicked two fingers his way in a gesture that could be universally translated.

At the back of the store was a steel door, and Dan reached past me to push it open, then gave me a shove through. The back room was twice as large as the store, and two other men were seated at a Formica table there, watching the Mets play baseball on a flat-screen television that had been propped on some cardboard boxes. The boxes had labels of different electronics manufacturers. Neither of the men looked our way.

A flight of stairs ran up to the left, and Dan indicated I was to start climbing, so I did. Best as I could figure, Drama just wanted me moved around right now, and my guess was that I'd get shuffled about for a while before we got to settle down.

I found myself in a carpeted reception area, with peeling wallpaper of yellow and orange flowers, three new leather couches, and a desk. An air conditioner whirred in a nearby window whose glass had been covered with orange paint. The carpet was green, an old shag peppered with stains.

Behind the desk sat an overweight white woman in her forties, wearing a hot pink tank top that revealed the fact she'd gone braless for the day. She had a can of Diet Coke beside her, a telephone, an intercom, and an open copy of one of the Russian-language dailies. She sat waiting for us with a bored expression that lasted until she saw Dan. Then she smiled.

Dan draped his right arm over my shoulders, speaking rapidly to the woman and giving me a friendly shake as he did. As she listened she nodded, and when he had finished she pressed a button on the intercom and said something, quickly.

A door at the back opened almost immediately, and a young woman who couldn't have been older than eighteen emerged wearing something that would only ever look arousing in lingerie catalogues. Her hair was black, loose about her face, and she was just close enough to pretty that I supposed she would be if I saw her anywhere but here. Her body was entirely visible under the fabric, her breasts still winning against gravity and her nipples erect from their contact with the air-conditioned air. Her pubic area was barely hidden by a black thong.

She stopped in the doorway and put one arm up on the frame, striking a pose, then turned to give me a view of her from behind. Her body was small and slight, and there were bruises on the back of one thigh. All of her nails—fingers and toes—were painted red.

"This is Katrina," Dan said. "You're going to go with her."

I realized I was in a whorehouse, and I saw where this was heading, and I said, "No, I'm not."

Then I stamped my right foot down on his, going for his instep. The move clipped him, enough that he growled, trying to pivot and drive his knee into my stomach, but I twisted away from him, out from under his grip, and the knee missed, but his right grabbed the collar of my jacket, keeping me from backing away. Before I had the HK up he'd grabbed the gun with his left, twisting it down so fast and so hard that I had to let it go or risk him tearing my index finger off in the trigger guard. The gun landed on the floor between us and I pitched myself forward, hitting him in the nose with my forehead. That rocked him, but he didn't let go of my collar, and with his left he shot two quick and mean punches into my right side, going for my kidney. Heat and pain chased each other around my middle and I almost lost control of my bladder, and the part of my brain that thinks these kinds of things at the worst possible moment wondered if I'd ever been hit so hard in my life.

He still had my collar, and I tried to get my arms up to his, turning to break his hold, but the kidney punches had done a number on my legs, and I got halfway through the turn before he shifted his balance and drove me into the desk, ramming the edge into my belly. I doubled over and he used his left to slam my face down onto the desktop so hard, the can of Diet Coke fell over. As the pool of carbonation swept into my eyes and hair, he changed his grip, using both hands to hold my head down, putting all of his weight against me, and I could feel his thumbs digging into my right temple.

Points of light began swimming before my eyes. The soda had found its way into one nostril, the carbon dioxide burning, and I sputtered and struggled, and Dan didn't relent.

"No more, okay?" He sounded as if I'd hurt his feelings more than his body. I probably had.

There really wasn't any choice. I tried to nod, realized that was never going to work given my current posture, and choked out a noise of assent. Again, his grip changed, and while one hand remained on my head, thumb still applying pressure, the other ran down my leg and located the Smith & Wesson. He threw that aside, then went through my pockets and took my wallet, my knife, every slip of paper I'd gathered during the day.

Satisfied that I'd been disarmed, he released me, and I pushed myself back up, feeling humiliated and angry and in a fair amount of pain. Katrina was still in the doorway, looking bashfully at her red toenails. The fat woman was already mopping up the spill on her desk, as if this sort of thing happened all the time.

Dan took me by the shoulders, straightening me up, and adjusting my glasses before letting me go. His mouth and nose were leaking blood, but he smiled as if he was having the time of his life.

"Okay, we're friends again?" he asked.

I sneezed, trying to get the carbonation out of my nose. "Friends," I said.

Dan tucked his arm around my shoulder once more, and together we followed Katrina into the back.

The room had a queen bed, a wet bar, and a speckled mirror on the ceiling. Attached to the head and footboard of the bed were leather manacles, lined with fur. There was also a couch, a Sony television with a Toshiba VCR, an ornate coffee table, and a cheap particleboard armoire. Despite all I've seen and done in my life, it was my first time in a brothel, and for some reason, I hadn't believed that people really liked this sort of thing.

Katrina crossed the room to another door, holding it open and beckoning for me to follow. It was a bathroom, the main fixture of which was a raised Jacuzzi. A shower filled the opposite wall, separated by a toilet and sink, both of which could have used a scrubbing. There were more mirrors.

As soon as I'd stepped inside, Katrina started to remove my jacket.

"Don't," I said.

Her attention stayed focused on my chest, and she cooed something I didn't understand and tried to lift my jacket off again. I caught her hands, felt them small and cold, and tried to get her to meet my eyes.

"I don't want to get undressed," I told her.

She turned and looked at Dan, who was standing in the doorway, said something in whatever it was they all seemed to speak. Dan, who was wiping at his nose and mouth with a handkerchief, grunted a response.

"You have to strip," he told me, studying the bloodstains on the fabric in his hand. "Either she helps you or I do."

The frustration made it into my voice. "I'm not looking to get laid."

Katrina glanced from me to Dan, then back, then cooed something again. Dan shook his head in response. This seemed to satisfy her, because she reached out for the side of my face, touching my skin where the soda had dried.

"Huh?" she said. "This? Yes?"

"You don't have to fuck her," Dan told me.

I brushed her hand away, trying to be gentle about it, though the truth was that my anger was threatening to get the better of me. She understood or she didn't, but either way she mimicked the gesture, perhaps mocking, and then moved to the Jacuzzi and sat at the edge.

"I gave you a choice." Dan dabbed at his nose once more, then folded the handkerchief tidily and put it in his back pocket. "Look, Mr. Kodiak, this is how it goes. You're staying here couple hours, okay? Maybe five, six. All paid for, best girl in the house, best room in the house, you get everything, all paid for."

"I don't want—"

"Yeah, I know, you don't. That's okay, you don't have to have her, nothing like that. But I need your clothes."

At the Jacuzzi, Katrina was gently splashing the water with her feet.

Dan was watching me closely, serious, and I saw in his eyes that I had misread him earlier. If he was a hood now, he hadn't always been one, and something in his expression reminded me of Moore.

This was what I'd been afraid of, what I knew would happen, and if Dan and I mixed it up again, I was pretty sure the result would be the same. Only this time, he wouldn't be concerned that we remain "friends." When he said he needed my clothes, I knew he meant that he needed all of them, and I knew that once I lost them they'd be gone for good, most likely burnt or dumped. I wasn't going to be able to keep the tracker, either; there was no way I'd be able to get it loose and hide it on my person with him watching.

I could only hope that the tracker had worked, that Natalie or Corry had been able to mark my location, and that someone was on the way.

"All right," I said.

He looked relieved, spoke quickly to Katrina, who swung her legs out of the water and reached around to the back of the door, pulling a terrycloth bathrobe from the hook there. I took my jacket off, then my shirt, and when she saw my vest, she made a comment to Dan. He answered, and she nodded, as if his explanation was perfectly valid.

I stripped down and stood in the middle of the bathroom, both of them looking at me, and I decided that I was still too pissed off to be embarrassed, so I looked right back at them. Katrina moved forward with the robe, and Dan stopped her.

"Your watch," he told me. "Your earrings."

I unfastened the Oris and handed it to him, saying, "I'm going to want that back."

He was turning it in his hand, and he nodded, and I was pretty certain I'd never see it again.

The earrings were another matter entirely. I hadn't removed the two hoops since I'd first gotten them over twelve years earlier, and while they moved easily enough in their holes, I couldn't get them unfastened, even using the mirror over the sink as a guide. My fingers kept slipping off the tiny bead that closed the gap in each hoop, and I couldn't get a grip to free them. After almost two minutes of my struggling, naked, tugging on my ear, Katrina took pity on me and draped the robe across the sink, then moved in to help. She had to lean against me to get a good grip on the hoops, and the heat of her body touched mine, and her breasts pressed against my arm and chest, and my body reacted.

When they were out, she handed them to Dan, then offered me the robe.

"You have anything up in your ass?" Dan asked.

I needed a second to properly parse the sentence. "No."

"You telling the truth or do I need to check you?"

"I'm telling the truth."

He rubbed at his goatee, then held out his hand. "Glasses, now, please. You will get them back."

I gave him my glasses, and finally felt naked.

"Okay, this is good, now," Dan said. "Take the hot tub or the shower, Katrina will stay with you."

Katrina closed the door after him, then went back to the Jacuzzi, shucking what little she was wearing and lowering herself into the water with a gasp and a sigh.

"You come in?" she asked, and I caught a blurry motion of her hand that I assumed was an attempt to beckon me closer. "Come here, *da*?"

I took a shower instead.

When I emerged wearing my robe, Katrina was on her back on the bed, idly toying with one of the manacles from the headboard, her hair carefully draped across her breasts. I shook my head and she finally took the hint that I had no plans to avail myself of her body. She left the bed and took some clothes from the armoire, putting on a pair of cutoffs and a yellow *Powerpuff Girls* T-shirt, then moved to the couch and switched on MTV. Every so often she would glance my way, and a couple of times she tried communicating with me in broken English, asking if I wanted anything, and each time I said no.

There were no clocks in the room but for the VCR, and that one hadn't been set. Best as I could figure from the television, it was over an hour before the woman who had been at the desk came back to check on us, carrying my glasses. I checked them before slipping them back on, but nothing seemed different about them. Katrina and she had a brief conversation that seemed to be about me, with the older woman making some interesting gestures and sounding unhappy or, at least, displeased, though whether that was with Katrina or with me, I never knew. Then she left us alone again.

This was clearly a holding position, someplace Drama wanted me stored until she was ready to move me to the next phase of the game, ideally the return of Lady Ainsley-Hunter. The longer I was in the same place, the greater the chance that someone would be able to locate me. What they did then would depend on whose head prevailed, but I suspected it would be Moore who assumed command in the field. Bridgett would be all for rushing in to save me—she felt I was one up on her in that regard, and I think it bothered her—but Moore would try to set up surveillance and wait for me to move again.

That was what I thought at first.

Sometime in the afternoon, though, I started wondering if maybe it had been more than simple radio trouble that had made me lose contact with everyone but Bridgett. Until I'd met Dan, I was relatively confident that Drama was working solo, and in that case she couldn't have been in two places at once, which meant she couldn't have been in position at the cemetery *and* have been in position to do harm to Moore, Dale, and Corry. But Dan's presence meant that she knew people, was willing to work with them, and consequently it was possible that she'd had someone take my friends out, in one fashion or another.

It wasn't a thought that made sitting on the couch, watching yet another overproduced and underlit music video, easy to take. I got up and started to pace around the room. I opened the armoire, looked inside for something that might fit me. Not only was there nothing I could put on without splitting, there was nothing appropriate to my gender. I contemplated trying to leave the room, but had a strong suspicion that I'd just end up in a lot of pain, or worse, unconscious. I didn't want that; I didn't want to miss anything.

Just as I thought I was going to go well and truly stir-crazy, the door opened and Dan returned, carrying a paper sack from The Gap.

"Clothes," he informed me, throwing the bag on the bed. "Put them on quickly, please, we have to go."

He turned to Katrina and the two began talking as I dumped out the contents. None of my original clothes were there; everything was new. There was a set of replacement underwear still in its wrapping, and a box of Nike sneakers. The pants were black with cargo pockets, and the shirt was a simple white T-shirt with a pocket over the left breast. There was even a belt.

Everything fit, and I was dressed before Dan and Katrina had stopped talking.

"Where's my watch?" I asked.

"Sorry."

"My father gave me that watch for my thirtieth birthday. I want it back."

"You talk to 'Tasha about the watch, okay?"

"Am I going to see her?"

"Soon now, very soon." He studied me with something like approval. "Katrina says you didn't touch her."

"She's lying. We broke the bed."

He laughed. "Sure you did, sure, okay. Now we go, you follow me."

"I follow you," I said, and I did, right out the door and into the two men I'd seen downstairs when I'd first arrived.

It was my own fault, I'd let my guard down and I walked right into it, and as each of the men grabbed my arms, Dan turned around and nailed me in the solar plexus. I lost my breath and most of my balance and before I'd begun to recover either, he'd taken my glasses and pocketed them. From another pocket he produced a black cloth bag, and he had it over my head, had it tied, before I could protest, yet alone resist.

"Sorry," he said. "Saves time."

Then something hit me on the back of the head, and instead of just seeing black because my head was in a bag, I saw a whole different darkness.

CHAPTER SIXTEEN

He used ammonia to bring me back, waving the broken ampoule under my nose until the shock and pain charging through my sinuses forced my eyes open. The disorientation was instant and, for seconds, total, and my first instinct was to fight, so I tried swinging at the man who was causing me pain. The punch connected with his jaw and he grunted, dropped the ammonia, and grabbed my arms. It took another couple of seconds with him shouting at me before I understood what it was he was trying to tell me.

"You're to meet her!" Dan was saying. "Now, you're going now, Mr. Kodiak! Stop fighting me, you're going now!"

I stopped struggling, trying to recognize the face in front of me. I was on my back, on something hard, and when I tried to sit up, Dan shoved me back down. He was hard to see, and the space past him was utterly dark, and I knew I'd lost my glasses again.

"You're done, yes? No more fighting?"

"No more fighting," I agreed.

He let me go, moving back on his haunches, his head down. From his jacket pocket he produced my glasses. I put them on, realized I was in the back of a delivery van of some kind. As I sat up the ammonia still lingering in my sinuses made me sneeze, and my head hurt so badly I wanted to weep.

"You going to puke?" Dan asked.

"No." I massaged my forehead, trying to soothe the pain. "You didn't have to knock me out."

Again, he sounded apologetic. " 'Tasha's orders. We had to take you back to the street, long drive, she didn't want you making talk, you understand."

"You could have gagged me."

"She said knock you out, I do what she says."

He reached past me and pushed open the doors at the back of the van, climbed out, and offered me a hand. I ignored it, swung my legs around slowly, and got out.

It was night, though how late I couldn't tell, and at some point while I'd been out it had rained, because everything around us glistened with reflected light. The humid air stank of feces and rotten food, and I looked around and saw water and then the length of Manhattan in the distance, and I realized I was smelling the Hudson. A sign at the corner of the street said we were at Frank Sinatra Park.

"Hoboken."

"Hoboken," Dan confirmed cheerfully, slamming the rear doors. Then he came around to where I stood, handed me a paper lunch bag, and then passed me and climbed behind the wheel.

"Wait," I said.

"No. No more waiting," he replied, starting the engine with one hand and slamming the door with the other. He leaned out the open window. "Good to meet you, Mr. Kodiak."

For some reason, I shook his hand when he offered it. Maybe it was my expression or my grip, but it gave him a last laugh, and then he put the van in gear and pulled out. I watched as the taillights went down the block, then slipped around a distant corner.

There didn't seem to be anyone else around. A couple of boats were out on the Hudson, moving lazily on the water, and I saw the lights of a helicopter as it lifted off from the heliport on Thirty-fourth Street. Seconds later, the sound of the rotors reached me, then faded. From Hoboken I could hear traffic, automobiles on the main roads, but there didn't seem to be a lot of them, and I thought it had to be past midnight, if not later. To the north, over the river, I could see the lights spanning the GW Bridge. A couple cars were parked along the curb nearby, though there was no sign of any of the owners. One of them was a Ford Escort, and I looked at the license plate and confirmed that it was the same one I'd driven from the cemetery.

I remembered that I had a paper bag in my hand and decided now would be the best time to open it. Inside was a key, another cheap Motorola walkie-talkie—this one blue—and my watch. The key went with the Escort.

I put the watch on my wrist, the key in my pocket, and dumped the bag in a trash can at the edge of the park before switching on the walkie-talkie. Then I pressed the transmit button.

"I'm here," I said.

"I know," Drama said. *"How's your head?"*

"It hurts. Are we almost finished? It's been a long day."

"For us both. If you're asking if I'm ready to return her, the answer is yes. Shall I tell you how this will work?"

"Please."

"I am sitting behind an Accuracy International AWM, which is pointed at your principal's head. As long as you do as I say, sighting her will be all that I do. However . . ."

"I understand."

"I never doubted that you would. You will keep the radio on and I will direct you to her location. Begin by turning to your left and proceeding to the corner. Stay to the sidewalk. At the corner, turn right and keep walking. I'll let you know where to stop."

Turning left meant leaving the park and walking down Third Street about twenty yards, putting my back to the Hudson. On my right, a chain-link fence stood about eight feet high, topped with barbed wire. Beyond it, in the darkness, I could see what had once been space for piers and warehouses, but was now nothing more than an enormous expanse of broken pavement, scattered with rusting pieces of scaffolding and some very determined weeds that had managed to push through the cracks in the concrete.

The corner was River Street, and I made the right, still following the fence. Fifteen feet or so along, the weeds thickened, spilling through the fence, and a large sign hung on the chain-link, stating that the area was slated for development, to be "reborn" as something called The South Waterfront. I'd read about it in the papers, but never actually been down here before. A lot of construction was planned for the area, Sinatra Park being only a small part of it. Office buildings and hotels were supposed to start going up soon, financed by the likes of Trump and Lefrak. There had even been talk of attempting to move the Stock Exchange from New York to the location, but it would never happen.

"What did you think of Dan?" Drama asked.

"Interesting fellow," I said. " 'Tasha?"

"Just a name." She said it dismissively. *"There's an opening in the fence another five meters or so from your position. You can make it if you crawl."*

It took another minute before I found the gap, obscured by weeds. The ground nearby was deep with broken glass and trash, and I had to belly-crawl to get through the gap, and I took it slow. Even knowing that Drama was nearby with a rifle, I found myself more afraid of catching tetanus from a rusty nail. I couldn't remember the last time I'd been immunized.

When I was through I got to my feet, brushing myself off, looking around. A couple of towers for power cables stood nearby, anchored to concrete slabs. Past them were chunks of abandoned machinery, broken and rusted pieces. As I came around a tower, I got a good look at the space. There was almost no cover to speak of for at least one hundred yards, and even though the streetlights didn't do much to illuminate the area, anyone looking with Nightvision or infrared would have no difficulties picking me out.

"Walk forward, as if going to the water."

I picked my way around the largest piles of junk. As I crossed out into the open, there was a rumble of thunder, and distant lightning jumped clouds. My heart was surprisingly steady in my chest, and my breathing was easy, and I wondered what I should make of that. Drama had to have line of sight on me, I had to be close to my principal, and I should have been very scared. But I wasn't.

"Stop. Turn left."

Looking past the scattered garbage, I could see the length of the shattered pier, all the way to the far fence on the north side. Beyond its edge, maybe half a mile away, a building sat just on the water, a road running between it and a sharp slope to the east. At the top of the slope I saw the nimbus of sodium lights, but not the lights themselves.

She had to be on the slope, on the high ground, and the odds were that I was looking right at her.

"There's an oil drum ahead of you," Drama said. *"She's inside."*

I lowered the radio, saw the container, and walked toward it. As I approached I could see that the cover had been removed, but I was almost on top of it before I could look inside, and when I did I saw Antonia Ainsley-Hunter, shivering, bound, a black cloth bag over her head.

"Antonia," I said. "It's Atticus, I'm here."

She jerked at the sound of my voice, turning her head, trying to see me with her covered eyes. She made a noise, and I realized that she'd been gagged, too. The Motorola had a clip, and I hung the walkie-talkie from my belt before reaching for her.

"I'm going to touch you," I said. "I'm going to remove the hood."

She tried to nod, made another sound that would probably have been inaudible if not for the amplification from the metal that surrounded her. I touched her as gently as I could, knowing that she'd had unwelcome hands on her too much already, and got my fingers along the edge of the bag at her neck, feeling around until I found where it had been tied. The knot was easy, and I undid it, then pulled the bag off and threw it down.

The look in her eyes was desperate gratitude, but there were no tears. A ball-gag was in her mouth, but I decided that could wait, and reached in to take her beneath the arms. She tried to move to assist me, but there was nowhere for her to go, and in the end I had to almost fold my upper body in with her to get a grip. I pulled her up against the edge of the barrel where I was leaning, tipping it against my body, backing up a little at a time to ease her out. I had her mostly out when the barrel finally tipped all the way, and its hollow clang on the concrete was followed closely by another roll of thunder.

She couldn't stand, and I lowered her to the ground, stretching her legs out in front of her. Her hands and feet had been bound with cord, and again the knots weren't too difficult, and I freed her extremities, then removed the gag. When it came free she leaned forward, coughing dry heaves, and I crouched beside her, putting a hand on her back. She was choking and coughing and trying to speak all at once. I ran my hands over her body quickly, feeling for injuries. As far as I could tell, she wasn't hurt beyond the effects of having been held captive for almost thirty-six hours.

"Just breathe," I told her. "You're going to be fine, just breathe."

It took another minute before she could control herself enough to manage any speech at all.

"Get me the hell out of here," she rasped.

She needed most of ten minutes before she could compose herself, before she was willing to try to get to her feet. Drama remained silent the whole time, though I knew she was watching, and I knew the crosshairs were still resting on Her Ladyship. When Antonia finally was willing to stand, I had to help her to her feet, and when she tried her first steps, she almost fell, and I had to catch her.

"I'm all right." Antonia's voice was raw and disused. "I can do this."

"Take your time."

"No, I want to go now, I need to get out of here."

"All right," I said, and I gave her my arm and together we started to make our way to the fence.

"You're not going with her," Drama said softly.

The voice had an immediate effect on Lady Ainsley-Hunter, and despite her fatigue and her pain, she recoiled from me, looking frantically for the source of the sound. Her ankle glanced off a piece of broken pipe as she moved back, but I caught her before she tripped.

"Walkie-talkie," I explained, helping her upright once more, seeing her confusion, her near-panic. "It's all right, I won't let her hurt you."

"Where . . . where is she?"

"No idea." Still holding her with one hand, I took the Motorola off my belt and keyed the transmitter, saying, "I'm going to walk her to the car."

"No." She was stern, but her voice remained soft. A teacher instructing a rebellious student. *"Tell her where it is, give her the key. You're not going with her."*

I moved Antonia around so that I stood between her and the distant slope.

"Atticus."

"I've done everything you've asked," I said. "You'll get what you want. But I want *this*. I need to see her to the car, I need to see her drive away. It's my job."

The Motorola went silent.

"You'll get nothing," I added.

"She goes, I'll get what I want?"

"You have my word."

More silence.

"One condition. You make her promise that she goes straight to your apartment, that she stops for no one, she contacts no one, until she's there."

"Done."

"I want to hear her say it."

I held the Motorola out for Antonia. "I need you to tell her you'll do exactly as she asks."

"You're not coming with me?"

"I'll follow later," I said.

"I don't understand."

"I need you to promise."

"I promise," Antonia said, and then repeated, to the radio, "I promise."

"Then go ahead," Drama said.

Halfway to the car there was a percussive clap of thunder and an almost instant flare of lightning, and the rain began to pour, hammering the ground with heavy drops that soaked us both, filling my new clothes with water.

Antonia stayed on my arm, concentrating on putting one step in front of the other, and though I didn't ask her, she told me anyway.

"I remember the elevator and the lights going out and the noise. After that things get horribly disjointed. I remember waking up as she was binding me, and I tried to scream and she'd gagged me. I don't even know where I was half the time. She wouldn't tell me *anything,* Atticus, she wouldn't tell me *why*. She wouldn't tell me anything. . . ."

By the time we made the turn back to the park she'd forced her way through the trauma, and her legs weren't all water anymore, and she was willing to try walking on her own. When we reached the car, I took the key from my pocket, unlocked the door, and helped her get behind the wheel. On the passenger seat, Drama had left an open Triple-A map, a route highlighted on the paper. Antonia dropped into the seat and stared over the dash for a couple of seconds, massaging her wrists one after the other, then noticed the map.

"Directions," I explained. "Back to my place."

"What do I say to them?" she asked. The rain pounding the roof of the car made it hard to hear her.

"I don't know," I said, because it was the truth.

Antonia searched my face. "She's going to kill you, isn't she?"

I didn't say anything. It seemed like Drama had gone through a lot of trouble just to put a bullet in my head, but I wasn't taking bets on how the night was going to end.

"Atticus—come with me."

I pressed the car key into her palm. "You want to take the Holland Tunnel. You have to go now, Your Ladyship."

She looked at the piece of metal I'd put in her hand as if she'd never seen anything quite like it before, then put it in the ignition. The engine started, and I stepped back, one hand still on the door.

"Put your seat belt on," I said.

She tried to laugh, but all she managed was a wobbly smile. Once she'd snapped the belt into place, she said, "Thank you."

"For you, anytime," I said, and I shut the door, stepping back from the vehicle. Through the water streaming down the window, I thought I could see her giving me one last look, and then the headlights came on and she pulled away.

When the Escort had disappeared into the rain and the night, I turned and started making my way to the slope, to where Drama waited for me.

She met me in the parking lot just past the restaurant that sat on the water. The restaurant turned out to be named after Frank Sinatra, too, and I toyed with the idea that Drama was maybe a Sinatra fan herself, and that was why she'd picked the location. But I realized it wasn't; she'd picked it because farther north and a little east was the campus for the Stevens Institute, and from there she'd had a clear view of everything going on below.

It had taken me just over twelve minutes to make the walk, and the rain had begun to taper off, and now the thunder came in distant and irregular growls, and the lightning couldn't be seen at all. Her directions had been calm and quiet, and had given me no indication of how much farther I needed to go.

As I came around the north side of the restaurant, she ordered me to turn right and approach the Hudson and toss the Motorola into the water. I did, and when I turned back around, she was there, standing beneath the awning of the building, out of the shadow, and I realized I'd walked right past her and not even noticed.

I thought she would leave some kind of distance between us, but she just walked right up to me, stopping only long enough to toss her Motorola into the river after mine. Once she did that, her hands appeared empty.

Each time we'd been this close before, her face had been concealed. This time she hadn't bothered. Finally, the fear that had been absent on the dilapidated pier made itself known, and beneath my soaked shirt I swear I could feel my heartbeat trying to pound its way out. I closed and opened my hands, wishing they would stop shaking, and then I wished that I was someplace else, warm and dry and going to live.

She was almost as I remembered her, and that surprised me. After describing her so many times I'd begun to think I was fabricating details I'd never actually known. She was just under my height, slender, though her shoulders were a little broad, hinting at upper-body strength. The clothes she wore were ordinary, jeans and a shirt and a fabric jacket that was either blue or black. Her hair had been cut very short, and when she turned her head, I could see it was almost shaved at the back of her neck.

I waited for her to stop, but still she kept coming forward, and when she was close enough to touch me without needing to fully extend her arm, she did, pressing her left palm on my chest. Through the wet fabric, her touch seemed hot. The gesture itself was not hostile, but it terrified me, and I couldn't bring myself to move, to look away from her.

We stared at each other.

She had a full mouth, a narrow chin, a slender and small nose. Her eyes seemed large, and she didn't blink, and in the weak light I couldn't tell their color. Her ears were small, laid against the sides of her head, and she wore no jewelry. Her cheekbones were high, making all of the angles of her face that much sharper.

"My name is Alena Cizkova," she said.

I opened my mouth and heard my voice. I don't remember what I said.

There was a tiny, hot pain from my left thigh, and I forced myself to look down, saw her withdrawing the needle, saw her drop the syringe. It was a thin plastic one, disposable, and the plunger had fallen all the way, and I watched as it hit the pavement beneath us, making a little splash in a puddle as it landed.

I brought my eyes back up and said, "That's a stupid way to kill me."

She blinked. The corner of her mouth moved, and her lips parted, and she tilted her head back, and she started to laugh. My mouth was filling with foam, and I told her that it wasn't funny, and I tried to grab hold of her, grabbing at her arm where her hand was still on my chest. She stepped back, and I tried to move forward some more, to grab her again, and my left leg understood but my right wanted to stay exactly where it was, and I ended up on the wet asphalt on one knee, then both, then on my hands.

She laughed like my death was the funniest thing she'd ever seen.

PART TWO

CHAPTER ONE

There was a Doberman.

The dog was a he, and he didn't have a collar, and he weighed at least sixty pounds, and his eyes, soulful dog eyes, seemed to be telling me that the jury was still out, and until it came back, I'd better be on my best behavior. A puffy scar ran along his neck, width-wise all across the throat, white-pink flesh that would never grow fur again. He put his muzzle beneath my left hand, nudging it with his wet nose, and when I moved my fingers he turned away, his nails clicking on a hard floor.

It was day and the sunlight was strange, washing out colors and already heavy with heat, and I tried to make some sense of my surroundings as best I could without my glasses. Mostly I was seeing hues, light green and blue, past the foot of the bed, broken by a rectangle that was an open door. To my right, the wall continued, though it was disrupted halfway along with a painting, a swirl of colors that blended together.

The sheet across me was white, and there was no blanket. I lifted it and saw that my left leg was intact, and felt an enormous relief, so great that I fell back and just lay still, staring at the ceiling, at the fixture positioned high above me, at the blades of the fan as they whirred in silent rotation. There had been hallucinations, and there had been many of them, filled with people I'd known or still knew; the boy who'd beaten me up every day after school when I was ten;

the drill sergeant who'd given me a faceful of Mace in AIT, then ordered me to run the obstacle course; the teacher who had humiliated me when I couldn't conjugate my Latin fast enough. All those people, faces I hadn't seen in decades, tormenting me each in different ways.

And there had been the people I still knew, the ones I loved. Bridgett saying that unless I could stop her she'd go back on the junk, and then making me watch as she cooked up her heroin, injected it, all the while begging me to stop her. Scott Fowler with a folder of photographs, the Backroom Boys, Gracey and Bowles, standing behind him, and each photo was of Antonia, and each picture was worse than the first, her body bent, stripped, broken, torn. One snapshot had Her Ladyship facedown on a concrete floor, her face obviously missing, like Michael Ortez in a warehouse in Dallas.

"That's what really happened," Fowler had said. "And why didn't you tell me?"

Those weren't the worst, and thankfully, all were already sinking into lost memory. But in one I'd lost my left leg, the tiny puncture in my thigh growing alive with gangrene, until rotting flesh had invaded my lower body. Then Drama had come and told me not to worry, that it was to be expected, and when I'd looked again, the leg was gone and she was walking away, taking it with her.

It had seemed real.

Birds were singing, and I turned my head to the left and saw sky and the tops of trees, and the color of the sky was a solid, vivid blue, and there didn't look to be a cloud in it. I listened longer, and there were a lot of birds, and then, behind their calls, the constant white noise of surf meeting shore.

There was a stand beside the bed on the left side, and on it were my glasses, a glass of water, and two tablets of Advil. I sat up and let the sheet fall and put the glasses on. Just that much movement left me breathless. My head felt swollen, and my mouth parched. My back was sore, the muscles along my neck and shoulder full of dull pressure, as if I'd held them in the same position for too long.

I took the Advil dry, then contemplated the water before draining the glass. It was tepid, but tasted pure. I got to my feet, standing naked by the bed. The floor was cool, red and brown tile in an ornate star pattern that repeated over and over to the walls. The air was warm and a little moist. My legs felt steady.

There was a square of gauze on the inside of my right arm at the elbow, held in place with a strip of cloth tape. I pulled it free, saw dried blood on the gauze, the bruising on my skin.

A pair of pants, the color of wet sand, was draped over the end of the bed. They were baggy and a little long, and secured around the waist with a drawstring. As I pulled them on, the Doberman came back, stopping in the doorway to look at me.

"Hi, dog," I said.

The Doberman's nostrils flared. But for the scar, he probably would have been show-worthy, and as it was he was clearly healthy, clearly strong. Without blinking he watched me tie the drawstring, then followed me as I went to the veranda.

I was on the second story of the house, and the house was atop a hill. It was constructed of concrete, painted a pale orange, and the veranda itself was open, twelve feet wide and long, closed to my right but open to the left where it stretched along the length of the house and turned a corner, out of sight. The ocean was perhaps half a mile away. The strip of beach was white, and the water was green near the shore, and then it turned the same blue of the sky as it stretched to meet the horizon. In the distance I could see a yacht with a white sail. The sun was behind me, blocked by the house, and it felt early in the morning. I knew the afternoon would be hot.

The hillside down to the beach was covered with trees and plants, flowers in bloom, and the growth was so thick I couldn't make out a path. The trees were palm and cedar and bamboo and mahogany, and there were others I didn't recognize, including several that seemed to be bearing fruit. The foliage confirmed it as much as the bird that was perched nearby on the rail, eyeing me suspiciously. The bird was small, yellow-bellied, with an almost hummingbird-like narrow beak, marking it as a nectar feeder. I'd never seen a bird like it before.

Not only was I no longer in New York, I wasn't certain if I was still in the same hemisphere.

The Doberman was looking from me to the bird on the railing.

"Wouldn't happen to know where I can find a phone, would you?" I asked him.

He didn't answer, looking back at the bird, and then his ears pricked, and he turned and loped out of the room, his steps clicking on the tile. I looked for the little bird, discovered it had flown away, and then started along the veranda, around the side of the house. I knew I wasn't going to find a phone, and even if I did, I wasn't quite sure what good it would do me. Placing a call to New York would probably take time, and the first thing Natalie or Dale or Bridgett or Corry would demand to know would be a question I couldn't answer. "Maybe the Caribbean" wasn't going to get any of us far.

The veranda ended around the corner, past another set of French doors, open, and another bedroom. The bed was a queen, unmade, and identical to the one I'd just left. In an open closet hung a small selection of clothes, most of them women's and some of them expensive. There were two more doors, and through one was a master bathroom with double sink, toilet, tub, and shower, that exited back into the room where I'd started. The other door led to a hall and a flight of stairs. The Doberman was nowhere to be seen, and was apparently staying quiet.

The stairs ended in a square, central room with a high gabled ceiling. The roof beams were exposed, dark varnished wood that was maybe teak. Two more sets of French doors were open to the left, leading out to a covered patio and another view of the water. Since I was now looking in the opposite direction I had been above, it struck me that if we were on an island, it was a small one. I headed out the door.

Drama was sitting in a white wicker chair at a glass-topped table. The Doberman lay at her feet. On the table was a pitcher, and a French press of coffee, two mugs, and two glasses. A plate of fruit was by her arm, mangoes, green oranges, grapefruit, and papaya, and on another plate were four muffins. By her left hand was a Walther P88 semiautomatic pistol. She was wearing shorts over a black one-piece bathing suit, a no-nonsense Speedo. In the sunlight, the hair I had once thought was brown or black was now almost copper. Her arms and legs were tanned, and along her left bicep, curling just inside of the elbow and then around and up to her shoulder, disappearing beneath the bathing suit, was a hard white scar. Other scars crisscrossed her forearms, signs of cuts and tears, and on her leg was a starburst discoloration, where a bullet once had found its way inside.

She lowered a book to watch me approach, marking her place with a finger. Her eyes were almost drowsy.

The book she was reading was *Drama: A Window into the World of Protection and Assassination*.

She let me finish looking over the table, then said, "The coffee was just brewed," and turned her attention back to the book.

Feeling hungry, I took a seat. The juice was fresh, pineapple mixed with orange, and I drained one glass and finished half of another before I reached for the coffee. When I went for the plate of fruit, my hand was less than five inches from the Walther. She didn't seem to mind, or care; she just turned a page.

There was a slight breeze rustling leaves, and the scent of salt water was in it. A flight of six steps ran from the patio to a driveway, and the driveway curved into a gravel road. There was no sign of a car, but a blue bicycle leaned against the railing at the bottom of the stairs, and a large Honda dirt bike was parked beneath an overhang a little farther down.

The coffee was hot and strong, and I drank it looking at the pistol on the table and tried to figure out what it meant. She had gone to a lot of trouble to get me here alone, and I didn't think she'd have made the effort just to shoot me over breakfast. If she needed the gun for self-defense, I was flattered, but she was overrating me, and that wasn't something she'd ever done before. If she was expecting someone besides me who might need shooting, she wasn't acting like it.

Which left one thing.

I picked up the gun. The Walther P88 is a very nice, very expensive semi-automatic pistol that was originally designed to be a potential replacement for the M1911 Colt, the tried-and-true sidearm of the U.S. Army. It did quite well in its trials but failed the adverse-conditions test, where the military likes to bury, freeze, burn, drop, crush, and otherwise torture equipment. Even so, the Walther's considered by many a pistol aficionado as one of the finest combat pistols ever produced. It's a fully ambidextrous gun, meaning that the magazine release and decocking levers are mirrored on both sides.

The magazine was full. I slipped it back into place and racked the slide, putting a round into the breech. Then I raised the gun.

"I wouldn't," she said, lowering the book.

"Sure you would."

She gestured off to her left, my right. "You'll have to kill him, too."

I glanced down, saw that the Doberman had moved soundlessly to my side, and was now in a crouch, prepared to spring. His lips were back, and his fur was up, and he should have been growling but he wasn't, and the scar at his throat finally made sense.

"Call him off," I said.

"Or what?"

"It's a double-action. I don't even have to cock it. Call him off."

She used the flap of the book jacket to mark her place, then set the book beside her empty coffee cup. As she poured from the French press, she said softly, "Miata, *tovarisch*."

The Doberman's lips fell back around his teeth, and he moved back to her seat, then lay down once more beneath the table.

She picked up her cup. "You haven't tried the muffins."

"I'm not certain I trust your food."

"But you trust the drink."

"No. I was thirsty."

The corner of her mouth curled gently.

"What did you spike my OJ with, by the way?" I asked.

"Interferon."

"Made me good and sick."

"I wanted to slow you down, then. I don't now. I left the gun out so you would not be afraid."

"It's working," I told her. "Where are we?"

"This is my home."

So we were in the Caribbean. It had been one of the last things she'd said before trying to kill Pugh, her voice calling through the barricaded door, where Dale and I had retreated with our principal, trying to buy time for Natalie and the others to arrive. Drama had used an explosive, set it against the wall in a final attempt to blow us up. Just before she'd armed the device, she'd talked of pineapple muffins and Bequia.

I indicated the muffins with my chin. "These the ones you were talking about?"

It pleased her that I had remembered. I didn't tell her I'd searched through two atlases before I'd found Bequia on a map. It was part of the island nation of St. Vincent and the Grenadines, nine miles south of St. Vincent itself, about a hundred miles west of Barbados, and I'd never heard of it until she'd mentioned it that day. I'd had a hell of a time finding out anything more about the island other than the location. Settled by the English and the French, it had been an independent member of the British Commonwealth since 1979. It was off the major tourist track, and its main industries were fishing and boatbuilding. Mostly the harbor served visiting yachts. Apparently there was a regatta of some sort every Easter.

"You never told them," she said.

"No."

"I thought that perhaps you'd forgotten, or misunderstood."

"I understood." My arm was getting tired, and I couldn't see myself shooting her in the next few minutes, so I set the Walther down on the table but kept my hand on it.

I asked, "How long was I out?"

"Five days. I injected you with Ketalar, then used an IV to keep you nourished and hydrated during the journey. The hallucinations only occurred when you were regaining consciousness, which you did twice before we got here." She put her elbows on the table and crossed her hands under her chin, and I realized she wanted to keep talking, that there probably weren't that many people she got to tell about her work. "Would you like to know how I moved you?"

"Oh, absolutely."

"I had a boat waiting up the Hudson. When you lost consciousness, I moved you aboard and took you to Brooklyn, where I transferred you to another boat, a 38 Scarab AVS. Then we went down the coast. We stopped to refuel in Virginia Beach, Charleston, Nassau, Cockburn Harbour—in the Turks and Caicos—then again in Tortola in the U.K. Virgin Islands, before reaching Kingstown in St. Vincent. The journey took just over four days."

"You manned the boat yourself?"

"No, you had to be monitored, the boat had to be controlled, and I had to sleep."

"Was it Dan? Danilov?"

She nodded.

"Did you kill him?"

Her chin came off her hands and she sat back, and either she really was indignant or she was damn good at faking it, because she looked both hurt and appalled. "Dan is my friend. There was no need to kill him."

"You let him come all the way here?"

That clarified the question for her, and she nodded, understanding me. "You and I left him in Kingstown, with the boat. No one knows I am in this place."

"But me."

"But you."

I felt the gun under my hand, the grip beneath my fingertips. There's a gag used in the military a lot, so much so that it's worked into the popular culture, as a way of evading an uncomfortable question, a way to avoid divulging a secret.

I could tell you, I thought, but then I'd have to kill you.

So maybe the gun was to be used on me, after all.

"I am not going to kill you, Atticus," she said, reading my mind. "You could leave here now. The magazine is loaded, and the gun is ready. If you were to raise it and shoot, I could not escape with my life."

"There's your dog."

"We both know that Miata is a very particular kind of threat, and one that would not stop you."

For a moment, I considered doing it. Wrapping my fingers around the butt, raising the gun and pulling the trigger, punching her out of her chair with the force of two bullets. By the time the Doberman had gotten in position to take my throat, I could put him down, too.

I considered it.

"Maybe it's time you told me why I'm here," I said.

CHAPTER TWO

She didn't know her real name, the one she'd been born with. At the orphanage in Magadan, she'd been called Alena. Alena Cizkova. But because Oksana Zurkowska had read a book on Egyptian mythology, and because in that book there were pictures, and because Oksana thought the picture of Osiris's bride bore a slight resemblance to the small girl she liked to tease, the other children in the orphanage called her Isis.

She'd been put in the orphanage quite young, she told me, and all she knew of her parents was that they must have both been negligent. She remembered being perhaps only two years old and a man with a beard putting his cigarettes out on her back. She didn't know why he did this, and she thought that perhaps the man was her father.

Then the State came and took her to the orphanage, and she stayed there until she murdered Oksana.

"I had wanted her dead," she told me, "the way that children want their tormentors dead, and so I plotted it, and so I stole her life."

It was the shirt that had given her away. The old drunk who tended the boilers in the orphanage basement saw her trying to stuff it in the furnace, and he had stopped her and seen the blood, and had held her while a search was made for Oksana. When the girl's body was found, one of the wardens beat Alena in the body until blood came out of her mouth. Then the police were called.

She said they questioned her for several hours and that she didn't say a word. She was placed in a cell with men three and four times her age.

When she got to that part, she bent to pet the dog. After several seconds, she added, "That was a bad night. I will never allow another night like that."

The next day, two men in uniforms came and took her from the cell. They put her in another room, where they asked her different questions than before. She knew they were Government, and that they were powerful, because the police in the station were afraid of them, and because of the long night and all that had happened, this time she did talk. The two men gave her papers with problems on them for her to solve, showed her photographs and asked what she thought of them. One told her a story and then, an hour later, asked her to write down everything she could remember of the tale. Then they gave her a lunch of black bread and dried fish and water, and when she had finished, they called a doctor in to examine her, but she fought with them when they tried to undress her for the physical exam. In the end, two of them had to hold her down.

Then they put her back in a cell, but this time a different one, where she was alone. No one came to see her. No one spoke to her. She spent a second night listening to adults crying and yelling in cells all around her, and she cried a lot, too. It was the last time, she said, that she could remember crying.

At dawn the third day, one of the Government men returned, and she was released into his custody, given new clothes and a small breakfast, and then taken away, to a school in the northern Caucasus, in Vladikavkaz, then called Ordzhonikidze, a thousand and a half miles from Magadan. The school was dedicated to the education of the children of high-ranking military officers. There were strict rules, and the students all wore black uniforms with scarlet stripes as trimming.

She was there less than a month when the man from the Government returned, this time with others, and they asked her more questions, gave her more tests. These tests were more extensive, and lasted several days. She was given another physical exam, and this time she did not fight.

Five or six days after the last test had been given and the last Government man had left, she was moved to another school. This one was on a military base outside the city of Omsk, which, like Magadan, was closed.

"That was where they trained me," she said.

The day she arrived, an administrative officer recorded all of her data carefully, her height, her weight, her hair and eye color. The distinguishing marks on her body. He had pictures taken of her teeth and fingerprints lifted from her hands. On the sheet, she saw that he left her name blank.

She was surprised when she saw that the officer recorded her age as nine years old.

Her instruction was handled by the GRU, the intelligence arm of the Soviet Army, and subtlety was not their strong suit. She was made first, as she put it, into a "blunt instrument."

"Starting with physical conditioning," she said. "Then beginning tradecraft, languages. Then advanced techniques, escape-and-evasion, construction of trade devices, electronics, IEDs, so on."

She told me she could speak Russian, English, French, and German, all fluently. When she really wanted, her English could sound almost native, and her French perfectly so. Some days, she was forbidden to speak Russian, and if she was caught doing so, she was punished. As she grew older, such periods would last for a week or more. Languages were hard for her, and she didn't enjoy them, because she didn't think she was good at them.

It was in other skills that she excelled. She was an excellent shot, had earned the designation of Master Sniper by the time she was twelve. She didn't like pistols so much until she reached mid-puberty and her hands had grown large enough to control them reliably. The courses that required her to build things she loved, the courses where she was asked to construct an improvised explosive device, or a timer, or to rewire a radio, or to build and plant and retrieve a bug or other surveillance device. A lot of the time, the courses, such as they were, were actually practical exams, live fire exercises. She was so young that the GRU was anxious to take advantage of her apparent innocence.

"When I was thirteen, I planted bugs in the French Embassy," she told me. "As far as I know, they're still there."

She wasn't actually asked to kill anybody until she was fourteen. All she would say about the murder was that it occurred in Afghanistan, and that it was a Western journalist who had been writing about the Soviet Union's war there. It was her first time in Afghanistan; before Gorbachev pulled Soviet troops out of the country, she would return another eight times, each time leaving a body in her wake.

"Nine," she said. "I remember all of them."

She held a military rank, she told me, at least she had until she'd gone independent. But before she struck out on her own, she said, she was a major in the GRU, and had been decorated many times for service to the U.S.S.R. In the course of six years, she had traveled all over Europe and Asia, had been to the United States twice. She told me she was partial to the U.S., that she liked working there.

Then she turned twenty-one, and, as she put it, "The war ended and I lost my job."

The decision was motivated by two things: greed and self-preservation. When the Wall came down, when the East opened itself to the rest of the world, the money dried up instantly. The perks and benefits she had known most of her life vanished. Work came less and less.

What made it worse was the "new openness," the information now being swapped freely in the intelligence community. Secrets were suddenly being shared with former enemies, or secrets were leaking, or secrets were simply being sold.

"If I stayed, there would be another job. And that job would fail, and I would be blown, and I would end up arrested or dead."

It was the memory of that first night in the police station, the memory of Magadan, that motivated her. She wasn't ever going to allow that to happen again. She would never be a captive.

It was then, too, that she discovered she was afraid to die.

She made preparations.

And the job came, just as she had anticipated, and she left for Amsterdam as directed, and as soon as she arrived she took another flight to Paris, and then another to Rome, then Malta, then New York, and, finally, Tel Aviv. In Tel Aviv she put word in the proper ears that she could contact someone who could arrange death, if the price was right. She built an elaborate protocol for those who wanted to hire such a service, pretending that she had a partner, an employer. She used classified ads and answering services and dead drops, and then, later, the Internet, all the tradecraft she had been taught.

It took eight months, and she was nearly broke before the first job came. She investigated the source, investigated the mark, and decided it was a job she could do successfully. She spent another seven weeks preparing for it, and when she believed everything was right, she flew to London and killed a very wealthy man's wife, and made it look like the woman had stroked-out while standing in line at Harrods.

She'd earned just under three million dollars for her efforts, and never looked back.

When I pressed her, she told me that she had murdered nine men and two women for money. I rephrased the question.

"How many people have died at your hands?" I asked.

She didn't want to answer. She took her time. Then she said, "Thirty-seven."

But only eleven had been for money, she added.

She thought it was ironic that, since going independent, she'd actually committed less murder than before.

I told her that I thought it was ironic, too.

Then I told her that, while all of this was very interesting and deeply disturbing, it still didn't explain what the hell I was doing with her on Bequia.

"I want to hire you, Atticus. Someone is trying to kill me."

CHAPTER THREE

Miata circled ahead of us as we followed a dirt footpath beneath the trees. The sand was fine and hot beneath my feet, and the sun had risen to almost directly above us. We sat on the beach.

She had put on a pair of sunglasses. I'd taken the Walther with me, holding it in my hand, but now, as she sat watching the water and talked, it seemed a both ridiculous and obscene thing to be carrying around.

"You are fucking out of your mind," I told her.

"I do not want to die." Her eyes tracked Miata's movement, as the dog played in the surf. "Why is that insane?"

"There are too many places to begin, but for a start, I don't believe you—"

"I am telling you the truth."

"—and even if someone *is* trying to kill you, you sure as hell don't need my help to keep you alive. You've got to be one of the most dangerous people in the world, and I mean physically, lethally, dangerous. I don't even like sitting this close to you, and I've got a goddamn *gun* in my hand."

Her mouth twitched. "Thank you."

"It's not a compliment. Even if I accept everything you've told me—and I'm not saying that I do—you have in your head more knowledge about death, about causing it, about preventing it, than any person I've ever met. And I've met some very skilled killers in my time."

She removed the sunglasses, squinting at the water. "The man after me . . . he is one of The Ten."

Oh, I should have seen that coming, I thought. I should have seen the headlights on that one a mile away, coming through the tunnel and making straight for me.

"Oxford?" I asked, but it was rhetorical, and even as I said it, I hoped she wouldn't answer.

"You know of Oxford?"

"I was briefed on him four days before you snatched Lady Ainsley-Hunter. Told he was coming to New York."

"He is searching for me." Miata came trotting back up the beach, sand stuck to his paws. She scratched his ears, then brushed his coat clean. When she glanced at me, she saw that I was staring at her, and she read the suspicion in my face. "What?"

"I'm trying to figure out if Miata's for show."

"He is my dog. He relies on me."

"Is that why you cut out his voice box?"

She was up and shouting down at me so quickly it made me remember just how true everything I'd said about her, thought about her, was. In her anger, she'd turned the sunglasses in her fist, now holding them like they could double as a knife. In her hands, they could.

"Poshol v pizdu!" she spat at me. "You think I would do that? You think I would do that to an animal, to a dog, to something that cannot even understand? *Nu tebya k chortu!"*

The gun was still in my hand and I thought I could bring it up and maybe save my life, but she had already turned away, was striding down to the water. Miata looked at me accusingly, then followed her.

Like she cares about a dog as anything other than a tool.

Like she really needs help, anyone's help, and mine specifically.

She'd stopped at the edge of the water, letting the foam splash over her feet, and I watched as she swiped sand from the seat of her shorts, then crossed her arms over her chest. Miata was pawing at some driftwood that had washed up on the shore nearby.

I went down to join her.

She stood watching the ocean, where a boat had stopped about a mile out, at the edge of the cove. Small figures wearing snorkeling gear were preparing to dive.

"I did not cut his throat," she said. "A man in Miami did that, and he is dead now, and yes, I did kill him, and yes, I was paid to do it. But I would have killed him for free."

One of the skin divers, a woman, went over the edge of the boat. There was a small splash.

"Do you know why Miata's throat was cut?" she asked. "The man I killed, he had houses where he kept drugs, and in them he had men and dogs on guard. He set traps in the houses, grenades screwed into light sockets so that when the switches were thrown the grenades would detonate. He made pits, cut holes in his floors and then filled his basement with sharp metal and broken glass.

"And he cut the throats of his dogs so the police would not hear the animals coming. He took their voices because it would make them crazy and silent and savage. I had been paid by his competition to shut down his businesses. His guards, his men, they fled when I killed him. But the dogs did not, they were mad and they were loyal, and I had to kill them to save my own life. Miata, he was still alive when it was over, and I took him away with me."

She opened her hand, unfolded the sunglasses and then, using both hands, put them back on her face. Her mouth was closed, still angry.

"I am not a monster, I am not some freak who can only achieve climax through another's pain or death. I am—I *was*—an assassin. Everyone who has died by my hand, they died for a very specific reason, either because they were the mark, because they led to the mark, or because they were trying to kill me."

She turned her head to see my expression, but I kept my eyes on the divers in the water.

"I do not torture animals," she said.

We watched the skin divers in the water for a while as they surfaced and dove and surfaced again.

"Why does Oxford want to kill you?" I asked her.

"Because of you," she said, and turned and walked away, calling for Miata to follow her.

"Bullshit," I told the Caribbean.

"I should have killed you," Drama said. "I should have gone through the door after the explosion, and shot you, and Dale Matsui, and Pugh."

"You would have died, too."

"Yes. But that should not have stopped me."

We had moved back into the house, into the kitchen, which was a narrow rectangle with the same earth-toned tile that covered the second floor. Drama was washing the dishes from breakfast, dumping the grounds from the French press into a trash can beneath the double sink. For a moment, I flashed on her as a kind of lethal Donna Reed, and the mental image had me grinning without meaning to.

She saw it and frowned. "When I was younger, Atticus, when I was training, death did not frighten me. Now it does. I knew if I went through the door, if I finished the job and killed you and Pugh, I would die as a result. And I wanted to live. So I ran."

A stainless steel bowl was on the floor by her feet, and she picked it up, then filled it with fresh water from the tap. When she bent to grab it, the muscles in her legs were taut and defined. I realized that she shaved her legs and pits, found that surprising. The bullet she'd taken to the thigh was a through-and-through, and it looked like she'd been lucky, that the round hadn't expanded as it passed through her body. It made me remember when I'd been shot.

"Then your friend, Chris Havel, she writes this book," Drama said. "I should have stopped her. I didn't. I should have come back and killed her, and you, and Dale, and Natalie, and Corry. I should have made the statement."

"Why didn't you?" I asked.

She moved her eyes from me, looking out the window. The breeze had picked up, and shadows came and went as the branches randomly blocked the sunlight. After a minute, I realized she wasn't going to answer.

"Why did you tell me where you live?" I asked.

Still no reply.

"Alena," I said.

Her head whipped around, and there was the hint of distraction in her look, as if I'd caught her attention by accident, as if the usage of the name amused her. Her lips came together, the corner of her mouth rose briefly.

"You will laugh," she said. "I didn't like Pugh, but I saw things in you that I saw in myself. You understand this, I know you do, it happens in your profession as well. The sense of artificial intimacy. I watched you for several weeks, and although I knew it was false, I felt it anyway. So I wanted to give you something that was special to me, something that no one else had. I gave you my home."

I nodded, thinking that I should be surprised, and finding that I wasn't. What she was describing wasn't that unique a phenomenon. There was a reason, after all, that so many bodyguards ended up sleeping with, romancing, or in some cases, marrying their principals. The nature of the relationship is intimate and high stress, and in such an environment connections between individuals develop in unexpected ways and with an alarming intensity. More than once I'd had a principal indicate a willingness to let our relationship stray from professional to personal, and I knew that Natalie had experienced the same thing with an even greater frequency. What Drama did and what I did were different sides of the same coin.

I thought about the last night I'd spent with Bridgett, the argument we'd had.

Alena took a blue-and-white dish towel from the hook by the sink. She started drying the dishes.

"By letting Havel publish her book, I made myself a target," she said. "There is too much truth in it. It generates interest, attention, pressure. And it marks me specifically. An assassin is supposed to be invisible. I let Havel inform the world about me."

"And Oxford's been hired to keep the world from learning anything more?"

"Oxford will try to discredit Havel, and possibly you as well. He will most certainly destroy me."

"So it's in my best interest to help you?"

"It is in your best interest to keep Oxford from succeeding. Keeping me alive is only part of that." She assembled the now clean and dry French press and folded the towel. "You believe I should die?"

"I believe you should be punished for what you've done," I answered. "Thirty-seven people are dead because of you, eleven of them murdered to line your own pockets."

"General Augustus Ndanga," she said.

"Who?"

"General Augustus Albertus Usuf Kiwane Ndanga, Uganda, four years ago. I shot him through the head at six hundred and forty meters."

"Nice shot."

She moved closer, leaning on the counter to meet my eyes. "Ndanga would enter villages with his army and murder all the men, even the boys, even the infant boys. He would kill the women, even the little girls, but those who could bear children, he would rape them repeatedly, until he was certain he had made them pregnant. I killed him. I should die for that?"

"Depends who hired you for the job."

"The CIA paid me four million dollars for his death," she replied. "You have killed. You must understand."

"Yes. I have killed. But I have never committed murder. If a man comes at my principal, I'll draw my gun not to kill him but to stop him, and there is a world of difference in that. For me a gun is a tool, used to force an assailant to stop their assault. For you, it's a means of ending a life as efficiently as possible."

"You shot Erika Wyatt's mother, four times. One bullet would have stopped her."

"One bullet *might* have stopped her," I said, more harshly than I intended. "She had a gun and I had to be sure."

"And being sure, that is more or less a reason to kill than organizing the rape of a whole people?"

"I'm not about to argue the necessity of Hitler's death, or Stalin's. We had this conversation the first time we met. What I do and what you do are very different."

She stared at me for a moment longer, then moved away from the counter, back to the sink. I'd seen nothing in her eyes. She hung the dish towel on the hook.

"Has it not occurred to you that I didn't kill anyone when I took Lady Ainsley-Hunter from you?" she asked. "That I did not kill you, or Natalie Trent, or Corry Herrera? That I did not kill Bridgett Logan or Dale Matsui or Robert Moore?"

"It has occurred to me. And I think the only reason you didn't is because you want something from me, and you know that if you'd killed any of them, I'd make it my mission in life to . . ." and I shut up, because I realized what it was I was about to say.

She didn't press it, just opened the refrigerator and, after viewing the contents, asked me if I wanted fish for lunch.

We ate on the patio, grilled yellowtail with thick slices of pineapple. It was the kind of lunch I'd have chased with a beer if she'd had any, but there was no alcohol in the house, so we both drank water. The Walther stayed by my plate, but I was getting tired of lugging it around, which I supposed was one of the things she'd thought would happen.

She'd put music on her little stereo before taking her seat, and I could hear the Beatles singing softly inside. The album was *Rubber Soul*.

"I couldn't simply approach you in New York and ask to hire you," Alena said. "You understand why I had to do it this way."

"I would have run screaming," I admitted.

"Yes."

I put my utensils down and looked at the bare bones on my plate. "Why me? You've certainly encountered other PSAs."

"None that I respect." She drank some water, gauging my reaction. From what she saw, she felt the need to clarify. "You beat me. No one has ever done that before."

"I didn't beat you."

"My job was to kill Pugh. I failed."

"I was lucky and I was working with people who were outstanding at their jobs," I said. "What you're asking me to do, you're asking me to do alone. You, of all people, should know what that means."

"You're forgetting that I will be your principal. Pugh could not fire a gun, Lady Ainsley-Hunter could not rig an explosive. Pugh was an old man, diabetic and possibly alcoholic. Ainsley-Hunter is an activist, a public figure and a zealot. I am a thirty-one-year-old woman in excellent physical condition, mentally acute and—despite what you would care to believe—emotionally stable."

I hated the fact that I was actually considering what she was saying. I hated it even more that, once again, she knew what I was thinking.

"There is more," she said. "No one you have ever protected before can teach you what I can teach you, Atticus. I can teach you everything Oxford knows, because I know it, too."

"You're offering to turn me into an assassin?"

"I'm offering to show you how we work, how we think. How we see the world. How we see ourselves." She looked at me across the table. "There's something else. You *need* to do this."

I didn't quite laugh, but it came close to an outright snort. If I'd had water in my mouth, she'd have gotten an impromptu shower.

"You are losing yourself," Alena said softly. "Fame does not suit you. It is distracting to you, and perhaps even offensive. The money is nice, it allows you comforts, allows you to provide for Erika and even Logan—"

"Logan makes a fine living without my help."

She blinked at me, waiting to see if I was finished, then continued. "It allows you to provide for Erika, but that is not enough for you. It has allowed you to meet those people who, culturally, you have been told it is desirable to know, women like Skye Van Brandt. But your association with people like Van Brandt has not made you happy. It has, in fact, made you weak."

"Hold on—"

"Last year would what I did in the elevator a week ago have worked? Last year, given the same situation, would you have debussed your principal to a publicly known location after an attempt had been made?"

"The 'attempt' was a man playing with himself."

"That should not have mattered in the slightest," she said, annoyed with me.

I drank water and didn't say anything.

"The man who beat me a year ago never would have made that mistake."

I set the glass down empty. It wasn't actually made of glass, but instead a clear molded plastic, light blue. Hers was from the same set, but pale green. "Then why would you want to hire that man?"

"You are also the man who put himself between an Accuracy International AWM and Ainsley-Hunter, and then demanded to see his principal safely to the car. You are the man who bid his principal goodbye, and then came to meet me, believing that his life was a fair trade for hers. You are the man I want to protect me."

"Her life was worth saving."

Now it was her turn to drink water and not respond.

I shook my head and looked off the patio. The breeze was moving palm fronds and branches, as if they were waving me to either come closer, or to make a discreet exit. It was getting warmer as the day progressed, but in the shade of the patio, surrounded by the concrete and tile, it remained comfortable.

"You killed three men in Dallas, Texas, ten days ago," I said. "Video surveillance caught you leaving the scene."

"No I didn't." She said it with conviction and almost surprise.

"There were pictures, Alena. Three men—Ortez, Montrose, and a third whose name I don't remember. All had been shot. There was a picture of you leaving, driving a car out the gate."

"It was not me. The photograph was a fake."

"Sure."

"I have not been to Dallas in over three years. Who showed you these pictures?"

"It's not important."

"I did not do it."

I looked at the trees some more, felt her looking at me. I said, "Tell me about Oxford."

"He is like me."

"Another Russian?"

"No, American, I think. Maybe British. I'm not certain who trained him, but he is from the West. What little I know about him suggests a military and intelligence background."

"I heard he specializes."

"Scandal," she confirmed. "He uses sex, it is the way he stages his bodies. But it means nothing, it is simply a *kind* of job, one that takes its own special planning, the way a bombing or a poisoning takes special planning. He knows what I know."

I had to wonder about that. It could be as simple and straightforward as she made it sound, staging bodies the way other people move their furniture. But I doubted it. Someone who kept returning to the sex angle was probably someone who liked playing with naked bodies. Maybe Drama wasn't a monster, but I wasn't willing to extend the same faith to Oxford.

"Is there a history between you two?" I asked.

"No."

"And you're sure he's coming after you? You've confirmed that?"

"Yes. I have sources."

"Sources like Dan?"

"My sources say Oxford is looking for me. I take that kind of threat seriously, so I checked."

"But you don't know who bought the hit?"

"No."

"And you're sure it has been bought, that he's not doing this on his own?"

"Oxford would not undertake such an operation for free. *Pro bono,* as you say. To kill me, he would demand a substantial payment."

"How much?"

"Four million dollars, at least. More, perhaps."

"How long has he had the contract? Or whatever it is you folks call it."

"Job. I call it a job. Just as you call it."

I was silent.

She took a green orange from the bowl at the center of the table and began peeling the skin. The bowl was white porcelain, with two thin, sky blue stripes running around its center. "He has had the job only a month or two."

"If he was in New York looking for you, he knew you were in the U.S. That means he's close."

"New York is a clearinghouse." She was removing the skin from the orange as a single piece, using only her fingers, trying to keep it from tearing. "It is the place to acquire everything, from equipment to people. Everyone goes through there. New York means nothing."

"Does he know about this place?"

She hesitated.

"Does he?"

"He knows about the connection between you and me, about Pugh. I'm certain he's read Havel's book." She looked up from her work with the orange. "It will take him some time, but he will find me here."

"How much time?"

She finished removing the skin, coiling it on her empty plate. She offered me a wedge of the orange, and when I shook my head, ate it herself, her eyes wandering to the water. She was quiet long enough for "Girl" to end, and John and Paul's harmony on "I'm Looking Through You" to begin, and it was clear she was thinking about it, considering how she would search if the positions were reversed.

"At least three months," she said, finally. "Possibly four. Maybe longer. I do not think any less—he would have to have extraordinary luck. It will cost him a lot of money. He will start by establishing what occurred between you and me and Ainsley-Hunter, then attempt to recreate your route. He will try to track the equipment I used. The rifle would be the weakest link, and with time, it would lead him to Brighton Beach. There he will learn about the Scarab, and he will know we took the boat. He will calculate the range of the vessel, and then he will begin a methodical search of all those places where we made landfall, where we refueled. He will lose us for a while once he reaches the Caribbean. He will have to move from island to island, carefully, because he will believe he is close, and he will not want to show himself. It will take him at least six weeks before he narrows his search to the Lesser Grenadines. He will lose us again at Kingstown, realizing that was where we left the Scarab. It will take him at least another week before he reaches Bequia.

"But once he reaches Bequia, it will not take him long at all. The island and the population are both small, and it will take him less than a day to locate this house, to verify that I am here. Then he will withdraw and plan.

"And then he will kill me."

"And me."

"Yes." She ate another wedge of the orange, holding it on the pads of her fingers. "He will be surprised you are here, because he believes you are dead, that I killed you, and that your body is rotting at the bottom of the Hudson River. He cannot conceive that I spared you. He will not expect you here."

"But he'll spot me during the surveillance," I said.

She finished the orange, dropping her right hand and allowing Miata to lick the juice from her fingers. "There is an optometrist in Port Elizabeth, we will get you contact lenses. You will cut your hair and dye it. You will grow a beard. With the sun, the tan, it will make recognition difficult."

"You're getting ahead of yourself," I said. "I didn't say I was staying."

This silence lasted long enough for *Rubber Soul* to end.

"You should leave here," I told her. "Keep moving."

"Movement is exposure."

"So you're just going to wait until Oxford shows up? And then kill him?"

"If you can think of another way to stop him, I'd be quite interested in hearing it."

I ignored that. "Do you have any idea how he'll come at you?"

Again, she gave it some thought before answering. "He will want to verify the kill with his own eyes. Pistol, probably. It will be close work, inside the critical space."

That was both surprising and distressing. Jeppeson's attempt on Lady Ainsley-Hunter had been inside the critical space, and I'd gotten her out of that with dumb luck and nothing else. I doubted there would be anything dumb about Oxford's try when it came. Survival would hinge on reaction times, how quickly I could spot the threat and respond, how quickly Drama could do the same.

"He can get that close?"

"I can," she said simply.

You're thinking about this, I realized. You're considering it seriously. You're out of your miserable little mind.

She was petting Miata's neck, waiting for me, as if she could see me teetering on the brink.

"Most principals, they hire a BG because the BG knows something they don't, namely how to keep them alive," I finally said. "They're buying that knowledge far more than they're buying the body. They normally get their money's worth. But this is different, this is a whole different level of play. This isn't lunatic-in-the-crowd stuff, this isn't some overzealous fan. This is a professional killer. That's your territory. You have knowledge I don't."

"Some of the knowledge, yes."

"Which makes me think that I'd be cannon fodder for you, nothing more."

"I have already said that I will teach you what I know. I will teach you everything."

I took off my glasses. The left lens had taken a hairline scratch at some point, probably before I'd left New York. I hadn't noticed it. I put my glasses back on.

"If you stay," she said, "I will have no secrets from you."

She waited for me to respond for nearly a minute, and when it was clear to her that I wasn't going to answer, she cleared the table and went inside. I heard the faucet in the sink open, the water splashing. Miata moved from where he had parked by her chair to me, resting his muzzle on my lap. I decided that scratching him on the head would not be wholesale collaboration with the enemy.

If I believe her, I thought. If I can believe her. And I know I can't, so why am I even thinking about this?

The photographs that Gracey and Bowles had shown me, they could have been faked, it was true. Why they would fake them, why they would go to the time and the effort to put a scare into me, I couldn't begin to imagine. It had been in that same meeting that Oxford had been mentioned, that I had seen a picture that connected him to Drama. That meeting had put the players on the table, linked them all together.

There just wasn't any logic to it that I could see other than a means to set me up. So maybe the Backroom Boys were in on it with Drama; she'd already admitted to having worked for the CIA, or at least she had if I was willing, once again, to believe her. It was like following a loop of lies, a Möbius strip that, no matter where I began to follow it, fell back on itself. I couldn't even see a fundamental truth anymore, a place to start. I was being played, sure; by whom, why, I no longer had any idea.

Then there was the other thing, the chance, however remote, that she was telling me the truth. That Oxford had been hired to kill her, that the CIA had misread their intelligence, had overreacted to the presence of two of The Ten arriving in the United States at the same time. If that held, then Drama was lying about Dallas, but that could be explained.

It was, in fact, harder to do what she had done to me in New York *without* killing people than the other way around. If the deal in Dallas had gone sour, if she'd had to defend herself, then it made sense she would lie to me, deny having been there at all, for fear of pushing me away.

Of course, I didn't actually know if Drama was telling the truth, if my friends were still alive.

Too many variables, too many things I didn't know.

She emerged from the house, carrying a beach towel and no longer wearing the shorts, now just in the one-piece bathing suit.

"I must exercise," she said without looking at me, and headed down the path back to the beach. Miata left me and followed her.

I stayed at the table.

There was only one door that I couldn't open, in the basement. Shielded wiring ran along the basement ceiling, into the room. Throughout the house I found signs of an alarm system, though I couldn't locate the controls. Motion detectors had been discreetly placed in the foyer, the living room, and the kitchen. Another was at the head of the stairs, and on the second floor, after some looking, I found sensors at both ends of the hall, and the bedrooms. The only room that wasn't covered was the master bathroom.

I didn't find any video surveillance equipment, no cameras or the like, but I didn't take a lot of time to look, so I could have easily missed them.

There was no telephone that I could find, and no television. The only household electronic was an Aiwa compact stereo system with multidisc CD player, sitting on a shelf in the living room with a stack of discs beside it. She seemed to be a big fan of the Fab Four, had a copy of everything they'd ever released, as well as orchestral recordings of their songs, pure instrumental versions. There was a scattering of classical music.

The house was Spartan. A framed poster for the Easter Regatta hung beside an ugly oil painting of a milkmaid working a cow. The only bookcases I found were in the living room, filled with tired paperbacks, their spines creased and broken, most of them at least ten years old. There were several spy stories, and a lot of true-crime books. Most were in English or French, but there were a handful written in German.

In the kitchen, in a cupboard by the sink, she kept cookbooks. The majority of these were in French, lessons in the preparation of fine foods, and none looked to have ever been opened. The rest were in English, titles that talked of maximizing your potential through food, the power of fresh fruits, healthy vegetarian cooking, performance diets.

Aside from the knives in the kitchen, the only weapon I found was upstairs in the master bathroom, a Korth .357 Combat Magnum, resting on a box of tampons in a drawer by the sink. I'd never actually seen a Korth before. It is a six-thousand-dollar gun, handmade and superbly tooled.

If you're going to be attacked in the john, I thought, you might as well defend yourself with the best.

I dropped the Korth back on the tampon box and headed back outside.

The sun had dried most of the water from her skin and swimsuit. She sat on the towel, tossing a piece of driftwood for Miata to fetch. The Doberman seemed ecstatic with the game, running back and forth with his mouth open and his tongue flapping, and if he'd had his voice, I'm sure he'd have been barking in delight.

"I want to use a phone," I said.

She didn't look at me. "I can't allow that."

"I have to know if my friends are still alive."

"If you call them, you will tell them where you are. They will come for you. They will alert the authorities. I can't permit that." She held out her hands as Miata returned with the stick, and they played a short game of tug-of-war before he dropped it and crouched, ready to resume the chase again. She hurled the stick end over end a good twenty feet, and he was after it almost before it had left her hand.

"I won't tell them," I said.

She'd been sitting with her hands on her knees, her legs drawn up, and now she stood on the towel. With her index fingers, she pulled the elastic at the seat of the suit, making the fabric taut again. She had a swimmer's body, with a powerful torso and defined muscles in her shoulders and arms.

When Miata had returned and then left again in pursuit of the same stick, she said, "You will do the job?"

"I can't answer that until I talk to my friends."

"I will pay you three million dollars, and provide you with any equipment you require. I will transfer the money to the accounts you specify, or show you how to establish a new one, one that will keep the money safe and hidden."

"I haven't said I'll do it. I need to use a phone first."

She picked up the towel and shook it out. Miata came back and dropped the stick at her feet, and she said something to the dog in Russian, and the dog, for a moment, looked annoyed.

"Follow," she commanded.

I wasn't sure if she was talking to me or to the Doberman.

The keypad to unlock the basement door was hidden behind the light switch, and the code was long and she blocked my view of the sequence with her body.

The room was enormous, though mostly empty, a concrete bunker with a low ceiling. A couple of mats were spread out on the floor in the middle of the space; heavy, sway, and speed bags hung just past them. A weight bench was in the corner, a stack of plates beside it. A single column stood in the center of the mats, wrapped in gray and black foam and held in place with duct tape. At the far end of the room was a man-shaped silhouette, plywood painted black, and farther along more mats, these positioned in front of a series of floor-length mirrors. A dance *barre* was bolted to the wall nearby. On the left-hand wall as I entered, about halfway down, was an alcove, and another door, closed. The scent of cordite lingered, stale in the air.

She led the way in without stopping, saying only, "My hard room."

To the right of the door ran a long metal counter that turned at the corner and continued down for several more feet. There was only one chair, positioned in front of a battery of video monitors, all on, that fed their images into a stack of VCRs to one side. The monitors covered both interior and exterior access to the house, and stretched along a fair portion of the beach. A laptop computer handled the alarm system, with a map of the house on the screen, showing all the open doors and windows.

At the end of the counter was the handset for a satellite phone, and she switched the power on, waiting for the red light on its face to stop blinking and verify a signal lock. The dish for the phone had to be outside somewhere, but with all the foliage, she could have left it unconcealed and nobody would ever find it.

"Who are you calling?" she asked.

"My home."

She knew the number, activating the speaker and then dialing. She leaned back against the console, giving me room to access the phone, but keeping one finger on the power switch. From the grill, I heard the beep and whistle of the satellite. The phone rang three times before it was answered by Erika Wyatt.

"Hello?" The connection was clear, as if I was calling from Midge's apartment below, and Erika's voice was full of fatigue.

"It's Atticus."

She shrieked so loudly, the noise echoed off the concrete all around us, clearly delighted that I was alive. I tried not to let Alena see me grin.

"Oh my God!" Erika said. "Where have you been? Where are you?"

Alena was moving her finger lightly back and forth over the switch. Her expression said to hurry up.

"Where have you been, Atticus? Are you all right? Jesus, everyone's been so worried about you—"

"I'm fine," I said. "Is Bridgett there? Natalie?"

"No, no, I mean, Natalie's at the office and Bridgett went with Agent Dude to look for you, they sent divers into the Hudson looking for you, you know that? Oh my God, it's so good to hear your voice—"

"Erika, listen. I need you to tell me what happened."

"What happened? You disappeared, that's what happened, you should be telling *me* what happened—"

Alena was making a whirling motion with the index finger of her free hand, telling me to wrap it up. I said, "Erika, I'm all right. But I need to know if everyone there is okay."

"They've been really worried about you, it's even been in the papers—"

"Dale and Corry and everyone?"

"They're *all* fine. What's going on? Where are you?"

"It may be a while before I get back."

"But *why*? Where are you—"

"I'll be in touch as soon as I can," I said, but Erika never heard it, because Drama had already killed the connection.

"You didn't have to do that," I said. "I was wrapping it up."

"You were wasting time."

"I wanted her to know I was all right. You made a choice to remove yourself from humanity, to live on an island. But I have people, and I owe them consideration for their feelings."

She shut off the power to the phone and folded her arms over her chest. It was cooler in the basement, and goose bumps had risen on her arms and legs.

"He'll kill us both," I said.

"I don't think he will. I think we can stop him."

"And then what happens? Whichever way this goes, it'll end in death."

"Yes. It will be him or me."

"And if it's him . . ."

"I will not kill you," she said.

"I am a fool, I admit that without provision," I said. "But I'm not an idiot. If Oxford dies, and you live, and I'm alive, you've got to kill me, or else your little Paradise Island is revealed for all to see."

"You don't understand. I am done, I have quit. Oxford will be the last life I take. After that, I am an assassin no more. I would not harm you."

"How can I believe you?"

She gestured to the phone, and when I shook my head, she got angry. "I do not know what else to do! I have shown you my life, Atticus, I have asked you for your help, and I have kept my word to you each and every time it was given! What more can I do to earn your trust?"

"Let me walk out of here. Now."

She pushed off the counter and practically ran to the door, yanking it open and gesturing for me to go through.

"Go. Go ahead! Go!"

I went out the door and up the stairs, hearing her swearing in Russian behind me. On the ground floor I crossed the living room and went out onto the patio, then down the steps. The abrupt change in temperature brought sweat onto my skin. Across the driveway I met up with the little road, following it under the shade of a grove of mahogany trees. Birds were singing.

Something rustled in the foliage, and I turned around, ready to shout at her that I'd known she was a liar, and that at least she could be bothered not to shoot me in the back.

Miata was standing on the road, looking at me, and I scowled. He blinked, curious perhaps as to why I was suddenly so angry at him. Then he snuffed the air and turned back toward the house.

I followed the dog.

CHAPTER FOUR

It is always about you and your body.

It's how you see yourself, and as a result, how you see the rest of the world.

The body dictates everything. It's where it all starts.

What you can make it do. What you can make it endure. How quick you can be. How precise. How quiet, and strong, and flexible, and still. It is the one tool you always have at your disposal, no matter where you travel, the one weapon that can never be discovered going through customs, never be spotted by a watchful guard or an attentive police officer. It is at the heart of everything you do, and you must be able to trust it absolutely.

The body.

This is what it takes.

You're up at sunrise, with at least eight and sometimes nine hours of sleep already at your back. The rest is as important as the exercise, and you should avail yourself of the luxury while you can; there will be times when you must go without sleep, when you are running or hunting, and when those times come you must be strong.

Take the rest when you can.

When the sunlight or—if it's raining—your internal clock wakes you, you shut off the alarms and check the perimeter to make certain nothing happened during the night, though you already know nothing did. This is vigilance, not paranoia; this is a constant awareness of your environment, and you must rely on it wherever you go. Getting lazy gets you killed. Secure though you may be now, there is always someone hunting the hunter.

Certain that nothing requires your immediate attention, you move out to the veranda, or for variety, the patio, and begin your day. You start with yoga.

Initially, you used the Hatha style, though over the years you have adapted it to something more suitable to your needs. The metaphysical and spiritual aspects of the tradition hold no interest for you; you are strictly interested in the practical. Yoga promotes flexibility, keeps your joints loose and strong, builds endurance and strength, teaches a control of your breathing. It requires self-awareness, and allows you to monitor your body for changes or injuries, for anything that could later develop into a problem.

You are so practiced at this that you can easily support your entire body weight on a single appendage, on your foot or your hand or your head.

Yoga can take up to an hour, and now it's time for breakfast, since you cannot train without nutrition. You throw fresh fruit into a blender, perhaps with some plain yogurt, though an egg once a week is not out of the question, and sometimes you have a muffin or some toast. Whatever you decide, once there is something in your stomach, you take the supplements. Silica, magnesium, B-vitamins, micronutrients, Siberian ginseng, lutein, taurine, carnetine, glutamine, creatine, chromium, all natural, all taken to keep you at your peak. Some of these you mix into your juice or the smoothie you make. Some of these come from pills.

You don't supplement vitamin C or potassium simply because you're getting all you need from your fruit intake. If you're female, you supplement iron; if you're male, you take zinc.

You avoid artificial chemicals, and you never take steroids or other engineered drugs. You cannot risk a dependence. Addiction will dull you, teach your body how to lie, and that cannot be permitted.

You go downstairs, to the basement and the mirror.

You begin at the *barre* bolted to the wall. First position through fifth, standing straight, then in *demi-plié,* then *grand-plié*. You do *port de bras,* a whole series of *battements,* extending and returning your arms and legs. After a time, you move onto the floor, watching yourself in the mirror, and you repeat the exercises, faster now, and assembling steps into what could charitably be called a dance. A *grand temps lié, arabesques* from different positions and angles, then the turns.

These lessons in ballet, this practice, is as vital as any exercise with weights or guns, and thus you give it your total concentration and effort. Ballet develops a sense of rhythm and timing; it focuses breathing; it requires control. In ballet, every aspect of the body in motion is the body in control. Each inch of your body is trained to respond precisely to your will, with strength and speed. These are skills that serve you well.

It's an easy transition to go from a *jeté en tournant* on the floor into the padded post, turning your dance into an attack, working on your hand-to-hand skills and your footwork. This is shadow-boxing, fighting invisible enemies at full speed, with all of your power. You're not practicing any specific martial art, you've no interest in Kung Fu *katas*. What you use is a combat *style,* uniquely your own, a hodgepodge of maneuvers and moves acquired over the years or developed on your own, picked for speed, savagery, finesse, efficiency.

You work freestyle, stringing moves together and often surprising yourself with new combinations, new ways to move from wrist to elbow to knee. You prefer the post to the heavy bag because you can move around the post, attacking from any angle, any direction, any height. You weave and duck across the floor, defending yourself against invisible assailants, then attacking again, holding nothing back.

If it weren't so damn exhausting, it might be fun.

When you're soaked with perspiration and your lungs are crackling with each breath, you redouble and push harder, because you've never yet been in a fight that ended merely because you wanted a breather.

Often you practice with weapons, using a stick or a knife or both on the pole. Sometimes you wield a set of keys, or a box of wooden matches, or a plastic comb, or a drinking glass, or your shoe, or belt, or watch. You use anything you can think of, anything that might, one day, be at hand. All that matters is where it connects and how hard it hits when it does.

You stop. You're out of breath, sore, thirsty as hell.

Dehydration is a killer.

It may work for those models in magazines, the ones whose muscles are so cut, who look sculpted from clay, but you know the truth behind it. You're actually stronger, in better form and shape and condition than any of those hard bodies, and if you went without water for three days before a photo shoot, your skin would be as thin as paper and your abs would look like that, too.

But of course, then you'd be weak, sick, and dying.

So you damn well stay hydrated.

There's a roll of tape on the end of the *barre,* and you use it on your wrists before moving to the heavy bag, the one you filled with water, rather than sand, because water makes the bag feel more like a human being would feel. You throw punches, knees, elbows. You practice kicks, always low, because anything higher is too slow and renders you too vulnerable. You practice eye gouges and throat shots and organ hits, always visualizing the anatomy of your target, the solar plexus, the liver, the kidneys, even the frail projection of the xiphoid process, where one blow can send slivers of bone into the vital organs.

You don't ever go for the face unless you want to send a message.

Then to the speed bag, practicing tempo, rhythm, endurance. Then you jump rope, practicing your footwork, staying light and quick.

When you finish, you've been at this for over three hours.

You drink more water, and remind yourself that this was the easy part.

You swim two miles in about forty-five minutes, and with the tide and the waves and the current, you're working out your whole body. The salt water keeps your skin healthy and strong, and you've noticed that cuts and scrapes heal faster as a result of your relationship with the ocean.

Back on shore you stretch, drink water, then you pick up the two-by-four and start your run, holding it in front of you, always in an overhand grip, because carrying it on your shoulders or your back would be too easy. One day you'll have to run carrying something, maybe a rifle, maybe something more awkward and heavy. You begin along the beach, but there are paths all around the house, and you vary your route every day, never allowing your body to become too familiar with any one routine.

At different points along your run, you stop. You grab a branch and do pull-ups or dips. You drop on your back and do sit-ups. Each exercise you do has been picked for its practicality, was long ago evaluated and added to the repertoire on the basis of, first and foremost, how well it trained you to move your own weight, and to move it quickly. You don't do crunches, for instance, because you're not interested in having a washboard upper abdomen; you do sit-ups simply to get to your feet as swiftly as possible, to allow you to perform a kippup, where you can go from flat on your back to your feet with one motion. You do pull-ups because you know one day you will need to lift yourself into cover, or over an obstacle.

You don't do push-ups because you see no possible offensive or defensive use for that motion.

Because you've done these exercises so much, done them so often, your body adapts quickly. That's too close to complacency for you, and so you've got to break it up, vary the routine. Instead of a two-mile swim, you push yourself sometimes to five, swimming the circumference of the lagoon and all the way out to the open sea.

Once a week, you run the equivalent of a marathon, all the way around the island. It's not a very big island, and you can end up running its length multiple times.

Three days a week you train with free weights, but you only work the major muscle groups, and this is to keep your body active in different ways. You're not looking to develop more muscle, only to stimulate what you've already got. Squats and squat thrusts and leg presses to keep the lower body active. Military and bench presses for the upper body and shoulders.

Two days a week you take off to let your body recover. This means you do yoga in the morning, and then a light swim, only a mile. You alternate the days, to keep your body fresh, but you never skip two in a row.

Twice a week, unless there is a need to do otherwise, you work with the firearms. Wearing eye and ear protection in the basement, you fire two hundred rounds through different pistols, different calibers, just keeping in practice. You work with your off hand, you train standing, kneeling, prone, even on your back. You use the shotgun and the submachine gun and the rifle, just to maintain familiarity. Then you clean all the weapons, making certain they work as they were designed to, that they will be ready when you call upon them.

You pick your food carefully. Lean meat, fish, lots of fruit, lots of vegetables. You are partial to watermelon, not only because it has such a high water content, but also because it is an exceptionally nutritious fruit. You drink water constantly, juice occasionally, green tea rarely.

You avoid caffeine. It is the worst possible natural stimulant, addictive and draining to the adrenal gland.

Since you have almost no fat on your body, you include it in your diet because you need that fuel, and don't want to burn the sugar out of your muscles. Nuts are good, and olive oil. It's hard to get dairy, but whole milk is acceptable. Your taste for artificial sweets, desserts, is limited—fruit is much more appealing.

That's the process.

These are the effects.

The first week is hell, you know you're going to die.

It doesn't matter if you've trained for the Olympics or gone through Basic or reached your umpteenth-level black belt in Tae Kwon Do, your body has never been asked to work like this, to adapt and change to so much so fast. It rebels, sending out every signal it knows in an attempt to get your attention, begging you to quit. When you run, you get sick to your stomach. Your shins feel knotted, your legs are in chaos, the ballet training giving pain everywhere, from the arches of your feet to your calves and knees and hips. When you carry the two-by-four, you see a muscle in your forearms pop up beneath the skin like a golf ball. Your shoulders, arms, chest, and back ache. There are times when you cannot stand up, and each time you try, your thighs cut out on you again, your quadriceps utterly useless, and you find yourself falling to your knees and powerless to resist gravity. The first time it happens, it's alarming. The sixth time, it's pathetically funny.

Muscles don't hurt; they burn, and by the second day, all of them have come together in one bonfire that rages all along your body.

To combat the agony, you receive regular rubdowns, to drive the lactic acid from your calves and thighs and back, and that hurts, too. Every night before falling into the exhausted stupor that is substituting for sleep, you use a liniment that smells at once of camphor and molasses—*dit da jow* it's called, and if you could fill a tub with the stuff and soak in it, you would. It stains your skin amber, but you don't care—it works, seeping into your muscles while you sleep, soothing the pain.

But when you wake the next morning, that little gift is gone. You're stiff and sore and the act of getting out of bed makes you want to weep.

You're constantly hungry, too, because fruits and vegetables and a little sliver of fish, that's not food, it's not *enough*. You think you drink water just to have something in your gut. Because of all the supplements, your urine has turned neon yellow.

The burning in your muscles continues, and you live on faith that, if you stick with it for long enough, it will pass.

But you're seeing no signs that it will.

The second week is a study in disaster. You think you've pinched the sciatic nerve, but learn that, instead, the iliopsoas—the muscles that work your thighs at the hips and secure the pelvic girdle—have seized up as a result of all of the ballet training. The constant spasm is pulling your back and legs out of whack, and the pain shoots down your hamstrings as if on razor-wire.

On day ten, while shadow-boxing at full speed and full power, something spasms and for a time you can't turn your neck. Then the muscle relaxes, and you can move your head again, though now it feels like someone is resting their whole weight on their knees, and their knees are somehow on your shoulders. That soreness remains for the next several days.

The general muscle burn continues, but now it is endurable. The rubdowns at the end of each day are so essential that you shave your legs to avoid the constant hair-pulling. And while one burn may be preparing to leave you, another has arrived, a sunburn so bad that blisters have risen on your back and shoulders, the result of constant exposure to the sun. Sunblock has proven worthless, it simply sweats right off your skin, even the brands advertised as waterproof. Maybe it would be different if you were just taking a quick dip and then drying off on your towel, but because you're running after the swim, because it feels as if you are constantly in motion, you'll never really know.

Day twelve, while running the trails, your ankle twists and you take a header into the ground, ramming the two-by-four into your chest. The bruises appear within hours, your skin rising taut with the edema, and you learn that the best way to deal with the injury is by massaging the swelling out, getting the fluid and blood to dissipate. It hurts a lot. You end up soaking your sprained ankle in a bowl of *dit da jow*.

You are so hungry you think that maybe you dreamt of a cheeseburger last night.

The third week you start to turn the corner.

The pain in your muscles is less constant, though you're still relying on those rubdowns to keep your body from seizing up like a rusted engine, and you stink constantly of camphor and molasses. The ten-mile run that left you puking two weeks earlier is now negotiable, though certainly not easy, and that two-by-four is still the bane of your existence. All the same, you're surprised by the strength in your grip, the power in your fingers. You have opportunity to marvel at how swiftly your body adapts, and there are moments when your focus broadens, when you can see past the constant work to slivers of the results—you smell the ocean and it is different, cleaner, sharper. The trees have their own odors. Colors are sometimes shockingly vivid. Your skin has cleared up with the exercise and constant exposure to sunlight and salt water, and it feels different on you, tighter and stronger.

You're growing to rely on yoga the way you once relied on coffee. You've learned enough that you try that headstand you've been seeing, and it's going well until you lose your balance completely and nearly kill yourself by going over the veranda.

Your neck, recovered from the week prior, spasms again.

The one part of you that seems to have endured thus far without complaint, your wrists, begin aching. You realize you haven't been taping them well enough before working the post and bags. Or maybe you're not punching right, and suddenly you're reexamining the mechanics of the movement, trying to work out what it is you're doing wrong.

On the off days you download video, PBS's *Dance in America,* footage of the New York City Ballet, the Bolshoi. Dances choreographed by Balanchine, performances by Baryshnikov and Nureyev. An art that never held much appeal before now is fascinating, and you can break down patterns and steps, attempt to recreate what you see. You stink at it, and you know that, but that's not the point. You're beginning to understand the motion.

The food tastes better, though your diet has remained fundamentally the same. Watermelon is astonishingly more delicious than tiramisu. For the first time you're not ravenously hungry.

The fourth week, stepping from the shower and reaching for the towel, you see yourself in the mirror, and for a moment honestly do not recognize yourself.

You stare for quite a while, wondering.

By the eighth week, when you move, swimming in the water or running on the beach or working at the *barre,* you are completely aware of yourself, the space you consume in your environment and how to travel through it. You see for the first time, perfectly, the nearly infinite ways you can move your body, and with that comes an epiphany: you understand why yoga and ballet have survived for as long as they have. It is no longer just enough to do the exercises; now you strive for proper form and grace.

You understand the beauty and benefits of being able to move your own weight, with mastery, completely. When you hit the heavy bag with your hips driving the blow and not just your arms, you're both delighted and horrified with the understanding of just what that blow would do to another body.

Then one morning you rise with the sun and you look out at the water as you start your morning yoga and you realize you are up first, you are folding yourself out of your handstand before she even emerges from her bedroom. You greet one another, say good morning. You settle into the day.

You realize you have been doing this for almost four months.

And you know it's got to end soon, one way or another.

CHAPTER FIVE

She cried in her sleep.

It took me a while to figure out that was what I was hearing. During the remainder of August I was too blitzed from the regimen to do anything but sleep through the night, and my physical exhaustion was so total that nothing short of gunfire could have roused me, anyway. It was mid-September before I actually heard the sound, and even then I couldn't identify it. It was faint and small, inconsistent, and there were nights when I heard nothing at all. If Miata had been able to speak, I'd have blamed it on him; instead, I convinced myself it was wildlife playing about in the trees, a manicou or a bananaquit up past its bedtime.

It was October, fourteen weeks since I'd been taken from New York, when I woke in the predawn and heard it again. A warning had been issued earlier that week for Hurricane Josephine, and though the storm had missed the Lesser Grenadines, Bequia had taken some collateral fallout, with winds and heavy rain. While I had been concerned, thinking that if he were close, Oxford could use the storm to good effect, Alena hadn't seemed to care one way or another. Josephine was the fourth named hurricane to have traveled the Caribbean since my arrival; clearly she was used to them.

My concerns about Oxford had been growing daily; for the last two weeks I'd carried a gun whenever and wherever I could, an HK P7 from Alena's substantial weapons locker. I'd urged her to carry, but she'd been surprisingly resistant to the suggestion, acquiescing only when we were out of the house, either exercising or during the occasional trips into Port Elizabeth.

We didn't talk about it, but we both knew there wasn't much time left.

Thoughts like that made it understandably hard to sleep.

There were other things, too, though, more complex and somehow more potent than Oxford's impending arrival. I hadn't spoken to anyone in New York since the call to Erika, and the guilt had begun to eat at me. It was no longer a question of getting to a phone, because I now had the run of the house; the satellite phone was there for me to use if I wanted it, and Alena had given me the codes both to the hard room in the basement and to the general alarm system. I could call if I really wanted to.

But Alena had asked that I not, and at first I'd told myself that I was respecting the wishes of my principal, so I hadn't. And the longer I went without making contact, the worse I felt about the situation. When I thought about it, which was normally at night after we'd each retired to our separate beds and me staring at the blur of the fan, I knew why the guilt was growing to be so strong. The people I'd left behind deserved to know that I was all right; it was a cruelty to keep them ignorant. And it really wasn't my honoring Alena's request that was keeping me from the phone.

I was scared. I didn't know what I would say. I didn't know how to describe the situation. I didn't know how I could convince Bridgett or Dale or Natalie or Scott that I was not only fine, healthy—hell, *very* healthy—and relatively safe, but that I was doing something I wanted to do. That I wanted to be here.

As sprung as it sounded, that I was happy.

That wouldn't play in the Big Apple. I could practically hear Natalie lecturing me on the history of hostage/terrorist brainwashing.

They wouldn't believe me. They wouldn't understand.

I wasn't certain I did, myself, and I was the guy it was happening to.

Thoughts that keep you awake at night.

It wasn't the wind, the sound was too varied, too sharp, and without the customary rise and fall that one hears when a breeze finds cracks and corners. It came to me broken, past the sound of the rain pounding the roof and slapping the leaves and branches outside the house. I lay on my back and listened, and abandoned the idea that it was some creature outside. It was coming from inside, and it was coming from her room.

I got my glasses and rose. I'd switched to contacts almost two months ago, and the difference in lenses was briefly disorienting. I thought about taking the gun, and decided that if I was going into her room in the middle of the night, carrying a firearm was possibly a version of suicide.

I went slowly and quietly, crossing through the bathroom rather than through the hallway along the stairs. I left the light on in my room, using the door to block its spill.

The noise was now entirely human, a whimper, and I knew it was her. It stopped me, kept me motionless with my palm pressed against her door, gave me time to consider whether I should open it or not. The sound stopped. The silence filled only with the sound of the rain.

I took over a minute to open the door, letting the pressure from my hand increase a little at a time until it had swung out. I heard the sound again, sharper and briefer and louder.

She was twisted on the mattress, her legs drawn up almost fetal, the thin sheet tangled around her. She slept topless, wearing shorts, and a bandanna was tied around her neck, loose, as if it had slipped from her forehead. Her expression was pained.

Miata trotted over to where I was standing, pressed the side of his face to my thigh.

Her breath was ragged, deep nightmare breathing, and she made another short cry, then twisted again, her leg straightening suddenly as if kicking in her dream. Her breathing quickened, and Miata turned his head to look her way. She was waking up, would break the surface in a few seconds. I thought about trying to retreat, to keep her from seeing me. I wished I hadn't come through the door, regretted switching on a light, and I wondered what I had thought I would find when I had.

She stopped moving, her breathing calmer. In the ambient light, I saw her eyes open. Her legs straightened, and she sat up. We stared at one another for several seconds.

She hooked the bandanna at her neck with her thumbs, lifted it up over her chin, fitted it back into her mouth. Then she put her head back on the pillow and shut her eyes again.

I closed the door, went back through the bathroom, and climbed into my own bed.

She didn't offer and I didn't ask.

The next day was marked for rest, and after yoga and a swim, we rode the motorcycle into Port Elizabeth late in the morning. We did some general grocery shopping at the S&W Supermarket and then restocked on fruits and veggies at the produce market. We hit a couple of the shops along the shoreline walkway, passing the windows filled with batik and silk-screened clothing, model boats, and the like, getting some extra supplies. We also picked up my new identities, false papers. Alena had informed me that I would need false papers in case we had to move quickly, and I had agreed without argument; I hadn't needed a passport to get this far, but neither of us knew when or how we'd be leaving.

She knew the right people, of course, and the same day I'd gone to the optometrist to be fitted for contacts, we'd met with a couple who owned a yacht named *The Lutra*. They were a man and a woman in their early thirties, with the look of healthy Euro-trash, and knew Alena as Giselle Roux. In exchange for fifty thousand dollars in cash, they were more than delighted to take the passport-sized photographs of me and to promise a speedy return.

Today, almost eight weeks later, *The Lutra* was back in the harbor. I parked the motorcycle at the edge of the Shoreline Road, near the Bequia Marina, thinking we'd head aboard together, but Alena told me to wait while she headed down the pier. Scattered vendors were working on the beach, selling T-shirts and handmade dolls. The storm had left humidity in the air, but the heat, still in the high seventies, had already evaporated most every puddle. What little tourist season there was to Bequia seemed to have ended, though there were a couple of other yachts at anchor, mostly manned by European Old Money dilettantes who couldn't make landfall in Mustique, to the south. A couple kids were splashing in the waves.

If we were being surveilled, it was happening from a distance and via optics, or perhaps from a more direct concealment. But in watching the movement of those people around me, there was nothing to give me alarm. One of the results of my becoming more attuned to my own movement and carriage was that I could now more easily see it in others, who had good posture, who carried their weight in their hips and pelvis or in their back or at their knees.

Alena came off the boat and back down the pier, a brown envelope tucked under her arm. She handed the envelope to me to hold while we did our shopping. I kept my eyes on the crowd as she picked fruit, bantering with the peddlers in the French-English patois that served as Bequia's unofficial language. She took almost fifteen minutes to fill the two bags we'd brought.

A uniformed policeman from the station by the ferry dock was examining the motorcycle as we made our way back to it, though he moved away from it as we approached, giving us a smile and a wave of his hand. We smiled and waved back, and pretended to be sorting the contents of the two bags until he was out of sight. Then I got down on my haunches and gave the bike a good looking-over while Alena covered my back, watching our surroundings.

"Nothing," I said.

"Check the oil cap."

"I did. Nothing."

I straightened up and started the bike without climbing aboard, and the engine ran just as it had, and so I swung my leg over and got the stand up. Alena climbed on the back, and I pulled out, heading north.

"You're going the wrong way on purpose?" she asked in my ear.

I nodded, checking the mirrors and accelerating. The roads weren't in the best shape for high-speed anything, and I knew I was taking it a little fast, but I figured it was an effective way of flushing any possible tails. The road ran along the edge of the island, uphill, with the ocean on our right. After putting a couple of miles between us and Port Elizabeth, I took a turn and slowed down, taking us onto a dirt track that cut through a lemon grove. Behind me, Alena made an approving noise. We'd taken the route before, but only on foot while running.

The track forked and I turned us south, following it another quarter of a mile before breaking direction and cutting down a hillside to the road that ran along the west side of the island. When I got to the bottom I put in the clutch and stopped, craning my head to look back and around.

There was a lens flare from the trees, sunlight hitting glass.

"Fuck," I said.

"We should double back, try to flank him."

I gave it a couple seconds of thought before I said, "If it's him and he's trying to kill you, the worst thing we can do is split up here out in the open."

"If it's him."

"We're going back to the house." I put the bike into gear and opened the throttle, heading down the road. The acceleration was sudden enough that she tightened her grip around my waist, and I felt her lean back.

"Anything?" I asked.

"Nothing. No one following." She had to shout, and then I felt her turn, put her mouth closer to my ear. "Could have been a false alarm. Did you see anyone in Port Elizabeth?"

"Aside from the cop, no one suspicious."

"That was just your paranoia, the cop was honest. He's been here since before I arrived."

"You could have told me that," I said.

"I wanted for you to feel useful."

I nodded and put on more speed, making for the house, hoping that she was right, that it was just my paranoia.

Miata greeted us when we got back, and Alena took the bags into the kitchen while I headed to the basement to check the monitors and the laptop. No breaches had been recorded anywhere, and everything on the system was still running as it had been designed to. Electronic assurance notwithstanding, I took a pair of binoculars and headed upstairs to the veranda, where I spent the next half an hour surveying the surrounding terrain all along the hillside and out onto the water.

I had just finished the full three hundred and sixty degrees when I felt her at my elbow. She took the binoculars from me without comment, handing over the envelope we'd collected in Port Elizabeth. While she made her own survey of the area, I moved back inside to the bed, and dumped the contents.

There were three complete sets of papers, two U.S. and one Canadian. All gave me a driver's license, a passport, and various other sundry bits of identity and detail—library cards, Social Security cards for the U.S. identities. The Canadian I.D. also included a membership card in the Ducatti Rider Program, and I noted that all of the licenses had motorcycle endorsements. The U.S. papers contained membership cards to Blockbuster Video.

The work was excellent, and on close examination I couldn't see any flaws. The documents were so good, in fact, that I was pretty certain they weren't strictly forgeries. In all likelihood, the crew of the good ship *Lutra* had a connection somewhere to get blanks of everything they needed. The first U.S. set said my name was Dennis Murphy, from Gahanna, Ohio, married, thirty years old. The other U.S. said I was Alex Klein, and that I lived in New York City, single, also thirty. The Canadian said my name was Paul Lieberg, from Vancouver, British Columbia, also single, but this time I was thirty-two. I appreciated the fact that none of the identities required my needing fluency in a second language.

Alena had finished her survey, was lowering the binos. "Nothing."

I stowed the papers in the envelope, and we headed back downstairs. I put the binoculars and the papers away. We grilled some fish for lunch, and after we had done the dishes, Alena said that maybe it was time that I assembled a go-bag.

"We'll be leaving in a hurry?"

"Good tradecraft demands you always be ready to go," she replied. "Now that you have the papers, we should not waste more time."

It was hard logic to argue with, even if I'd been inclined to, which I wasn't. She gave me a leather gym bag, and together we loaded it with a change of clothes for me, extra underwear and some basic toiletries. From the weapons locker in the hard room she took a little over a hundred and fifty thousand dollars in cash, most of it in dollars, the rest in French francs, Swiss francs, and deutsche marks. I laid the money at the bottom of the bag. I put the Gahanna I.D. in one of the outside pockets, the Vancouver in the other. The New York I.D. we put in a FedEx envelope, and after some thought, I addressed it to Moore, adding a note asking him to hold it for Mr. Klein. I signed it, dropped it into the envelope, and sealed the whole thing up. The envelope went into the bag along with everything else, to be sent if and when we ever had to hoof it.

Alena took my bag and set it in the front closet beside her own. Then we headed back to the basement and watched a download of the Bolshoi performing *Swan Lake*.

There were no sounds from her room during the night, but the next morning, while we were working at the *barre,* Alena caught my eyes in the mirror's reflection and said, "I have nightmares."

"It happens," I said.

She had one hand on the *barre,* her left out in a curve, her left leg extended and raised behind her almost one hundred and twenty degrees. Her eyes stayed on me, steady.

"I have them often. Sometimes I cry out. It's not something I can help."

She was still watching me in the mirror, as if expecting a judgment.

"Sounds bad," I said lamely.

She brought her leg down, switched to the right, extending and raising it. "You're not curious?"

"You mean do I want to know what your nightmares are about?"

"Yes."

"No."

She considered that, then turned her attention back to her reflection. We finished our warm-ups, moving to the center, and I started working on a series of leaps that I'd watched the night before. The problem was I kept pulling my upper body out of line when I went into the air, so instead of making the move elegant or at least somewhat graceful, I felt that I was instead doing a rather convincing impersonation of an ox that had just been shoved from a passing plane. I spent a good twenty minutes trying to get the leap down, and finally I surprised myself by actually pulling it off, and then I really surprised myself by being able to do it again.

When I came down the second time I looked over to Alena, hoping that she'd seen my success, and was somewhat disappointed to find that she hadn't, engrossed in a problem of her own. She was launching a series of pirouettes, and at first it looked to me like she was doing fine—certainly a world better than my own sad attempts at dancing—turning around and around in *demi-pointe,* three, then four, then five times. It took me another minute of watching to realize that she was trying to push it to six, and that she was growing frustrated, or at the least, annoyed.

I waited for her to try again, and when she started spinning, opening her arms to second position, I moved in to spot her, putting my hands to her hips. She turned from the fifth to the sixth easily, and I thought she would stop, but she kept going another two times around before stopping.

"Try it again," she said, and I let her go, stepping back.

She put her weight on her working leg, swung the other up and into the turn, her arms again opening to second position, and again I moved in. She gave me some of her weight, spinning in my hands and then, at the sixth pirouette, coming out of it, pausing, and then going into a leap. I brought her up, set her down again, assisting as she went into a low arabesque. Her arms swept forward and up, and I guided her as she rose, her torso straightening as her right leg stayed extended behind her. I brought her against me, my hands on her hips, and when she was upright, the leg perfectly perpendicular to us, I lifted and turned. She spun fast, putting distance between us. I moved, trying the first of the leaps I'd been practicing, and I wasn't an ox, and when I turned back, the length of the floor was between us. She paused, then launched a *grand jeté*. I tried one of my own, and we ended an arm's length apart. She took my hand, and spun back into me, her arms raised, her body arched back against mine, my hands on each side of her chest. After another moment, she let her arms descend.

Neither of us moved.

We had ended facing the mirror, and I saw her reflected, her eyes closed. Beneath my palms I could feel her breathing, her heart pounding. Mine was doing the same; we were both out of breath.

Her eyes opened and she watched me in the mirror. She gave me more of her weight to hold.

"*That* was dancing." She was still out of breath, and perhaps even surprised.

I managed a nod, still focused on our reflections.

I wasn't sure I liked what I was seeing.

I wasn't sure I didn't, either.

I thought about the fact that I needed to let go of her, and that after almost four months of contact between the two of us, of rubdowns and massages and teaching, her body and my own had become simply tools. Intimate though the knowledge of them was, they had become almost abstractions.

Now they seemed very real.

She turned her head from the reflection.

"Have you thought about it?" she asked, looking directly at me.

"I have." I let go, backing off a step, moving my eyes from her reflection to her person. "We shouldn't. We can't."

"No." Her voice was low. "We can't."

After a second, she moved to the post and began fighting her invisible foes.

The laptop on the counter began screaming for attention.

She beat me to the computer. The P7 was on the counter by one of the monitors, and I took it up as she checked the screen.

"Perimeter, someone on the driveway," she said. "One vehicle, coming to the house."

"Stay here," I said. As I hit the stairs she called something after me and I shouted back, "I mean it! Stay there!"

I didn't hear her answer, taking the steps two at a time to find Miata waiting for me at the top. With the gun in my right, I glanced around the corner into the living room, and seeing it clear, moved through to the back. I stopped and checked again, this time looking outside, and I saw no one. I doubled back across the space, sweeping the gun around with my survey. Alena stood at the top of the stairs, holding the Neostead shotgun from the weapons locker. I glared at her.

"It's not him," she told me.

I intensified my glare and gestured to her to back off. She shrugged and fell back to the stairs, backing up them and out of sight. There was a knock on the door, heavy and rapid and hard. I made my way to it, Miata at my heels.

There was another pounding at the door, and I thought that if it wasn't Oxford, whoever was outside was either forward, foolish, or insane. Using the wall to cover my back, I edged to the window that looked out to the front porch, taking a quick peek.

She'd been right. It wasn't him.

It was Chris Havel.

And Bridgett was with her, holding a gun, and looking like she meant to use it.

CHAPTER SIX

The only thing I could think to say as I opened the door was, "It's not what you think."

She had the gun up to my face before I'd finished the sentence, was starting forward with a snarl.

"Fuck you, where is she, you sack of—" Bridgett said, and then she stopped, the barrel of her SIG perhaps an inch from my nose, and for the first time since I'd known her, she looked like she couldn't think of a thing to say. In my peripheral vision, I could see Miata hesitating, looking up at Bridgett, and then he lowered his head and headed out the open door, brushing past her bare legs.

Bridgett didn't even notice, didn't move at all, the gun still in my face.

"Hi, Chris," I said. I didn't look at her.

"Atticus," Chris said. "What happened to the glasses?"

"Contacts."

"Oh yeah?"

"Yeah. Soft lenses, Bausch and Lomb."

"Those are nice. The Vandyke doesn't really suit you, though."

"It's temporary. I'm hoping to shave soon."

"Sure," Havel said. "You going to invite us in?"

"I'd like Bridgett to lower her weapon first."

Havel waited. I waited. Bridgett held the gun on me a moment longer, then lowered it. She left the hammer up. Her expression had frozen, but now it was starting to crack. Bridgett doesn't hide her feelings well, and I was reading a long string of emotions that started with shock, touched on relief, switched to rage, and now was mostly suspicion. After another second's silence she looked past my shoulder, into the house.

"Where is she?" Bridgett demanded.

"Why?"

She tightened her jaw, pushed past me, bringing the gun up again. I gestured for Chris to follow her through, then checked outside. An old Army Jeep, painted a combination of rust and blue, was parked in the drive. I didn't see anyone else. I closed and locked the door.

They had made it into the living room, each of them reacting very differently to the space. Havel had the same leather book-bag hanging from her shoulder as the last time I'd seen her, and was reaching into one of the pockets while taking in her surroundings. She was grinning, and when her hand came out of the bag, she'd produced a pad and a pen. If she'd been a six-year-old about to meet Mickey Mouse, I don't think she could have looked more delighted.

Bridgett, on the other hand, was scanning the room as if searching for someone to shoot, which I suspect was just what she wanted to do. When I came back to join them, she stopped long enough to glare at me, her rage once again naked and in control.

"What the fuck do you think you're doing?" she demanded.

"It's complicated."

"Fuck you, uncomplicate it, uncomplicate it now. You look like an asshole, you look like you've gone fucking diesel on me, here, as well as crazy. Jesus Christ, what have you been doing?"

Havel, who had started taking notes, stopped long enough to glance up at me. "You look really good. Except for the Vandyke. You lose weight?"

"Some," I said.

"Where is she?" Bridgett asked. "Is she here?"

"She's here," I said.

"I'm going to kill her."

"Why?"

She looked at me much as she had just moments earlier over the barrel of the gun. "How about she's a motherfucking professional killer to start with? How about she tried to shoot me through the head? How about she fucking kidnapped you and apparently has turned you into the poster goddamn child for Stockholm fucking Syndrome?"

"It's not Stockholm Syndrome," I said. "I'm here because I want to be."

"You and Patty Hearst."

Chris had moved to the bookshelves, was examining the titles there. "She a Beatles fan?"

"Yeah."

"Let me guess," Bridgett said. *"Revolver."*

"Help!" I said.

Bridgett laughed, and it wasn't amusement. "Oh, is that it? She *needs* somebody?"

I hadn't actually considered that, but I said, "Pretty much."

She stepped closer to me, holding the gun against her thigh, the hammer still up. I'd never noticed the way she carried her weight before, how much of it rested in her lower back and her knees. She poked me in the chest with the index finger of her empty hand.

"You know what we've been through the last few months?" she hissed. "You know what Erika's been through? Not to mention Scott and Dale and Corry? Not to mention your family, who saw in the paper that you had disappeared?"

"I've an idea."

"You've an idea. That's good. Does that mean your incredible selfishness has some sort of justification?"

"I'm a bodyguard," I said.

"What is that, is that an answer?"

"She's my principal."

Havel stopped thumbing through the titles on the shelf to look at me. If I'd introduced her to Mickey before, now I'd presented her with a lifetime pass to the Magic Kingdom.

"Brilliant," she said.

Bridgett didn't think so. For a moment I thought she was going to pistol-whip me. "I want to see her, I want to talk to this bitch."

"Give me the gun," I said.

"Fuck off."

"I can take it from you."

"You can try."

The P7 was in my right hand, so I used my left, grabbing the SIG and twisting it from her grip in one motion. I had it before she could resist. Before she could find words I'd turned the pistol in my hand and lowered the hammer, then tossed it onto one of the empty chairs.

"You son of a bitch," Bridgett said, and she tried to punch me in the face, but I moved out of it and she bruised only air, and that just made her angrier. "You son of a bitch."

"You need to calm down."

She turned, moving to the chair where I'd sent her pistol.

"Don't," I said.

Havel was watching us, her delight long gone. She wasn't even taking notes any longer.

Bridgett stopped but didn't turn. Her voice was tight, coming from high in her chest.

"You going to shoot me, Atticus?" she asked. "Has she got you so wound up you'd shoot me in the back?"

"It's complicated," I said. "And if you go at her with a gun, one of you will end up dead."

"God dammit, Atticus. I've been looking for you for three months. I thought you needed help, I thought you might be dead." Her shoulders dropped, and she turned to look at me again, and she even managed a crooked smile. "Sound familiar?"

"It does," I said. "Look, you're here, both of you are here, now's not the time to hash this out. You want to meet her?"

"Yeah, I do."

"As long as you don't try to kill her, that'll be fine," I said. "Wait here."

Bridgett nodded, and Havel resumed scribbling madly in her pad. I went around the corner, out of the living room, to the foot of the stairs, thinking it would be better for me to head up and talk to Alena first rather than to just call her name and ask her to come on down. I doubted getting her to relinquish the shotgun would be as difficult as it had been getting Bridgett to give up the SIG, but I was sure some talk was going to be required, whatever the case.

I never got the chance to find out.

CHAPTER SEVEN

She was lying at the foot of the stairs, in a heap, and the shock stopped me cold, and before I could think to look away from her body, I felt the metal chill of a barrel pressing against my neck.

"Gun," a man said in a friendly whisper. He sounded very calm. "Unload it quietly. Then set it on the ground. Do it right or your head comes off."

I did it right, emptying the gun and leaving the breech open so he could see that the chamber was empty. The shotgun Alena had been carrying was gone, and I realized it was the Neostead that was now pressed into my skin. I didn't dare turn my head, couldn't see him to my side. From the living room, I heard Havel saying that she hadn't dreamt they would get this lucky.

"Hands behind your head, lace the fingers," he whispered.

I laced my fingers behind my head. I couldn't see any blood on the ground, and it looked like she was breathing, and I decided that was at least something.

"Back it up."

I backed it up, and he stepped out from where he'd been pressed against the wall. He was almost entirely bald, but for a thin film of short brown hair running from the sides to the back of his head. His face was a long oval, his eyes very blue. He had crow's-feet, like he enjoyed laughing. I put him somewhere in his late thirties or perhaps early forties.

Havel was still talking to Bridgett as I backed up into the living room, and then her sentence faltered. I heard one of them start to move, probably Bridgett going for her gun in the chair, or perhaps she'd already picked it up and was trying to find a shot, but it was useless. He was walking directly in front of me, using the Neostead as a prod, and there was no way she'd get a shot past me.

As if to prove me right, he said, "Toss the gun over here, Ms. Logan, or I'll open him."

There was the clatter of the SIG hitting the tile, rattling to a stop by my feet. He didn't spare it a look, kept his eyes on me. He was wearing surgical gloves, and had a black fanny pack strapped around his waist.

"You're not Drama," Chris said.

"Is it that obvious, Ms. Havel?" he asked. "Kodiak, if you'd turn around and join the ladies in the center of the room, please. Once you're there you may lower your arms."

I hesitated and he gave me the barest shake of his head, a warning. I turned, saw that Chris was still standing by the bookshelves. She had lost her color, the pad and pen held limply in one hand, the book-bag now in danger of sliding from her shoulder. Bridgett was a few feet to her left, her eyes moving from him to me. There was nothing in her posture or face to suggest she was happy with this development. I brought my arms down and turned slowly and when he didn't tell me to stop, kept going until I could face him.

He had moved the Neostead to his shoulder, sighting it properly, keeping the barrel on me. His clothes were entirely ordinary, long tan pants and a lightweight short-sleeved shirt, dark blue, and he looked as if he'd just come off one of the yachts in Port Elizabeth. There was a watch on his left wrist, visible beneath the thin latex of the gloves, but no other jewelry was apparent.

"Who the hell are you?" Bridgett asked.

"No one important." Everything he was saying came out in the same conversational tone. "Took you two long enough to get here. I've been waiting almost six weeks."

"The fuck are you talking about?"

"He's called Oxford," I said. "He's another assassin, he's been hired to kill Drama."

"Partial credit for the answer," Oxford said. He moved a couple of steps closer, surveying the space briefly before settling his gaze back on us. "It's a bit more complicated than that, actually."

"Complicated how?" Bridgett asked.

"In a second," he said. "Ms. Havel?"

It took Chris a moment to find her voice, and she coughed before she could say, "Yes?"

"Come over here, please. Just up the step." When she didn't move, he added, "I could start shooting at any time."

I heard her move past me on the right, stepping up out of the living room, into the hallway that led from the front door. As she did, Oxford sidestepped his way around, as if to block her from making a break for it. Bridgett risked a glance at me, but I didn't move and I didn't speak. There was nothing to do and nothing to say.

"You can stop there," Oxford instructed, and he glanced quickly over his shoulder, as if to assure himself that the door was directly behind him.

Chris stopped moving. Her hands were visibly trembling. The book-bag looked like it would fall any second.

"This'll work," Oxford said, more to himself than to us.

Then he shot her in the chest.

The shotgun had been loaded with buckshot rather than slugs, and the close-range blast punched through Havel in a mist of blood and gore that fell on the tile like paint spattered from a shaken brush. Bridgett choked back a cry, took a step forward, then stopped as Oxford moved the barrel level to her chest. I didn't move, feeling my own hands shake, my whole inside turning wild and cold.

Havel staggered, then fell on her back, her neck craned and her eyes open, staring at us, already dead.

"I'm having to improvise," Oxford told us. "But this'll do."

"Holy Mother of God," Bridgett whispered. "Why . . . ?"

"The problem has always been how to discredit the whole thing, you see, not just her or Kodiak or, uh, 'Drama' back there." He began inching back to where the SIG lay on the floor, used his head to gesture to where Alena lay, out of sight. "Initially I was planning to stage the two women together, then use Mr. Kodiak as the jealous lover. But this is really much better, because it's closer to the truth."

He had reached the discarded pistol, perhaps twelve feet away, and now crouched, keeping his eyes on us. I thought maybe he was about to give me an opening, but he wedged the stock of the shotgun against his hip before reaching for the gun, still keeping his finger on the trigger. If I tried anything, either Bridgett or I would end up dead. When he had the gun, he reached around behind his back and stowed it in his belt. Then he rose again and gave us a smile.

"I have no idea what the fuck you're talking about," Bridgett said.

"That's okay," he said. "Kodiak does, don't you?"

"Who hired you?" I asked.

"This isn't James Bond, Kodiak. This is the real deal. If you know, you know, that's fine, you'll die with the knowledge. Otherwise, you die curious."

"He's been hired to do more than just kill Drama." I kept my eyes on him while I spoke. "He's a . . . character assassin, I guess is the best description."

"That's the best description." He risked a glance over his shoulder, to the stairs, and apparently Alena hadn't regained consciousness, because when he looked back our way, he was still smiling. "Okay, I think we're ready. I can finish down here when we're done. Ms. Logan, if you'll step this way?"

"Fuck off and die," she said.

Oxford made a sound that was part exasperation, part laugh, then moved the barrel of the Neostead back to me. "Do it or I'll kill him here. I won't like it, it's not the effect I'm after, but as I already said, I improvise superbly. Trust me, I can make it work."

"The effect you're after?"

"God is in the details, Ms. Logan."

She looked at me, and she had her fear under control, but it was obvious that the leverage was working. She started to where he was standing and he let her close to about six feet before ordering her to stop and turn around. When she did, he pushed the barrel of the shotgun to the base of her skull hard enough to keep it there with one hand. With his other, he took hold of her by the hair.

"Kodiak, to the foot of the stairs and pick her up," he said. "You're not going to be able to rouse her. I hit her with etorphine, she's going to be down for several hours yet. If it makes you feel better, she won't feel a thing."

Alena still hadn't moved, still unconscious, and I crouched and got my arms beneath her. It was a different lift than before, and she was heavier in my arms.

When I was up again, he said, "Her bedroom. Put her on the bed."

I started up the stairs, desperately sorting through my options. There wasn't a lot in Alena's bedroom that could double as a weapon, at least nothing that I could think of off the top of my head. The Korth was still in the bathroom, as far as I knew, but there was no way I could get to it without getting Bridgett killed. If Miata had been inside maybe I'd have had a chance, but he wasn't, and it was just as likely that Miata was dead. I had no idea how long Oxford had been in the house before he'd revealed himself to me, though I suspected he had entered when Havel and Bridgett had, using them as cover.

Behind me, I heard Oxford ordering Bridgett to follow me, to take it slow.

I reached the top of the stairs, moved through the open doorway into Alena's bedroom, and set her on the bed. The clock and lamp were on the near-side nightstand, but neither could do me any good; the clock was too light to use as a weapon, and the lamp too clumsy.

They entered close after me, as I was turning from the bed, and as soon as Oxford was through the door he gave Bridgett's hair a tug, halting her. She grimaced, furious.

"When was the last time you fucked our friend on the bed there?" Oxford asked me.

"Never."

"Please. I'm asking because it's important, and I need the truth."

"Never," I repeated.

"I understand how awkward this is, confessing your infidelity in Ms. Logan's presence, but I don't have time for this. Now, when was the last time you fucked her?"

"I've never had intercourse with her."

"After all this time here, just the two of you?"

"Shocking, I know," I said.

"What did you do all those long nights?" he wondered.

"We watched a lot of ballet."

"Huh." He considered. "Ms. Logan, turn around. Face me."

The muscles in Bridgett's jaw were jumping as she turned. He still hadn't let go of her hair. When she was facing him, he set the barrel of the shotgun beneath her chin.

"There's a bottle in the fanny pack. Reach inside with your left hand, slowly, and remove it. If you make any sudden moves, you'll die. And Mr. Kodiak . . ."

"I understand," I said.

She took almost half a minute to do it, but it felt a decade longer. When the bottle was in her hand he ordered her to turn around again and hand it to me. I took it, feeling the sweat from her fingers on the plastic. I could hear pills rattling around inside as I turned it to read the label. It was a bottle of Viagra, 50mg tablets, the prescription in my name.

"Take two of them. Then set the bottle on the nightstand."

Bridgett looked at me, and the horror that was creeping onto her face told me that she'd finally figured out the full extent of what Oxford had planned.

I stared at the bottle in my hand but didn't open it.

"Take them."

"No."

He sighed, then twisted the handful of Bridgett's hair until she winced. "If you're saying you don't need any help to get it up, that's one thing. There are guys who can climax easily under these circumstances, believe it or not. You don't strike me as one of them. So you'll take the pills, because if you do, there is a chance I will let Ms. Logan live. If you do not take the pills, I'll kill all three of you."

Just buy the time, I thought. Take the pills and buy the time. There is a way out of this, you just haven't seen it yet. Take the pills, buy the time.

After I'd swallowed the second pill I put the bottle on the nightstand as he'd directed.

"Good," Oxford said, and he gave Bridgett a shove, letting go of her hair and again taking hold of the shotgun with both hands. The push put her off balance, and she bared her teeth as she righted herself, pulling up just in front of me. Her eyes met mine briefly, the look in them tormented.

"Back away from him. Just past the foot of the bed. Stay there and don't move."

She took the position as ordered, and he tracked her with the gun the whole time. When she stopped, her eyes fell to where Alena lay.

"Don't let her fool you," Oxford said. "She was extremely dangerous once."

"Once?" Bridgett asked.

"Before she lost her nerve."

"Now what?" I asked.

"It'll be about thirty minutes before the drug kicks in, so we'll take things slowly," he said, adjusting his grip. "Undress her. Start with her shoes."

Time, I thought. Time. There is a way out.

I started with her shoes.

He was very particular about each article of clothing, where he wanted me to set it in the room. The shoes were actually her ballet slippers, and Oxford had me toss those out the door, so that they fell on the stairs. Her shirt ended up just inside the room. She wore a sports bra, and that he had me fling to an opposite corner.

"The touch of passion," he called it.

The rest of her clothes ended up in a heap by the side of the bed.

"How you feeling?" he asked when I'd finished.

"Sick."

"And how's the cock? Any rumblings?"

"All's quiet on the western front." I wasn't lying. So far, the only thing I was feeling was nausea, though I couldn't tell if that was the drug or the fear.

Bridgett, who had remained motionless at the foot of the bed, said, "It doesn't matter if you do what he says or don't, he's going to kill all of us."

"No, Ms. Logan," Oxford said. "If Kodiak does what I require, you'll live. You'll be the subject of a massive manhunt, obviously, but you're resourceful. You can probably stay free for a while, at least."

"My ass," she said. "If you let me go free I just tell the police what happened here."

"They won't believe you."

"They will."

"They won't, trust me. I've done this before. When the cops are done, they'll have mountains of evidence, both circumstantial and physical. And your word in the face of that, Ms. Logan, will be less than liquid goose shit."

"No one will believe—"

"Goddamn, you're naïve! You don't even see it, do you?"

She glared at him, hatred pure and savage. "It won't work."

He seemed encouraged by that. "Kodiak here is hardly a model citizen. The public, the authorities will find it quite easy to turn on him. The media's been kind so far, but with a little digging, a little light cast in the right corners, a different picture will develop. He'll be seen as a failure and a fraud, as a man who has gotten not only his friends killed through his own negligence, but also his clients. A man who has worked in sex clubs, who has lived with the daughter of a woman he shot to death. A girl who is a minor, in a relationship that could easily be interpreted as sordid.

"Take all of that, Ms. Logan, and now consider . . . suddenly he is famous, he is wealthy, due in part to his success in defeating a 'world-famous assassin.' People believe that Havel's book is truth. But once they see her dead here, presumably by your hands, once they see a sordid sexual relationship between Kodiak and his sworn enemy, they will be outraged. And when the authorities discover that money has traded hands, that Ms. Havel paid Kodiak, either to help perpetuate the fraud, or, better, because he's blackmailing Havel, they'll believe they have been conned. For that, they will hate him. They will hate Ms. Havel. They will disregard everything they ever heard about Drama or The Ten, because if the public detests one thing more than any other, they detest betrayal."

"There are people who know the truth," Bridgett said. "People who will—"

"Inconsequential." He hit each syllable with equal emphasis. "What is one hundred or five hundred or even a thousand men and women who know the truth in the face of millions of beer-chugging natives who believe a lie? The damage will be irreparable."

"I'll know," she said.

"Which brings us back to my point, Ms. Logan. No one will believe you. If Kodiak is a failure and a fraud, you are even worse. A cursory investigation will confirm that you've been his lover. A cursory investigation will reveal that you're a junkie, which the authorities and the public will both take to mean that you are unreliable at best, a criminal at the least, and most certainly never to be trusted. And when the forensic examination of the scene here comes into play, when your prints are found on the shotgun and Kodiak's semen is found inside Drama, the theory of the crime will suggest itself naturally. Kodiak vanished with his new lover, you forced Havel to lead you to them. You arrive, find them in bed together, and in a fit of rage, you shotgun them to death. In an attempt to conceal your crime, you murder Havel.

"Then you flee, or, if you prefer, you turn yourself in, and spin a tale of assassins and treachery that no one will ever believe."

Bridgett was using the edge of the bed for support, her eyes moving from him to me to the woman on the bed. If I felt ill, she looked it.

"You're evil," she spat. "You are purely evil."

"I'm a professional doing a job," Oxford replied easily. "Unlike the bitch on the bed, I don't betray my employers or my profession. I do what I'm paid to do."

I cleared my throat. "And she didn't, and that's why you hate her?"

"Normally I don't give a good goddamn about who I kill or why." He looked at me. "Anyone can be a killer, Kodiak. Few can be an assassin. She let her name be known, she let her own life be more important than the job. That's despicable and unforgivable, because the job, by definition, is more important than life. I'll be happy to have capped her ass."

He stopped suddenly, as if realizing that he'd let his emotions show, then checked his watch quickly.

"You'll forgive me, I don't get to talk about my work often," he said.

"Sure, I understand. Now what?"

"Now you take off your shirt, toss it in the corner there."

I pulled the T-shirt over my head, threw it away. My heart was starting to race, and I could feel the heat of blood, the first humiliating rising of my penis. It wasn't an erection out of arousal, and it was horrifying, and I tried not to think about it. My skin felt hot all over my body.

"Pants, now."

"I have to remove my shoes."

"Yes, yes you do. You may sit on the bed and remove your shoes."

I sat down, the pressure of my body causing Alena to shift on the mattress, her bare leg resting against my back. I remembered practicing on the post with my sneakers, rejected them as a weapon. If I was closer, maybe, but at this distance they'd do nothing but annoy him. I started to unlace them, but he stopped me.

"Just pull them off. You were in a hurry, remember?"

"Sorry, I forgot." I pulled them off and tossed them.

He watched as I did so, then checked my crotch and smiled. "Okay, that's good. Now the pants."

"I need to stand up for that." I kept my eyes on him, trying not to see Bridgett trembling. The humiliation was stronger than the fear.

"Start seated. When they're below your knees you can stand."

I untied the pants, pulled them down to my thighs, then stood, seeing the legs bunch around my calves.

Ranged weapon, I thought.

I bent down and took the cuffs of each leg, stepping out of them, then straightening up again, holding them upside down.

"Where do you want them?" I asked.

"Near the door. Men tend to lose their pants as soon as they can."

"True enough," I agreed, and then I sprang, sweeping the pants up as hard and fast as I could, and he was totally unprepared for the assault. The crotch of the pants caught the barrel of the Neostead, forcing it up in his grip, and he fired high, instinctively, and the buckshot tore hell out of the ceiling, shattered the panes in the French door, and Bridgett was down on the floor but coming up again.

I kept going forward, twisting the pant legs around the shotgun as he moved to jack the next round into place, pulling left with a spin, and he fired again, this time at where I had been seated on the bed. I yanked, and the pump locked back, preventing him from bringing another round up, and all the while I was shouting that there was a gun in the bathroom, screaming for Bridgett to get the Korth from the drawer and to shoot this son of a bitch and I kept turning, driving from my hips and thighs with the pants now bound tight around the barrel, tearing the weapon free of his grip. I finished spinning, facing him again, the gun in both hands by the barrel; Oxford was trying to step back and pull Bridgett's SIG from behind his back, and I swung the butt of the shotgun into his jaw, heard the bone crack. He staggered and dropped, and I flipped the gun in my hand, and that was the mistake, because it gave him time. He came up as I turned the gun and worked the action, diving forward past the edge of the bed, past the open bathroom door, making for the broken window. I got my finger on the trigger and fired at his head, but the full blast missed him, only a portion of the buckshot raking his face. He screamed but kept going, and before I could fire again he was on the veranda, over the railing, dropping out of sight.

Bridgett came out of the bathroom with the Korth in her hands, and we raced each other to the ledge, reached it in time to see Oxford scrambling to his feet, running for the cover of the woods. The shotgun was useless at this range and in that cover, but Bridgett had faith in the Korth, and she fired three shots at him, but I couldn't tell if any of them had hit.

"Motherfucker I'm gonna kill that motherfucker," she ranted, turning and making for the door.

I spun to follow and stopped like I'd run into a wall.

Blood soaked the bed beneath Alena's lower body in a long inverted teardrop that began beneath her left leg and ended in an expanding point at the end of the sheet, drops seeping from the sodden fabric to form a puddle on the tile floor. I let go of the shotgun and went to her side even as Bridgett was going out the door. My heart was pounding from the exertion and the Viagra and the relief and the new fear, and I called for Bridgett to wait but she didn't, just kept going, her boots echoing as she slammed down the stairs three and four at a time.

I'd laid her head on a pillow, and now I pulled it from beneath her, folding it over and jamming it beneath her knee, trying to elevate it. Oxford had caught her with the second blast, indirectly, along the calf and shin. Her lower leg looked like raw and poorly ground meat, chewed and torn from the buckshot. Alena hadn't moved at all, her expression hadn't changed, and I hoped that meant the etorphine that Oxford had given her stole only her pain and consciousness, nothing more. I swore, tried to apply pressure to the leg, and got blood all over my hands and myself. I readjusted my grip, tried the pressure higher, and the blood flow slowed a bit but didn't stop.

"He's gone now," I told her. "You can wake up."

There was no sign that she'd heard me. I kept the pressure on, hoping the blood would slow, but it didn't. The contact lenses in my eyes were itching, making my vision blur, and I blinked tears out of them. I felt light-headed as I gave up on the direct pressure, went tumbling over the bed to the closet. I yanked the doors open, going through the clothes, pulling them from their hangers, and, not finding what I wanted, went to the bureau, began dumping out the drawers.

There were a couple of belts in the third drawer, and I grabbed the thickest and moved back to Alena, wrapping it around her leg, above the knee. I looped the belt and ran it through the buckle, pulling it tight, and there was no easy way to secure it, so I ended up making a knot. The bleeding slowed further, an ooze from the brutalized muscle rather than a flow.

I couldn't take her to the hospital in Bequia. It would be too risky, it would involve the police. But she needed medical attention, and fast, and there was only one solution I could think of. I wrapped her in the sheet and lifted her off the bed. She was breathing, shallow breaths that hadn't turned rapid yet. It wouldn't be long before she went into shock.

Bridgett came back up the stairs as I was lifting her, much slower than she had descended them. "He got away." She was out of breath. "She dead?"

"I can't get the bleeding to stop. I put a tourniquet on her leg but it's not enough."

"She needs a hospital."

"If I take her to a hospital the police will get involved."

"And that's bad? Chris is dead downstairs—"

"That's not her fault!"

Bridgett stared at me. She was still in the doorway, blocking the path, the Korth in her hand. I started forward, but she didn't budge.

"Where are you going to take her?"

"Are you going to help me?"

"Where are you taking her?"

"Dammit, Bridgett, either help me or get out of the way!"

She looked at the naked woman in my arms, at the blood staining the sheet. She looked at me in my underwear, the look on my face, the ruins of the room.

"Chris had the keys to the Jeep," she said.

CHAPTER EIGHT

I'd pulled on the pants I had in my go-bag while Bridgett was driving us into Port Elizabeth, and when we hit the pier I jumped out of the vehicle and sprinted barefoot along the water until I reached *The Lutra,* in the process driving a splinter into the sole of my left foot. The gangplank was down and the woman was on the foredeck, in shorts and a tank top, coiling a rope. When she heard me coming she called out something in French, and her partner or lover or husband or whoever he was appeared at the stairs from below. He used the frame to block the right side of his body, and I knew he had a gun in his hand.

"Giselle's been hurt," I said, and when neither of them moved, I repeated it in my atrocious French. *"Giselle été blessé."*

The man answered me in English, "Bring her aboard."

"I need help."

He spoke to the woman, coming the rest of the way up the steps and onto the deck. He was wearing shorts and sandals, with an unbuttoned tropical-style shirt. He tucked a Smith & Wesson revolver into his waistband, then followed me back down the gangplank to the Jeep. Bridgett kept an eye out while we lifted Alena out of the vehicle, still wrapped in the sheet, and we carried her quickly on board. It was mid-afternoon, and we got a couple of stares, and I hoped that we'd be at sea before someone had the presence of mind to call the police.

Bridgett followed us, carrying the two go-bags, and the man led us from the deck down into the ship, leading us to a cabin where the woman had already pulled down one of the folding bunks. She had a basin of water ready, and an open first-aid kit. As soon as we had laid Alena on the bed, he spoke to the woman in rapid French, then went back out. Bridgett dropped the bags, and I gave her a quick nod, and she followed him up.

"I'm Carrie," the woman told me as she pulled the sheet from around Alena's body, exposing the mutilated leg. She sounded American, maybe West Coast.

"Paul," I said.

She nodded, tearing open a couple packets of gauze. If she cared that the name I'd given her was, in fact, a name she had helped to give me, she showed no sign of it. "When was the last time you released the tourniquet, Paul?"

"Fifteen minutes ago, maybe more."

"Unfasten it."

When I crouched by the bed, my head started spinning again, and I had to catch myself on the side of the bunk. I was still erect, and it hurt, and I tried to not care who knew or saw as I unfastened the tourniquet, allowing some blood to flow back into Alena's leg. The wound began bleeding again. It meant that the leg wasn't a total loss, but it also meant that unless something was done and soon, Alena would bleed out. She was still unconscious but beginning the journey to the surface, and when Carrie prodded the injury, pressing gauze against the torn skin, Alena rolled her head and made an almost inaudible moan.

Beneath my knees, I felt the boat begin to vibrate, the slight lurch as we pulled away from the pier.

"How bad is it?"

"I'm not qualified to say," Carrie told me. "She's lost a lot of blood, obviously, and she's going to need a doctor. Go up to the bridge, tell Jerry that he should call Bennet."

"Who's Bennet?"

"Someone who doesn't ask questions. He's in St. Vincent, we can be there in an hour. I'll stay with Giselle and watch the tourniquet."

I scooped up my go-bag and left the cabin, climbing the steep steps back to the deck, then climbing a short ladder to the bridge. Jerry was at the wheel, opening the throttle. Bridgett was at the rail by the ladder, watching him closely. When I got up to them, she tapped my shoulder and motioned back at the pier, which was rapidly disappearing in the distance. There didn't seem to be anyone milling about the Jeep, anyone intent on pursuing us.

"Carrie says to call Bennet," I told Jerry.

"Then we shall call Bennet." He took a hand from the wheel, reached over to the console beside him where a variety of electronics were resting. There was a small sonar array, and something that I presumed would feed him the latest weather, and a GPS reader. There was also a satellite phone, already on, and he picked up the handset and, with his index finger, began punching in a sequence of numbers. After a couple of seconds whoever he'd dialed answered.

"It's Gerard for Bennet. Quickly, please." He turned the wheel slightly, then let go of it long enough to open the throttle further. "Bennet, yes, I'll be there in an hour . . . gunshot wound, leg . . . no, no, clear out the office, it'll be me and the injured and two others . . . looks like shotgun . . . let me ask, *un moment*."

Jerry moved the handset down, poked the mute button on the satellite phone. "How much?" he asked me.

"Fifty U.S.," I said.

Bridgett opened her mouth to speak, probably objecting to my total lack of business sense, but Jerry nodded as if I'd named an appropriate price, took the mute off the phone again, and said, "Twenty thousand, U.S. . . . *bien,* and no paper, Bennet, none."

He hung up the phone, went back to handling the wheel. "You will pay us before we arrive," Jerry said. "Give the money to Carrie."

"No problem." I headed back for the ladder, dropped back down to the deck. When I landed, my head spun again, and I wobbled, but this time didn't need to grab anything to keep myself from falling. I hoped that meant the Viagra was starting to wear off.

Bridgett followed. "Is there a plan or are you just flying blind?"

"We're going to get her stabilized, and then we're going to get her back to New York." We were moving along the water at a fast clip, and the wind was forcing me to raise my voice. "I have to get her secure, someplace where she can be defended. Then I'll figure out what to do next."

Bridgett produced her Ray-Bans from inside her jacket. She wasn't wearing her traditional leather, but the windbreaker was still black. Even though she'd hidden her eyes, her mouth had turned sour. "You think that sprung motherfucker's going to try again?"

"He ran because he lost control of the situation. You heard what he said, he's not going to stop."

"So you're not going to, either?"

"She hired me for a job. I'm going to do it."

"What the hell is going on between the two of you?" Bridgett asked.

I stopped counting out bills and looked up at her. The sun was behind her, and I had to squint. "You want to ask something, Bridie?"

"Were you honest with Oxford or was that a lie?"

"I don't think that's the question," I said, zipping the bag closed and standing up again. "You're not just asking if I've slept with her."

She ran a hand through her hair, looked away from me to the Caribbean. "You not banging her isn't really the assurance you might think it is after you've lived with her for four fucking months."

"You'd be happier if I had?"

"You're wound around her and she's yanking your chain. You're a god-damn pushover, you know that? You arm yourself so tough, you go diesel, you go fucking hand-to-hand with killers, and yet when you meet a pair of tits who bats her eyelashes and says 'help me help me,' you go all to putty."

"I hope you're including yourself in that," I said.

"Oh, I am. But I've never asked you to kill for me, babe. I never asked you to break the law."

"But it's fine when you've done it yourself."

"I'm not a killer. She is."

"Was."

Her laugh was sharp and mean. "Your wishing her a conscience doesn't change what she is. She's a fucking murderer, and you need to remember that."

"You should maybe wait until you have the facts before you go passing judgment."

"I have all the facts I need."

"Then we've got nothing more to discuss."

Bridgett finally looked from the ocean back to me. Her mouth had gone tight. Then she turned and walked away, heading for the bow and a view where she didn't have to look at anything she didn't want to see.

I took my bag and went down below, where I gave Carrie fifty thousand American dollars and then sat beside the bunk. She'd put a pair of shorts on Alena, and a shirt, and it made her look less vulnerable. Every ten minutes I released the tourniquet to let blood flow back into Alena's lower leg, and then I tightened it again. Carrie kept changing the bandages.

Alena continued to stay down. I got the splinter out of my foot.

Bennet was a middle-aged black man with a Jamaican accent who ran a clinic in Kingstown, St. Vincent. Jerry avoided the main harbor in Kingstown and instead landed us at Barrouallie, off Wallilabou Bay, and Carrie dealt with the one man at customs while we snuck Alena off the boat and into the back of a truck. Twelve minutes later we were in a surgery with dingy white paint on the walls and ceiling and cracked robin's-egg tile on the floor. Jerry handed Bennet his money as soon as we were alone, and while Bridgett waited outside, he and I watched as the doctor started to work.

"She's doped." He'd already started giving her blood, and had just hooked up an I.V. "What'd she take?"

"Etorphine," I said.

He glanced up from where Alena lay on the bed, shaking his head. "Not recreational."

"No."

"Maybe for the best. Narcotic, she's not feeling a thing right now. I can bring her back up with a hit of diprenorphine when I'm done working on her leg."

"Just stop the bleeding," I said.

He snapped on a clean pair of latex gloves, prodding the wound gingerly. "Deep wound, bone shards. I go digging in there, burning things closed and picking this shot out, could be a permanent disability."

"Is there another option?"

He scratched the bridge of his nose with a latex-covered thumb. "You take her to the hospital, they have surgeons could maybe do it. Tibia and fibula, problem is you can't break one without the other, and they're both ground up in here."

"No hospital," Jerry said.

"But I'm saying to you that I do this, she may not have everything in this leg that she once did, you understand?"

Jerry looked at me. I nodded.

"Okay, that's fine," Bennet said. "It's going to take me some time."

"Take all the time you want," I said. "Just make sure you do it right."

"Okay, that's fine," Bennet said again, and he began to work.

As soon as I'd stepped into the hall, Bridgett asked, "Well?"

"He's working on her. It'll take a few hours."

"In the meanwhile we do what?"

"I've asked Jerry to take me back to Bequia. I have some things I have to do there."

"Things that you don't want to tell me about?"

"No, things I need to do alone."

"And you want me to stay here?"

"I want you to stay with her, watch her. Make sure nothing happens to her."

For a second she considered that, then brushed some stray hair back behind her ear, glancing down the hall. When she looked back to me her expression had hardened, she'd made her decision.

Bridgett said, "This is what's going to happen, Atticus. I'll stay here. I'll watch her. I'll make sure no harm comes to your precious principal. I'll help you get her back to New York. But that's it, that's all. After that, we don't know each other anymore."

"You're going to write us off because of this?"

"There is no us, not anymore."

"I'm not talking about as lovers."

"Not lovers, not friends, not colleagues. We've been through a lot, Atticus, we've hurt each other plenty. But I never doubted who you were until now. Everything has changed. Please tell me that you can see that."

I could. I did.

I said so.

And she said she was glad that I understood, and she followed me back into the surgery, and I left her there with Bennet and Alena, and a sadness that I couldn't name.

CHAPTER NINE

Jerry guided *The Lutra* back to Bequia, and it was dark when he reached the mouth of the lagoon that footed the house. He'd killed the running lights before we'd arrived, and he dropped the anchor and told me that he would wait an hour but no longer. I told him that an hour was all I'd need, and if he was waiting for me when I got back, he'd get another twenty grand.

"Then I hope you can swim well," he told me.

I stripped to my shorts, then dove over the side of the boat and into the water, feeling its warmth surround me. It was an easy swim, but I pushed it. The exercise and the sensation of the water were welcome and liberating, and as I swam I finally felt that the last of the Viagra had been driven from my system. I was breathing hard when I reached the beach.

Outside the house, I climbed one of the mahogany trees and used it to jump to the roof. I didn't think Oxford would be lying in wait—I knew I'd winged him, and he was obligated to tend to himself before finishing with me—but I wanted to be careful. At the overhang outside of Alena's room I lowered myself onto the veranda, walking carefully, feeling the broken glass beneath my bare feet. I stepped inside, made a quick search of the closets and the bureau, looking for anything incriminating that might come back to haunt Alena or myself. From her bedroom I moved to the bathroom, then to my room. Everything was clean.

I headed to the basement, to the hard room, and punched in the code to open the weapons locker. Even with the P7 and the Neostead removed, there was still a substantial amount of hardware, including some explosives—some plastique with blasting caps and kitchen timers, and a couple of grenades. Another safe was set inside the locker, at the back, and I keyed the combination. Inside was a short stack of documents, extra identities that Alena had worked up over the years, as well as the paperwork for Alena's various accounts worldwide, including the trust she'd established to finance all of the credit cards she used in her different aliases. I took everything from the safe, including the money, which I estimated at almost a quarter of a million in mixed currency. I left the safe and the locker open, grabbed the explosives.

I hadn't used explosives since I'd been in the Army, and I took my time with them, working carefully. I used one of the blocks of plastique for the work space by the basement door. The explosion would destroy the electronics, make it impossible to salvage any useful information from them.

I set the timers for thirty minutes, checked my watch, set them running.

Outside of the hard room there was a small gas generator that Alena had kept in case the power went down, and by it stood two five-gallon jerry cans of gasoline. I took the cans with me as I went up the stairs.

On the ground floor I found Chris where she had fallen. The heat had already started working on her body, and a cloud of flies had found her. I passed her without stopping, moved into the kitchen, and grabbed a handful of plastic trash bags from beneath the sink. I loaded all of the papers I'd grabbed from the hard room inside, triple-bagged them, and then squeezed the air out. Then I sealed the bag with duct tape, and then I duct-taped the bag to my stomach. It was going to hurt later and it would cost me some skin, but it was the best I could think of; I was going to have to swim back to *The Lutra,* and I didn't want to lose anything halfway there.

I took a book of matches from the drawer by the sink, where Alena had kept candles and flashlights. Then I went back to Chris's body and started going through her pockets.

She had some loose cash, a couple of receipts, and a pack of chewing gum. In the book-bag I found her wallet and passport, as well as a selection of pens, two more notepads, and a Macintosh laptop. The other pad, the one she'd used to take her notes, was on the floor by her right hand. I dropped it in the book-bag, then moved everything into the center of the room.

I took one of the jerry cans to the top of the stairs, opened it, and backed down again, splashing as I went. I splashed the contents of the second can throughout the living room, pouring it on the book-bag, the shelves, the furniture.

The smell of the gasoline followed me outside when I stepped out onto the porch. I checked my watch and saw that I had twenty-three minutes before the plastique went off, perhaps thirty before Jerry left me behind.

That gave me at least ten minutes to try and find Miata, and it turned out I only needed three of them. I found him under the porch, curled up, nervous and watchful, and when I crouched and offered my hand, his ears flattened back against his broad head for a moment before he began creeping forward. When he came out I gave him a good scratch behind the ears, using my other hand to stroke his coat, checking his body for wounds.

"She's okay," I told him. "Wait here."

I went back to the porch, opened the book of matches, and used one to light the rest. Then I tossed the book into the living room, turned my back to the sudden heat. Miata followed me down to the water without prodding, but when I started to wade in, he hesitated. I kept going another couple of yards, until the water was at my chest, then turned.

He was looking at me from the beach. Beyond him, I could see the fire in the house beginning to spread. It would destroy the evidence of the lives there, and the plastique, when it detonated, would bury the hard room. There would be questions, there would be a mystery, and Chris Havel's body would be discovered. Perhaps she would be mistaken for the woman who had lived there, for the woman she had made infamous.

"Come on," I called. "I know you can swim, come on."

Miata took a couple of steps to the water, the waves splashing his paws, then skittered back onto the beach.

"I can't carry you. It's too far."

He dared the water again, backed off again. I looked at my watch. The plastique would go off in sixteen minutes. *The Lutra* would leave in twenty. Coming in had been easier, I'd been working with the tide, but swimming back would take longer, and I couldn't wait.

I backed away, the water now at my neck, the waves occasionally splashing over my head. Miata paced back and forth on the sand, looking after me, and then he turned and ran back toward the house, where the fire was beginning to lick out of the windows. I could hear the sound of the flames over the ocean. I checked my watch a last time and swore. I started back to the beach, had my feet on the sand again, when Miata reemerged from the woods, running hard. He hit the water without breaking stride, splashing his way to me, and I turned and started swimming.

I made it back to *The Lutra* with under three minutes to spare, grabbing the rope ladder that was dangling over the side. Jerry reached out a hand to help me up, but I waved him off, looking back for Miata.

The dog was clearly struggling, perhaps thirty feet back. I pushed off the side of the ship and swam toward him. The Doberman is a strong breed, but the swim had been hard on him, and he was fighting to keep his head above the water. I took his forepaws and pulled them onto my shoulders, and the extra sixty pounds of dog threatened to drown me then and there. I got a hand around his middle, kicking hard, and started swimming on my back. My muscles began to burn the way the house had gone up, and when Miata, reasonably frightened, struggled on me, I got a mouthful of water.

Then I bumped into the side of the boat, and Jerry was holding onto the ladder with one hand, reaching down to assist me. I manhandled Miata onto my shoulder, pushed him up to where Jerry could grab him. As soon as the dog was on the deck, I followed.

Back on the shore, the fire glowed on the hilltop. A muffled concussion rolled out to us across the water as the plastique detonated. Flame guttered up, higher than the main blaze. Then the fire settled again.

The ship vibrated once more as Jerry started the engines, and we pulled away from Bequia. I sat on the deck, catching my breath, Miata's head on my lap, watching as the fire faded below the horizon.

PART THREE

CHAPTER ONE

It took five days from the burn in Bequia to reach New York City.

The Lutra had returned me to St. Vincent, waiting in the harbor until I had collected Alena and Bridgett, and we had set off again that night for Miami. Jerry and Carrie had taken another ten grand for the trip, and I suppose they were giving us a discount rate because we had been so good for business. Their fee had included a handling of all requisite paperwork, with the promise that when we reached Florida, it would be as registered members of the crew.

Alena had been conscious when we boarded in Kingstown, still groggy from the narcotic, and suffering a fair amount of pain. Bennet had provided her with a brace for her leg and set of crutches. I told her about Havel's death, and Bridgett watched her like a hawk for a reaction.

"I did not know her," Alena said. "I'm sorry."

To which Bridgett had spun on a heel and marched off to find a berth of her own. I'd used some nail polish remover provided by Carrie to get the duct tape off my skin, and I tried to present Alena with the documents, but by that time she was already fading fast. Bennet had given her some Percodan to help with the pain as the local on her leg wore off, and the last thing she did before falling asleep was to hand me the bottle and ask me to throw the pills overboard.

I left her and went to find a bed of my own, only to discover that Bridgett and I were sharing a room. She was already in her bunk when I arrived, and she waited until I'd folded my bed down and gotten the blanket over me before speaking.

"She'd hired me, you know that?" Bridgett said softly. "Two weeks after you'd vanished, Havel came to my office and hired me to find you. Someone had told her that you'd made contact, Natalie or Dale or Corry, I don't know which, and she was certain you were with Drama and she was certain I could lead her to you both."

"She was right."

She rolled in the bunk, and I heard her feet bumping against the bulkhead. My bed was too small for me; I could only imagine how uncomfortable Bridgett was.

"All she talked about was what a great book it was going to be. She was so excited. It took me over three months to track you down, I went port by fucking port, and Havel was with me the entire time, and she never got discouraged, she never got disappointed. She just kept talking about what a great fucking book it was going to be."

Over the throbbing of the engines, I could hear the water lapping against the hull.

"And all along," Bridgett said, "we were just playing into that motherfucker's hands, we were just doing what he wanted us to do."

"Don't," I said.

"I'll feel guilty if I want to."

"If you hadn't brought her to Bequia, he'd have gotten her there some other way. His initial plan never included you, it was always Chris and Alena and me."

"If I hadn't found you . . ."

"Then maybe all of us would be dead instead of just her."

She moved in her bunk again, rolling, and I turned my head to see that she was staring at me, one hand beneath her cheek, her knees up against her chest. "It doesn't seem a fair trade."

"It isn't."

"You were willing to die for . . ." She made a gesture with her free hand, indicating the rough direction where Alena was sleeping.

"Bridgett, no bodyguard *wants* to take a bullet. That's a myth. No one in their right mind would catch a shot for someone else."

"But you'd do it."

"I'd do it. I'd do it for anyone who hired me. It's my choice, not theirs. It's what people pay me for."

"Chris should have hired you instead of me," Bridgett said.

The ship rocked on a swell, creaking softly. For a long time, there was nothing but the sounds of the boat and the water.

"That doctor," Bridgett said.

"Yeah?"

"He says she's never going to walk right again."

"Oh."

She moved in her bunk, and when she spoke again, her voice was more diffused, coming at me off the wall, indirect.

"It's still not a fair trade," she said.

There was only one snag during the voyage to Miami, when *The Lutra* put in at Cockburn Harbour in South Caicos for refueling. We were almost three days out from St. Vincent, and I'd been spending my waking hours with Alena and Miata. Bridgett gave us a wide berth. We still shared a cabin, but after the conversation that first night aboard, she hadn't uttered more than five words to me, and her silence seemed alternately hostile and sullen.

I actually hadn't expected to see much of Cockburn Harbour, since there was no immediate reason to leave the ship. The waterfront looked pleasant enough, though a little run-down, with a couple of empty warehouses skirting the edges of the harbor. Carrie mentioned in passing that the major industry had once been salt; she couldn't tell me what it was now, and seemed surprised when I asked.

We docked early in the morning, and Jerry went ashore immediately to arrange for refueling. After he left, Alena and I went on deck and tried to do the morning yoga routine, but it was difficult for each of us to relax; there was no question she was in constant pain, and I was more concerned with her well-being than my own. Add to that Bridgett's scornful look when she emerged, and it made finding the right state of mind nearly impossible.

Alena and I were still sitting on deck when Jerry returned, and he didn't look happy. Without a word to us he went below, and then, after only two minutes, came up again and headed our way.

"I'm afraid we're going to be delayed," he told us. "Albert says he cannot give us the fuel, it'll tap his stores. He asks that we wait until he has restocked."

"How long a wait?" I asked.

"Six, perhaps seven days."

Alena sucked a sharp breath. "That will not work."

"There is nothing I can do about it, Giselle."

"This man, Albert, you do business with him often?"

"Regularly."

"The kind of business you do with me?"

"Not exactly the same. But he has an idea the kind of things Carrie and I do to provide an income."

Alena looked at me, shook her head slightly. I understood. A week's delay would be more than enough time for Oxford to catch up with us, no matter how big a lead we might have on him at the moment. A confrontation with him on *The Lutra,* especially given the state Alena was in, could only end badly.

"Is there any other way to get the fuel?" I asked.

"The problem is the paperwork," Jerry said. "With the papers for the three of you, I need to keep my manifests appropriately doctored. We burned a lot of fuel racing from Bequia, and if I get called to explain that, it could be tied into whatever you left behind. This must remain off the books. Albert is the man I use for that."

"Does he have fuel now?" Alena asked.

Jerry grunted an affirmative. "He tells me he's already sold it to someone else, one of the other yachts in the harbor."

Alena looked at me again, then reached for her crutches. I watched as she got herself back to her feet, struggling with her wounded leg. It took her almost twenty seconds to stand, and once she did, she settled the crutches beneath her arms.

"Where is Albert?" she asked Jerry.

"He has an office in one of the abandoned warehouses near the edge of town," he said. "But you won't have any luck convincing him. I tried, I offered him twice what I normally pay him. He's not selling."

"Which warehouse?"

Jerry pointed out one of the less-abused structures near the edge of the harbor. "That one, with the green paint. His office is in the back."

"Be ready to leave once we're refueled," Alena said, and she began making her way to the gangplank.

Albert's office was behind a thin wooden door with a frosted glass panel set in it. The window once had the word "manager" stenciled on the glass, but at some point the glass had cracked and the "m" was distorted, and a shard where the second "a" had been painted was missing. It hadn't been more than a half a mile walk from *The Lutra* to the warehouse, but when we reached the door, Alena was perspiring and breathing hard. After taking a moment to catch her breath, she nodded at me.

I knocked on the door, and when a man inside said to come in, I opened it.

Albert was older than I'd thought he would be, maybe in his mid-sixties, white, but with the leather skin that comes from living years under a strong sun. His hair was more white than gray, his face lined like someone had worked him rather viciously in clay before bringing him to life. The office was as weathered as he, and when he came around his rickety particleboard desk to greet us, I heard the furniture creak. When he smiled at us, I saw that he was missing two incisors, and had a third capped in gold.

"Something I can do for you?" His accent was something between South London and North Jamaica.

"Are you Albert?" Alena asked.

He nodded, smiled again, looking from Alena to me.

"Jerry needs his ship refueled."

Maybe it was because she was on crutches, or maybe it was sexist, but Albert directed his response to me. "I already told Jerry, I can't help. Fuel I've got is spoken for, that's the way it is."

"Where is it?"

He glanced at her. "Why?"

"Do you refuel from a boat, do you use a truck, how do you do it?"

"A truck," he said, looking at Alena curiously. "But as I said, it's spoken for."

"You will move the truck to the dock and refuel *The Lutra*."

Albert laughed.

I saw it coming, saw the shift of weight indicating that she was going into motion, but by then, she already had.

Alena moved her weight almost entirely to the left crutch and swept the right one up sharply in between Albert's legs. The blow struck him squarely in the testicles, and it crumpled him forward, and he lost his balance. As swiftly as she'd struck, she pulled the crutch free and jabbed again, this time higher, hitting Albert just beneath the collarbone. He didn't have much air left, but what he had came out in a gurgle, and he fell back against the desk. The particleboard tore beneath him as he rode it onto the floor.

She lowered the crutch and covered the distance to Albert with one move, set the tip of the right crutch against his body again, resting it just above his stomach.

Albert's eyes were wide, bulging almost comically, and he wheezed in short spurts.

"If I push down, you will die," Alena told him.

Albert's expression indicated that he absolutely believed her.

"To live, you will do the following—you will get the keys to the truck. You will drive myself and my companion to *The Lutra.* You will refuel *The Lutra.* You will never mention us to anyone, ever. Do you understand?"

He nodded, then nodded again.

Alena moved the crutch from Albert's solar plexus. He avoided her gaze, tried to catch mine, silently pleading for help. What he saw gave him no comfort.

"I'm with her," I told him.

We left the South Caicos less than sixty minutes later, leaving Albert in the cab of his truck, parked on the pier. Jerry paid him for the fuel.

It took another day to reach Miami, and from there Alena, Bridgett, Miata, and I caught a flight to New York, landing at Kennedy. Not once during the trip did Bridgett speak to Alena, and for her part Alena never tried to engage her in conversation. From Bridgett's expression, I guessed she had a good idea of what had transpired in Cockburn Harbour, but she said nothing to me about that, either. I'm sure she thought that we'd left a body in our wake, and there seemed no point in my trying to explain otherwise.

It made for a fairly tense trip.

After we'd picked up Miata and moved out to the curb, Bridgett asked if I was headed home.

"Not yet," I said.

"You want me to tell anyone you're back?"

"I'll handle it."

"I'll rephrase. Is there anyone you *don't* want me to tell that you're back?"

"No."

"All right, then." She glanced at Alena, who was leaning on her crutches a couple feet away, talking to Miata in the dog carrier. Assured that she was out of earshot, Bridgett turned back to me. "You change your mind, all you have to do is call a cop," she said, and she headed for the taxi stand and climbed into a waiting cab.

We rented a car, and from the airport Alena directed me to one of her caches. It was in Queens, a tiny storage facility that abutted onto a junkyard and had easy access to the Cross Island Parkway. When we arrived, she told the manager that her name was Kim Gallagher, and that she needed to pick up some things for her brother. She showed him a current New York State driver's license to prove her identity, and when he checked his files, he saw that, indeed, her brother had given her permission to access the locker.

We brought the car in close, parked, and as we got out, I asked, "How many of these do you have?"

"In the five boroughs? Four." She handed me the key, leaning on her crutches. "At one point I had six, but one was broken into last year, and the other has most likely been compromised, so I won't go near it. This one is very clean, I haven't visited it in six years. It's never been used."

I unlocked the door and ran it up on its rails, and before we stepped inside she used one of her crutches to pull a piece of fishing line out of the darkness. The string had been run about five inches high, across the opening, and there was still tension on it.

"Safety," she said. "If it's broken, I know someone has been inside."

"Unless they replaced it."

"Unless they replaced it, yes. I don't think anyone has."

We stepped inside and I pulled the string that ran to the single bulb hung in the space. It was low wattage and didn't penetrate to the corners, but it didn't need to, because all that was inside were two pieces of luggage, a large blue duffel and a smaller black rolling bag. I put them in the car, closed the locker again, and we stopped at the manager's on the way out to return the key with thanks.

In Manhattan we checked into the SoHo Grand and got ourselves into a large room on one of the pet-friendly floors. I stuck with the Paul Lieberg identity; Alena called herself Jessica Bethier.

Before we headed up, I gave the FedEx envelope I'd been carrying in my go-bag to the young woman who checked us in, asked if she could send it out that afternoon. She assured me it would be no trouble at all.

Our room had a king bed and a couch that would convert to a queen. As soon as we were inside, Alena opened the carrier and Miata sprang out and stretched, then began snuffling his way through all of the corners. The hotel directory actually had a separate menu for pets, and Alena used it to order him something to drink and eat. The food arrived in under ten minutes, and Miata dove into his bowls. Once she saw that he was happy, Alena sat on the edge of the bed, pulling her crutches up after her. I opened the bags we'd taken from the cache and dumped them out on the bed, and Alena and I began going through the pile. She'd cached a couple changes of clothes, three pistols, and one HK PDW submachine gun. There were also three wads of well-used bills, twenties and tens bound with rubber bands.

"How much is there?" I asked.

"Here? A little under fifteen."

"And there's money in every cache?"

"Always. The U.S. is expensive."

"Oxford works the same way?"

"I'd expect he does. Money is pretty integral to the work." She started loading the pistols. "It's time we talked about what we're doing."

"I want to get you someplace secure, somewhere that you can recover from your injury."

She had been sliding bullets into the cylinder of a Colt revolver, and now she stopped and looked up at where I stood. "I will not recover. My left leg below the knee is permanently crippled. It cannot support my weight, it will never support it again."

To prove the point, she extended and raised her leg, then set it on the bed, her foot pointed at me. She reached down and pulled up the cuff of her pant leg, folding it back quickly to just below her knee. A large gauze rectangle was taped to her shin. She pulled it free, then turned her ankle to give me the full view. The stitches ran from just above her ankle to almost behind her knee, a zigzag of thread thick and black with dried blood. Her calf was only half as wide as it should have been.

"I've lost a large portion of my lower leg," Alena said, her face entirely neutral. "It's possible that the tibia and the fibula were both splintered, if not broken. The doctor in Kingstown did the best he could without a hospital and without more skill, and there is no infection, and the skin is knitting. But I will never walk on this leg again, not without assistance."

"We can get you proper medical help," I said. "Not some backroom surgeon. We can get you someone who knows what they are doing."

She folded the gauze back into place over the stitches, began rolling her pant leg down. "Atticus, even if you are correct, what you are saying requires time and money. Money I have. Time I do not. Oxford is on his way here, if not in New York already."

"All the more reason to get you someplace secure."

"I have not disputed that." She picked up the Colt, slid another round into the cylinder. "What do you suggest?"

"I want to bring in my colleagues," I said.

She finished loading the revolver, closing the cylinder with a push, a calm motion, very controlled. "Will you tell them who I am?"

"Yes."

She turned the gun in her hand, looking at it thoughtfully. "I will not go to prison. I will not allow that."

"They're my friends. They'll respect my wishes. If I tell them to keep it quiet, they'll honor that."

"You're sure?"

"Yes."

"Sure enough to bet my life on it?"

"Yes."

She smiled, setting the gun back onto the bed.

"You must have very good friends," she said.

"Absolutely not," Dale Matsui told me. "No way. I can't believe you'd even ask us to do this!"

He looked around the table, to Corry and Natalie, and then to Special Agent Scott Fowler, to see if they were going to offer him support. From their expressions, I suspected he would get it.

It was nearly midnight, and we were at the back of The Stoned Crow in Greenwich Village, the same bar where once, months ago, Lady Ainsley-Hunter was supposed to join students from NYU in merry pitchers of beer. All around us on the walls were representations of crows, paintings and pictures, some literal, some more loosely interpreted. Over Corry's head hung a poster from *The Crow* movie, and farther down the wall was a promotional flyer for a concert by the band of the same name.

It had taken a couple of hours to assemble everyone because I'd had to go carefully, unsure of who Oxford might already have under surveillance. In the end I'd made contact through Scott, thinking that he would be the most risky for Oxford to mark, and therefore the least likely to watch. Scott had taken it pretty well, saying only, "I was wondering when you'd call," and then he'd agreed to contact the others. He'd arrived at the bar first, with Natalie close on his heels, but he'd had just enough time to pull me aside.

"Gracey and Bowles are looking for you," he'd said. "We really need to talk."

Now he was staying silent, and I suspected he'd let the conversation run its course before weighing in with his own opinion and whatever facts he himself had.

Corry said, "I'm with Dale, Atticus."

"She's a paying client," I said. "Like any other."

"Uh, no, I don't think so," Dale said.

"Look, we take money to protect people we don't like all the time. It's never been our job to pass judgments—"

"Okay, hypocrisy readings are off the charts," Corry said. "Perhaps you may recall you're the guy who was complaining about spoiled-brat movie stars. Those are jobs you were all too willing to turn down."

"I never turned them down, I just never liked them," I replied.

Dale was shaking his head. "It's a personal choice, Atticus. I'm not going to protect the Grand Wizard of the KKK. I don't give a damn about how professional I'm being or not. I'd have thought you would agree with that."

"She's not who you think she is."

"She's the woman who nearly killed me twice," Dale replied. "So you tell me, Atticus—who am I supposed to think she is? How am I supposed to get past that?"

"I did," I said.

Natalie, who had been watching me closely the whole time, looked down at her beer, and I realized it had been the wrong thing to say.

"Yeah," Corry said, quieter. "Yeah, you did. And frankly, that's a problem for us."

"You've put us in a really bad position," Dale said. "You've put the whole firm at risk. If this gets out, what you've been doing, of what happened to Havel, of where you were and who you were with—"

"Wait just a fucking second," I said. I hadn't gotten as far as telling them about Havel. I hadn't told them about Oxford yet. I'd gotten only as far as telling them who my principal was and that I needed their help.

Natalie turned the glass of beer between her hands. "Bridgett came by the office this afternoon. She had us call Scott."

Hell, I thought.

"She told us everything that happened," Corry said.

"No, she didn't. She told you what she *thinks* happened. But she's got her facts assed up."

"Is Havel dead?"

"Yes."

"Were you living with Drama for over three months?"

"Yes."

"Was it more important to you to keep Drama from the authorities than it was to report the murder of a woman who was, ostensibly, if not a friend, at least an acquaintance?"

"Where are you going with this, Corry?"

He didn't like my tone, which was understandable, I suppose, because I certainly wasn't liking his. He put his elbows on the table, leaning forward, and Scott had to adjust how he was sitting to keep his eyes on me. I still couldn't get a bead off of him, of what he was thinking.

"You've abused your friendship with everyone at this table," Corry told me. "We've spent over a quarter of a year worried sick about you, waiting for a word or a sign that you were all right. We were your friends, and you abused our friendship. Did you even consider us?"

"I thought about you guys all the time," I said. "I wasn't in a position where I could just pick up the phone and call."

"You were absent for *four months,* dammit! Four fucking months! You should have found a way!"

"I couldn't! God dammit, if I had she would never have trusted me! If I had you wouldn't have understood! Don't you think I fucking agonized over this?"

Corry straightened, leaning back in his seat. He moved his beer around on the table, then lifted it and drained the glass dry.

Dale said, "Did you really think we'd greet you as the conquering hero?"

"I thought you'd give me the benefit of the doubt."

"We are giving you the benefit of the doubt," Corry said. "We're here, now."

"And when we're done, is Scott going to throw me down and slap the cuffs on?"

Natalie made a delicate snort. "Oh, please."

Corry spread his hands, as if sweeping all of our words from the air. "Okay, let's just forget the personal for a second. Let's talk about the professional. Do you know what happens to us if this gets out? We lose everything we've gained, everything we've worked hard for. We're back where we were when Trent had us blacklisted. You have no idea how we had to scramble after you vanished, Atticus, you have no idea the damage control we had to do. We lost two jobs as a result of your disappearance, and there was major footwork involved in keeping three others."

"Bottom line," I said.

That made him really angry. "Yes, bottom line. And you know what? I don't think I'm in that great a minority on this. I have a wife and a child and another on the way—"

"Esme's pregnant?"

"Yes, she's three months along, and you know what, Atticus? I want to keep a roof over my family's head, I want to send my children to college, I want to keep them fed and clothed and give them the things I never had. And to do that I need money, and I'd prefer to earn that money doing something I enjoy, something I take pride in. Like it or not, KTMH is a *business*. You had a responsibility to that, and you abdicated it."

"Then there's a solution," I said. "Buy me out."

Natalie looked across the table at Dale. She said, "I told you."

"I'm serious," I said. "Buy me out. What you don't seem to get, Corry, is that I *do* understand what you're saying, I *do* understand your concerns, and I sure as hell do know how this could look. I don't want to see the firm die, certainly not through any action of mine."

"Then why are you doing this?" Corry demanded.

"Because I have agreed to protect this life, I agreed to do this job. And because I believe her life is worth protecting."

There was silence at the table for a minute.

"I can't do this, Atticus," Dale said, finally. "I'm sorry, man. You're my friend, we were legs together, dammit. But I cannot do this thing."

"Neither can I," Corry said.

We all looked at Natalie. "You'll sell us your share of the firm?" she asked.

"Draw it up tomorrow morning, I'll sign it tomorrow afternoon," I told her.

"Then once it's signed, I'll take the job," she said.

Both Dale and Corry opened their mouths, objections flying, but she cut them off.

"We've each got our own shares, we've each got our own jobs in the firm. I'm taking this one. But I agree with Atticus. We don't judge our principals. We protect them to the best of our abilities. That's always been the job."

"This goes bad for him, it'll be bad for you," Corry said. "And that'll be bad for us."

"If that's what happens, I'll deal with it."

Neither of them said anything. At the back of the booth, Scott hadn't moved.

Dale slid out of his seat, taking his coat from the peg on the side of the booth. He put it on and headed out of the bar. Corry followed, but he stopped while zipping up his coat.

"When it's all said and done, you know this isn't personal."

"I'm remembering when you were working for Sentinel," I said to him. "The way you hated Trent and how everything was about the bottom line."

He frowned. "If you can change, so can I."

"Hell yeah," I said.

He offered me his hand, and I shook it, then watched him walk away.

Scott cleared his throat. "Hi, remember me? I'm the guy whose face you lied in."

"I'm sorry about that, Scott."

"I figured you were, but I wanted to hear it."

"So," Natalie said. "When do we start?"

"I'm working on getting a house," I said. "She's got some connections. I want to button her up, then we'll start working this thing."

"Working it how?"

"How much did Bridgett tell you?"

Natalie looked at Scott, and Scott held up a hand, ticking off points. "Drama. Oxford. Book. Sex. Stockholm Syndrome."

"She really doesn't want to believe I'm doing this of my own volition," I said.

"She thinks *you* think it's your own volition, but no, she really doesn't," Natalie agreed.

"And what do you think?"

"I don't know enough."

"Scott?"

"I don't care," he said. "Gracey and Bowles have contacted me three times in the past week, wanting me to contact them if I heard from you. They said you were in trouble."

"Did you?"

"Of course not. Bridgett wasn't the only person playing detective these past months. Someone hired Oxford to do the job, and it's not just a coincidence that within days of that job going south I start being pestered for information about you. Whatever's going on here, I want to know about it. For the time being, that's more than enough incentive to make me forget who your principal is, provided everything remains on the up-and-up."

"You're thinking it was Gracey and Bowles?" Natalie asked.

"It had to be. If not them directly, someone who supervises them."

"Why?"

"I've got a theory. Not much evidence for it, but I kinda like it."

"Share," I said.

Scott adjusted his glasses, smiled again, a little embarrassed. "Look at it like this. Havel writes this book, gets a lot of attention. I mean, big-ass attention, pop-culture attention. Suddenly prime time television is doing episodes about cops chasing professional killers, about lawyers defending assassins. There's a movie in the works. Everybody is suddenly talking about this thing that, up until a few months ago, nobody really gave much credit to.

"That kind of interest, it keeps building until it reaches a sort of critical mass. And the more people who are thinking about it, the more people who are saying, Jesus Christ, there are *assassins* for God's sake, the more people start asking questions."

"Questions like who and what and why and how," I said.

"Yeah, exactly. Now imagine that you're a Backroom Boy, and you've trained someone like Drama, you've created her. And now you're suddenly thinking, oh shit, I'm maybe three weeks away from a Congressional Oversight Committee. You can't stop people from talking about this thing, you can't undo it. But maybe you can get their attention elsewhere."

Natalie nodded. "According to Bridgett's version, that's pretty much what Oxford was trying to do."

"That's almost exactly what he said," I confirmed.

"There are very few people who stand to lose as a result of Havel's book," Scott said. "If two of them aren't Gracey and Bowles, then I'll give you even money that their bosses are."

"Finding evidence for this is going to be rough."

"But possible," Scott said. "Especially if you've got access to someone who knows how the system works. Especially if you're protecting someone who has been on the inside."

"You're a mercenary bastard," I told him.

"Call it payback for lying to a friend. I'm going to start digging, see if I can rattle a few cages. And I'd like to talk to, uh . . . Alena, is it?"

"Alena," I said.

"I'd like to talk to her in the next couple days. It can wait until she's buttoned up."

"She won't like it."

"Change her mind."

"And I can start tomorrow," Natalie said. "After getting the papers drawn up, of course."

"Just pay me my share, that's all I ask."

"You'll get what you're due."

"That's kind of what I'm afraid of," I said.

CHAPTER TWO

November in Brighton Beach has none of the charm reserved for New England, it's as if the autumn palette ignores the neighborhood altogether. Everything is gray, and a stormy sky only serves to reinforce it, as if saying, what the hell's the point?

I parked the car on Avenue Y, just a couple blocks west of Coney Island, and watched the street. Clouds were riding a chill wind off the water, and the few people on the street wore gloves or walked with hands in pockets. Nobody looked happy to be outside. I checked my mirrors, followed a clump of twenty-something tough guys with my eyes as they scowled their way down the block. They turned the corner at Hubbard, into a restaurant with a name written in Cyrillic. Condensation from inside stuck to the windows, and they disappeared out of sight like wraiths.

The gun in the glove compartment was clean and untraceable, one of the pistols from the cache Alena and I had cleared the previous afternoon. It was a Czech semiauto, the CZ75, and it could be carried cocked and locked.

I took the gun out of the glove compartment. I cocked it, locked it, and then put it in my belt at the small of my back.

Then I got out of the car and headed for the restaurant. Before I'd even opened the door I could smell the grease frying inside, hear the noise of the patrons. There was no liquor license posted anywhere I could see, but that didn't seem to bother anyone within, and there looked to be a bottle of vodka for everyone present. Cigarette smoke choked the air. I moved inside as if I knew exactly where I was going, and it helped that Alena had given me explicit directions, and because I didn't look out of place and I didn't act out of place, no one gave me more than a cursory glance.

I worked my way along the aisle between the counter and the crowded tables, giving an eyefuck to anyone who looked my way too long. Almost everyone present was male but for one very busty brunette working the register, and a couple of older women in a booth near the bathroom doors. At least a hundred horses had gone to their great reward to provide the occupants with leather, from boots to jackets to, in a couple of cases, pants. On a lot of the men I saw tattoos, especially on their hands and fingers, Russian mafia call-signs.

At the back of the room was a door marked with a plastic sign in English, ordering me to keep out. I went on through into the back room, passing a very large teenager who was listening to a Walkman as he sat on a stack of plastic crates. He slipped from his perch as I passed him and asked me something in Russian, and I waved my left hand at him in such a way as to indicate he didn't want to mess with me. I was at the next door and going up a flight of stairs as he settled back down.

I'd half expected another whorehouse, because Alena hadn't been clear on what I would be walking into, but it was merely a furnished room with two men doing paperwork at two wooden desks. As I came in both looked up, and from their expressions I could tell they'd been expecting someone else. The one at the closer desk, bespectacled and chunky, asked me something I didn't understand.

There was a couch and a coffee table, so I sat down like I owned the place. The chunky one repeated what he'd said, this time not so friendly. The other one, who was both older and smaller, rose, suspicion on his face.

"I want to see Danilov Korckeva," I said in the Russian Alena had made me practice over and over again until she was certain I could sound authentic. "Tell him I'm a friend of Natasha's."

Then I waggled my hand at the thin man, indicating that I wanted him to either use the phone, sit down, or possibly do the hokey-pokey.

He decided I meant for him to sit down. As the chunky one got on the phone, the older one studied me curiously, then asked me something in Russian. I gave him a look that said I wasn't in the mood for chatter, he nodded, and went back to his paperwork.

I kept smiling, though it was more honest this time. "Just act as if you own them," Alena had told me. "Say nothing after you ask for Dan. If they try to speak to you, scowl. If they do it a second time, draw the gun, but do not point it at them. Otherwise, look as if you don't have a care in the world. The longer you sit there and wait, the more afraid of you they will become. They can't help it. It's the Russian mentality. The only thing they fear is their own, and they will take you for one of their own, but one who is unknown, and that will truly frighten them."

And damn if she wasn't right, because I sat there for thirty-seven minutes, and each time I caught one of them looking at me I stared right back and scowled, and they lowered their eyes, caught, and hastily resumed their work. They didn't speak to me. They didn't speak to each other. The chunky one got up once and went to the small television that sat on a metal stand against the wall between their desks, and he looked at me before switching it on, the question in his eyes. I shrugged, and he smiled and switched on ESPN, then went back to his work.

A little after noon the door opened and Dan came in, wearing designer jeans and biker boots and the same leather jacket as before, plucking a pair of sunglasses from his face. There was no need for them on a day like today, but they seemed to suit the image. He saw me on the couch and stopped cold, squinting, and I had to remind myself that the last time he'd seen me I'd worn glasses and been clean-shaven. It took him almost three seconds, and then his face cracked into a grin.

"Holy fuck, it's Mr. Atticus!" He loomed in, offering one mammoth hand for a shake, the other going to my shoulder. It didn't rattle me as much as it had when we'd first met. "Natasha sent you? That's for real? You're not giving me the bullshit?"

"She needs a favor."

Dan waved a hand, warning me to say no more. "We don't talk here, not about 'Tasha. You come with me."

He waited until I was up, then held the door open for me, gesturing, and I grinned and didn't go through, and he laughed and nodded and went first. I followed him out into the hall and back down the stairs. When we reached the teenager with the Walkman, Dan cuffed him alongside the head, growling in Russian, and the kid yelped. We went back through the restaurant, then out onto the street, where the Kompressor was parked illegally in front of a fire hydrant. The top was down. He climbed over the side and forced himself behind the wheel, and I opened the door and took the passenger seat. The engine came to life and he did a moderately illegal turn, then put us on Coney Island Avenue, heading to the water.

"You're not dead," Dan said. "That's surprising."

"No one's more surprised than me."

He roared with laughter. " 'Tasha sent you, you walk in like an old-time commissar, you have balls. What does she need, anything she needs if I can give it, it's for her."

"She needs a house."

"Big house? Little house? Apartment? Condo?"

"A secure house, somewhere access can be restricted, someplace that she can hole up."

We turned onto Brighton Beach Avenue, Dan nodding. "And she sends you to get this for her? Why does she not come herself?"

"She's finding it difficult to move around right now."

"Police?"

"Almost."

He scratched his chin, sniffing the air. "Okay, I can get a house, a good house. But it's not cheap."

"It needs to be secure."

"Real secure, this house, in Jersey. Comes with alarms, cameras, I can even give her guards, she wants them."

"She may."

"Guards, those will be extra. I will pick them myself. Only the best for 'Tasha." He looked over at me, and his tone changed, and the enthusiasm, the friendliness, disappeared. "You tell her I get her the best, okay?"

"She said you always do."

He put his attention back on the road. "That's right, I always do. You don't fuck with 'Tasha unless you have your will in order."

"How long will it take you?"

"By tonight, I can do this. Where do I contact you?"

"Doesn't work like that, Dan. I'll contact you."

He took a moment, then nodded and rattled off a phone number. I repeated it back, as much to aid my memory as to check that I'd heard him right.

"How much will it cost?" I asked.

"With guards, for 'Tasha—she gets discount—I say five large a day."

"I'll have to check with her about the guards," I said.

"Of course, of course."

"She'll want to see you there when she arrives."

"Yes, of course, okay." He nodded a couple of times, then asked where he could drop me off. I told him back at the restaurant would be fine, and he turned the car around and headed back to where we'd started, driving in silence. Then he asked, "So, you were with her? All this time, you were with her?"

"All this time," I confirmed.

We were back on Hubbard, and once again he parked in front of the hydrant, then killed the engine. I opened the door and climbed out of the car, and he watched me as I started to go, then called out, waving me back. I came around to his side of the car.

"Was it hell or heaven?" he asked.

"I'm still trying to figure that out myself," I told him.

I got back to the SoHo Grand just before two, used the house phone in the lobby to ring the room once, hung up, and then took the elevator up. Natalie opened the door for me as soon as I got there, her Glock in her hand, and when she confirmed I was alone, let me pass, saying, "It's him."

Alena came out of the bathroom on her crutches, the PDW slung from her shoulder, and the tension seeped from her face when she saw me. From where he lay on the floor, Miata acknowledged me with a slight raising of his head.

Natalie had arrived late that morning, just before I'd left for the meeting with Dan, bringing with her a short stack of legalese that roughly meant I'd get three-quarters of a million dollars for my share of KTMH. The figure had been much higher than I expected, and Natalie explained that it would be paid out over the next six months. I'd signed the agreement, and then I'd introduced her to Alena.

The two women had greeted one another politely, with some awkwardness but nothing like the tension that had existed between Alena and Bridgett. I figured that Natalie wouldn't have very much to say to Alena, either, but as I came into the room, that no longer seemed to be the case. There was a pad of paper on the desk, covered with figures written in Natalie's hand, along with rough diagrams that made it look as if she'd been working on a calculus equation, and I realized they'd found a common interest to discuss.

"We've been talking about sniping," Natalie told me as she locked the door. "Alena was telling me about the Dragunov."

"I trained on the Dragunov," Alena explained. "How was Dan?"

"I hadn't realized how afraid of you he is," I said.

She hobbled to the bed, dropping one of the crutches and then taking the submachine gun off her arm. "Is he?"

"I think so."

"Then he will do what we ask." She sat down carefully, folding her hands in her lap. "How long does he need?"

"He says he can have a house for us by nightfall, one with basic security and a few guards."

"How many guards?" Natalie asked.

"I don't know. Three or four, I'd expect." I looked back to Alena. "I told him that you'd want to see him in person. He's asking five grand a day."

She made a face as if she'd hoped for better and expected worse. Natalie said, "We don't even charge that much."

"It's a seller's market," I told her. "We've got enough loose cash here to cover a week and a half or so, but there's no way this'll be over by then. We're going to need more money."

"I'll arrange it." Alena slid along the bed to the nightstand and picked up the phone, began dialing. It was a long string of numbers, and when she got an answer, she started speaking in German.

I moved to the couch and sat down, taking the pistol out of my belt. I unlocked it and lowered the hammer carefully, making it safe again. Natalie took her seat at the desk, began examining the figures on her pad. It took Alena another minute on the phone before she hung up.

"It's done. There is a Credit Suisse branch in midtown. If you go there tomorrow, they'll have the money. Two hundred thousand. You'll give half of it to Dan." She looked me over. "You should exercise."

"I'm kind of working right now," I said.

"Natalie is here, I am safe for the time being. You should at least do some cardio."

Natalie laughed, then caught herself.

"My personal trainer," I said.

"I noticed," Natalie replied.

"I'm serious, Atticus," Alena said. "Don't lose everything you've gained."

I really didn't want to work out, but she was right, and in fact I was already feeling the effects of not having exercised in almost a week. I did feel stiff, not as loose or as fluid, and the thing that surprised me most was just how aware of the changes in my body I was.

Alena used one of her crutches to prod me. "Go."

"I'm gone," I said, and went to the gym.

The house was in Mahwah, New Jersey, about an hour's drive from Manhattan. I left Alena with Natalie at the SoHo Grand and took Miata with me when I went out to see it, and I met Dan on the Franklin Turnpike in what could charitably be called the middle of town. He was parked outside of a Dunkin' Donuts, the roof now up on the Kompressor, but only because a light, cold rain had begun falling.

I followed him in my rental, and we wound our way along thin streets lined with trees, most of which had lost their leaves. Mahwah was on the edge of the New Jersey boonies, close to Mount Campgaw, though skiing at the resort wouldn't start until around Thanksgiving. The countryside was quiet and pleasant and hilly, the houses separated not only by wide spaces but also by age, some of the houses a century or more old, others built the year before. Farther into the mountains were New Jersey's infamous hillbillies, the Jackson Whites, inbred families with atavistic brows and six-fingered hands.

I followed the Kompressor onto a small side road that wound its way down another slope, then leveled into a small valley, then into another turn and up a short drive that ended at a seven-foot-tall gate supported by two stone pillars. There was no fence, but past the pillars on either side of the drive, the road dropped into foliage, more trees and bushes grown thick together.

Dan climbed out of the Kompressor and opened the gate, waved me through, and I pulled forward and then off the road, parking half on the unkempt lawn. I stopped the engine and climbed out, Miata springing down after me and looking suspiciously around him. Dan pulled forward and stopped beside me, his engine still running.

"You don't want to see the house?" He pointed up the road, at the building that was perhaps two hundred feet away.

"Go ahead, I'll meet you there."

He creased his brow, then put the car back in gear and drove away. Miata looked after him, then began sniffing around on the grass.

I started with a walk of the perimeter, taking almost three-quarters of an hour before approaching to the house. There was no fencing to speak of, and no cameras or other perimeter security. Even with the autumn assault, the woods around the grounds were still capable of providing heavy cover. At the back of the house was a high hill, and anyone coming over it would have a view of the whole area.

I didn't like it.

Miata loped behind me as I walked back up the drive. The house was built in the colonial style, and from the outside appeared to have been recently renovated. A wide set of stairs came off the drive to a porch, painted white. Dan was waiting for me by the front door, smoking a cigarette, and when I came up the steps he flicked the butt away; it hit a puddle and died with a sizzle. He looked at Miata, and Miata looked at him, and I swore they were sizing one another up.

"No dogs inside," Dan said.

"The dog is hers."

The pained look he gave me vanished quickly, replaced by a question that he didn't feel safe in asking. Then he shrugged and opened the front door, heading inside. I went in after him, and Miata took up the rear. As we came inside I could hear the warning tone from an alarm system, one long bleet, and Dan turned the first corner we came to and rapidly tapped in a code on the keypad. The bleeting stopped, and Dan began walking through the house, turning on the lights.

I took another hour just going through the house, checking all of the doors and windows and corners, hoisting myself up into the insulated crawlspace above the second floor, checking out the cellar. The security inside was better, and every portal on both the ground and second floor was wired, though obviously so. Everything ran through a locked junction box in the basement. The house was entirely furnished, decorated to match the colonial exterior. On the second floor were three bedrooms, one master and two smaller, and two bathrooms. The ground floor had a kitchen, dining room, living room, and guest room. There was a hot tub on the back deck.

Dan was waiting for me at the table in the kitchen, drinking from a longneck of Budweiser. Another bottle was in front of him, and he gestured that it was mine, but I shook my head and went to the cupboards, started opening them. The shelves had been filled with canned foods, ravioli and chili and other junk. The freezer was brimming with T.V. dinners and frozen pizzas, and the refrigerator held mostly soda, beer, and condiments. There was a sad head of lettuce wilting in the back of the crisper. I threw that in the trash can by the sink.

"What do you think?" Dan asked.

"Tell me about the alarm, what's it tied to?"

"The monitoring service. If it goes off, they notify the police."

"Who owns the house?"

"Bank in Brooklyn." When I frowned, he added, "All the paper is good."

"Yeah, but by Brooklyn you mean it's a front, that there's no name on it. It can be traced."

"Not easily."

"You're going to need to change that tomorrow, put the ownership in a name, a married couple, I don't care who. Just make it look good, and if you can backdate the sale, that's even better."

"Anything else?" He sounded testy.

"I want you to start looking into doctors, we need someone good, someone who specializes in sports injuries. Has to be completely off the record, but that shouldn't be too hard, and I'm sure you can find someone who lost their license because they started stealing from their own drug cabinet. Make sure whoever you find is discreet, because he or she may have to come out here several times."

"Is this for 'Tasha?"

"Can you do it?"

"All it takes is money. I ask again, is this for 'Tasha, is she hurt?"

I ignored the question, checked out the kitchen window into the backyard. It was night now, and there were no lights from outside.

"You will want the guards, too?" he asked. "I've got some boys, four of them. All good with arms, I can equip them however 'Tasha wants, automatics, submachine guns, even grenades. I can have them here tonight, if that's what she wants."

"Tomorrow will be fine. These are your guys?"

"They work for me."

"They know anything about protection? I mean real protection, not shakedowns."

The chair scraped as he shifted around, and I turned back to see that he was getting up, and looking pissed. "You listen, Mr. Kodiak, you can just drop that shit with me, okay? Your attitude I don't need, I know what I'm about here, I do this shit right."

"You going to answer my question?"

"I beat you down once," he reminded me.

"You did. You want to try again?"

Dan stared at me, his weight shifting into his torso. The longneck was in his right hand, and I figured he'd start with that. I didn't look away from him, and I didn't move, just started cataloguing all of the kitchen utensils and supplies that I saw in my periphery, picking which ones I'd use to stop him if he decided things needed to go that far.

Then he relaxed, his weight settling lower again, and he took a swig from the bottle.

"No," he said, after he had swallowed. "No, I don't think I will."

Back on the Franklin Turnpike I found a pay phone and called the hotel, asking for Mr. Lieberg's room. When the phone was answered, I spoke first.

"It'll do. It's not what I hoped for, and we'll need the extras, but it'll do. Her friend is waiting for me there now."

"Where?" Natalie asked.

"Franklin Turnpike in Mahwah. I'll be outside the Dunkin' Donuts."

"Take us an hour."

"Take two, make sure you're clean when you get here."

"Got it."

I hung up and got back in the car, then headed along the turnpike to the Interstate Mall, which was just a couple miles away. I cracked the window and left Miata in the car, telling him I'd be back shortly, then headed inside. At a GNC in the mall I dropped almost two hundred dollars on various supplements, then headed over to the Radio Shack and picked up another hundred or so dollars' worth of electronics. I did a little clothes shopping, as well, buying some extra underwear and the like for both Alena and myself. When I was finished I brought everything back to the car and went back into Mahwah and stopped at the first grocery store I saw. I bought food, mostly fruits and veggies, some fish, two gallons of juice, a gallon of milk, a couple of pretty lean-looking steaks. I also grabbed a ten-pound bag of Science Diet for Miata. When I'd finished loading the car, the trunk was full.

Then I headed back to the Dunkin' Donuts and waited in the car, watching the traffic and thinking. After a couple of minutes I got out again and went back to the phone, but this time I called Scott.

"You free tonight?" I asked him.

"You say such things and my heart leaps with joy."

"You've always been my number one guy, you know that. I'm going to call you in another hour or so, give you a location. Take your time coming out, but when you do, bring your pad and pencil."

"She's cool with this?"

"She will be."

"I'll expect your call," he said, and hung up.

They arrived just over two hours after I'd called, pulling into the lot in Natalie's new Audi. Alena was in the front passenger seat, a coat in her lap, the submachine gun under the coat.

"Any trouble?" I asked.

"None," Natalie said. "If he's in New York, he didn't know you were at the Grand."

"You checked us out?"

"All taken care of."

"New car."

"You like it?"

"What happened to the old one?"

"Sold it."

"Nat, you go through cars the way most people go through socks."

"I like that new-car smell," she said. "We'll follow you."

I climbed back into the rental and got back on the road, and they followed me the ten minutes it took to reach the house. The Kompressor was still where Dan had parked it, and the lights inside the house were still blazing bright. I stopped my car and let Miata out, told Natalie and Alena to wait. Dan was still in the kitchen, where he'd killed another two longnecks, talking on his cell phone in Russian. When he saw me he changed his tone, making a quick end to the conversation, then stowed the phone back in his pocket.

"She's here?"

I gestured for him to follow me.

They were still in the Audi, the engine idling, and when Natalie saw us coming, she shut off the car and opened her door. Dan started around for Alena's side, and I looked past him to her, trying to read what she wanted. She didn't seem to have any objection to Dan's approach, and so I let him help her out of the vehicle while I started unloading the rental. Between Natalie and myself we had my shopping unloaded and the bags from the Audi inside in three trips, just as Alena had reached the top of the porch. Dan was walking behind her, and his manner reminded me of nothing as much as an overprotective sibling watching out for his little sister. But when he offered to give her his elbow for support, she snapped something in Russian at him, and again it was clear that, whatever else he felt for her, she scared him.

Natalie set about a quick walk-through of the house while I unloaded the groceries, and Alena settled into one of the chairs in the kitchen, Dan again back at the table. I didn't say anything while I restocked the cabinets and fridge. The two of them spoke in Russian to one another, voices soft, though twice Alena's tone sharpened, and Dan said something conciliatory. I was folding the shopping bags and putting them away when I realized the conversation, whatever it had been about before, had now turned and made me the subject.

Natalie came back and rolled her eyes at me, and I moved to join her in the hall, saying, "I know, it's not good. It's not god-awful, but it's not good."

"The hot tub helps," she said.

"Sure, if you want to be picked off from outside."

"She taught you how to snipe, did she?"

"No," I said. "Sniping's woman's work."

"Well, let's talk about man's work, then. What do you want to do about the alarms?"

"I picked up some stuff at Radio Shack. Tomorrow we can wire a panic button to whatever room we're putting her in. Other than that, I'm not sure what else we can do."

"Be nice if we had Corry for this," she mused.

"And Dale for the vehicles, but we don't. Which room do you like for her?"

"The second bedroom upstairs, the one between the master bedroom and the smaller bathroom. You and I can take the beds on either side, she'll be covered."

I moved my head to indicate the flight of stairs. "Be trouble if we have to get her out in a hurry."

"Atticus," Natalie said. "If we have to get her out in a hurry, odds are none of us will be leaving alive anyway."

"We'll ask her what she wants."

Natalie looked past me, back into the kitchen. "You have any idea what they're talking about?"

"Probably me," I said.

"Oh, that's egocentric."

"Maybe. But I heard Dan use my name, and I don't think it was in passing. Not sure what the relationship is there."

"Not sure what the relationship is, here," Natalie pointed out.

I started to respond when, from the kitchen, Alena called, "Dan's going to go back into the city, get things ready for tomorrow."

Natalie and I stepped back into the kitchen, saw that Dan was already on his feet. He looked at me and asked, "If that's all right with you?"

There was no condescension in his tone at all.

"That's fine," I answered. "Thanks."

" 'Tasha says you'll pay me tomorrow."

"I'll have the money by the afternoon."

"That's good, then."

He adjusted his coat, glanced at Alena, then made his way out of the house. Natalie turned and followed him to the door, locking it after he left, staying at the window until his car was out of sight. I pulled out one of the chairs at the table and sat down with Alena.

"How do you feel about being upstairs?"

"The stairs will be difficult, but I'll manage. It will be fine." She set her crutches aside, propping them against the table. "Dan says you were unhappy with him."

"Not with him. There are problems with the house, it's not ideal. But it'll serve."

"He says I changed you."

"You did."

"He says I made you like me."

"That I'm not so sure about. But at least I'm no longer addicted to caffeine."

She smiled, but didn't laugh. "When is Fowler coming to speak with me?"

I was only a little surprised. "He's waiting for my call."

"Tonight would be best."

That was more surprising. "I thought you'd take some convincing."

"No, it was to be expected, and if you had not already contacted him, I would have asked you to. I will give him information."

"Like?"

"Oxford has certainly been hired by the same people who told you I had killed in Dallas. They lied to you, hoping you would make their jobs easier. They hoped I would contact you, and that you in turn would contact them. They most certainly planned to then forward that information to Oxford, helping him to narrow his search. Since they are Oxford's employers, only they can end the contract. But if I give information to Fowler, information embarrassing to those people, Fowler will share it with his superiors, and that will force them back into hiding."

"Nice plan if it'll work. Do you think it'll work?"

She shook her head. "But it will complicate things for Oxford at the least, perhaps buy us more time. Understand, I will speak to Fowler only because we can use him."

"He doesn't want to arrest you."

"I'm glad to hear that, because I won't allow it to happen."

"I'll make sure he understands," I said. "You don't have to worry about Scott, he's a good guy."

"Another of your friends."

"He's a good friend."

"I noticed that only Natalie agreed to help you."

"Dale and Corry are still my friends."

"And yet they are not here."

She shut her eyes, tired. It occurred to me that her leg was giving her a lot of pain. She opened her eyes again, then leaned over to where I was sitting and put her lips lightly against my cheek.

"Call your friend," she said.

CHAPTER THREE

She talked to Scott for almost three and a half hours, from shortly after midnight until almost four in the morning. They stayed at the kitchen table, Alena drinking juice and Scott mainlining coffee, and he filled page after page of his notebook with what she said. Mostly she gave him histories, incidences where she knew an assassin had been hired for a job, and she gave him enough facts, enough names and dates, explained enough about how such a contract would be carried out, that Scott could take the information and fill in the rest. She never implicated herself, though at least one of the assassinations she told him of was the execution of General Augustus Albertus Usuf Kiwane Ndanga. She told him about tradecraft, things she hadn't even shared with me, explaining to Scott the sorts of things he should look for if we wanted to tie Oxford to the people who had hired him. She explained contact protocols, cutouts, dead drops, authorizations.

Half of Scott's questions were about money, and he asked Alena to explain how payments were made, how an organization would arrange the funding for such jobs, how the transfers would be handled, in general, how she—and presumably others of her profession—handled their finances. In this she was more forthcoming, all things considered, and when she told Scott that, in fact, she didn't actually handle her money herself, he was incredulous.

"You actually trust it to someone else?"

"Of course. To a bank, in fact."

"A bank?"

"There is no other way," Alena answered. "Suppose I require a rental car, or a hotel room. I would need a credit card, one that is not only legitimate but also matches the identity I am using. A trustworthy banker can supply all of that."

"How does that work?"

"The majority of my money is in a trust with a safe and very private bank, and there is a man who handles the accounts for me. That man receives instructions from me to do certain things."

"Like?"

"If I need a credit card, I tell him to authorize an account payable from my trust in the name I require. If I am renting a storage unit in, say, Queens, he is told to write a check to the firm on the first of every month until ordered otherwise. Like that."

"So this person theoretically knows who you are, he could be used to find you."

"He knows the identity of the holder of the trust," she replied. "He has only met that woman on two occasions. He is well paid, Agent Fowler, extremely discreet, and he has ascertained enough about how I make my living to remain careful."

He stopped focusing on his notepad for a moment to look at her. "You threatened him?"

"I never have needed to."

I spoke up. "Does Oxford use the same procedure? A banker and a trust, like that?"

"Not the same, but almost certainly similar."

"How much money do you think he has?" I asked.

She considered, adjusting her weight slightly and frowning down at her left leg. "Probably more than I do. I'd guess—and this is only a guess—in excess of twenty million dollars."

"How often do you think he contacts his banker?"

"Fairly frequently. Certainly he makes contact whenever a payment is expected, in order to confirm delivery."

"Do the people who have hired him, do they know who the banker is?" Scott asked.

"No. They would be asked to transfer the money to dummy accounts and the like. The banker then handles the rest."

"So the contractor or contractors can't contact Oxford through the banker?"

"No, though whoever has hired him, they must have a way to contact him, and vice versa. In most instances this would give him power over them, but not here—if he is tied to a government agency, working with someone in Langley, say, then he is their employee, beholden to the organization."

"Is there a direct line of contact?" Scott asked.

"I'm not certain I understand your question."

He adjusted his glasses, trying to find a way to rephrase. "Say someone at the CIA decided to bring Oxford in, to use him for this job, to kill you and Atticus and Havel. Is that person the same one who actually made contact with Oxford, negotiated the deal, things like that?"

She started shaking her head. "No, no, that would not happen. In a private contract, yes, A hires me to kill C, and either A hires me directly, or A uses a contact, B, and B hires me. But that can be traced back. With a government job one thing is universal—there is always insulation. The person or persons who gave Oxford the job, who have set up the accounts with which to pay him, they will not be the same people who decided to hire Oxford in the first place."

"So how do you find the source, where it started?"

"You don't. You can't."

Scott looked over to me, then to Natalie, then back to Alena. "I can't accept that."

"Agent Fowler, that has nothing to do with anything," Alena said. "We are not talking about a hiring that started with an individual. We are talking about a decision of policy. Oxford will be funded until he completes the job. Or until he becomes more of a liability than an asset to the people who wish to use him."

"And he becomes a liability when?"

She smiled. "When he allows a book to be written about him."

It got laughs from both Scott and Natalie, and it made her smile a little brighter.

"Is that the only way?" Scott asked.

"There are others. If Oxford were to begin blowing up buildings in Manhattan, if he began killing people without due caution, if his behavior became erratic, the contracting party would have to sever the relationship. Anything that would cause them embarrassment, that would do it, if used properly. The information I have given you will have the same effect."

Scott scribbled quickly on his pad, then looked at me. "How embarrassing would it be if you paid a visit to Gracey and Bowles?"

"Depends how we did it," I said. "If I contact them and ask for a meeting, they're likely to say sure, how about someplace dark and deserted at four in the morning, and why don't you bring that lovely lady friend of yours. And then they'd tell Oxford where to expect me."

"But if I contact them, ask to meet, and you arrive with me?"

"That'll give them pause."

"And then we tell them that we know about, say, the prime minister of Moldova, or a certain military officer in Africa."

Alena coughed softly. "That is precisely what you *should* do."

"The result being they'd leave you two alone?" Scott asked.

"Ideally."

"Is that likely?"

"They will stop. Whether or not Oxford will, too, that is another matter entirely. Either way, it would force an action."

"What kind of action?" Natalie asked.

"They might cancel the contract, call him off altogether. They might put the operation on hold, although that seems less likely. They might attempt to buy Atticus off, bring him into the fold, encourage him to sell me out. There are any number of choices."

"I won't sell," I said.

She looked at her crutches propped against the table. "I know."

When Scott's cup had been emptied for the seventh time, I refilled it from the pot and then set another to brew. The smell of the coffee was strong, just a little burnt, and I was surprised that I didn't want any. Alena and Scott were still talking, and I was feeling stiff after all the sitting, so I headed down the hall to the foot of the stairs, where I used the banister as a makeshift *barre* and did some stretching. Natalie came and shut the door from the kitchen, leaned against the wall, watching me. She tried to stifle a yawn.

"You can go to sleep," I told her.

"Not quite yet." She rubbed her eyes. "What is that, ballet?"

"Yeah."

"She taught you ballet?"

"No, that would have taken eight or nine years."

"Russian school," she noted.

"Well, obviously."

"I took lessons when I was a kid." Natalie moved from the wall around to the stairs, sat down on the third step, still watching me. I went through a couple more motions, trying to get loose. The ballet wasn't as effective as yoga, but it helped. "Bridgett said you'd gone diesel. I didn't believe it until I saw you."

"Is diesel a bad thing?"

"Hell, no." She tapped my hand where it rested on the banister, getting me to look at her. "So, are you going to tell me what's going on between you two?"

"Me and Bridgett?"

"I've got the you-and-Bridgett part figured pretty well. The defining moment was when she blew into my office and called you a brainwashed fool and a fuckin' son of a bitch, to boot."

"She'll divorce you, too, she finds out you're helping me."

"Maybe so, but she's probably more inclined to cut me slack."

"Meaning she'd call you a fool and omit the brainwashed part."

"That's my thinking. So talk to me about you and Alena."

I stopped stretching. "It's kind of like working with you, actually."

"I think I'm flattered." She cocked her head. "Is that all?"

I sighed. "Why is it that everyone thinks I'm sleeping with her?"

"I'm not sure everyone does. I don't. I didn't. But if I had, it would be because you're a heterosexual male who has never showed an aversion to sex, and who spent a large amount of time with a not-unattractive woman who conceivably held a position of great power over you. And because it's not beyond the realm of possibility. And because I have a dirty mind."

I leaned both hands on the banister, looking at Natalie past the supports. "You put it like that, I'm wondering why I didn't."

"Because you were involved with someone when you left. And because it would have been icky."

"Both true. Bridgett didn't seem willing to get that far, though."

"It's probably easier for her to believe that you've fallen for Alena than for her to accept that you changed of your own free will. And the fact is, you cheated on her once."

"That was your fault, you tempted me with your feminine wiles," I said.

"Well, you know, when I'm drunk off my ass I'm extremely seductive."

"Bridgett said that I'd fallen for her?"

"Not in so many words. But the brainwashing comment and the repeated references to Patty Hearst made it clear to me that she wanted to believe you were a victim rather than a participant, that you'd been manipulated emotionally."

"And what do you think?"

"I actually don't think you've changed that much," Natalie said. "I'm in the minority, but I think I know you pretty well. You've always tilted at windmills. You know what's funny?"

"What's funny?" I asked.

"I like her, too," Natalie said. "I know who she is and what she's done, I spent three hours this morning with her discussing wind shear and ballistic drop, the relative merits of bolt versus semiautomatic rifles, and I had a thoroughly enjoyable time. It's not just that I like her, it's that she's *likable.* Why is that?"

"She wants to be liked."

"Yeah, but why?"

"I don't know. It could be psychological. From what she's said, I expect a large portion of her childhood was spent seeking approval from adults who rarely gave it. Oxford was almost the same way, though he didn't seem to want me to like him, so much as to understand where he was coming from. He wouldn't shut up once he got rolling. These are people who don't have many honest interactions, who every time they speak to someone, they're always calculating a result or an angle. I'd think it's pretty liberating to just be able to say what's on your mind."

She chewed her lower lip for a couple of seconds, and then the door from the kitchen opened and Alena came through on her crutches.

"All finished?" I asked.

"Yes. Agent Fowler is using the bathroom, I think all of the coffee caught up with him."

"How are you feeling?"

"I'm tired and my leg aches. I want to sleep."

Natalie got up, clearing the stairs, but Alena stopped before reaching them, at my side. She touched my elbow.

"What he and you are thinking of doing is very dangerous," she said. "I tried to explain that to him, but I'm not sure he understood."

"I'm sure he did, he's a smart guy," I said.

"I don't dispute his intelligence, Atticus. But I am worried that if too much pressure is put on Oxford's masters, Oxford himself will become even more unpredictable. It could make things worse, not better."

"I'll tell him you said so."

"Please do." She moved to the stairs, started painfully up them, Natalie and I watching, and after the fifth step it began to feel very awkward, and I wanted to help her. A shine of perspiration appeared on her forehead, and her hands on the crutches turned white from the strength of her grip.

When she reached the second floor she looked down at us.

"How long did it take me?" she demanded.

"Eighty seconds, about." Natalie sounded embarrassed.

"Eighty seconds. Tomorrow I'll do it in seventy."

Natalie went up shortly after to double-check that Alena had gotten settled, and I joined Scott in the kitchen where he was finishing his notes. My watch read three minutes past four when he capped his pen and stowed his pad, and I walked with him as he went to his car.

"She's a fucking gold mine, you know that?" he asked. "She practically gave me too much information, I'm not even sure where to begin. We can hit Gracey and Bowles tomorrow."

"Not yet," I said. "I want something more to hold over Oxford, not just his bosses."

"Like what?"

I didn't answer, and we continued along the path to where he had parked. The rain had stopped early in the evening, and everything smelled wet. It was cold enough outside, now, that a slight film of frost had covered the windshield of Scott's car. He wiped it off with a gloved hand. A few leaves blew across the lawn.

"Alena is afraid you're not aware of the danger here," I said. "She's afraid that if we pressure Gracey and Bowles, it could backfire."

"Everything I took down tonight I'm forwarding to the SAIC," Scott said. "He'll send it straight to Washington, you can bet on that."

"That may not be enough insurance."

"Can you think of anything else to do?"

"That's the problem. Oxford's going to keep coming until either he's dead, we're dead, or he's been called off. And I'm not so sure about that last one. That's why I want some insurance."

"And again I ask, like what?"

"His money."

He opened the door to the car, slipped behind the wheel, then started the engine and cranked the defroster to full. "I'll start sending faxes tomorrow morning, but I have to tell you, based on what she said, I don't think we're going to get very far. If Oxford's drawing government pay, they're in a very strong position to block any inquiry I make."

"Then don't inquire," I said. "Let me handle it."

"You asking me to sit on my hands?"

"I'm not saying that, I'm just saying don't go looking for his money. If you've got other avenues to pursue, do it. Oxford made some noise about cash moving between me and Havel, you could look into that, see how he managed it. But if you start trying to dig up stuff about his funds, that'll set off alarms."

"You just said we need to find his money."

"I'll handle it."

He blinked at me. "Jesus, you will, too, won't you?"

"I'm going to be gone for a week, maybe longer. If you need to contact me, go through Natalie."

"Do you have that much time?"

"Oxford was wounded when he left Bequia, and we've been careful since then. It'll take him time before he finds us again."

"Long enough for you to be gone a week or maybe longer?"

"I'm optimistic."

"That's fine as long as the optimism isn't foolish."

"I think I've got the time," I said.

Scott grunted and swung his legs into the car. I put a hand on his door, pushing it shut. He drove away, the gate opening automatically as he approached it. I watched the specter of his taillights disappear behind the trees.

He'd gone out of sight when I realized that I'd forgotten to tell him to be careful.

CHAPTER FOUR

Alena was already up when I woke, and I joined her in her room for some yoga. We kept it short, and she took it easy, then went to take a shower in the master bathroom. I headed downstairs and put together some breakfast, coffee for Natalie, and some rather lumpy smoothies for myself and Alena. She came into the kitchen as I was finishing up, moving energetically on the crutches, and when she saw the bottles for all of the supplements I'd bought, she laughed.

I waited until she'd finished her drink and her vitamins before telling her what I was planning. Natalie came in as I was starting, but since the coffee didn't kick in until I was almost halfway through, I ended up repeating myself a lot. Alena listened intently, and after I'd finished she told me that the plan sounded solid enough, but that I should use Austria instead of Switzerland if everything worked out as I intended.

"You want a *Sparbuch* account," she told me. "It's a passbook account, but anonymous. You'll need to find a willing Austrian national to set it up."

I said that I didn't think it would be a problem, then went upstairs to shower and pack my bag. Dan arrived while I was getting dressed, the four guards he'd promised in tow, all of them smaller and younger-looking versions of himself. I immediately recognized two of the faces from the Brighton Beach restaurant, though it took a little longer before I could place the other two. They were the ones who had held me outside of Katrina's room at the brothel. All of them came armed, pistols and rifles, and all of them spoke fluent English, with accents ranging from almost negligible to nearly impenetrable. It made giving them their marching orders interesting. Natalie gave them the rundown of the location, broke them up into shifts, and put them to work guarding the house and the perimeter.

While she was briefing the guards, a car pulled up to the gate. The doctor Dan had located was in his early fifties with watery and bloodshot eyes, white and thin like a distance runner or a junkie. He never gave his name and never asked any of us for ours, and he brought two bags with him, and I searched them both before letting him into the house. Aside from medical tools he had a small pharmacy in one of the bags. The other held a variety of braces and equipment for making casts.

Alena had come to watch Natalie's briefing, and when I came in with the doctor, she moved to the guest room on the ground floor for his exam. I put Dan on the door and followed them in, watching while the doctor asked Alena to lie on the bed. She removed her pants and lay back, and the doctor pulled the gauze from her shin and began poking and prodding from her foot to about midway up her thigh. He asked her a few questions about range of motion and sensation. A couple of times his fingers dug into her skin, and she winced, but never made any sound.

After twenty minutes he was ready to diagnose, and it wasn't good.

"Without an X ray I can't be sure. You've shattered the two bones that run from your knee to your foot, and while the splinters have been removed, the bones aren't knitting. I don't know who the butcher was who practiced his needlepoint on your leg, darling, but if I were you I'd ask for my money back. Not even counting the tib-fib clusterfuck in there, the muscle damage is tremendous. That you've got any sensation in your left foot at all is surprising as hell, and that you're not screaming in constant agony is truly amazing. I've seen members of the New York Jets crying like babies with injuries less severe than this."

"Is there anything you can do?" I asked, not liking his mirth.

"Surgery, but that's not my arena. You want someone to get in there and clean the thing up, maybe replace the bone with a rod. That's all speculative, though. Like I said, I'd need to see an X ray to be sure what is going on in there."

"If I have surgery will I get my leg back?" Alena asked.

"Probably not. There's nerve damage as well as muscle trauma. With extensive physical therapy you could put some weight on the leg, but it will never be able to hold you again. You're looking at needing a crutch or a cane for the rest of your life, toots."

"You've got a great bedside manner, doc," I said.

He turned to me, wiping at his eyes. "Hey, chew me, smartass. I'm here because the ugly Russian outside gave me two grand to drive up to Mahwah, and he promised me another three when I left. This lady's lower leg has been mangled, and from what I can see that's because she got it shot up. So it looks to me like you're illegals or criminals or something I don't even want to know about. You get her to a surgeon, they can maybe do something for her. Otherwise, the leg stays useless."

Alena propped herself up on her elbows and muttered something in Russian.

"What *can* you do, doctor?" I asked.

"I can put a brace on the knee to help immobilize the lower leg, that should help with some of the pain. And I can hook her up with some Percodan or another pain reliever of her choice."

"I'll take the brace," she said. "You can keep the drugs. You'll probably get more use out of them."

"No argument there." He dug into the bag that held the braces, selected one and eyeballed Alena's knee. Then he discarded it and pulled another one out, this one longer, and began strapping it to her leg. She swore once as he was tightening the straps, and when he was done she had a combination of metal and rubber running from her ankle to above her knee.

"She's going to need some help getting her pants back on," the doctor told me, closing his bags. "You kids have fun, now. Where's Ugly with my dough?"

I led him from the room and told Dan to see him the rest of the way out. Dan nodded and glanced back at where Alena was sitting up on the bed and asked her something in Russian. She responded tartly. Dan nodded again, rested his big hand on the doctor's shoulder, and left.

When Alena was up, she put tentative weight on her left foot, and it didn't look like much at all, but just that action made her suck a sharp breath and brought water into her eyes. I handed her one of her crutches, then held the door for her while she limped out of the room and back to the stairs.

"Time me," she said, and started up.

It took her fifty-six seconds. Instead of being pleased, she scowled all the way back into her room, where she settled into a chair and stared out the window.

"I should go with you."

"No, you really shouldn't," I said. "Aside from the injury, it would just leave you more exposed."

She nodded grudgingly. "When you get the money at the bank, leave yourself at least fifty thousand to travel on. Withdraw ten thousand in Swiss francs before you leave."

"I will."

"The rest you can exchange in England."

"I will."

"The cache near Kent, that one should be safe, although the papers there will be useless to you. The one in Geneva is good, too. I don't have anything in Austria."

"It's all right, Alena, I'll be fine."

She didn't speak for a couple minutes, and I saw her hands turn to fists, balling tighter and tighter until the blood had run from her fingers, turning them the color of white chalk. "I hate this. I hate my leg. I hate this brace. I hate this house. I hate this view, that doctor."

"If this works you won't be here much longer."

"You are certain Moore will help you? Even after what happened to Ainsley-Hunter?"

"Moore owes me."

She gave me a serious appraisal. "If you find Oxford's banker, you will have to be savage, Atticus. You will have to hurt him. Not permanently, perhaps, but enough so that he will fear you."

"I thought I'd leave a clue of some sort," I said. "One of the false names, something Oxford could work with."

She looked appalled at the suggestion. "No, no, no. When you have the banker, when you are finished, you must threaten his life, you must say something like, 'if you talk, the only part of your body they will ever find is your tongue,' something like that. You must say it like you mean it."

"What if he believes me?"

"It doesn't matter. You will be the devil he doesn't know. Oxford is the devil he does. And I assure you, he is more afraid of Oxford, has feared him more completely and for longer than he will fear you. Their entire relationship is founded on two things: fear and greed. So far, greed has held the higher ground. You must play on the fear, and by threatening his life, he will not even consider that you are manipulating him. He will believe that he is being brave, that Oxford will reward him for his courage and loyalty."

"You think it's a he?"

"Almost positive," Alena said. "Most of them are."

"I should be back in a week."

"I shall be here," she said sourly.

Early in the afternoon, Dan drove me into Manhattan in the Kompressor and waited while I handled the money at the Credit Suisse branch off Madison Avenue. I presented myself as Paul Lieberg with the papers to prove it, and the woman behind the desk went from pleasant to solicitous when she ran my name through the computer. Of the two hundred thousand Alena had transferred, I put a hundred thousand in a cashier's check made out to a name Dan had given me in the car, another fifty in a check made out to Jessica Bethier. I took the remaining fifty thousand in cash. As instructed, I withdrew ten of it in Swiss francs, then another ten in pounds.

Back at the car I handed Dan the two checks, telling him that the smaller one was to go to Natasha. We parted company, me carrying my bag and he pulling back into traffic.

My watch said it was eight minutes to two, and that meant I had over five hours until I needed to catch the plane, more than enough time to do the thing I'd been considering doing since I'd returned to New York three days earlier. It was a risky, if not an outright stupid, thing, and if I'd told Alena or Natalie where I wanted to go and who I wanted to see, both would have gone through the roof.

I did it anyway, though, catching one of the Lexington line trains down to Astor Place. I came back aboveground beside the giant Starbucks and walked over to Broadway, heading south a couple blocks and then west, until I was on the campus of NYU. I found the dormitory I wanted, debated about using the intercom to call up, and was spared the trouble when a knot of girls emerged. I went through as the door swung shut behind them, and took the elevator up to the sixth floor.

The door to her room was decorated with all sorts of paper, postcard reprints of classic movie posters and a bumper sticker ordering me to question authority. At the center was an eight-by-five piece of paper that had been run through a printer. It read K.C. & ERIKA and THIS HAD BETTER BE **GOOD**!

The door was open, so I didn't need to knock. I stuck my head in, and saw her seated at a desk, typing furiously on a laptop. She had a cigarette going, too.

"Can I come in?" I asked.

Erika turned in the chair before I'd finished speaking, yelped, yanked the cigarette from her mouth, and jumped up and ran to me, into a hug that nearly put me back into the hall. She also nearly put the cigarette out in my neck.

"What the hell kept you?" she demanded, her face in my chest. Then she let me go and stepped back and asked it again.

"Let's go somewhere and talk."

"K.C.'s not here, she's at her playwriting class, you can come in."

"Let me buy you coffee."

Erika opened her mouth to invite me in again, and in the process introduced me to the fact that she'd gotten her tongue pierced at some point in the past few months. Without another word she turned back to her desk, saved the document she'd been working on, and set the computer to shut down. Then she grabbed her black leather biker's jacket, the one Bridgett and I had bought her over the holidays the previous year, and joined me out in the hall.

We were silent in the elevator and out of the building, and when we hit the street, she zipped up her jacket and asked, "Now?"

"Not yet," I said.

"There's a place on Christopher with good java, big fucking cups. You need a crane to lift them."

"Lead on."

She did, with me walking beside her, and after another block and a half, she asked again. "Now?"

"Now," I said, and she threw her arms around my chest and squeezed me tight, and I returned the hug just as fiercely.

"I am so fucking angry at you," she told my chest.

"So am I," I said. "You started smoking."

Erika pulled back and punched me lightly in the chest. "Not the same! Not the same at all!"

"And you got your tongue pierced."

"And you got rid of the glasses and grew a dead animal on your face. Oh, excuse me, that's a *beard,* my mistake."

"I'm in disguise."

"As what, a pimp?"

"That's cold. I don't look like a pimp."

"I don't know what you look like." She moved her head back, as if trying to adjust the focus on me. "Well, shit. Bridgett said you'd gone—"

"Diesel," I said.

"No, not diesel—crazy. You don't look crazy."

"Us lunatics seldom do."

"You gonna tell me where you've been?"

"I'm going to tell you everything," I said.

Erika listened to me holding her cup of coffee, which, though big, did not require a crane. She held the cup in front of her the way Tibetan monks hold their prayer bowls, her blue eyes intent on my face as I spoke. Her hair had been its natural dirty blond the last time I'd seen her, but she'd since dyed it a matte black that matched her jacket. As ever, her hair hung long on the left side of her face, concealing the ear that had been mutilated by a man with a knife four years earlier.

She looked different to me, no longer the teenager who'd come into my home years ago, pulling chaos in her wake. She was nineteen now, a young woman and, to my eyes, coming of age very nicely. I was so glad to be with her I didn't even give her grief when she set the cup down and lit herself another cigarette.

After I'd finished she started giggling, and then she started laughing, and then she choked on the smoke she'd inhaled and coughed. Then she laughed some more.

"Only you," she said. "Only you would go away as someone's prisoner and come back as that same person's knight in shining armor."

"It's a unique gift," I admitted.

"Bridgett's right, you are *totally* mad."

"When'd she talk to you?"

"Yesterday, we had lunch at Anglers and Writers. She says she doesn't want anything to do with you. I asked if she meant until this was over or forever or what, and she said she didn't know."

"Bridgett's got her reasons, and they're good ones. I understand why she's angry."

"I think she's overreacting."

That surprised me. "Really?"

"Yeah, really. Last year she pulled the vanishing act on all of us, remember? And when you found her—*you*—she was strung out on smack and sitting in her own shit. You took her home, you cleaned her up, you watched her back when she got into the heavy stuff. I think she owes you the same courtesy here."

"It's not the same situation," I pointed out.

"You've always given her more slack than she's given you." She took another drag from the cigarette, then blew a jet of smoke up at the ceiling. When she'd finished the display, she indicated my bag, which I'd set on the floor by my chair. "Either you're going somewhere, or you've got something in there for me."

"I'm going somewhere."

"I'm disappointed. I was hoping something like a shirt, you know, one that said, 'My Legal Guardian Went To A Caribbean Island With A Professional Assassin And All I Got Was This Lousy T-Shirt.' "

"Tell you what, I'll have one made especially for you."

"Make sure it's black with white lettering if you do. Can you tell me where you're going?"

"No."

"So you just came by to say hi-and-goodbye?"

"That and something else. This thing with Alena could get dangerous. I want you to be careful."

"I am always careful, big brother."

"I'm not talking about condoms in your purse, Erika. Don't take any stupid risks. If you go out, go out with friends. Don't get drunk, don't smoke pot, any of that wacky college stuff."

"I've never smoked grass," she said, indignant.

"I'm speaking generally. You want specifics, here's a list. Don't go by the apartment, not for any reason at all, it's probably under surveillance. Lock your door whenever you're in your dorm room, don't leave it open like it was just now. I want you on your guard until I tell you otherwise, and when I do that, I'll do it in person. If someone tells you that I sent them and you don't know who they are, you raise an alarm and run like hell. If I want you I'll get you in person or it'll be someone you know very well, and I mean someone like Natalie or Scott or Bridgett. And if you see anything—anything at all—that makes you just the tiniest bit suspicious, I want you to call one of them ASAP. Don't worry about overreacting, don't worry about looking foolish. We're talking about your life."

"You're totally serious, aren't you?"

"If anything happened to you, Erika, I *would* go crazy," I said. "Please be careful."

"I will."

"Your word?"

"You know you have it."

"Good." I checked my watch, saw that I had just over two and a half hours to make the flight. From one of my pockets I took a bundle of bills, counted out five thousand dollars beneath the cover of the table, then folded the money and handed it over. "Emergency funds. Don't blow it on fast boys and loose cars."

She pocketed the money without bothering to see how much I'd given her. She'd already put the cigarette out, and she could tell I was getting ready to leave, because she was up before I was, and she gave me another hug.

"I'll be back as soon as I can," I told the top of her head.

"I know," she said. "You always come back for me."

At seven fifty-three that evening, I was a man named Dennis Murphy, in seat 29B on a British Airways 747, making my way to London.

CHAPTER FIVE

It took looking in the first copy of *The Sun* that I could find to confirm that Lady Antonia Ainsley-Hunter was in London, and I caught a cab from Heathrow into the city, got dropped off in front of the Burns Hotel in Kensington. It was just past seven in the morning when I checked into my room, a double with an almost queen and a passable bathroom, and I fiddled with the alarm clock until I got it to work, then crashed on the bed until a quarter past ten. When I woke I did some yoga and some sit-ups, showered, then headed out in search of a pay phone. When I found one I liked, I called Robert Moore on his cellular phone.

"Moore."

"This is Mr. Klein," I said. "You're holding a letter for me."

He didn't miss a beat. "Yes, it arrived several days ago. Do you need it delivered?"

"If that's possible, and the sooner the better."

"Where can I meet you?"

"There's a tube stop at Earl's Court."

"I can be there in fifty minutes."

"That would be fine."

"I'll come in on the train." Then he added, "Mind the gap."

I was laughing as I hung up the phone.

London subway stations, even at their worst, make New York's look like they were constructed by giant rats, and that the giant rats still reside in them. Those in London are also, for the most part, far less crowded, and as a result I spotted Moore as he came off the train. He was wearing a Burberry coat and holding a black plastic shopping bag, and he waited by the tracks until the train had pulled away again before moving forward.

I let him pass me before saying, "Hey."

He stopped and said, "I thought it was you, but the hair threw me. You've been in the sun."

"Lots of sun," I admitted, and I took his offered hand and shook it warmly.

"Christ Almighty, but I'm glad you're okay."

"I figured you might be pissed."

"You daft? You got her back, and that was the most important thing." Moore looked around the station, then handed me the shopping bag. "Is this what you were after, then?"

"Actually, no," I said. "I need a little help."

"You always do. Buy me a pint and we'll chat about it."

We had a late lunch at a well-hidden pub in Chelsea called The Surprise, on a crooked street called Christchurch Street, about a block from Oscar Wilde's townhouse. It was comfortable and quiet inside, with bare oak floors and wood on the walls. A small dining area was at the rear and we got a table and some food. Moore tried to get me to try one of the ales, saying that it was a good, living brew and that I owed it to myself to try some. I drank a ginger beer instead.

"How's Her Ladyship?"

"Running great guns, as you might expect," he said. "She'll be disappointed that she didn't get to see you."

"I don't want anyone to know I'm here."

"That much I'd already gathered." He nudged the plastic bag with the toe of his shoe, pushing it farther against the legs of my chair. "I opened it when it arrived, of course. It's well done."

"It is."

"Made me curious, you might imagine. Wondered what you were doing sending me paper like that, after everything that had happened. You care to explain it?"

"Not right now."

"All business, then?"

"What I need, I need as quickly as possible."

"And what you need is . . . ?"

"A name and an address. And I can't get them through my sources."

He opened his pack of Dunhills, lit one. "Think you perhaps better tell me a little more."

"There is an individual, could be female, most likely male. This individual is an accountant or a banker or possibly a lawyer. Most likely working in Europe, in one of the major financial centers."

"This a hypothetical person?"

"No, this person exists. And aside from his normal job crunching numbers or selling loans, he handles accounts and investments for one very specific, very particular client. He does this with absolute discretion and more than a little fear, and in exchange for this work, he makes at least a million dollars a year himself."

"Powerful client."

"Oxford," I said.

Moore leaked smoke from his nose studying me. His eyes were thoughtful, but I couldn't tell if the thoughts were pleasant or not.

"You're looking for Oxford's banker?" he asked. "You sure he's got one?"

"I have it on reliable authority."

"And this authority would be who?"

"Someone who knows."

He took another drag, looking sidelong towards the bar and the door. Then he brought his eyes back to me, and it was clear he knew who I meant. He asked, "Why come to me? You've got contacts on your side of the ocean, why not use them?"

"If they make inquiries, the wrong people will notice."

"Wrong how?"

"Wrong as in the people who've hired Oxford in the first place are also the people one would normally ask about this sort of thing. You've got to understand, Robert—he's not just after my principal, he's after me, too. I'm part of the contract, and he already got too close once."

"So you're appealing to me on the basis of . . . what? Our history?"

"If that's what it takes."

He shook his head. "No, that won't wash. This is a business transaction between us, all right? We keep it on that level, it won't arse up the friendship."

"Business."

That actually had a visible effect on him, and he relaxed in his seat. "I'll need two thousand pounds and a way to reach you."

"How long will it take?"

"I'll talk to the blokes I know tonight, all goes well, I'll have something for you by morning."

"Then I'll call you tomorrow morning." I dug out my wallet, counted ten of the hundred-pound notes I'd acquired earlier, and handed them over. "You get the rest when I get your report."

He counted the money, then folded it away in his pocket. "Your business sense has improved."

"I need this information, and I need it fast, Robert," I said. "Every day that passes, this guy gets closer to me, to my principal, to the people I love."

"Supposing I bring you what you want tomorrow, what're you doing then? Sharing that with your—ahem—principal?"

"You don't have to worry about that."

"Actually, I do, and if I don't get an answer I can work with, you can take your damn money back."

I shook my head. "You're the one who made this business."

"That I did." He finished his cigarette, ground it out with a grin, then drained the last of his living ale from its glass and got to his feet. "Call me after nine."

He was already on his cell phone before he had left the pub.

I spent the rest of the day wandering through the bookstores on Charing Cross Road, not buying anything. I found another pub around seven and got myself a very limp salad and some very bland fish, and I walked all the way back to the Burns Hotel fighting the craving for some deep-fried food. At the desk I got directions to a twenty-four-hour gym nearby, and spent three hours in it working myself into a lather. When I was done I didn't want fried food, just sleep, so I returned to the hotel and went to bed.

At nine the next morning I called Moore from a different pay phone.

"I'll have something by the end of the day," he said. "But the price is going up."

"How much?"

"There's a rental fee, I'll explain when I see you. Call me at five."

When I contacted him again at five, he told me that Mr. Klein should get a room at the Hilton before nine that evening, and hung up. I went to the Hilton and did as ordered, found that I had most of four hours before anyone would come calling, and used the pool at the hotel for a long swim. Then I went for a run in the rain. Then I went back to the hotel, took a shower, and tried not to think about how slow Alena was on the stairs, about the four men and one woman who were standing guard over her, about the fact that Oxford would go through them like they were made of tissue.

At one past nine Moore knocked on the door and I let him inside, then checked the hall.

"I came clean," he said. "No one's following me."

He was wearing the same raincoat from the day before, and beneath it a well-tailored navy suit. He was also carrying a burgundy leather briefcase, and he set it on the floor between his legs after I'd shut and double locked the door.

"Four thousand," Moore said.

"You taking advantage of my generous nature?"

"Like I said, it's a rental fee. The people I got this information from, they did it as a favor to me, but they didn't do it for free. I'm covering my expenses." He folded his overcoat once and draped it over the back of the nearest chair. "I'm keeping this business."

"I'd like to see what I'm getting for the money."

"You're not getting anything, you're borrowing." He picked up the case and laid it flat on the bed, then popped open the locks. Inside were several folders, manila with red stenciled warnings about violations of The Official Secrets Act. Moore looked at me to see if I understood.

"When do they have to be back?" I asked, gesturing at the folders.

"By oh-five-hundred, no later, otherwise they'll be missed. Gives you shy of eight hours to review them."

I dug out my wallet and handed over the bills. Moore pocketed the money, this time without counting it, then removed the folders from the case, handing them to me.

"Where will you be?" I asked.

"Right bloody here. Those don't leave my sight."

"I'm not going to steal them."

"I'm committing an act of treason for you." He sounded angry. "That should give you some idea of the measure of my trust. But trust you as I do, I don't want to leave and find out someone else blew through here and walked out with Her Majesty's documents. So I'll stay. You can order up some dinner. But those papers never leave my sight."

"The menu's by the phone," I told him, and then sat down at the desk and opened the first folder.

The files had been prepared by someone in military intelligence, using data compiled from a wide variety of sources that included British Intelligence, Interpol, the DEA, and the CIA. As I began working, Moore told me that one of the problems had been in actually assembling the data; apparently no one had ever bothered to try and track down Oxford's money man before.

"Bloke who helped me on this didn't give you much hope," Moore told me as I got started.

There were files on five men, each of whom had earned government or law enforcement attention through their financial dealings. The files were piecemeal assemblies, printouts and copies and faxes and copies of copies and copies of faxes, slips of paper stapled together, the occasional photograph. It took me nearly an hour just to get everything sorted into usable piles. Once I had that done, though, things went fairly quickly, mostly because I knew what I was looking for.

The first file was of an Englishman named Meadows living in London and employed by Lloyd's. A notation in the file said he was on his third marriage, no children. Along with the personal data were copies of various police reports, indicating two arrests for drunk driving and one for the solicitation of a prostitute who had turned out to be an undercover officer. Meadows had earned his file courtesy of the DEA, who suspected him of laundering money for a group of arms dealers out of the Middle East.

There was no way Alena would have trusted this guy with her money.

The next file was on a Swiss named Junot, an attorney in his early forties, living in Geneva, on the lake. Employed by Brunschwig Wittmer, twenty-two years of service. His personal information was at the bottom of the file, stated that he was divorced and that his ex-wife and their nine-year-old son had subsequently died in an avalanche during a skiing holiday in the Alps. He had earned Interpol's notice by purchasing a marble bust of Nike at an auction three years earlier, and the only reason they'd noticed him at all was that the seller had been the point man for an organization out of Turkey that trafficked in a lot of heroin. A note queried where Junot had gotten the money to purchase the statue, but the investigation had apparently ended there when no one could find a connection between him and the seller other than that single transaction.

He was a possible, and I set him aside.

The third was an American named Collier who worked for Bank of America, which I found kind of amusing. Collier specialized in loans for foreign development, was in his late thirties, married with three children, all girls. He was also financing foreign loans, and while many of those loans had been high-risk, that wasn't what had earned him CIA attention: six years ago he'd gone to China on some sort of trade junket and begun an affair with a woman who said she was in software development in Taiwan, but was actually part of the Chinese Security Force. Collier had been leaking her technology information as opportunity allowed.

Another discard.

The fourth was another Swiss, living in Zurich, named Blanc. I discarded him immediately when I saw that he had served ten years for killing a pedestrian in a hit-and-run accident. I never bothered to see why he'd made the file.

The fifth was a South African named Martins, single, never married, fifty-six years old. He was another banker, and had been identified by Interpol, the DEA, and the CIA as a bookkeeper for the Sicilian mafia, though apparently that employment had ended some ten years ago.

He, too, was a possible.

It was nearly one when I finished going through the paperwork.

"Any joy?" Moore asked.

"Maybe. I've got two guys here that I'd trust to do the job if it were mine. The others are all too unreliable—either histories with drugs or the authorities or potential personality problems that would make them untrustworthy."

Moore moved from where he'd been slumped on the couch, watching television, and came to the desk, looking over my shoulder. "Fifty-fifty chance."

"Problem is I don't have time for those odds," I said. "I'm leaning toward Junot."

"Let me see."

I handed the folders over, then got up and went to the window. There wasn't much of a view, just scattered lights filtering through the fog. I heard Moore rustling papers as he flipped through the files.

"Why Junot?" he asked.

"No prior history."

"Martins is pretty clean."

"But he's known."

"Oxford an American?"

"I'm pretty sure he is."

"That would connect him with the CIA."

"And Martins is known to the CIA."

"What I'm thinking, yes."

"No. The more I think about it, the more it's got to be Junot if it's any of them."

"You don't think the dead wife and child would be a problem?"

"It's a bonus, actually. Junot's isolated, doesn't have people. Won't be talking to anyone about the money."

"People who collect ancient pieces of art tend to show it off."

"Depends why they like the art. You look at Junot's file, you tell me if that looks like the kind of man who shows off. To me it reads like a man who spends an awful lot of his time alone."

"Martins . . ." Moore mused. "Looks like he's a homosexual. Mid-fifties, never married. Could mean he's discreet."

"Problem is that the file doesn't actually say that he's queer," I said. "Which could mean he's so far in the closet, it's an issue for him. That could be used against him as blackmail. It would make him a potential risk."

"In this day?" Moore asked.

"I've never been to South Africa, I don't know what the public perception of gays there is." I turned and went back to the desk, gathered up the remaining files and handed them to Moore, who dropped them back in the briefcase. "Thanks."

"You're welcome." He latched the case shut. "This isn't the kind of thing I do for just anyone, you understand that."

"I do. And I appreciate the risk you've taken."

"It levels the field."

"I thought this was just business."

"If it was just business, I'd have told you to sod off when you called this morning. You need anything else?"

"Actually, I do," I said. "This should be easier, though. I need a contact in Austria, someone who'd be willing to make a couple bucks doing something marginally illegal."

"How much and how marginal?"

"Say ten grand? They'd have to open an account for me at a bank, a specific kind of account. The account has to be opened by an Austrian national, and I don't have the German or the papers to do it myself."

He took his coat from the back of the chair, slipping into it, thinking. "There's a woman I know, she could do it. I'd have to ask her first, of course."

"Of course," I replied. "It may be a couple of days before I need her."

He took the briefcase off the bed. "Give me a call when you do."

"I will," I said.

When he reached the open door, Moore said, "You're walking a very narrow rope. Be careful you don't fall off."

"I'm not going to kill anyone, Robert. . . ."

"See that you don't."

"At least no one who doesn't have it coming," I said, shutting the door after him.

CHAPTER SIX

The alarm began sounding a warning the moment the man opened the door for me, and before he got any ideas I shoved him the rest of the way through, jamming the barrel of the Browning against his neck. He nearly fell as we came over the threshold but I jerked him back to his feet and when his ear was closer to my mouth, I said one of the phrases I'd been practicing since leaving London almost fifteen hours earlier. I'd practiced it in French, German, and Italian, not knowing which language I would need, and while I wasn't sure I had captured the letter of my order in each language, I know my tone made the spirit plain.

"Shut off the alarm or you're fucking dead," I said in German.

He nodded vigorously, already straining to reach the keypad, and I waited while he punched in the numbers, six of them. The keypad had an LCD and three lights, and right now one of the lights was bright red, and getting angry. Then the last number went in and the pad chirped and the red light went out, and another, green, came on.

The man with my gun against his neck began whispering a rapid and frightened string of German, and he strained to see me without turning his head, his eyes white and wide. I pulled the gun from his neck and then clubbed him with the barrel, which was bad for the gun but worse for him. He went down on his knees, caught himself on his hands. I saw blood seeping through the thinning black hair at the back of his skull, and before I looked at it too long and really started thinking about what I was doing, I hit him again.

The man fell to the floor, still.

I dropped a knee onto his back, holding the Browning out, sighting down the hallway, into the darkness of what I took to be the kitchen, but there was nothing, no movement, no noise. With my free hand I felt for his pulse, got one off the carotid, strong and rapid. Assuming that the blows to his head didn't cause a cerebral edema or a sudden clot, he'd be okay.

The carpet in the hall was thick and silk and looked like it had come from Turkey, or maybe farther in Asia, and when I set the gun on it there was no noise. From the left pocket of my coat I removed the duct tape and wound it rapidly around the man's wrists, binding them behind his back. I did the same with his feet, then pulled off his necktie and gagged him with it, tight. I didn't want to use the duct tape and risk him suffocating, but I didn't want him playing possum and raising an alarm as soon as I moved away. I probably didn't need to worry, but it made me feel like I hadn't hit him all that hard, wasn't being all that callous, if I kept telling myself he wasn't truly unconscious.

But he was, and when I rose, he didn't move.

I put the duct tape back in my jacket and listened again. From above I heard the sound of water as it began running through pipes. Past that, the only noises came from a grandfather clock at the end of the hallway and the muted slap of Lake Geneva as it met the shore outside.

My shoes silent on the expensive rug, I started down the hall, looking for my target.

I'd given it twenty minutes after Moore left before heading down myself, checking out of the room and then catching a cab back to the Burns and falling into bed. At six I was up again, and by seven I was at Heathrow with a Swissair ticket to Geneva. I was still moving as Dennis Murphy, and passed through passport control without the slightest hitch. Outside, I caught the train into the city, a ride of seven minutes that let me off in the downtown of one of the world's nerve centers. The last time I'd been through Switzerland I'd been in my teens, with a EurailPass in my pocket and a list of youth hostels in my hand. The places I'd stayed had been utterly without frills but absolutely clean. This time I stayed at the Intercontinental Hotel on Petit-Saconnex, a huge and modern high-rise, where everything was just as clean as the last time, but far more welcoming. My room had soft beige carpet and the bedspread was the color of brass, and out the window I could see the lake and the Alps and the city.

The cache was actually twenty-nine kilometers outside of Geneva, near Nyon, on a small boat berthed at one of the tiny marinas that dotted the shores of the lake. I caught a cab and managed to convey to the driver where I needed to go with a combination of English and French, and when we reached our destination it took me another three minutes to make him understand that I wanted him to wait for me. There were perhaps sixteen boats moored to a floating pier that jutted out over the clear and cold water, the access from the road blocked by a token gate, the kind of structure that is more a polite request to keep a distance than a warning to steer clear. I walked out over the water, not seeing anyone, counting berths, until I found the craft I wanted.

The boat was named *La Petite Marie,* and the deck was clear and empty. The cabin door was held shut with a combination lock, and for what felt like a lifetime I stared at it, racking my brain for the numbers Alena had given me, the numbers she'd told me I mustn't write down, that I had to memorize. It took me three tries before I got it right, and the relief I felt when the lock snapped open left me wanting to laugh.

The boat had been built to hold two people intimately at best, and the interior smelled of musty fabric and mildew, and something vaguely fruity, as if the last occupant had eaten an orange and forgotten to throw out the skin. A cushioned bench ran along one side of the cabin and against the far wall, where it met with a narrow closet. Pulling the cushions back revealed cabinets built into the side of the boat, and in the one nearest the prow on the starboard side I found a powder blue grip made of vinyl. I took the bag, replaced the cushions, and locked the door on my way out.

A boy, perhaps fourteen years old, stood at the end of the pier as I came back, and he watched me approach. When I hopped the fence again he asked me a question in German, and I answered in the best French I could manage that I didn't understand. He gestured out to the *La Petite Marie,* asking another question, and I shrugged and grinned and climbed into the cab. The boy watched as we departed, and as the car turned to take me back to Geneva, I saw him walking out on the pier, presumably making for the boat.

I doubted that the kid worked for Interpol or even the CIA, but all the same I had the cab drop me off at the headquarters for the International Red Cross, then walked a couple blocks until I found an open clothing boutique. I purchased a pair of leather gloves that weren't so thick that they would impede my manual dexterity, then got directions to an English language bookstore on

Rue Versonnex, where I purchased a French-English phrase book. I made my way back to the hotel, and was in my room, behind its locked door, before I ever opened the grip.

Alena had cached two pistols—a Browning and a Beretta—with ammunition for each. The money came to almost thirty thousand in Swiss francs, with another ten thousand in dollars. There were also papers for Genevieve Pontchardier, a young woman who lived in Bern and worked for one of the banks there, as well as a mix of toiletries and clothes. There were also binoculars and a thirty-five millimeter camera. Except for the weapons and the cash, it was the kind of bag someone might pack for a weekend excursion along Lac Léman.

I burned Genevieve Pontchardier's papers over the toilet, then moved everything to my bag, except for the money. This I put into three hotel envelopes, then put the envelopes inside my coat. I dumped the grip in the trash and went down to the lobby. Most of the staff spoke English fluently. The concierge smiled knowingly when I asked him if he could suggest a discreet bank nearby.

"All of our banks are quite discreet, Monsieur Murphy," he told me, and then he took one of the paper maps of Geneva he kept by his desk, and conscientiously traced out my route for me. "Their English is very good, and you will find them extremely helpful."

I thanked him, then asked if he could suggest someplace for lunch. He could and I enjoyed some of the finest trout I've ever eaten at a restaurant that charged me more for fish than I'd ever paid. Then I went to the bank, and less than an hour later I had my very own numbered account, with a starting balance of thirty thousand Swiss francs and ten thousand American dollars. It was distressingly simple to do. I'd given basic, anonymous information, and then been asked to sign a form declaring that the money I was depositing was, in fact, legally my own. That was pretty much it, and I left wondering if all of the things I'd read about the Swiss tightening their banking laws hadn't been just smoke.

Finally, with all of my groundwork laid, I returned to my room and loaded the Browning, then stuck it in my coat. I unwrapped my new gloves and stuffed them in another pocket, along with the roll of duct tape. I took the binoculars, and then I headed out again, this time behind the wheel of a rented car, and went to see the villa of M. Laurent Junot.

If I'd had time, if Oxford hadn't been breathing down our necks, I would have hired five people through Moore and put everything under a magnifying glass, would have worked the whole thing up as if I'd been preparing the advance for someone like Antonia Ainsley-Hunter. I'd have put Junot under surveillance for at least six or seven days, watching him while he went from home to work to play, noting who he met, where, and when, and why. I would have invested in some pricey electronics and tried to tap the phones and bug the house, and I certainly would have devoted a fair chunk of time and resources to learning the details of the alarm. I'd have taken a small mountain of photographs. In short, I'd have been very careful.

But I didn't have the time, and as I sat in the rental car, peering at the house through the binoculars, I could feel the nervousness rising. It wasn't just what I had to do next that was causing it; it was the knowledge that the clock was running, that Oxford was certainly in New York, and maybe closer to Mahwah than I wanted, that perhaps he was already doing all of those things I didn't have time to do myself. Another city across the world, another man was marking another target, and if I didn't hurry things up, there wasn't going to be anything I could do to stop him. I was beginning to regret having told Scott to wait for me before approaching Gracey and Bowles.

I was running out of time.

I started with a drive around the area, then abandoned the car half a mile up the road and moved in on foot for a closer look. It was late afternoon by the time I actually stepped onto the grounds, and there was a chill breeze coasting off the lake. I put on my new pair of gloves and took in as much as I could.

The villa was stately, with grounds that wound down to the shore of the lake. A boathouse rose beside a private pier, and moored to it was a boat the size of the *La Petite Marie,* but of a quality to suggest it would rather sink than be tied near its lesser cousin. The grounds were pristine, and even with winter closing in, looked capable of withstanding nature's entropy for a while longer. There was a back door that led onto a small patio for summer dining and, farther along, another door, smaller, that looked to be the servants' entrance.

The structure itself was built of gray stone with dark wood framing its portals, and all of the doors looked heavy enough to withstand gunfire, although I doubt that had ever been a consideration of the owner. Twice I saw people moving around inside the house, once a man, wearing a black suit, and once a woman, also in black, though this time in a dress.

At seven-nineteen, a black Bentley pulled up in front of the house, and I watched as the driver let M. Laurent Junot out of the car. If the photographs from Moore's file were to be believed, I had the right man, white, in his mid-forties and balding. Junot's shoulders were rounded and his back was straight, and he walked like a man who spent all of his days and perhaps the majority of his nights sitting at a desk. Nothing about him struck me as out of the ordinary, and I thought that if I was Oxford, that would be just as I wanted it.

When Junot reached the house, he was greeted by the man in the black suit, and apparently whatever words they exchanged were brief, because Junot barely broke stride as he continued inside. The driver then brought a black barrister's case from the car to the other man, and they spoke for a while longer before the driver returned to the Bentley. The woman came outside, spoke to the man who now held the case, and then headed for the garage. The man with the case went back inside as the driver moved the Bentley out of the drive and into the garage. I caught a glimpse of a Porsche also parked in the garage before the door shut. Beside the garage were two other cars, an older Audi and a Peugeot.

The woman followed the driver, and when he emerged again she gave him a kiss on the cheek. He opened the passenger door on the Audi for the woman, then got in himself. They drove away.

Lights continued to burn on the first and second floors of the house, and I retreated to the cover of some red spruce and pines that formed a privacy screen along the south side of the estate. If my surveillance so far had worked, there were only two people in the house, and one of them was my target. That was manageable, but I needed to be sure there were only two of them inside. For a few seconds I toyed with retreating to a phone, trying to reach Alena to talk it out with her.

I knew what she would say, though. I knew exactly how she'd get inside if she were in my place, if the clock was pressing for action. Not liking what I would have to do wasn't going to change anything, and the sooner I accepted that, the easier it would be to do the rest. It was a question of efficiency, and I knew the value of that—it had been Alena's guiding principle; if Bequia really had been—as Bridgett had told any and all who would listen—my indoctrination, then that lesson had indeed taken firm hold.

For another hour and a half I watched the house from the perimeter, catching glimpses of silhouettes moving past windows. It grew into full darkness, and my hands and feet began to ache with chill. No exterior lights came on to illuminate the grounds. I hadn't seen any security lights mounted on or around the house, although if that was because they'd been deemed unnecessary by the occupant or rejected out of a sense of aesthetics I would never know. Shortly before nine-thirty I crept onto the grounds, trying to get a closer look.

As I was working my way around to the back of the house, lights began going off on the first floor. I stopped and listened, and my heart began to race. Perhaps twenty seconds passed before I heard the service door open, and I ducked low. The man in the black suit had emerged, was now turning in the doorway and calling out "good night" in German. I heard the electronic sound of an alarm arming, and that was what spurred me, finally, told me that there would be no better time than the present.

I was on him before he'd closed the door, pressing the barrel to the back of his head with one hand, grabbing him by the throat with the other. With my index finger and my thumb I squeezed either side of his larynx, keeping him silent, and before he had begun to respond I had him back through the door, pulling him up at the threshold, and I was inside the villa.

The sounds of running water stopped as I left the kitchen. I emerged in a room with an elaborate sideboard and a crystal chandelier suspended over the polished rectangle of the table. Light filtered in from the main hall, and I could see the edge of a flight of stairs running to the floor above. I moved quietly and quickly, the sound of my feet disappearing into the layers of carpet, halting at the foot of the stairs to see Junot passing above me. He was in silk pajamas, a book in his hand, and he didn't break stride and he didn't see me. Forty seconds later I heard a switch being thrown, and another light went off, dropping darkness down the steps.

The grandfather clock in the hall chimed the hour. I started up, hearing the stairs squeak beneath me, and I shifted my weight and tried to stay light on my toes, and the noise continued, but wasn't as loud. Coming around the landing at the top, I saw another spill of light, this flowing from beneath a closed door, probably the bedroom. I waited and didn't move. The last chime of the clock striking ten echoed and faded.

I heard the sound of paper brushing paper, pages turning in a binding. The ticking of the clock below seemed to grow louder.

I kept waiting.

The grandfather clock marked a quarter past, and then half past. The light stayed on. When the clock chimed a quarter to, as the last tone vanished from the air, the light beneath the door went out.

The grip of the Browning had grown warm in my hand. An ache crawled across my shoulders, tracing a line from the trapezius on down. I began marking the time in my head, counting the ticks of the clock. There was no noise coming from the bedroom.

The thought struck me that I could well be wrong, that Junot wasn't who I wanted at all, that I should be in the house of some man in South Africa instead. I didn't like that thought, but it persisted, and I wondered if I had missed something, wondered what else I should have done.

When the clock chimed eleven, I moved to the bedroom door and put my hand on the knob, and again settled my weight.

I spent the next six minutes opening the door, moving the handle from its position parallel to the floor to perpendicular to it, applying constant pressure until I felt the latch slip from its housing. The door opened silently, from a fraction to a sliver to an inch. My eyes had long since adjusted to the darkness, and through the gap I could see a portion of the bed, the shape of a form in it. Just from the sound of him I knew he was asleep, I knew he had no idea I was there.

The sensation of power in that instant was acute and absolute, the feeling of control so complete it seemed to radiate from my body outward, to everything I could see, everything I could touch. In my chest I felt something else, something that reminded me of grief.

It was easy to reach the bed, to stand beside him and look down on him sleeping, and just as easy to raise the gun in my hand. The lamp beside the bed was an orb seated on a pyramid base, with a digital clock glowing at its center. A push-button at its side brought it to life, the bulb increasing in strength like a rapidly rising sun. As color began to bleed into the room I brought the barrel down across his nose, not swinging hard, not needing to.

M. Laurent Junot awoke bleeding, crying out and starting up, then crying again in horror at the slick of blood running over his lips, and the sight of me, in his home, with the Browning pointed at his face. His mouth worked, then shut, and another noise escaped him like distant tires squealing around a turn. His eyes, blue and wet, searched me first for recognition, and failing that, for understanding.

"I'm not him," I said in English. "But you know that already."

There was comprehension in his face, and then he tried to conceal it, backing up beneath his sheets until his pillows parted behind him, one of them thumping to the floor. His tongue stabbed out over his lips, then retreated.

When he began to open his mouth again I pounded my left hand into the softness of his stomach, once. The pain and the pressure sent him lurching forward, mouth gaping, breath coming free in a rushing gasp. With my left I grabbed him by the collar of his pajamas, feeling silk threads pop as I yanked him out of bed, pushing him onto the floor. He sprawled, hands scrabbling at yet another Oriental rug, and when he got his middle off the ground, I kicked him in the ribs, putting him on his back, then immediately bending over him and pulling him to his feet once more. He couldn't support his weight, and I shoved the Browning into his stomach and with it pushed him against the wall, my left hand going to his forehead, forcing his face back and level, forcing him to look at me.

"I'm not him," I said again. "Do you understand?"

Junot tried to nod, realized he couldn't. He coughed, and it was painful for him, because the spasm of his muscles made him need to move, and I wouldn't let him. He forced out enough air to say, "Yes, yes. I understand."

"You're going to give me all of his money," I said, and I took the gun from where it was pressed against his belly and rested it instead against the lower orbit of his left eye. "You're going to do it now, or we'll repaint your fucking bedroom in an interesting new shade called Hint of Banker's Brain."

He sagged and I put more pressure on the bone beneath his eye, and he scrabbled and found his footing and straightened again. The blood from his nose was staining his pajama top to the hem.

"Say you understand," I told him.

"Yes, yes, I understand," he said.

I shoved both the gun and my hand against him, then pushed off, and he slid down the wall partway before he could catch himself, his legs working on the rug to find traction. He got upright once more, nodding at me, raising his hands.

"I have a computer in the study," he said. "My computer—I can access accounts from there."

Again using my left, I grabbed the pajama collar and twisted it so he would turn. The collar was wet with his blood. With the Browning against his skull I marched him to the door.

"Lead," I said. "And nothing for nothing, asshole, but you're not quick enough to get any ideas."

"No, no ideas," he echoed, his voice meek.

We crossed the hall at the head of the stairs, leaving the light of the bedroom behind us. Another door was ahead, and he reached for the knob, opened it, moving slowly. The caution wasn't simply for my benefit, I knew;

he was trying to think of an advantage, a plan, any way out of this that would keep him from doing what I was forcing him to do.

"Turn on the light," I said.

The switch was to the left of the door, and he fumbled for a moment before finding it. A lamp in the corner came on suddenly bright, and I tightened my grip and reapplied pressure with the gun to keep him from moving. He tensed when I did, but didn't try anything.

The study was less ornate than I'd have thought, but just as perfectly appointed as every other room I had seen. Bookshelves covered three walls, floor to ceiling, like wallpaper, broken only at one point by a large display case of wristwatches by Patek Philippe. The case was ornate, as detailed as the timepieces inside, and turned slowly, keeping each watch wound. The desk was modular and black, and it should have been out of place, but wasn't. The computer on it was black, too, the monitor thin and sleek.

I pushed him toward it, and when he tried to sit in the chair, I hooked it with my right foot and shoved it out of the way.

"Stand."

He began to nod twice, then switched the computer on with a slow and deliberate press of his right index finger.

"It will take a minute," he whispered.

I didn't say anything, knowing that he wanted me to. Beads of sweat formed at his hairline; I watched as they met the barrel of the Browning and broke to either side. The computer ground through its boot cycle, its internal fan not quite as loud as the rasp of Junot's frightened breathing.

When the monitor asked for his password he began typing, didn't even hesitate. The program he was after was marked on the desktop, and the interface window opened and I knew enough to know I was looking at what I was after.

Junot cleared his throat. "I . . . you understand, I cannot do it all from here . . . some money, yes . . . but . . . but in the morning, if we were to go to my bank, you see, it would be—"

So that was going to be his play, that was what he'd been thinking of as we'd crossed the hall. I grinned.

"How much money?"

"Only two, three million dollars, perhaps." He sounded apologetic.

I moved the gun from his neck down along his spine, until it was in the middle of his back.

"You're lying," I said. "I want all of it."

"No, *monsieur,* please under—"

"Shut up!" I shouted, and he did, and he cringed.

I waited a couple of seconds, letting him wonder if I was going to kill him. I let the silence build.

"How much?" I repeated.

"Maybe four or five—"

I punched him in the left side with my left hand, where I had kicked him, and he groaned and bent, and I pushed the gun harder into his spine.

"Listen to me, you soon-to-be-quadriplegic," I said. "Don't try to tell me that if you get a call at three in the morning from a man you fear more than Satan himself saying he needs twenty million dollars transferred to Bogotá in ten minutes you can't do it, because we both know that's a fucking lie. You will transfer his money, all of it, to the account I tell you, or I'll start pulling the trigger and I won't stop until I hear the hammer go dry."

He had begun trembling halfway through my tirade, and when I finished he simply began typing. His voice was shaking like his body when he asked me for the account number, the name of the bank. I gave both to him, the account I'd established earlier that day, and he bent over the keyboard and his fingers fumbled on the keys, but I watched the monitor, and I saw the numbers moving, and I knew I had him.

It took him under three and a half minutes, and when he was done, I had twenty-seven million, three hundred and forty-two thousand, eight hundred and sixteen dollars and seventeen cents more in my account than when I'd arrived. I waited until he had logged out and shut down the computer before letting up on the gun in his back.

When the monitor was charcoal again, Laurent Junot lowered his head and said, "*Monsieur* . . . please, I do not want to die like this. . . ."

I pulled him back from the desk, stepping away as I turned him to face me. "You tell him anything about me, that I was here, anything at all, and I'll come back and put so many holes in you, your body will whistle in a breeze."

The idiom seemed to confuse him, or perhaps he was too afraid to understand. The blood from his nose came in slow drops that broke free when he nodded.

"Please," he said again, and it was pitiful, and it made me sick.

For a moment I looked at him, wrecked and terrified, and felt the same burden of grief and power I'd had when I'd seen him asleep in his bed. Then I flipped the Browning in my hand and struck him with the butt. He saw the movement coming, but was too slow to do anything in his defense, and perhaps his hands were coming up to protect his temple.

The butt of the pistol cracked against his skull, the shudder of metal meeting bone, and he toppled to the floor, landing hard enough to rattle the case of watches on the wall.

I needed a moment before I could bring myself to crouch beside him, to check him for a pulse. Like the manservant below, he was still alive, and like the manservant below, I hoped the only thing I'd left Junot with was a rotten headache.

I switched off the lights before leaving, exited the villa through the same door by which I'd entered. When I got outside, my watch said it was three minutes past midnight.

The air was cold and I started shaking as soon as it hit me, and I felt giddy, almost drunk, and I nearly tripped twice as I made my way the short twenty feet to the edge of Lake Geneva. I threw the Browning into the water, followed it with the duct tape, then turned and made my way back to the car, half-jogging, half-walking. It was where I'd left it parked, and I started the engine and pulled out, and my foot felt heavy on the gas. The streets were mostly deserted, and I took them carefully, mindful of the posted limits.

At the rental agency, I left the car in the lot and the keys in the slot, then stripped off my bloodied gloves and dumped them in a trash can on the corner before hailing a cab. The lobby of the Intercontinental was quiet and deserted but for the attendant at the desk, who greeted me in English as Mr. Murphy, and who had to say it twice before I realized she was talking to me.

"Enjoying Geneva?" she asked.

"Time of my life," I assured her, and went up to my room.

It took me a while to fall asleep, staring at the ceiling, feeling the sorrow gnawing at my bones.

CHAPTER SEVEN

When the bank opened the next morning I withdrew twenty thousand in American dollars cash, the rest in a draft. Then I closed the account and went back to the Intercontinental, where I cleaned out my room and checked out of the hotel. At the Gare de Cornavin I stopped in the men's room long enough to dump the Beretta in a trash can, then got a second-class ticket on the next train to Austria. I found a pay phone and fed it a lot of coins for the privilege of speaking with Robert Moore.

"Klein," I said when he picked up.

"How's business, then, Mr. Klein?"

"Lucrative."

"Oh, well, I'm delighted to hear that." From his tone, I couldn't tell if he was lying or not.

"I'm looking to do some business in Vienna," I said.

"So you'd mentioned. I've got someone I think would be perfect for you. Her name's Sigrid Koller, and I've already told her all about you."

"Where can I meet her?"

"There's a bar on Stephansplatz called Onyx, opens early, nine in the morning in fact. Perfect for you business types. Ms. Koller will be there tomorrow at a quarter to ten, looking for you."

"What does she look like?"

Moore laughed. "Don't worry about that, mate. Shall I tell her it's on?"

"I'll be there."

"Right. Good luck with your business, Mr. Klein."

"Thanks," I said, but he'd already hung up.

I slept most of the way to Vienna, which was better than being awake, because awake I worried. By now, Junot had certainly contacted Oxford, or at least had tried to; it would take him time to reach his employer, to put the word in the right locations that they needed to talk. But assuming that Junot had regained his courage shortly after his consciousness, that meant that Oxford either knew he'd been robbed, or was soon to find out.

Then what? It wouldn't take long to track the account number, to find out that Dennis Murphy had received the twenty-seven-million-dollar deposit, and that Dennis Murphy had the next morning withdrawn the whole amount. With a little more legwork, some routine inquiries, Oxford would find out where I'd stayed, would get my description. Even assuming that he didn't know I was behind the theft when Junot contacted him, once he had a physical description, there wouldn't be any doubt.

The real question was: how long would it take him? I was operating on the theory that he was still in the United States, that he was in fact in New York, and perhaps even closing in on Mahwah. Would the theft be enough to delay him? Would he abandon the hunt long enough to fly to Geneva and have words with Junot, to investigate the theft? Or would he assume it had been me? And if he assumed it was me, would he assume Alena was with me?

That last potential gave me the most hope, because if he believed that Alena and I had done the robbery together, he would have to assume that we were in Europe together. That would bring him out of the country, and if I was very lucky, he'd be arriving in Geneva about the same time I was headed back to New York.

If I was lucky indeed.

That didn't seem likely. If Gracey and Bowles were still in contact with him, Oxford wouldn't have to leave the U.S. He'd simply have them look into it. With their resources, Oxford would know exactly who had done what with his fortune by the time I landed at Kennedy. In that case, we'd be pretty much back where we'd started, but with a slight advantage in my court.

After all, I had his money, and I didn't care how professional or committed Oxford was or said he was—nearly thirty million dollars was enough incentive to make him change his tactics, if not his plans.

That gave me comfort, until I started thinking about Alena, and her timing herself up and down the stairs in Mahwah.

The Vienna Hilton was across the street from the train station, so I took a room there using the Klein I.D. The nonsmoking floor was booked up, and I ended up with a queen bed in a room that was surprisingly un-Hilton in terms of décor and style, but that reeked of cigarettes and heavy air freshener. I dropped off my bags and changed and headed down to the fitness center, where I killed four hours. My energy surprised me. I'd never imagined an adrenaline rush could last so long.

I stayed in that night, dining in the room and watching Austrian television, which I found bewildering and vaguely disturbing for no reason that I could articulate. I fell asleep early, but woke once during the night, in the darkness, certain I wasn't alone in my room. I lay on my back, motionless, trying to control my breathing, to sound like I was still nursing my dreams, listening for any sound, any indication of where the intruder might be. The noise of the hotel was a muted rustle, and from the corner, by the window, I was sure I heard carpet crushing under someone's feet as they pitched their balance, trying to stay steady and still.

There was nothing more, no other noise, and the fear slipped over my skin until I was fighting to stay calm, and when I couldn't take it any longer I pushed into motion with a frantic rush, tumbling out of the bed and putting it between myself and the intruder. I yanked the clock radio from the nightstand and threw it at the intruder, ducking low, coming up again, finally getting a good look.

I was alone.

I turned on the light, saw the clock, broken, resting between the television cabinet and the window. I looked at the curtain, checked behind it, found the window closed and locked, and I was up too high for anyone to have come in that way, anyway. I picked up the clock and tried to plug it back in, found that I'd snapped the cord, too. I dropped it in the trash, feeling foolish and embarrassed and deeply frightened.

I filled a glass of water at the bathroom sink, drained it, filled another, drained that, and climbed back into bed, feeling my heart racing.

No wonder Alena had nightmares.

The Onyx was an American bar, meaning it was an Austrian version of what an American bar should be, which I suppose explained why it opened at nine in the morning. It was on the sixth floor of the Haas Haus, one level below Do & Co., which turned out to be a sushi restaurant, so I figured the whole building was basically a cross-culture experiment gone terribly, horribly awry. Out the windows was a nice view of St. Stephen's Cathedral, and when I arrived at twenty to ten, I was surprised to see a number of very well-dressed men and women already enjoying their first martinis and Bloody Marys of the day.

I got myself an orange juice from the bartender and took a seat at a table, and hadn't been there for more than a minute when a woman took the chair opposite me, and the moment she sat I knew why Moore had told me not to worry. She was in her mid- to late thirties, skin as dark as Moore's, and lovely. She wore black leather pants, the kind that, whenever I see women in them, I wonder how they pull them on and never doubt that they have to peel them off. Her turtleneck was the color of dried blood, and she wore a man's tweed jacket.

"Mr. Klein?" she asked as she sat, the Austrian accent tripping over an upper-class English one.

"Ms. Koller," I said. "Nice to meet you."

"Robert says that you want to pay me a lot of money to do something very small."

"I need to do some banking."

"Perhaps you'd rather be in Switzerland, then?"

"I've been there, they don't have what I need. I want to open a *Sparbuch* account."

"Passbook, you mean."

"This is a very specific kind of account."

Sigrid Koller reached across the table and took my untouched orange juice, sipping it. Her eyes ran over me, then to the bar, then to the view. She set the orange juice back down.

"I know the account you mean," she replied. "It won't take long."

"I'm glad to hear it."

She rose, adjusting her tweed jacket, and smiled at me, so I got up too, and we left the bar together. A couple of the Bloody Mary pioneers watched us go. When we got to the elevator, I took two envelopes from my coat and handed them to her. She put them in the pockets of her jacket, one on either side.

"Each has ten thousand dollars in it," I said. "One is for the account. The other one is yours."

"You're paying me all up front?" Koller asked.

"Robert's word carries a lot of weight."

"It does for me, as well. Give me until noon. Where shall I meet you?"

"I'll be in the lobby of the Hilton across from the train station."

The elevator stopped, the doors sliding apart.

"Noon," she repeated, and we each went our separate ways.

I made reservations for a five o'clock flight to Heathrow, and then a connection from there back to JFK. Then I checked out of the room and left my bag with the bell captain and went for a short walk around Vienna. It was colder here than it had been in Geneva, and almost as clean. I did some window-shopping, and at an antique store picked up a fountain pen that I thought Erika might like as a present. I was back in the lobby of the Hilton by five of twelve, and Sigrid Koller was there waiting, reading what I assumed was a local newspaper at one of the chairs in the lobby. I went to the bell captain and got my bag, then headed out again, and she followed me onto the street and into the train station.

As I came through the doors she caught up with me, pressing the newspaper into my free hand and saying, "Sir? You dropped this."

"Thank you," I said.

She nodded and murmured, "It was nothing," and then she turned and went back out to the street. When I stepped out a minute later, there was no sign of her.

In the fold of the newspaper was an envelope, and in the envelope was a slip of paper and a plastic credit card. The paper had the name of a bank and a four-digit number, presumably the PIN code for the card. I dumped the newspaper in the trash, put the card in my wallet, told the first cabdriver I found that I wanted to go to the bank named on the slip of paper.

The beauty of a *Sparbuch* account, as Alena had explained it, was this: While Switzerland allowed for anonymous banking, it was a relatively simple task to force someone to access an account—just as I had forced Junot to do. This account was far more secure, because while it remained anonymous, it required three separate checks before funds could be accessed. Not only did the account have to be identified and the proper PIN code provided, but the right card had to be used—and the card was virtually impossible to forge. Created by Motorola, the card contained a transmitter that, when in range of the bank, would broadcast and receive a specific, encrypted clearance code. One could have the account number and the PIN, but if one didn't have the *right* card, the bank's computers would shut down the transaction instantly.

In essence, the card became the money in the account. Without the card, the money was untouchable.

After I deposited the draft, I withdrew another check, this for half a million dollars. If nothing else, Oxford could finance my little operation against him. Then I caught another cab to the airport.

Twenty-nine hours later, Scott Fowler and I went to meet two men from the CIA in a hotel room at the Holiday Inn overlooking Times Square.

CHAPTER EIGHT

I'd reached Mahwah just past two that morning, exhausted physically and emotionally, the strain of the last several days finally catching up with me. One of the Russians who let me through the gate used a radio to contact the guards inside the house, and by the time I reached the front door, Natalie was there, clearly having just woken up. She gave me a hug once I'd gotten inside, and before I could even ask, she told me.

"No signs of him. Dan says that someone's been asking a lot of questions in Brooklyn, especially in Brighton Beach, and everyone is assuming it's Oxford. But no one has seen him, and there's been no contact, to anyone's knowledge."

"If he's working Brighton Beach, he's not far from finding us here."

"Not the way Dan talks," Natalie said. "The way he talks, his people will kill or die to keep their secrets secret."

"Dan talks big."

Her mouth curved in a wry smile. "Well, he's a big guy."

I blinked at her, and maybe it was the fatigue that let me see it, but it hit me and I practically choked. "You've got a crush on a Russian mafia hood?"

Natalie looked at me, indignant. "Hello, pot."

"Hello, kettle. At least I was abducted and brainwashed. What's your excuse?"

"And you don't think being locked up here for five days is a kind of Stockholm Syndrome?"

"You best be careful, young lady. Otherwise you'll find yourself being bought out by your partners."

"Unlike some people, I can keep a secret. You look fuck-awful, Atticus. Didn't you sleep on the plane?"

"Some."

"You need some more."

"Soon. How's Alena?"

"She is fine, thank you." From the top of the stairs, Alena cleared her throat.

She had abandoned the crutches at some point, and now, in her left hand, was a metal cane like the ones I'd seen often in hospitals, with a black rubber grip for her hand, and a small platform with four feet at its base. The brace was on the outside of her sweat pants, a different one than she'd worn when I left.

From my wallet I produced the *Sparbuch* card and held it for her to see.

"Victory," I told her.

Alena nodded and perhaps contemplated smiling. She turned from the railing and rested her weight on the metal cane, looking down at me, and I understood that she wanted me to come up the stairs to her. I turned my attention back to Natalie, who was watching me, rather than her.

"We should plan to move tomorrow," I said. "A new location, I don't really care where, just outside of Manhattan. If we can arrange it without going through Dan, so much the better."

"I've got a place in Allendale lined up," Natalie said. "Smaller than this one."

"Does it have stairs?" Alena asked.

"I'm afraid so." Natalie turned back to me. "We can be ready to move by mid-afternoon."

"I'm still in the master bedroom?" I asked, gesturing upstairs.

"You are still the master, yes. I put some stuff away for you up there. There's a gun in the bureau drawer. Couldn't get a P7 for you, though, sorry about that."

"You should have talked to Dan," I said.

"You need to go away now," Natalie told me.

I nodded and headed up the stairs, and when I reached the landing, Alena pivoted on her good foot, letting me pass. I went into the master bedroom, saw that the bed was made, as Natalie had said it would be, and tossed the bag onto it. Alena followed me in and perched on the corner by the footboard, resting the cane between her feet, and I handed her the *Sparbuch* card, then went to the bureau and opened the top drawer. There was an unopened package of Munsingwear undershorts, and another unopened package of tube socks, and between them was a box of 9mm ammunition and a SIG P225. The drawer had been lined with contact paper, and the paper was blue with white and red roses on it. I took out the ammunition and the gun, and figured the gun must have come from Dan because there was no sign of a serial number anywhere on it. I checked the magazine, saw it was empty, and started loading the gun.

"How did it go?" Alena asked.

"Successfully. I took nearly thirty million dollars from him."

"A lifetime's work."

"Think it'll get his attention?"

"It would get mine."

"I don't think it was everything. There must have been investments, too."

"It would have taken too long to liquidate all of his assets. Thirty million . . . that is enough."

I finished loading the clip and put the magazine in the SIG, but I didn't chamber the first round. I put the gun on the bureau and the box of ammunition back in the drawer, then turned my attention entirely to Alena. She had shifted on the bed, the *Sparbuch* card still beside her, and was watching me closely.

"Did you exercise?" she asked, finally.

"I tried."

"It's hard to keep it up when you're working."

"It is."

"And the diet?"

"I forgot the supplements, but other than that I stuck to it best I could."

She considered that, nodding slightly. "You're shifting your weight, it is climbing into your back again. You need to practice your ballet."

"There wasn't anyplace that I could. I managed yoga in the hotel rooms."

"When I was traveling, ballet was always the first to go." She looked at the card beside her, then back to me. "You will see Agent Fowler in the morning?"

"Maybe. Ideally we'll arrange to meet Gracey and Bowles at the same time Natalie is moving you to Allendale. Oxford can't be in two places at once."

"It's a good tactic. It is more likely that they will notify Oxford where you will be meeting, and he will attempt to back-tail you from that location to me."

"Only if Gracey and Bowles know that I'm coming. They won't. Scott will arrange to meet them alone."

She pushed hair off of her cheek, nodding again, the same slight movement of her head. "Are you going to tell me what you did?"

"There's not much to tell."

"I would like to hear it."

"I'd rather not talk about it, actually, Alena. I'd rather get some sleep."

She understood what I meant, shifting her weight to the cane and using it to rise. Her walk was quicker than it had been before I'd left, but I suspected that the pain was as bad, maybe worse. She made her way to the open door, then stopped and turned back to face me.

"And how are you sleeping?"

"Not very well. Any suggestions?"

She just shook her head.

We did yoga together the next morning, and after breakfast I took one of the cars and drove into Mahwah, using a different pay phone on the Franklin Turnpike to call Scott. I told him we were on and that I'd call him back in an hour, and he told me that was fine and I hung up. There was a comic book shop on the street nearby, and I went inside and looked at the glossy covers and remembered I'd bought the pen for Erika, wondered when I'd be able to give it to her. Hopefully soon.

It occurred to me then that I wasn't going home again, no matter what happened. Even if everything worked, if Oxford could be bought—or, more precisely—blackmailed off, I could no longer imagine a way to fit into my old life. Too much had happened to me, to the people around me, I wasn't going to just slip back in as if I'd never been gone.

I wondered where I'd go, and I didn't see anything that gave me an answer.

I left the shop without making any purchases and got back into the car, driving another few miles along Franklin until I found another pay phone. I checked my watch and killed another fifteen minutes in the car, watching the traffic and my mirrors. When the hour was up I used the phone.

"They can't make a meeting until tomorrow morning," Scott told me. "Seven A.M., the Holiday Inn on Times Square. I told them I'd found a connection between Havel and Drama. They seemed eager."

"But not eager enough to make it today."

"No. Could be trying to buy Oxford more time."

"They suggest the place or you?"

"They suggested an out-of-the-office meeting. I suggested the Holiday Inn. This'll work for you?"

"It'll do," I said. "You've taken care of everything else?"

"The SAIC has my report, and it'll go to Washington today. I fudged some of the details, but most of what Alena told me checked, and it didn't take much digging to find corroborating facts. I took some flak for not registering my CI, but the stuff I've turned up is enough to keep that a minor concern for the time being. As long as what she told us can be independently verified, I think I can keep her out of it."

"You don't have a choice. She won't play ball."

"I've explained that to my supervisor. He doesn't accept it. But, like I said, it's not an issue right now."

"Just see that it doesn't become one."

He got testy. "Stop badgering me, Atticus. I'm on top of this. You know I've got your back, I always have."

"You always have," I agreed. "See you seven A.M. tomorrow."

Natalie and I moved Alena to Allendale that afternoon, another two-story house, off Crescent Avenue. It was a relatively new neighborhood, and the house itself had gone up perhaps twenty years ago, in what had once-upon-a-time been a celery field.

"It's a rental property," Natalie said. "We've got it for the winter."

"Florida?" I asked.

"Bermuda," she said.

The alarm system was much the same as on the Mahwah house, but without motion detectors. The backyard spilled down a slope to a fence that abutted a still-intact wetland, and neither Natalie nor I liked the exposure, but once again we had to work with what we were given. There was a covered swimming pool in the yard, and Miata ran out onto the cover, then raced back to the deck when water began creeping around his paws. Either it brought back bad memories for him or, like us, he knew it was too cold to swim.

We spent the rest of the day getting the guards into position, and it took a while before Natalie and I could agree on how to protect the front. Here, there was no clear border to the street, no fence, just a short strip of grass that met with the asphalt, the driveway coming up on the left side of the house as one faced it. In the end we put one of the guards in the front room, behind the curtains, with orders to watch the street and nothing else, and, to cover the back, another in one of the bedrooms on the second floor, with a similar directive. I took the master bedroom again, Alena the one beside it, and Natalie the one across the hall.

At eight that night Dan arrived with replacements for the boys who'd been on post during the day, and they each entered the house with a rucksack over their shoulder and a pizza box in their hands. After we ate, the old guards departed, the new guards dug in, and I took Alena back upstairs. She did not ask me to time her.

I checked her room and found it as secure as the last time I'd looked, then checked on the guard on the floor, and found him sitting in a straight-backed chair, in the dark, watching the yard through a pair of infrared goggles. I left him alone and went downstairs, where Dan and Natalie were talking in the kitchen over cups of coffee.

"Dan," I said. "The I.R. goggles. Nice touch."

"Thank you," he said, and honest to God he looked pleased.

I told them I was going to bed, went back upstairs and looked in on Alena once more.

Either Gracey or Bowles had ordered up a pot of room-service coffee, and there was a tray with three cups and a pitcher of half-and-half, and a bowl stuffed with packets of sugar and artificial sweeteners on the coffee table by the couch. Bowles, at the desk with the laptop in front of him, squinted at me as if trying to place my face, and the expression hid any surprise he might have been feeling. Gracey recovered by indicating the coffee service with a sweep of his empty hand.

"We only have three cups," he said.

"It's all right," I told him. "We're not staying long. You guys taping this?"

Bowles frowned. Gracey just shook his head. "We didn't think we'd need to. You've been getting around, Atticus. We heard you were in Europe."

"Not me. I haven't been to Europe in years."

"Someone who looks like you, then." Gracey poured himself a cup of coffee, added cream, then two packets of sugar. He used one of the spoons to stir, then licked it clean before setting it down again on the tray. It took him almost a minute to get everything the way he wanted it, and I knew the wheels were spinning, but he was doing a fine job of keeping his thoughts and feelings to himself. Bowles turned back to the laptop and began typing lightly on the keyboard.

When Gracey had tasted the coffee and satisfied himself that it was palatable, he targeted Scott. "You've been fucking us around, Special Agent Fowler. You told us you didn't know where Atticus here was at. That wasn't very nice of you. A thing like that, it could come back and bite a big chunk out of your ass."

"Gosh, I hope that's not a threat, Mr. Gracey." Scott settled his briefcase on the bed and snapped it open. "Especially since I've already written up everything Mr. Kodiak here is going to tell you, and my supervisor found it interesting enough that he's forwarded it to Washington. It's probably going to the Director as we speak."

Gracey pulled out the big, amused grin he'd used so much when we'd first met almost five months earlier, and gestured with his pen at the folder Scott was now offering to him. "Is that copy for us?"

Scott waited, and Gracey didn't take the folder, so he spun it out of his hand onto the bed, closer to where Bowles was seated. Bowles leaned forward from the desk and picked it up, began leafing through it as if it could only hold minor amusement for him, at best.

"Cash flow," Bowles told Gracey.

"No kidding?"

"No kidding," Scott confirmed. "Looks like person or persons unknown tried to make it appear that Ms. Christian Havel was paying Mr. Atticus Kodiak over three hundred thousand dollars for a variety of unspecified services. Oddly enough, all of the money moving between the two seems to have done so without either of the participants' knowledge."

Gracey glanced over his colleague's shoulder, then to me. "Who knew you were so flush?"

"I've been saving for a rainy day," I told him.

"Looks good and cloudy outside right now. I guess we'd better hear it, then. Don't you think we should hear it, Matthew?"

"I suppose we should, yes, probably," Bowles replied, closing the folder and extending it back to Scott.

"You can keep it. I've got copies," Scott said.

Bowles set the folder beside his laptop. "Yes, I think we'd better hear it."

"I'll start with the hypothetical," I said.

Gracey laughed and sat back on the couch beneath the window, bent to refill his cup. Past him I could see the neon and billboards over Times Square, the pedestrian traffic increasing as the workday began. There were new ads up for Broadway shows I'd never heard of before, reminding me that I'd been away for a long time. Bowles turned the laptop slightly so he could see me over the monitor, still tapping away.

"Once upon a time, someone wrote a book about a professional assassin," I said. "The author got a lot of attention for it. The book did very well. It hit bestseller lists. People talked about it. And the more people talked about it, the more people read it. Before this book, people never thought much about professional killers and murder-for-hire and things like that; they thought it was all Hollywood. Sure, most of them would admit that they believe governments have people killed; this was the first time they began to see how it is really done.

"Other books had come before, of course, but those had been dismissed. For some reason this book wasn't. Maybe because the killer, the subject, was a woman; maybe because it had better press. It doesn't matter.

"What matters is that people began asking questions. They wanted to know how this killer could exist. They wanted to know how she was trained. How she worked. How she was funded. And they wanted to know if there were others.

"Now other people are taking notice, and they're getting worried, because these other people, they're the killer's employers. And they're getting nervous. They're remembering things like Iran-Contra and phrases like 'oversight committee.' They don't want that. They need this problem to go away.

"So they hire another killer, one who is like the assassin in the book, but different. This killer has a specialty, and he can make the problem disappear. He can discredit the author of the book, the subject of the book, even another one of the players. And once they're all discredited, once they're dead and the sordid details of their relationship emerge, the book will be forgotten. Business will continue as before."

Bowles stopped typing, his eyebrows rising slightly. Gracey set his empty cup down on the tray and began twirling his pen, poking the inside of his cheek with his tongue.

"You couldn't stand a cotton ball on that crap," he told me. "Even if you got someone to sit still and listen to this, no one would buy it. It's impossible to prove."

"It's a theory," I said. "I don't have to prove it."

"You came here to give us that piece-of-crap theory?"

"Not really." I looked at Bowles. "You got all that?"

"I'm fine."

"Good, because I really want you to get the next part."

Gracey fell back against the cushions on the couch, spreading his arms with a shrug.

"Three years and two months ago," I said, "the Undersecretary of Housing and Urban Development authorized four million dollars deposited to a fund to study how better to assist children suffering from autism and their families who live in public housing in the United States. Over the following six months that four million was distributed to A&M Consulting in Bethesda, Maryland, and Corsair Industries in Providence, Rhode Island. Four months after the final payment was made, both companies returned a forty-eight-page joint report to HUD."

"Sounds about right," Gracey said.

"In reality, and without the Undersecretary's knowledge, the four million was diverted to a Mr. Simon Freidich—" and here I spelled out the name "—as payment for the murder-for-hire of Alexander Akhmetov, then Kazhaki Minister of Energy. Akhmetov—a hard-line Muslim with ties to groups in Afghanistan and Libya—opposed the construction of an oil pipeline that, in part, would allow light sweet crude to be sold to Israel at below-market cost. His murder ensured the delivery of that oil, and as such made good on promises made by the then Secretary of State, in essence assuring the success of the U.S. foreign policy in the Middle East, at least for the next year and a half.

"Simon Freidich is, of course, known to everyone present as Oxford."

Beside me, Scott adjusted his glasses. Gracey stopped playing with his pen.

I added, "If you'd like, I can tell you all about the CIA-financed murder of General Augustus Albertus Usuf Kiwane Ndanga in Uganda, as well."

"You have proof?" Gracey asked.

"I don't need it. You heard Agent Fowler. Enough people know that if they want to find it, they will."

Gracey made a snorting sound, as if halfheartedly clearing his nostrils, then moved forward to the edge of the couch, glancing at Bowles. Bowles closed the top of his computer and then removed a small and sleek cellular phone from inside his coat. He pressed a button and almost immediately got a connection.

"Mr. Harris?" Bowles said. "Yes, your order has arrived."

He hung up, replaced the phone in his coat, and took the laptop off the desk, tucking it beneath his arm as he rose. None of his previous jitters were evident. He looked at me, he looked at Scott, and then he looked at Gracey. Gracey sighed and pulled his coat from the back of a chair, slipping it on, adjusting the lapels. Bowles headed to the door.

"For the record, we have no fucking idea what you're talking about," Gracey said.

"Of course you don't," Scott said.

Gracey came closer to me. He looked pointedly at Scott.

"He stays," I said.

Gracey sighed. "Off the record?"

"Sure."

"We've pulled the plug. Whatever he does now, he does alone."

"I figured."

"He wants his money back."

"Then he can talk to me about it."

"He says you were with her for four months. Says that she trained you."

"You sure you can trust him?"

"You took out his eye."

"I was going for his brain."

"We're done with this. It was a stupid fucking idea in the first place. Shit like this happens every ten, fifteen years, it always ends up the same. Nothing changes. You understand that."

"Sure."

Gracey hesitated, then grinned. "You're either a lunatic or a zealot."

"Why can't I be both?"

He moved to join Bowles at the door. "It'll be a while, but we'll be in touch."

After they'd gone, Scott moved to the desk and picked up the file Bowles had left behind, stowing it inside his briefcase. "Did he just try to recruit you?"

"I already have a job," I reminded him.

"Sounds to me like you maybe have another one," he said, and then his cell phone rang and took the last word for the time being. He answered it, saying his name, then fell silent. After a couple of seconds he made an affirmative noise, then another, then glanced at me. I took the opportunity to move to the window and close the drapes; Gracey or Bowles had left them open, and there was a good line of sight from across the street, on the Seventh Avenue side, and I didn't like the idea of anyone trying a long shot on us.

Although, if Gracey was telling the truth, it wouldn't be Oxford; without two eyes, he'd be useless as a sniper.

Scott finished the call with a "thanks, detective," and that brought my attention to him fully. He put his phone away.

"What?" I asked.

"That was a detective at the Seventeenth with a very good memory. When you vanished, I had a notice put out to your precinct that I wanted to be contacted if anything happened at your apartment. Trying to look out for Erika, you know."

"My apartment's been tossed," I said. It made sense; Oxford was looking for his money, he'd gone through my home. I found it vaguely insulting that he didn't give me more credit.

Scott shook his head. "Do you know a Margaret Horne?"

"Midge? She lives in the apartment below mine."

"She's dead. Someone broke into her place and stabbed her to death, did a number on the body with a knife. They can't tell if there was a sexual assault involved."

A bubble of panic was inflating in my chest, pressing against my lungs, making it hard to breathe.

"I'm going to head over there, talk to the detectives, see if I can find out what happened," Scott said. "Give me a couple hours before you call."

"Oxford," I said.

"Could be random."

I wanted to scream at him that it wasn't random, that nothing here was random anymore, that everything had a reason and a purpose, and that Midge dead in the apartment below where I had lived for four years wasn't just a message. So what if I had Oxford's money: he knew there were things more precious to me than that. He had come to my home and failing to find me had settled for the next best thing, someone I knew. He'd come to my home to commit murder, and maybe it hadn't even been me he was after.

I thought of Erika and her stupid dorm room door wide open to the hall, her back presented to anyone who came walking by with a gun or a knife or a club.

I ran for her life.

CHAPTER NINE

The door was closed and the sign on it had changed and now read K.C. & ERIKA and NO WE'RE NOT BUT WE COULD IF WE WANTED TO.

I knocked hard, kept pounding on it until it was opened, and I'd started to say her name when I realized I wasn't looking at Erika but at another young woman entirely, one who was about Erika's height but whose hair was electric blue and shaggy, with a piercing below her lip and another just above it.

"Fucking knock it fucking off!" she yelled at me and then took a quick step back, probably realizing that I wasn't a student. Then she reached for the door and started to close it again.

"Where's Erika?"

"Get the fuck out of here or I'll start screaming," the woman said, and she put her weight against the door and tried to slam it in my face.

I moved forward and caught it before it closed, forcing it back. "Please—my name's Atticus, I have to find Erika."

"Let go of my door or I'll scream, I mean it, cocksucker."

"Where's Erika?"

She stopped shoving against the door, but didn't move her weight off it, keeping it partially closed. She peered through the gap at me. "Atticus doesn't have a fucking beard, cocksucker, and he wears glasses, and you better goddamn back off now because the rugby team is down the hall and they are personal friends of ours."

I fumbled through my thoughts, trying to find something to say, and came up with, "Leather jacket, the black one she wears, Bridgett and I gave it to her, Christmas, last year. She's a natural blond, always wears her hair long over her left ear because she's missing a piece of it, a chunk of the lobe and cartilage that a man named Sterritt cut out of her."

The woman's expression went from defiance and fear to confusion. "She never told me that."

"You're K.C., right? You're her roommate, you're taking playwriting classes, she told me that the last time I saw her, when I told her that I was going away and that there might be trouble. She told you that, too, or something like that, told you that if anyone came by and said his name was Atticus—"

"Let go of the door. Let go of the door and let me close it. If you're him you'll do it."

I let go of the door, and the second my weight was off it she slammed it closed and I heard the deadbolt slide. I cursed, wanted to stamp my feet, turning in the hall. A couple of the doors farther down had opened, and two young men were watching me with no attempt to conceal their suspicion. I resisted the urge to glare right back, faced the door again, raised my hand to knock once more, and the door unlocked and the woman pulled it open. She was holding a framed photograph in one hand, and she held it up next to my face, comparing the two for what felt like hours.

"You're him," she said. "I'm K.C."

"K.C., I need to find Erika. Now."

K.C. nodded quickly and left the door open as she went to Erika's desk, riffling through the papers scattered atop it. Erika's half of the room was distinguishable from K.C.'s as more disordered, with magazines and books strewn all over the bed and floor. I went for the closet, found the duffel bag that Erika had stolen from me when she'd started school, began stuffing it with clothes from her drawers.

K.C. had put the photo down on the chair, and I saw the picture, Erika and me at Yankee Stadium two years back, when Torre's Glory was really cooking. K.C. was talking as she searched the desk, as I packed the bag.

"I'm sorry about that, she told me to be careful and there are all sorts of freaks in this city, so I didn't know what to make of you. She's got a schedule here, somewhere, she's got a slew of classes this term, I mean, just so many—here, here it is! She's in English right now, Renaissance Playwrights, it's in Main."

"I don't know where Main is," I said.

She grabbed her coat off the hook on the back of the door, a blue-and-black overcoat with a fake fur lining. "I'll show you."

Class was in progress when we reached the lecture hall, and while that seemed to deter K.C. from heading on through, I opened the door and walked in, searching the seats for Erika. For a fraction of a second, as the professor went silent and the students all turned their attention on me, I couldn't see her anywhere, and I felt the panic return and redouble. Then she stood from her seat in the middle, gathering her things, and the relief I felt was so strong that I didn't even feel bad about embarrassing her in front of her peers.

She came down the steps to the floor of the hall, head down, books and bag pressed to her chest, and when we were outside and the door was closed behind her, she dumped most of the things into my arms to hold while she replaced them in her book-bag.

"Thank you for that particular mortification," Erika said.

"You're leaving town," I told her.

"I'm leaving town," she told K.C.

"Yeah, looks like," K.C. said. "So I assume this *is* Atticus?"

"Oh, yeah, only Atticus has the capacity to humiliate me like this."

She had her bag packed again, and was putting it back on her shoulder, so I put an arm around her and began guiding her out of the building. I was moving fast, and both Erika and K.C. struggled to keep up.

"Slow down, dammit!" Erika said. "At least tell me where I'm going!"

"I don't know and I don't care, but it's out of town, and K.C. should probably come with you."

"I have class," K.C. remarked.

I caught a portion of Erika's frown, and she pulled out from my grip but didn't slow, just clamped her bag harder against her side to keep it from bouncing. "This is the bad thing you were worried about, isn't it?"

"It is," I said. "Midge is dead."

"Who's Midge?" K.C. asked.

Neither of us answered, and K.C. understood that this wasn't a joke, and she lost some of her color as she followed us out onto University Place. I put a hand out on Erika again as we went north to East Eighth, just to keep track of her, while I tried to find a cab to hail. There weren't any, and I took us west to Fifth Avenue to where more cars were moving along the street, then tried again. Three cabs passed with fares before one slowed along Fifth Avenue. I got to the door first, pulled it open and all but shoved Erika inside. K.C. stopped and looked at me like I'd dropped from a hovering spaceship.

"You're serious?"

"Get in the fucking car now," I told her.

"Erika?"

"I'd do it," Erika said.

K.C. slid in, and I went after her, slamming the door shut and telling the driver the address I wanted in Chelsea.

"We're going to Bridgett's?" Erika asked. "Won't she be at work?"

"It's only nine-sixteen," I said. "She never gets into her office before ten."

"Bridgett's the one who's the private eye, right?" K.C. asked, excited.

"Where will she take us?" Erika asked me.

"I don't care as long as it's out of New York, out of the state."

"I've always wanted to see Machu Picchu."

"Unless you've got a passport with you, that's out," I said.

"New Orleans?" K.C. asked softly. "I've always wanted to visit New Orleans."

"New Orleans would be fine," Erika said. "Just tell me that it won't be another four months before I hear from you saying it's safe to come back."

"You'll hear from me in three days, tops," I promised. "Or you won't hear from me at all."

Bridgett opened the door on the second knock, and when she saw me and Erika and K.C., she greeted us warmly. "Motherfucking hell," she growled.

"I need you to get them out of town," I said. "They want to go to New Orleans."

"It was K.C.'s idea," Erika told Bridgett.

"And that would make you K.C.?"

K.C. offered Bridgett a hand, saying, "Yeah, hi, I'm K.C. You're Bridgett."

"This is all very nice," I said. "But we're still standing in the hall."

"They can come in," Bridgett said, and she moved aside to let them pass.

K.C. entered first, followed by Erika, who stopped just past the door and looked back at me. "Say goodbye this time, okay?"

"I will."

She went into the apartment, following K.C. out of sight. From the front room I heard the stereo, Joe Jackson singing on the speakers. It would have made me smile if Bridgett hadn't looked so upset with me and the situation; she'd gotten her appreciation of Joe from me.

I pulled out my wallet and emptied it of cash, then went through my pockets and gathered most of the money scattered in them, as well. All told, it looked to be almost seven thousand dollars. Bridgett took the money.

She didn't ask how bad it was, because she knew the answer already. If there was nothing we agreed upon anymore, Erika still meant the world to both of us. That I had brought her here, now, in this way, told her almost everything she needed to know.

"Who'd he kill?" she asked quietly.

"Midge. Last night or this morning. I don't know anything more."

The upset flickered into sadness, but she stayed silent.

"I'll contact you when it's safe to come back," I said. "If you need more money or anything—"

"I don't need your money. We'll be fine."

"Just get them gone, and fast. He's as liable to come after you as he is to go after Erika."

"You think I don't know that?" she snapped.

"I'm just saying—"

"I know what you're saying. You've lost control of the situation, the way I knew you would, and now you're falling fast, and so are the bodies, or if they aren't they soon will be. I hope you're happy. I hope this is what you wanted. I hope her life is worth it."

I swallowed and took it, and Bridgett stopped speaking and caught her breath.

"I hope yours is, too," she added.

I looked past her, down the hall. Joe was singing "Slow Song." I called out Erika's name, and she came around the corner fast enough that I knew she'd heard everything Bridgett and I had said. She came down the hall, and when she reached me I put my arms around her and pressed my lips to her forehead. She wrapped her hands around my middle and hugged me tight, and then she felt the SIG at the small of my back and let me go.

"It's worth it," she told Bridgett.

"Then he shouldn't squander it," Bridgett shot back.

I waited outside of Bridgett's building until I saw the three of them emerge, and I kept watch on them as they walked to the corner and hailed a cab. A cold rain was drizzling down from the clouds, dripping off the brick buildings all around me, and it soaked the shoulders of my coat and touched my skin. I watched the taxi as it went out of sight, then found a pay phone and called Scott's cellular.

"Where are you?" he asked.

"Chelsea. Bridgett and Erika are going out of town."

"Wise. If it was Oxford and not just some homicidal lunatic, he was definitely sending a message. Gracey said that you'd taken out one of his eyes?"

"Yeah."

"Which one?"

"It would've been the left."

"That fits."

I felt the sickness and the guilt, imagined what Oxford had done to Midge's left eye. I hoped to God that she'd been dead at the time.

"Still there?"

"Yeah."

"We should meet up."

"You're on foot?"

"Yeah. I can be at Madison Square Park in nine minutes."

"See you there."

It took me eight minutes to make it to the park, jogging the whole way, first up Eighth Avenue and then across on Twenty-third. The streets were crowded, as always, fields of umbrellas, mostly black, that had me weaving my way along the sidewalk and occasionally into the street. I put my left foot in a puddle at one point, felt my wet sock chafe as I ran. Pedestrians kept their heads down, either covered with their portable canopies or shielded beneath hoods or raised newspapers. Even though I was running, no less than three homeless people asked me for money as I went past.

I tried to think, tracking the thoughts I'd been ignoring since leaving Times Square. Oxford had to have gone for Midge early, before the meeting with Gracey and Bowles, and I couldn't imagine they'd given their blessing to her death. It meant that Oxford had sprung, that the theft had done what Alena had feared it would do—had made him either irrational or all the more ruthless, and neither prospect was a comfort. But it also meant that the money would bait him, that he would respond to it, and that still gave me an advantage, tawdry though it now seemed.

I reached the south side of the park and crossed against traffic, getting a face full of grimy mist from a passing delivery van. I stopped at the base of the statue of Seward on the south side of the park, my back to the Flatiron Building. I was only three minutes from the office of my attorney, but the information felt useless as it rattled around in my head, trivial and a waste of time and energy. I started along the path from the subway stop, scanning the park for Scott. In the dog park to my left, a peach-colored standard poodle chased a mutt, each dog wet and barking happily. The dog owners watched while leaning against the rail, chatting together beneath their umbrellas.

About halfway through the park I saw Scott coming in from the northeast side, and he raised a hand to me, and I nodded and stepped around a woman in a wheelchair, getting closer. He stopped just inside the park as a homeless man, shielded from the weather in a navy parka, reached out to him from behind. Scott turned, his hand going into his jacket for his wallet or for change, his back to me, and beneath the hood of the parka I saw a face, a bandage, and I realized who it was and what was happening, but it had already happened by then, and even as I brought my gun out Oxford was turning away from Scott and running across Twenty-Sixth, racing up Madison, and I didn't have a shot, and just as it had been with Havel, I didn't have a thing I could do.

Scott was on one knee when I reached him, and I said his name and he looked up at me from where he'd been staring at the handle of the knife in his chest.

"Jesus, this hurts," he said, and then fell back, pitching over.

I got a hand on his shoulder and righted him, shoved the SIG back into my pocket, and he made a horrible noise of pain and fear and his body began to shake. I heard people moving around me on either side, and I caught him in my arms and laid him on the wet asphalt, smelling dog shit and wet grass and spoiled food, seeing the handle of the knife that had pinned his tie to his shirt to his chest. Blood was spreading in an ever-growing oval. The poodle in the run was barking in outrage.

"Son of a bitch asked me for a dollar," Scott said.

Rain was splashing on the lenses of his glasses, smearing his eyes. I put my hands on his shoulders, then his face, feeling the cold of his skin. My head felt like it was going to explode, and I couldn't find my voice anywhere. The damn dog kept barking.

"For a dollar," Scott said.

Then he shook once more, gently this time, and his last air escaped him with a whisper, and he didn't move again.

CHAPTER TEN

I left him there, and told myself it was what I had to do. I pushed through the gawkers who had gathered around us and done nothing, and I grabbed the wrist of the one man who tried to stop me from leaving, and I twisted it until he fell to the sidewalk rather than fight me for its possession, and I never broke my stride. I walked, I did not run, to the corner of Broadway, and headed south down the street, then broke track and turned east to Park, where I changed direction again, this time north, up to the subway stop at Thirty-third. A train was loading when I got to the bottom of the stairs and I jumped the turnstile and rode the Six north.

At Grand Central I got off and made it to the base of the stairs before it caught me, and I grabbed the railing for support and threw up on the platform. When I was finished I continued up, and caught the Times Square Shuttle across town, and then another train, this one down to Penn Station. I went back aboveground and walked the block to the PATH train on Thirty-third, and there was one waiting and I took a seat and shoved my hands in my pockets and tried to keep from vomiting a second time. The PATH train stayed motionless for almost three more minutes before the doors shut, and it took me south, and then, ultimately, across the Hudson to Hoboken.

I used a pay phone at the station and called Natalie's cellular. When she answered, I said, "Erika and Bridgett and Erika's roommate K.C. have already left town, but I need you to call Dale and Corry and tell them to go, too, to get their people and go and go now, because I don't know who he's going after next—"

"Atticus," Natalie said. "Slow down. What's happened?"

"He killed Midge this morning. He's just getting started, Nat, and he must have been watching the apartment because that's the only way he could have known where we'd be. He did it on purpose, Natalie, he wanted me to see it—"

"Atticus!"

I stopped talking, got a breath. When I could let it out with control, I said, "He killed Scott, Nat. I was thirty feet from it and I couldn't do anything to stop it."

There was no noise from her end of the phone.

"Couldn't do anything," I said.

"Wh—" and her voice snagged, thick, and she had to clear it. "Where are you?"

"Hoboken. The PATH station."

"Is there a building around, anywhere you can go and sit down?"

"There's a bar," I said. "The Rail Side Bar."

"Go inside. I'll be there as soon as I can."

"You've got to call them, Nat. Dale and Corry—"

"I'll call them from the car. Go inside. I'll be right there."

She hung up and I listened to the dial tone before replacing the handset in its cradle. It was still raining. I looked around and realized that I was only a ten-minute walk from where I'd found Lady Ainsley-Hunter, from where Alena had found me. Construction had begun on what was to be Hoboken's shining new hope, the great towers of Trump and Lefrak. I wondered if there was an irony in that, that I would be here again, and I thought about what had brought me back to New Jersey.

The bar was almost entirely empty, and my watch explained that was because it wasn't yet noon. There was an empty booth near the back and I put myself in it, pressing my back to the corner of the wall, watching the door. A tired woman who had painted her face to look otherwise asked me what I wanted to drink. I told her ginger ale.

"You sure?" she asked, peering at me. "Nothing stronger?"

"Just ginger ale," I said, and from a pocket I pulled some of my remaining bills and had to look at them in my hand before deciding how much to give her. In the end I handed over a twenty and told her to keep the change. She brought me the ginger ale and left me alone.

I looked at the bubbles climbing along the inside of the glass and thought about what I needed to do next. When the last of the soda was gone and the ice cubes were rattling at the bottom, I knew I'd already decided I would kill him.

More people came into the place, men dressed for construction work, and they bought bottles of beer at the bar and settled onto stools and glanced my way. The woman came back and silently replaced my empty glass with a full one.

By the time Natalie arrived my stomach had settled, and after she'd located me she stopped at the bar and bought herself a soda, then came to my booth. The construction workers who had noticed only her body and not her face stopped staring when they realized she was coming to join me, and went back to their third or fourth beers. I wondered if they would be operating any heavy machinery after lunch.

Her eyes looked puffy, the skin beneath them a little darker than usual, as if bruised, and perhaps she had cried already, or perhaps she was waiting for a better time. In a soft voice she told me to scoot over, and I let her in beside me, and after she'd sat she put her head to my shoulder, and for almost a minute neither of us moved.

Then she sighed and lifted her head and said, "I called them. They're on their way here."

"They shouldn't be. They should be heading to their homes and then the hills."

She shook her head. "He went to the office."

My stomach lurched. I couldn't speak.

Natalie read my mind. "They're okay, they didn't even see him, Dale just told me that some guy with a bandage over one eye came in and gave the receptionist a sealed box with a note on it, saying the box was for you. Then the guy left. That was all."

"They checked the box?"

"It's not transmitting anything and the chemical sniffer didn't detect any explosive, and when they used the portable X ray on it, Corry thought it looked like a cellular phone."

"Did they read the note?"

"It said that he would call at nine tonight. It said that if you didn't answer, more people would die."

—

The construction workers left, and were replaced by a few businessmen and women who had apparently all opted for a liquid lunch, and they were more gregarious than their predecessors, and soon they were laughing over their drinks. One of them, a guy perhaps my age with the body of a slipping jock, was especially loud, and I thought about climbing over the table and beating his face in just to make him go quiet.

Natalie didn't seem to like it, either, and after a few minutes of his prattling, began muttering about assholes and how everyone had them.

Dale came through the door first a little past one, Corry right behind him. Their expressions were stressed and grieving and worried. Corry slid me the box and the note without a word as the painted woman returned to the table.

"If this is a drug deal, you all have to order something," she said. It was meant as a joke, but it lay on the table much like the box itself, and when she saw our looks she added, "Not that you're dealing drugs or anything."

I ordered another ginger ale, and Natalie ordered another Diet Coke. Dale and Corry asked for mineral water. We waited in silence for the drinks to come, and after they had and the woman was gone, I read the note and it said exactly what Natalie had told me it did. Then I opened the box. The phone was small and cheap, no frills, lime green. I didn't turn it on, just put it in a pocket.

"It was on the news on the way over," Dale said. "FBI agent stabbed to death in Madison Square Park."

"Everyone's looking for the guy who did it," Corry said. "There's a description circulating for a possible suspect. It matches you."

That wasn't surprising, but it made the guilt come back as strong as ever, and the looks from Dale and Corry weren't helping.

"Get out of town," I told them quietly. "Get Ethan, get Esme, get the baby, and get out of town, and wherever you go, go there together. You'll be able to watch out for one another if you stay together. Natalie or I will let you know when it's safe."

"How?" Dale said.

Natalie said, "You closed the office up?"

"Of course," Corry said.

"I'll change the message on the answering service. When it says we're open, you'll know it's okay to come back."

"You have any idea how long that'll be?" He didn't ask her: he was looking at me.

"Just tonight," I said.

"That's all?" It was clear in his voice he didn't believe me.

"One way or another, it'll be over tonight. He left you guys the phone for only one reason, because he wants to communicate with me. When he calls, I'll offer him what he wants."

"You'll hand her over?"

"Do you really think this is still about her?" I asked.

"I don't know what the fuck any of this is about, Atticus," Corry said, and he got up from the table and waited for Dale to join him, no longer willing to look at me, focusing on the door to the bar.

Dale slid out along the bench, unfolding himself and rising to his feet. He left the bar without another word, Corry following after him.

The businessman who had once been a jock finished telling a joke where the key words seemed to be "Polack," "Jew," and "corn-bread."

"Let's get out of here before I kill him," I told Natalie.

We headed out of the bar, and Natalie stayed close to my side as we left, putting herself between me and the man I'd threatened, and it wasn't until we were outside and at her Audi that I understood she'd been afraid I was serious.

I didn't know how I felt about that.

It was almost four when we returned to the house in Allendale. Natalie had taken a roundabout route through several of the small townships that peppered 17 North, and we'd doubled back twice, just to make sure we were clear. There was no one tailing us that we could see, and I doubted that there was anyone tailing us that we couldn't. Oxford had a more efficient means of finding me; for now, I knew, he was content to wait.

Once during the drive, Natalie switched the radio on to one of the all-news AM stations out of New York, and it hadn't been three minutes before the report of the murdered federal agent came on the air. They weren't releasing Scott's name until his family could be notified, and the search was continuing for the man whom bystanders had seen kneeling over the dead man's body. More information was promised on the hour. When the report was over, Natalie switched the radio off, and we listened to the sound of the wipers clearing rain from the windshield for a couple of miles.

"What are we going to do?" she asked.

"You're going to protect Alena. I'm going to meet with him."

"He'll kill you."

"The deal will be he lets it go or he doesn't get the money back."

"He won't let it—"

"Natalie, his employers have pulled the plug, he's operating on his own now. He needs the money. He'll do what I say to get it back."

She frowned, adjusting her grip on the wheel, and I caught her toss me a glance that said she knew I was being simple and stupid, and she wasn't buying it.

"And you really think he'll leave it at that?"

"Of course he will," I lied. "We're all professionals."

Dan let us in the door with a gun in his hand, and I left Natalie to tell him we'd be moving again soon. There was concern on Dan's face as we entered, and I knew the concern wasn't for me, and I wondered once more what had passed between him and Natalie. The guard in the front room told me Alena was in the basement, and I went through the door, quickly shutting it behind me, and then to the stairs, descending three at a time. The owners had a variety of exercise equipment and hobby supplies scattered throughout the basement, and Alena was using an old workout machine with pulleys and rubber resistance straps to lift weights, doing lat pull-downs on a bench. She was wearing a black T-shirt and the brace was still wrapped around her leg, and the sweat was coming off her so I knew she'd been at it a long time.

When she saw me she released the bar, letting it go back into position.

"Who was it?" she asked.

"Scott."

"How?"

"He stuck a knife in his chest in the middle of Madison Square Park."

She reached for her cane and got to her feet. She used the corner of her shirt to wipe her face. Then she looked at me.

"Critical space," she said.

"I'm going to hear from him at nine tonight. He'll tell me that he knows where my parents live, where my brother lives, where my third-grade teacher lives, and he'll tell me that he'll kill them all unless I give him his money back."

She nodded, watching me as I came off the last step and began walking around the room. There were bowling trophies on a shelf with a box of Christmas tree lights and a half-finished model of a '68 Mustang convertible. On one wall was a reprint poster for *Treasure of the Sierra Madre*.

"And what will you tell him?"

"I'll tell him he can have his money and in exchange he leaves us alone. Gracey and Bowles pulled out on him this morning, he's working solo now, and I'll remind him of that, and I'll remind him that if he kills me he's never getting the cash. He'll listen to that."

She adjusted her weight on the cane, nodding. "He will."

"Then I'll name a place and a time for him to meet me. I'll tell him that I will meet him there. I'll give him every assurance that I'll be there alone, because I will be." I looked back at her, at her full mouth drawn tight with concern, at her brown eyes that always seemed just a little too big for her face. The perspiration on her brow had run along her cheeks, trailing lines that were like tears. It felt as if it had been years since we'd danced, instead of only two weeks.

"And then?" she asked.

"And then I'll kill him."

There was no visible reaction on her face, no sign that what I was saying disturbed or frightened or even amused her, and for an instant I felt a rage flash through me, blindingly hot, and I hated her for her calm and dead heart, and for what she was doing to mine.

"You will need a good location," Alena said.

"I've already got one in mind. If you're up for a short walk, I'd like you to check it with me."

I suppose she had already guessed where I was talking about, because she went to the stairs and said, "I will get a coat and meet you at the door."

There was a gate in the fence at the backyard, and Miata trotted out ahead of us as we crossed into the wetlands that had once been a farm. The earth was littered with dead leaves, dried and broken twigs, and the roots from the many trees made the ground uneven and poked out treacherously. We took it slow and I gave Alena my arm. With her arm through mine we probably looked like any other couple out for an early evening walk with their dog.

The path forked at an enormous maple that had been large when the farm was still in good order. An old tire hung from one of its branches. Empty bottles of beer and crumpled snack wrappers littered the wet ground around its base. We turned left, and the path narrowed. Miata snuffled along, nose to the ground. On our right, through gaps in the brush and trees, we could see the water beside us, reeds and more brush breaking its surface. It didn't look deep, more a marsh or a swamp than a pond.

After six minutes we passed a small stand that had been built by the State of New Jersey as a bird-watching post. It was made of wood, rotten in places, and had once been painted green. I climbed it while Alena waited below, and had a complete view of the water and the surroundings. The whole area was rimmed with trees, and I could hear the whisper of tires on the Franklin Turnpike to the east. Another bird-watching stand had been erected on the opposite side of the marsh, and it looked as dismal and frail as the one on which I stood. To the north, jutting into the water with its front stoop sagging, was an abandoned farmhouse.

When I climbed back down I told Alena what I'd seen, and we agreed that a closer inspection of the farmhouse was in order, and so she took my arm again and we continued on our way. Miata disappeared around the bend ahead of us, and when we rounded it we found him seated in the middle of the path, chewing on his thigh.

There was no clear path to the house, and I had to push my way through the brush and into the water before I could reach its side. It wasn't much of a home, only one room, and through the long-since-broken windows I saw a small empty space of broken floorboards, more trash. I left Alena on the path and crept around the side, and discovered the only door was the one I'd seen facing the water. I waded in, the cold water filling my shoes, opened the door, and stepped inside.

Kids had used it as a getaway, a make-out spot, although it was hard for me to imagine the place as romantic. Yellow newspapers and rusted tin cans were scattered about, and perhaps two or three hundred cigarette butts floated in the corner where the water was steadily rising over the floor. In another year, or two, or five, the building would collapse with its rot, but for now it was holding the line, fighting valiantly to stay stable. Teenagers would yet lose their virginity within its buckling walls.

This would be where I would do it, I decided, and went back to join Alena.

"There's only one way in," I said. "Unless he decides to break down the wall, he'll have to go around to the door. He'll have to come out the same way."

"Sounds perfect."

"I'll come back after we return to the house, put the card in the far corner."

She didn't reply, just took my arm again, and we continued to follow Miata around the marsh. By the time we reached the fence at the house, it was dusk, and my watch said it was just before six o'clock. We went back inside the house, upstairs, and Alena took the *Sparbuch* card from her go-bag, which she was keeping beside her bed. I went to place it, and it was full night when I returned in another twenty minutes, my feet and legs freezing from the cold water and the cold air.

I removed my wet shoes and socks and pants and threw them all in the dryer, then headed upstairs and put on my last pair of jeans. Alena was still in her room, but Natalie had now joined her.

"Where's the PDW?" I asked them.

"In the Audi," Natalie said.

"I need it."

Natalie looked at Alena, and when Alena didn't object, got to her feet, saying, "I'll get it."

"Good."

"He will need a vest," Alena said. "Get him a vest, too."

We waited in silence for her to return. Miata sat by the bed, and Alena scratched him idly behind the ears.

"Why did you name him Miata?" I asked suddenly.

She stroked the back of his neck. "I couldn't think of anything better."

"Yeah, but Miata?"

"He was the last dog. I'd shot him, but he was still alive, and as I was leaving he watched me and that was when I picked him up. I put him in my car, drove away, and when it was safe, I tried to stop the bleeding. I couldn't. It was night, and I went to an emergency animal hospital, and I said that he was my dog and that someone had shot him. They asked me his name, and the first thing I thought of was the name of the car I'd been driving. So I said his name was Miata."

"My parents named me Atticus because they liked the book," I said.

"What book?"

"*To Kill a Mockingbird.* You don't know it?"

"No."

"You'd like it."

"I'll get a copy."

She stopped stroking Miata and sighed. The dog sighed, too. "Atticus—I never wanted it this way."

I said nothing.

"Don't hesitate," she cautioned me. "When you have him, you must not hesitate. If you hesitate, you will die."

"I won't hesitate."

She seemed to want to say something more, but Natalie returned then, carrying the PDW and a Kevlar vest, and she handed both to me.

"I want you to move her," I told Natalie. "Tell Dan it doesn't have to be anyplace fancy, but it needs to be away from here."

"We've already got a location lined up near Cold Spring," Natalie said.

"I'll call you when I'm done, meet you there."

"If you can," Natalie said.

At ten minutes to nine I turned on the cellular phone and went into the backyard, taking a seat in one of the deck chairs around the covered pool. In the kitchen, Natalie and Dan stood talking at the stove, both of them watching me through the sliding glass doors. I could see the lights on in Alena's room, too, but not her silhouette. The guard's room was dark, and I knew he was in the chair once more, the I.R. goggles in place, scanning the trees. According to Natalie, the guards were all former Russian military, and two of them were even *spesnaz,* like Dan.

I put my head back against the chair and stared up at the sky, at the faint shapes of high clouds moving quickly in the wind. It was cold and going to get colder, and what few stars I could see flickered as if someone was playing with a galactic dimmer switch.

By my watch, it was two past nine when the phone rang.

"You're late," I said.

"Your watch is fast," Oxford said. "But then again, you are, too. I was going to hit Erika Wyatt this afternoon, but you robbed me of that."

"And more," I agreed. "How's the eye?"

He chuckled in my ear. "No, we're not going to banter. You know what I want, and you know what I'll do to get it. I underestimated you, and that was my mistake, but you pushed it. You know how hard it is to replace a good banker?"

"Junot covered for you as best he could."

"Is that why you killed him? Because he wouldn't give you all of my money?"

The clouds were growing farther apart and more stars were appearing. "He was alive when I left him."

"I'm sure he was," Oxford said. "But he was dead when the cops got there. That's the trouble with blows to the head, they're unpredictable."

"You want your money, I've got it. I'll give it back to you, tonight, but in exchange you let this whole thing go. It's over."

"Of course it's over, you fucking amateur. It was over the second those limp-dicks at the Company pulled my plug. You give me my money and we'll leave it at that. But if you don't, if you fuck with me, if I find that you've ripped me off, I'll kill every fucking person you've ever loved. And you know I can do it."

"The money for our lives."

"That's the deal. I'll honor it if you do. But I want it tonight, I want this over with tonight."

"You and me both," I agreed. "You in Manhattan?"

"I'm in the city, yeah."

"You're going to come out to New Jersey," I said. "Take the GW to Route Four. Four to Seventeen North. Seventeen North to the Allendale exit. Take Allendale Avenue to Franklin Turnpike, make a right, and about half a mile down the road on your right is the entrance to the Allendale Nature Preserve. It's unmarked, there's no sign, but if you watch for it, you'll spot the turn. Get out of your car and walk to the path, and ahead of you, through the brush, you'll see an old house. The card to access the account is in the house."

"I'll need the PIN, too, asshole," Oxford said.

"You'll get the PIN. While you're in the house, I'll leave a piece of paper with the appropriate code on it under your wiper. You arrive at three-thirty, you leave at three thirty-five. If you're late or early, if I see anything I don't like, you get the card but you don't get the code. Understand?"

"You verify my arrival, then you'll leave the code?"

"That's what I'm saying."

"How do I know you won't just cap me when I come back to the car?"

"How do I know you'll honor the agreement?"

"Because I'm a professional, that's why."

"Then that'll be your assurance as well as mine," I said. "Three-thirty, no earlier, and remember, my watch said you were two minutes late in calling."

Then I hung up, switched the phone off, and stared at the stars, wondering if Laurent Junot had been buried alone or by the side of his dead wife and child. I wondered where Scott's funeral would be held, and if I would attend it, if I could attend it.

I wondered what it meant that, despite my best intentions, I had become a murderer.

CHAPTER ELEVEN

Alena wouldn't look at me when I loaded her into Natalie's Audi, didn't say a word at all when I closed the door and watched them pull away from the house, Miata peering at me from the back window as Natalie followed Dan in his Kompressor and the other guards in their minivan. Alena's silence didn't change how I felt. I understood more than ever that there was nothing she could say; I understood more than ever why she was the way she was.

Back in the bedroom I stripped out of my clothes and took a long, hot shower, then used a scissors to cut off most of my mustache and beard. I went through two blades shaving off the rest of the hair, and when I saw myself in the mirror, I looked like someone I had known long ago and then fallen out of touch with, someone from summer camp and childhood.

I dressed again and put the vest on beneath my jacket, making certain the straps were snug and that the Kevlar wouldn't creep up my chest if I had to run or crawl or jump. I stuffed the rest of my things in my bag and took it out to the rental car that had been left behind for me, stowed everything in the trunk. Then I put the SIG in a jacket pocket, the PDW under my arm, and closed up the house, shutting off the lights and locking all the doors. When the owners returned from Bermuda, there'd be no sign that we were ever there.

By my watch it was six minutes to twelve when I crossed the fence back into the preserve, and there was no sign of life anywhere as I walked. Naked branches scraped against each other in the wind, and the water whispered around the reeds, but I didn't hear any animals, and even the traffic from the road was intermittent and distant. Diffused light came from distant streetlamps in the surrounding neighborhoods, reflected on the clouds.

When I passed the stand where I'd first surveyed the area, I swung out the stock on the PDW, dropped the handgrip from beneath the barrel, and flipped the selector to its three-round-burst setting. I settled the weapon against my shoulder, and moved on, slow and staying low, and I took twenty-three minutes to follow the path around to where I could see the house. I stopped and listened hard for almost five minutes more, and heard only traffic and wind and water, and I decided that he hadn't arrived yet. I didn't think he would have; it was the PIN code that had hobbled him—whatever he might have wanted to pull, he had to get the code from me, and that meant he had to play my game until I gave it up. After that, all bets were off.

The PDW isn't a long-range weapon, and that meant I would have to be fairly close to do it. If I'd been less ashamed of myself, I'd have asked Natalie to get me one of her rifles, and I'd have taken position in one of the birdwatching stands; but to do that would have been to admit to everything, and somehow I lacked the courage, and I realized something else, then: that murder is cowardice, no matter what anyone says.

On the east side of the rotting house was a small peninsula, and from its edge at the closest point, the door of the building was only ten yards away. I crept along the brush, hearing branches crack and break around me, and at the edge, lay down on my belly with a view of the building. The ground was cold and wet from the rain, and the smell of the earth and the wet and decomposing leaves was strong. Lying there felt like penance.

I listened to my watch tick and waited, felt the moisture of the earth seep into my clothes and body, felt myself growing colder and calmer. An earthworm, disturbed by my presence, made its way over my hand, and I felt its progress and didn't move. It seemed to know what it was doing, and after a while it buried itself again, unconcerned by my intrusion.

The first sound of his car reached me at three twenty-eight, and my watch had just marked three-thirty when I heard the engine die and a door open and shut. I lost the sound of him as he crossed from the car into the preserve, caught his steps again as he fought his way through the underbrush. The branches cracked and broke as he came, and he stopped abruptly, realizing the noise he was making, realizing, too, that he didn't have an alternative. The wood of the house creaked as he stepped onto the porch, and though his shoes no longer made a sound, the building betrayed his position with every move he made.

The water bounced what bare light there was back into the air, and when he came around the corner for the door, I could see him, though it wasn't easy. He had worn black in an attempt to make himself less visible, and had even covered the bandage on his face with ink or paint to keep the white gauze from becoming a target. With both hands he held a gun, and when he turned I confirmed it was a machine pistol, a Beretta. I had expected as much; he'd compensate for his new lack of depth perception with firepower, rejecting finesse in favor of volume.

When he reached the door he hesitated, then crouched along the hinge side. He took nearly a minute to open the door, and when he finally had it free of its swollen frame, he gave it a hard shove and pulled back, out of the line of sight. After five seconds of silence he peered into the darkness, leading with the gun, and then, satisfied I wasn't inside, he lowered the weapon and reached his free hand into his pocket. When it came out again, a thin beam of light shone into the house. He moved it methodically across the floors and walls, quickly but completely checking for tripwires or other booby traps. Then the light stopped moving, and I knew he'd seen the card.

He rose and stepped inside, and the house groaned with his entry, and the marsh sloshed against the foundation. Ripples rode out on the surface of the water.

I brought the PDW up to my shoulder, and put the sights on the doorway of the house, where his head would appear. My pulse raced against my temples, and the feeling made me think of Junot again, of his bone cracking with my blow, and blood filling the space between his brain and his skull, of pressure building until the organ began to collapse beneath the weight of it all.

He was standing in the doorway again, and I didn't know how he'd gotten there. With both hands on the Beretta, he swung it in a steady arc, searching the shore on either side, and I saw his head in my sights and I tried to put the pressure on the trigger. I thought of Scott and of Chris, thinking that would make it easier, but it didn't.

Something gave me away, some sense that he was in my sights or some noise I didn't know I'd made, but something alerted him. He turned and the Beretta found me, and I still couldn't pull the trigger, and then his left knee blew out and the gunshot followed it across the dark water.

Oxford wobbled, the Beretta dipping, and he looked to find my muzzle flash and I saw his hip rip open, and wood behind him splintered and flew apart, and he twisted with the force of the shot and collapsed onto his remaining knee, the Beretta bouncing out of his hands and into the water. He opened his mouth to scream and there was another flash and the back of his head came open, and the report echoed again.

He dropped to his side and rolled off the slope of the porch, into the water.

I found my feet and started running, following the path back to the bird-watching stand, the PDW in my hands. I came around the bend and saw Natalie by the ladder, and she didn't look at me as she helped Alena down from the platform. There was no sign of the rifle, and I guess it had already gone into the water, and I said nothing as Natalie guided Alena back to the path, handed her the cane once more.

I dropped the PDW and she hobbled forward and I caught her before she fell. Her arms went around me, her hands open and strong on my back, and her voice was thick and wet, choked with the tears that I hadn't seen in her eyes.

"He would have killed you or you would have killed him, and I couldn't let it happen. I couldn't let you die for me, you understand?"

Natalie stood still on the path, and she was blurring in my vision, and I almost didn't hear her saying that if we were going to go at all, we had to go now.

I was remembering Lady Ainsley-Hunter, and the way she had gone through Orin McLaughlin as if he wasn't there. I was remembering the look on Alena's face as she threatened to use her crutches to kill a man if he didn't give her what she wanted.

I thought of all the dead; of Oxford, and Scott, and Midge, and Chris.

And Junot, who had been between me and what I needed to do.

"I couldn't let you become me," Alena whispered.

"It's too late," I said, and I lifted her in my arms, and I followed Natalie as she led us back to her car, carrying the PDW and the cane, the evidence of all our crimes.

ABOUT THE AUTHOR

Born in San Francisco, GREG RUCKA was raised on the Monterey Peninsula. He has worked at a variety of jobs, from theatrical fight choreographer to emergency medical technician. He and his wife, Jennifer, reside in Portland, Oregon, where he is at work on his next novel.